About the Authors

Maya Blake's hopes of becoming a writer were born when she picked up her first romance aged thirteen. Little did she know her dream would come true! Does she still pinch herself every now and then, to make sure it's not a dream? Yes, she does!

Feel free to pinch her too, via Twitter, Facebook or Goodreads! Happy reading!

Jennifer Hayward has been a fan of romance since filching her sister's novels to escape her teenage angst. Her career in journalism and PR—including years of working alongside powerful, charismatic CEOs and travelling the world—has provided her with perfect fodder for the fast-paced, sexy stories she likes to write—always with a touch of humour. A native of Canada's east coast, Jennifer lives in Toronto with her Viking husband and young Viking-in-training.

Natalie Anderson adores a happy ending—which is why she always reads the back of a book first. Just to be sure. Along with happy endings she loves peppermint-filled dark chocolate, pineapple juice and extremely long showers. Not to mention spending hours teasing her imaginary friends with dating dilemmas. She lives in Christchurch, New Zealand, with her gorgeous husband and four fabulous children.

If, like her, you love a happy ending, be sure to come and say hi on facebook.com/authornataliea, follow @authornataliea on Twitter, or visit her website/blog, natalie-anderson.com.

The Love Islands

COLLECTION

March 2019   April 2019   May 2019

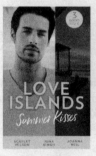

June 2019   July 2019   August 2019

Love Islands:
Swept Away

MAYA BLAKE

JENNIFER HAYWARD

NATALIE ANDERSON

MILLS & BOON

First published in Great Britain 2019
by Mills & Boon, an imprint of HarperCollins*Publishers*
1 London Bridge Street, London, SE1 9GF

Love Islands: Swept Away © 2019 Harlequin Books S.A.

Brunetti's Secret Son © 2015 Maya Blake
Claiming the Royal Innocent © 2016 Jennifer Hayward
The Mistress that Tamed De Santis © 2016 Natalie Anderson

ISBN: 978-0-263-27549-0

MIX
Paper from
responsible sources
FSC™ C007454

Printed and bound in Spain
by CPI, Barcelona

BRUNETTI'S
SECRET SON

MAYA BLAKE

CHAPTER ONE

THE HIDEOUS MANSION was just as he'd recalled in his night-mares, the gaudy orange exterior clashing wildly with the massive blue shutters. The only thing that didn't quite gel with the picture before him was the blaze of the sun glint-ing off the grotesquely opulent marble statues guarding the entry gates.

Romeo Brunetti's last memory of this place had been in the chilling rain, his threadbare clothes sticking to his skin as he'd huddled in the bushes outside the gates. A part of him had prayed he wouldn't be discovered, the other more than a tiny bit hopeful that discovery would mean the end to all the suffering, the hunger, the harrowing pain of rejec-tion that ate his thirteen-year-old body alive from morning to night. Back then he would've welcomed the beating his reluctant rescuer had received for daring to return Romeo to this place. Because the beating would have ended in obliv-ion, and the bitterness coursing through his veins like acid would have been no more.

Unfortunately, the fates had decreed otherwise. He'd hid-den in the bushes, cold and near catatonic, until the ever-present hunger had forced him to move.

Romeo stared up at the spears clutched in the hands of the statues, recalling his father's loud-bellied boast of them being made of solid gold.

The man who'd called him a bastard and a waste of space to his face. Right before he'd instructed his minion to throw him out and make sure he never returned. That he didn't care whether the spawn of the whore he'd rutted with in an alleyway in Palermo lived or died, as long as he, Agostino

Fattore, the head of the ruling crime family, didn't have to see the boy's face again.

No…not his *father*.

The man didn't deserve that title.

Romeo's hands tightened on the steering wheel of his Ferrari and he wondered for the thousandth time why he'd bothered to come to this place. Why he'd let a letter he'd shredded in a fit of cold rage seconds after reading it compel him into going back on the oath he'd made to himself over two decades ago. He looked over to the right where the towering outer wall to the late Agostino Fattore's estate rose into the sky, and sure enough, the bush was exactly as he remembered it, its leafy branches spread out, offering the same false sanctuary.

For a wild moment, Romeo fought the strong urge to lunge out of the car and rip the bush out of the earth with his bare hands, tear every leaf and branch to shreds. Tightening his jaw, he finally lowered his window and punched in the code his memory had cynically retained.

As the gates creaked open, he questioned again why he was doing this. So what if the letter had hinted at something else? What could the man whose rejection had been brutally cold and complete have to offer him in death that he'd failed so abjectly to offer in life?

Because he needed answers.

He needed to know that the blood running through his veins didn't have an unknown stranglehold over him that would turn his life upside down when he least expected it.

That the two times in his life when he'd lost control to the point of not recognising himself would be the only times he would feel savagely unmoored.

No one but Romeo knew how much he regretted wasting the four years of his life after the bitter night he'd been here last, looking for acceptance anywhere and any way he could find it. More than hating the man whose blood ran through his veins, Romeo hated the years he'd spent trying to find a replacement for Agostino Fattore.

Giving himself permission to close his heart off at seventeen had been the best decision he'd ever made.

So why are you here? You're nothing like him.

He needed to be sure. Agostino might no longer be alive, but he needed to look into the heart of Fattore's legacy and reassure himself that the lost little boy who'd thought his world would end because of another's rejection was obliterated completely.

Impatient with himself for prevaricating, Romeo smashed his foot on the accelerator and grunted in satisfaction as the tyres squealed on the asphalt road leading to the courtyard. Unfolding himself from the driver's seat, he stalked up to the iron-studded double doors and slammed them open.

Striding into the chequer-tiled hallway, he glared at the giant antique chandelier above his head. If he had cared whether this house stood or fell, that monstrosity would have been the first thing in the incinerator. But he wasn't here to ponder the ugly tastes of a dead man. He was here to finally slay ghosts.

Ghosts that had lingered at the back of his consciousness since he was a child but that had been resurrected one night five years ago, in the arms of a woman who'd made him lose control.

He turned as slow feet shuffled in his direction, followed by firmer footholds that drew a grim smile from Romeo. So, the old order hadn't changed. Or maybe the strength of Romeo's anger had somehow transmitted to Fattore's former second in command, prompting the old man who approached to seek the protection of his bodyguards.

Lorenzo Carmine threw out his hands in greeting, but Romeo glimpsed the wariness in the old man's eyes. 'Welcome, *mio figlio*. Come, I have lunch waiting for us.'

Romeo tensed. 'I'm not your son and this meeting will not last beyond five minutes, so I suggest you tell me what you withheld in your letter right now and stop wasting my time.' He didn't bother to hide the sneer in his voice.

Lorenzo's pale grey eyes flared with a temper Romeo had witnessed the last time he was here. But along with it came the recognition that Romeo was no longer a frightened little boy incapable of defending himself. Slowly, his expression altered into a placid smile.

'You have to pardon me. My constitution requires that I strictly regulate my mealtimes or I suffer for it.'

Romeo turned towards the door, again regretting his decision to come here. He was wasting his time looking for answers in stone and concrete. He was wasting his time, full stop.

'Then by all means go and look after your constitution. Enjoy the rest of your days and don't bother contacting me again.' He stepped towards the door, a note of relief spiking through him at the thought of leaving this place.

'Your father left something for you. Something you will want to see.'

Romeo stopped. 'He was not my father and there's nothing he possesses in this life or the next that could possibly interest me.'

Lorenzo sighed. 'And yet you came all this way at my request. Or was it just to stick out your middle finger at an old man?'

Romeo's jaw clenched, hating that the question he'd been asking himself fell from the lips of a man who'd spent his whole life being nothing but a vicious thug. 'Just spit it out, Carmine,' he gritted out.

Lorenzo glanced at the nearer bodyguard and nodded. The beefy minder headed down the long hallway and disappeared.

'For the sake of my friend, your father, the Almighty rest his soul, I will go against my doctor's wishes.' The remaining guard fell into step behind Lorenzo, who indicated a room to their left.

From memory, Romeo knew it was the holding room for visitors, a garishly decorated antechamber that led to the receiving room, where his father had loved to hold court.

The old man shuffled to a throne-like armchair and sank heavily into it. Romeo chose to remain standing and curbed the need to pace like a caged animal.

Although he'd come through the desolation of his ragged past, he didn't care for the brutal reminders everywhere he looked. The corner of this room was where he'd crouched when his father's loud lambasting of a minion had led to gunshots and horrific screams the first time he'd been brought here. The gilt-framed sofa was where his father had forced him to sit and watch as he'd instructed his lieutenants to beat Paolo Giordano into a pulp.

He didn't especially care for the reminder that it was possibly because of Fattore's blood running through his veins that he'd almost taken the same violent path when, tired of living on the streets, he'd almost joined a terror-loving gang feared for their ruthlessness.

Sì, he should've stayed far away, in the warmth of his newest and most lavish by-invitation-only Caribbean resort.

His eyes narrowed as the second bodyguard returned with a large ornately carved antique box and handed it to Lorenzo. 'It's a good thing your father chose to keep an eye on you, wasn't it?' Lorenzo said.

'Scusi?' Romeo rasped in astonishment.

Lorenzo waved his hand. 'Your mother, the Almighty rest *her* unfortunate soul, attempted to do her best, but we all knew she didn't have what it took, eh?'

Romeo barely stopped his lips from curling. The subject of his mother was one he'd sealed under strict lock and key, then thrown into a vault the night he'd buried her five years ago.

The same night he'd let his guard down spectacularly with a woman whose face continued to haunt him when he least expected it. A woman who had, for the first time in a long time, made him want to feel the warmth of human emotion.

A tremor went through him at the memory, its deep and disturbing effect as potent, if not more so, than it'd been that night when he'd realised that his emotions weren't as clinical and icy as he'd imagined them to be.

He shut down that line of thought.

Maisie O'Connell had had no place in his life then, save as a means of achieving a few hours of oblivion, and she most certainly didn't have one now, in this cursed place. Like the bush outside this miscreation of a mansion, she represented a time in his life he wanted banished for all time.

Because it makes you uncomfortable...vulnerable even? Basta!

'You seem to be under the misapprehension that I'll indulge you in fond trips down potholed memory lanes. Be assured that I will not. If I remember correctly, *you* helped to throw me out of the gates when I was a child. Your exact words, presumably passed down from my father, were—*I see you again, you leave in a body bag.*'

Lorenzo shrugged. 'Those were hot-headed days. Look at you now. You've done very well for yourself despite your less than salubrious beginning.' A touch of malice flared in his eyes. 'None of us imagined a boy conceived in the gutter would rise to such esteem.'

Romeo shoved his hands in his pockets so he wouldn't do the unthinkable and strangle the old man where he sat. 'Then I guess it's a good thing I was intelligent enough to realise early on that whether you were born in the gutter or with a dozen golden spoons clutched in your fist, our lives are what we make them. Otherwise, who knows where I'd be today? In a mental institution, perhaps? Bemoaning my fate while rocking back and forth in a straitjacket?'

The old man laughed, or he attempted to. When the sound veered into a bone-jarring coughing spell, his bodyguards exchanged wary glances before one stepped forward with a glass of water.

Lorenzo's violent refusal of help had the guard springing back into his designated position. When the coughing fit passed, Lorenzo opened the box and took out several papers.

'You were never going to go down without a fight. I saw that in you even when you were a boy. But you'll do well to remember where that intelligence comes from.'

'Are you really suggesting that I owe what I've made of myself to you or the pathetic band of thugs you call a family?' he asked, incredulous.

Lorenzo waved him away. 'We'll discuss what you owe in a bit. Your father meant to do this before he was tragically taken from us,' he muttered.

Romeo curbed the need to voice his suspicions that his father's departure from this life hadn't been tragic at all; that the boat explosion that had taken his life and those of his wife and the two half-sisters Romeo had never been allowed to meet hadn't been accidental, but the target of a carefully orchestrated assassination.

Instead, he watched Lorenzo pull out document after document and lay them on the desk.

'The first order of business is this house. It's yours free and clear from any financial obligations. All the lawyers need is your signature to take possession. It comes with the collection of cars, the horses and the three hundred acres of land, of course.'

Astonishment rendered Romeo speechless.

'Then there are the businesses. They're not doing as well as we'd hoped, and certainly not as well as your own businesses are doing. The Carmelo *famiglia* mistakenly believe this is an excuse for them to start making moves on Fattore business, but I suspect that will all turn around once our business has been brought under the umbrella of your company, Brunetti International—'

Romeo laughed. 'You must be out of your mind if you

think I want any part of this blood-soaked legacy. I'd rather return to the gutter than claim a single brick of this house, or associate myself in any way with the Fattore name and everything it stands for.'

'You may despise the Fattore name, but do you think *Brunetti, son of a two-bit whore* has a better ring?' Lorenzo sneered.

It didn't, but in the bleak, terrible hellhole of his childhood it had been the better of two evils. Especially since that greater evil had warned him never to use the name *Fattore*.

'This is your legacy, no matter how much you try to deny it,' Lorenzo insisted.

'You can sit there and rewrite history until the walls crumble around you,' Romeo enunciated with a burning intensity he suspected would erupt the longer he spent in this house. 'But your five minutes have come and gone, old man. And this meeting is well and truly over. Any problems you have with your extortion business and territorial wars with the Carmelo family are yours to deal with.'

He made it to the door before Lorenzo spoke.

'Your father suspected that when the time came you would prove intransigent. So he asked me to give you this.'

For the second time, Romeo froze, his instincts screeching at him to keep walking, but his brain warning that to do as he so desperately wanted would be unwise.

Lorenzo held out a large manila envelope, which he slid across the desk with a smug look.

'I told you I'm not interested in anything bearing the Fattore name. Whatever is in that envelope—'

'Is of a more…personal nature and will interest you, *mio figlio*. I'm confident of it.'

Romeo abandoned the need to remind the old man not to call him son. Lorenzo was enjoying needling him a little too much, and Romeo was fast reaching boiling point.

Striding across the room, he snatched up the envelope and ripped it open. The first picture punched him in the gut, expelling a harsh breath. It showed him standing at his mother's graveside, the only attendee besides the priest, as Ariana Brunetti was laid to rest.

He flung the picture on the desk, his mouth twisting as the next picture showed him in funereal black, sitting at his hotel bar, staring into a glass of cognac.

'So Fattore had me followed for an afternoon five years ago. Perhaps he would've better profited using that time to tend his businesses.'

Lorenzo tented his fingers. 'Keep going. The best is yet to come.'

Dark premonition crawled up Romeo's spine as he flipped to the next photo. It showed him walking out of his hotel and down the street that led to the trendy cafés near the waterfront.

He froze at the next picture and stared at the image of himself. And her.

Maisie O'Connell—the woman with the angelic face and the tempting, sinful body. The combination, although enthralling enough, wasn't what had made her linger in his mind long after he'd moved on to other women, and other experiences.

Something had happened with her in that hotel room, above and beyond mind-obliterating sex. He'd walked away from her feeling broken, fighting a yearning that had terrified him for a long time, until he'd finally forced it back under control.

He had no intention of resurrecting those brief, unsettling hours. He was in control of his life. In control of the fleeting moments of emotion he allowed himself these days.

He threw down the pictures, not caring when they fanned out in a careless arc on the desk. Eyes narrowed at Lorenzo, he snapped, 'It's almost laughable that you think documenting my sex life would cause me anything but acute irritation. Irritation that might just push me into having this house torn to the ground and the whole estate turned into a car park.'

The old man reached across, shuffled through the pictures, then sat back again.

Exhaling, Romeo looked down and saw more pictures of the woman he'd shared his most memorable one-night stand with. But these were different. Taken in another country, judging from the street signs. Dublin, most likely, where Maisie had said she was from during one of the brief times they'd conversed in that electric night they'd spent together.

Still caught up in riotous emotions, he nudged the picture impatiently with his fingernail.

Maisie O'Connell, striding down a busy street in a business suit and high heels, her thick, glorious hair caught up in an elaborate bun. A vision far removed from the sexy little sundress and flip-flops she'd been wearing the first time Romeo had seen her outside a waterfront café in Palermo. Her hair had been loose then, hanging to her waist in a ripple of dark fire.

Romeo unveiled the next picture.

Maisie, hailing a taxi outside a clinic, her features slightly pale and drawn, her normally bright blue eyes dark with worry.

Maisie, sitting on a park bench, her face turned up to the sun, her hand resting on her belly.

Her very distended belly.

Romeo swallowed hard and picked up the last picture, his body suspended in shock as he brought it up to his face.

Maisie, pushing a pram down a quiet Dublin street, her mouth tilted in a postcard-perfect picture of maternal bliss as she reached into the stroller.

'*Madre di Dio*, what is the meaning of this?' he breathed, his voice cold enough to chill the whole mausoleum of a mansion.

'I will not insult your deductive powers by spelling it out for you,' Lorenzo answered.

Romeo flung the photo down, but he could not look away from them. Spreading his fingers through the glossy images, he found further evidence of surveillance. Apparently his father had decided to stop following Romeo and focus instead on the woman he'd slept with on the day of his mother's funeral. A woman whose goodness had threatened to seep into him, to threaten the foundations of his carefully barricaded emotions.

'If these images are supposed to paint some sort of picture, then you've wasted your time. Sexually active individuals have brief encounters and go on to have relationships and families all the time. Or so I'm told.'

He'd never indulged in a relationship. In fact, he actively discouraged his lovers from even entertaining a glimmer of the idea. Romeo suppressed a grim smile. He knew his attitude to relationships had earned him the amusingly caustic label of *Weekend Lover*. Not that he cared. Hell, if it spelled out his intentions before he even asked a woman out, then all the better.

Affection was never on the table, the faintest idea of love strictly and actively forbidden. His interactions were about sex. Nothing more.

'So you don't care to know the time span during which these pictures were taken?'

'Fattore must have had his own warped reason, I'm sure.'

Lorenzo continued to stare at him. 'Then you won't want to know that the woman gave her child an Italian name?'

Romeo snorted in disbelief. He hadn't told Maisie his surname. He'd been very careful in that regard because he hadn't wanted any association with either his mother or his father discovered, as tenuous as the connection could've been, seeing that he hadn't set foot in Sicily in over fifteen years.

'You two must have been desperate to clutch at so many straws. My suggestion to you would be to leave this woman alone to raise her child. She means nothing to me other than a brief dalliance. Whatever leverage you seek through her has no teeth.'

Lorenzo shook his balding grey head. 'Once you have calmed down and learnt a little of our ways, you'll realise that we don't tend to leave stones unturned. Or facts unchecked. Your father certainly wouldn't pin the future of his organisation, of his *famiglia*, on a whim. No, *mio figlio*, we checked and double-checked our facts. Three DNA tests by three different doctors confirmed it.'

'How did you come by samples for these tests?'

'Contrary to what you think of us, we're not bumbling idiots. A strand of hair or a discarded juice cup is all we need, and quite easy to come by.'

The gross violation that deed would've entailed turned his stomach and primitive anger swelled through him. 'You set your thugs loose on a little boy?'

'He's not just any little boy. Your woman gave birth exactly nine months after your encounter. And your son is very much a Fattore.'

CHAPTER TWO

MAISIE O'CONNELL FLIPPED the Closed sign to Open and enjoyed the tingle of excitement that never failed to come with that little action.

It had been a long, hard slog, but *Maisie's* was finally ticking over very nicely, was making a steady profit, in fact. Putting her beloved restaurant in the hands of a professional chef while she'd taken the intensive course in gourmet Italian cooking had paid off. The added feature in one of Dublin's top newspapers had given *Maisie's* the extra boost that had seen her bookings go from half full to booked solid a month in advance.

Picking up the glass-topped menu stand, she pushed open the door and positioned it for maximum effect on the pavement.

As she turned to go back in, a stretch limo with blacked-out windows rolled by and stopped two doors down from where she'd paused. Maisie eyed the car. Although it wasn't strange for luxury cars to pass through the quiet little village of Ranelagh, seeing as they were close to Dublin city centre, the presence of this car caused a different sort of tingle. Telling herself she was being too fanciful, she swiped a dishcloth over the surface of the menu stand and went back in. She checked on her kitchen and waitstaff of twelve, made sure preparations were under way for their first booking at midday, then went into her office.

She had roughly half an hour to get to grips with the restaurant's accounts before she had to be back in the kitchen. As she sat down, her gaze fell on the picture propped up on her desk. The pulse of love that fired to her heart made her breath catch. Reaching out, she traced the contours of her son's face, her own face breaking into a smile at the toothy, wide-eyed happiness reflected in his eyes.

Gianlucca. The reason for her existence. The reason the hard decisions she'd made five years ago had been worth every moment of heartache. Turning her back on the career she'd trained so hard for had not been easy. Certainly her parents had piled on enough guilt to make walking away feel like the betrayal they'd accused her of committing. Her own guilt for confirming their fears that the apple didn't fall far from the tree was bone-deep and would probably always be. She hadn't planned on getting pregnant as her mother had at twenty-four but she refused to let the guilt prevent her from loving or caring for her child.

She'd known from a very young age that her parents, had they been given a choice, would've remained childless. As hard as it'd been, she'd tried to accept that not everyone was built to nurture a child. Her parents certainly had found raising her a challenge, one they hadn't deemed as worthy as the academic careers they'd pursued relentlessly. She'd always known she came an indifferent second to her parents' academic ambitions.

But she'd wanted Gianlucca the moment she'd found out he was growing inside her.

There had been nothing she wanted more than providing the very best for her son.

She had given him the very best.

The tiny niggle of ever-present guilt threatened to push its way through, but she smashed it down. She'd done everything she could when she'd found out she was pregnant. Even going against her parents' intense disapproval to make that daunting trip back to Sicily. She'd tried.

Yes, but did you try hard enough?

She dropped her hand from the picture and resolutely opened the account books. Indulging in *might have beens*

wouldn't get the chequebook balanced or the staff paid. She
was content enough. More important, her son was happy.

Her gaze drifted back to the almost-four-year-old face
that was already taking the shape of the man he would one
day be. To the deep hazel-gold eyes that looked so much
like his father's. Eyes that could sometimes make her believe he could see straight into her soul, just as the older
pair had done to her that long afternoon and longer night
in Palermo five years ago.

Romeo.

A portentous name if there ever was one. While her life
hadn't ended in fatal tragedy like the famous story, meeting
Romeo had significantly altered it, her son being the only
bright thing that had emerged from encountering that dangerously sexy, but deeply enigmatic Italian with eyes that
had reflected enough conflict to last him several lifetimes.

Enough.

She switched on her computer and had just activated the
payroll system when a knock sounded on her door.

'Come in.'

Lacey, her young reservations manager, poked her head
around the door, her eyes wide and brimming with interest.
'There's someone here to see you,' she stage-whispered.

Maisie suppressed a smile. Her young employee had a
flair for the dramatic and saw conspiracies and high drama
in the simplest situations.

'If it's someone else looking for a job, please tell them
I'm not hiring anyone. Not till the summer season really
kicks off…' She stopped speaking as Lacey shook her head
frantically.

'I don't think he's looking for a job. Actually, no offence,
Maisie, but he looks like he could buy this place a hundred
times over.' Her eyes widened and she blushed, then bit her
lip. 'Sorry, but he looks really, really rich, and really, really,
intense.' Lacey's eyes boggled some more. 'And he came

in a *limo*,' she whispered again, looking over her shoulder into the restaurant.

The tingling Maisie had experienced earlier returned full force. 'Did he give you a name?'

'No, he just asked if you were in and ordered me to come and get you.' Lacey glanced furtively over her shoulder again, as if expecting their visitor to materialise behind her. 'He's very…*full-on*.'

Recalling her own line of thoughts moments ago and the intensity of Romeo's personality, she shivered. Shaking it off, Maisie stood up and brushed her hands down the practical black skirt and pink shirt she'd chosen to wear today.

She'd left all that dangerous intensity back in Palermo. Or *it* had left her, seeing as she'd woken up alone the morning after, with only rumpled sheets and the trace of her lover's scent on the pillow as evidence that she hadn't imagined the whole encounter.

She was in Ranelagh, the serene village she'd chosen to build a life for herself and her son in, not the sultry decadence of Palermo and its dangerous residents.

No danger or intensity whatsoever welcome here.

'Okay, Lacey. I'll take care of it.' Lacey's head bobbed before she disappeared from the doorway.

Sucking in a breath and telling herself she was being silly to feel so apprehensive, Maisie stepped out from behind her desk. In her short but successful stint as a criminal lawyer, she'd faced her share of unsavoury and even dangerous characters.

Whatever unknown quantity faced her out there in her beloved restaurant, she could face it.

Maisie knew just how wrong she was even before the tall, broad-shouldered figure clad from head to toe in black turned around from his brooding inspection of his surroundings.

Outwardly, her body froze a few steps into the restaurant. But inside, her heart kicked into her stomach. *Hard.*

'Romeo.'

She realised she'd said the name rattling through her brain aloud when he turned slowly and pinned her with those brooding hazel-gold eyes. That impossibly rugged jaw she'd thought she'd blown out of all proportion tightened as his gaze raked her from head to toe and back again. His prominent, cut-glass cheekbones were more pronounced than she remembered and his hair was longer, wavier than it had been five years ago. But the man who stood a dozen paces away was no less dynamic, no less captivating than the man who'd sat across from her in the café that memorable day.

If anything, he commanded a more overpowering presence. Perhaps it was because they were so far away from the place they'd first met, or because her mind was turning itself inside out to decipher exactly why he was here. All the same she found herself bunching a fist against her heart as if that would stop its fierce pounding.

'I'm not certain whether to celebrate this moment or to condemn it,' he rasped in a tense, dark voice.

'How did you… How did you find me?'

One eyebrow spiked upwards. 'That is what you wish to know? How did I find you? Were you attempting to stay hidden, perhaps?' he enquired silkily.

'What?' Her brain grew fuzzier, her heart racing even faster at the ice in his tone. 'I'm not hiding. Why would I want to hide from anyone?'

He approached slowly, his eyes not leaving her face, nor his hands the deep pockets of his overcoat. Even though it was early June, the weather remained cool enough to require a coat, and he wore his as a dark lord wore a cape, with a flourish that demanded attention. 'We haven't seen each other in five years and your first request is to know how I found you. Pardon me if I find that curious.'

'What would you have me say?' She licked lips gone

dry as he took another step closer until she had to crane her neck to see his eyes.

Mesmeric, hypnotising eyes.

So like his son's.

The blood drained from her face and thinking became difficult. She'd imagined this scene countless times. Had imagined how she would say the words. How he would take it. How she would protect her son from even the slightest hint of rejection, the way she'd done when her parents had transmitted that same indifference they'd shown Maisie all her life to her beloved son.

But words wouldn't form in her brain. So she stared at him, her thoughts twisting and turning.

'*Hello*, perhaps? Or, *how have you been, Romeo?*'

She caught his chillingly mocking tone and stiffened.

'Why would I? I seem to recall waking up to find myself alone in a hotel suite rented by an anonymous stranger. You didn't bother to say goodbye then, so why should I bother to say hello now?' she replied.

His nostrils flared then and a memory struck through her jumbled thoughts. They'd been caught up in one of the few short bursts of conversation in his suite. She'd unwittingly let slip the fraught state of her relationship with her parents, how lonely and inconvenient she felt to them, as if she were an unwanted visitor sharing a house with them.

His nostrils had flared then, too, as he'd admonished her to be grateful she had parents at all—strangers or otherwise. That observation had rendered her silent and a little ashamed, not because she'd hated being chastised, but because she'd seen the naked agony in his eyes when he'd said that. As if the subject of parents was one that terrorised him.

Maisie pushed the memory away and struggled to stay calm when he finally released her from his stare and looked around.

'What do you do here when you're not dabbling in being a restaurateur?' he asked.

She bristled. 'I'm not dabbling. I own this restaurant. It's my career.'

'Really? I thought you were a high-powered lawyer.'

She frowned. Had she told him that in Palermo? Back then she'd been newly qualified and working on exciting cases. Back then her parents had finally, grudgingly, accepted her career choice. She would even go as far as to consider that for the first time in her life she'd achieved something they were proud of, even if they hadn't quite been able to show it in the warm, loving way she'd seen her friends' parents exhibit.

Of course, they hadn't been thrilled that she'd announced soon after that she was taking a whole month off to travel Europe.

Despite her having the full support of her bosses to take the time off, her parents had advised her against the trip. Their utter conviction that stepping off the career ladder, even briefly, would ruin her life had finally confirmed how much they rued bringing a child, bringing *her*, into their lives.

And once she'd returned and told them she was pregnant…

Her heart caught at their bitter disappointment when she'd finally revealed her news. Roberta O'Connell hadn't needed to spell out that she thought Maisie had ruined her life for ever. It'd been clear to see. And knowing that by definition they thought having *her* had been a mistake had been an ache she hadn't been able to dispel.

Maisie shook her head to dispel the memory. 'No, not any longer. I gave up practising four years ago,' she answered Romeo.

He frowned. 'Why would you give up the job you trained so hard for?'

So she *had* told him more than she thought. Because how else would he know? And why was he questioning her like this, probing her for answers he already knew? Was he try-ing to trip her up somehow?

She swallowed. 'My priorities changed,' she replied crisply and stepped back. 'Now if you were just passing through and stopped to catch up, I really must get on. My first customers will be here shortly and I need to make sure the kitchen's ready to start the day.'

'You think I came all this way simply *to catch up*?' He looked around again, as if searching for something. Or someone.

Apprehension flowed like excess adrenaline through her blood, making her dizzy for a moment.

Romeo couldn't know about Gianlucca. Because *she'd* searched for him to no avail. No one else knew who the fa-ther of her child was. The only people who she would've confessed Romeo's identity to—her parents—hadn't wanted to know after she'd confessed to the one-night stand. Which was just as well because Maisie wouldn't have liked to con-fess that she hadn't known the surname of the man who'd impregnated her.

Maisie had a hard time accepting the fact that the only time her mother had initiated a heart-to-heart conversa-tion had been to tell her to abandon her child's welfare to childminders and nannies. That her son, once he was born, should be left to others to raise, so Maisie could focus fully and solely on her career. There'd even been an offer of a fully paid boarding school once he was a toddler! Despite her knowing her parents' views on hands-on parenting, it'd still been harrowing to hear her mother's words, to know that had her parents had the choice when she was born, they'd have abandoned *her* to the same fate.

'I really don't know what you're doing here. But like I said, I need to be getting on—'

She gasped when he caught her upper arms in a firm, implacable hold.

'Where is he, Maisie? *Where is my son?*' he demanded, his voice a cold, deadly blade.

Several things happened at once. The door to the kitchen burst open and Lacey rushed through, just as the front door swung inward and a party of four walked in. The scene stopped in almost comical freeze-frame. No one moved except for Romeo, whose eyes narrowed as they went from the door to Lacey and then to Maisie's face.

When shock continued to hold her tongue prisoner, Romeo's lips compressed. Glancing at Lacey's name badge, he jerked his head imperiously. 'Lacey, you're in charge of reservations, yes?'

Lacey nodded, her wide-eyed look returning full force.

'Then see to the customers, *per favore.* Your boss and I will be in her office.'

Romeo marched her into the small room and shut the door behind him with a precise movement that suggested he was suppressing the need to slam it. Maisie was conquering equally intense emotions.

She put the width of her desk between them, then glared at him.

'I don't know who you think you are, but you can't walk in here and start bossing my employees about—'

'Deflecting won't help this situation. You know why I'm here. So let's dispense with trivialities. *Tell me where he is.*' That last remark was said with icy brevity that hammered a warning straight to her blood.

'Why?' she fired back, potent fear beginning to crawl up her spine.

Astonishment lit through his golden eyes. '*Why?* Are you completely insane? Because I want to see him.'

'Again, why?' A cloud descended on his face and Maisie held up her hand when he opened his mouth, no doubt to once again question her sanity. 'Let's stop for a moment and think about this rationally. We had a one-night stand.' She couldn't help the high colour that rushed into her face at the so very telling term. 'After which you walked away without so much as a thank-you-ma'am note. You used me, then disappeared into the night. A month later, I found out I was pregnant. Fast-forward five years later, you walk in the door and demand to see my son.' Maisie raised her hand and ticked off her fingers. 'I don't know your background. I don't know whether that aura of danger about you is just for show or the real thing. Hell, I don't even know your *last name*. And you think I should just expose you to my child?'

Several emotions flitted across his face—astonishment, anger, a touch of vulnerability that set her nape tingling, then grudging respect before settling into implacable determination.

He stared at her for a time, before he exhaled sharply. 'If the child is mine—'

She laughed in disbelief. 'Let me get this straight. You came here without even being sure that the child you're so desperate to see is yours?'

He folded his arms across his massive chest, the movement bunching his shoulders into even wider relief. Maisie became acutely aware of the room shrinking, and the very air being sucked up by his overwhelming presence. 'Since I've never met him, I cannot be one hundred per cent sure that he's mine, hence the request to see him. A man in my position has to verify allegations of fatherhood.'

Her eyes widened. 'Allegations? *Plural?* Are you saying this isn't the first time you've left a woman in a hotel room and found out there have been consequences to your actions?' Maisie wasn't sure why that stung so much. Had she imagined herself somehow unique? That a man who *looked* like him, kissed and made love as he had, would have limited the experience to her and only her? 'And what do you mean, a man in your position?'

Her barrage of questions caused his eyes to narrow further. 'You don't know who I am?'

'Would I be asking if I did?' she threw back. 'If you want

any semblance of cooperation from me, I demand to know your full name.'

His jaw flexed. 'My name is Romeo Brunetti.' The way he said it, the way he waited, as if the pronouncement should be accompanied by a round of trumpets and the clash of cymbals, set her spine tingling. When she didn't speak, a curious light entered his eyes. 'That means nothing to you?'

She shrugged. 'Should it?'

He continued to stare at her for another minute, before he shook his head and started to pace the small space in front of her desk. 'Not at all. So now we have our long-overdue introductions out of the way.'

Maisie cleared her throat. 'Mr Brunetti, I—' She froze as he let out a stunned breath.

Her gaze flew to his face to find his gaze transfixed on the photo on her desk. 'Is this… Is this him?' he asked in a tight, ragged whisper.

When she nodded, he reached forward in a jerky movement, then stopped. Apprehension slid over his face. He fisted and then flexed his hand, before he slowly plucked up the frame. In another person, she would've been certain he was borderline terrified of a mere picture.

Terrified or dreading?

The reminder of the cold indifference her parents had felt about their grandson, about her, made her itch to snatch the photo from him, protect her son's image the way she fought every day to keep him from the rejection she'd been forced to live with her whole life.

She glanced at the picture clutched in Romeo's large hand.

It had been taken at Ranelagh Gardens on the first day of spring. Dressed in a smart shirt, jeans and bright blue woollen jumper, Gianlucca had looked a perfect picture of health and happiness, and Maisie hadn't been able to resist capturing his image.

She watched now as Romeo brought the picture up close

to his face, his features drawn tight, his breathing slow and controlled. After almost a minute of staring at the photo without a hint of emotion, he raised his hand and brushed his fingers over Gianlucca's cheek, almost in direct imitation of what Maisie herself had done a mere half hour ago.

'*Mio figlio,*' he murmured.

'I don't know what that means,' Maisie replied in a matching whisper.

He blinked and sucked in a deep, chest-filling breath. 'My son. It means my son.' He looked up, his gaze deeply accusing. '*He's my son.* And you kept him from me,' he snarled, his voice still not quite as steady as it'd been moments ago.

Maisie stumbled backwards, bumping into the chair behind her. 'I did nothing of the kind. And if you stopped to think about it for a moment, you'd realise how ridiculous that allegation is.'

He shoved a hand through his thick dark hair, dislodging any semblance of order it'd been in. He began to pace again, the photo clutched in his large hand. 'How old is he?' he demanded when he paused for a moment.

'He's four in three weeks.'

He resumed pacing in tight circles. 'Four years… *Dio mio*, four years I've been in the dark,' he muttered to himself, slashing his hand through his hair again.

'How *exactly* were you enlightened?' It was a question he hadn't yet addressed.

He froze, as if her question had thrown him. 'We'll get to that in a moment. First, please tell me his name and where he is.'

The urgency in his voice bled through to Maisie. She wanted to refuse. Wanted to rewind time and have this meeting not happen. Not because being given the chance to reveal her son's existence to his father wasn't what she wanted.

From the moment she'd found out she was pregnant, she'd known she would give her child every opportunity to know his father. She'd gone to Palermo during her first trimester with that exact reason in mind and had given up after two weeks with no success in tracing Romeo.

No, the reason Maisie wanted to rewind time and take a different course was because she knew, deep in her bones, that Romeo's presence wasn't just about wanting to get to know his son. There was a quiet hint of danger about him that set her fear radar alight. And he hadn't yet shown her that the prospect of a son filled him with joy. All he'd done so far was put an alpha claim on a child he didn't know.

A child she would lay her life down to protect.

'Why are you really here?'

His brows clamped together. 'I believe we've tackled that particular question.'

She shook her head. Something was seriously, desperately wrong. Something to do with her precious son.

'No, we haven't. And I absolutely refuse to tell you anything about him until you tell me what's going on.'

CHAPTER THREE

ROMEO STARED DOWN at the picture one more time, his heart turning over as eyes the exact shade as his own stared back at him. The child…*his son*…was laughing, pure joy radiating from his face as he posed, chubby arms outstretched, for the camera. A deep shudder rattled up from his toes, engulfing him in a sense of peculiar bewilderment. And fear. Bone-deep fear.

He couldn't be a father. Not him, with the upbringing he'd had, the twisted, harrowing paths his life had taken before he'd wrestled control of it. He wasn't equipped to care for a dog, never mind a child. And with the blood flowing through his veins…the blood of a thug and a vicious criminal…

Dio mio.

Lorenzo hadn't been lying after all. A single wave of impotent rage blanketed him to know that the two men he despised most had known of the existence of the boy before he did. And while a part of him knew levelling accusations of subterfuge on the woman standing before him was unfair, Romeo couldn't help but feel bitter resentment for being kept in the dark, even while he continued to flounder at the reality stabbing him in the chest.

He pushed the emotion aside and concentrated on the reality he *could* deal with—her continued denial of access. Because whether he was equipped to handle the prospect of fatherhood or not, she was at this moment behaving like an irrational person…a mother bear—a concept acutely alien to him.

Inhaling deep to keep his emotions under control, he

rubbed his thumb over the face of his son. 'I have only just discovered I have a child.' He stopped when she raised her eyebrow again to remind him of her unanswered question. 'Through…business associates who wished to get my attention—'

She shook her head, her long ponytail swinging. 'What on earth does that mean? Why would business associates want to use your child to get your attention?' High colour had flown into her cheeks, reminding him of another time, another place when her emotions had run equally passionate. 'What type of business are you involved in?' she voiced suspiciously.

So she didn't know who he was. Something vaguely resembling relief speared through him. When his business partnership with Zaccheo Giordano had become public knowledge five years ago, his world had exploded with fawning acolytes and women falling over themselves to get his attention. That attention had increased a hundredfold when he'd opened his first super-luxury resort off the coast of Tahiti, a feat he'd repeated soon after with five more, seeing him skyrocket onto the World's Richest list.

It was curiously refreshing not to have to deal with the instant personality change that accompanied recognition of his name. But not refreshing enough to know his response had triggered suspicion that could keep him from his reason for being here. Even though her instinct might yet prove correct.

He needed to frame his words carefully.

'You have nothing to fear from me.' He'd managed to lock down his control after that gut punch he'd received on seeing her again. From here on in, he would be operating from a place of cold, hard intelligence.

She shook her head again. 'Sorry, that's not good enough. You'll have to do better than that.' Her gaze went to the picture frame he held on to, a fierce light of protection and possession burning in her striking blue eyes.

'Tell me the exact nature of your business or this conversation ends now.'

Romeo almost laughed. She was seriously deluded if she thought her heated threats would in any way dissuade him from seeing his son, from verifying for himself that the child truly belonged to him.

'I'm the CEO and owner of Brunetti International,' he replied.

She frowned for a moment, then her features morphed into astonishment. 'Brunetti...those resorts you need to sell an organ or a limb before you can afford a night there?'

He made a dismissive gesture. 'We cater to people from all walks of life.'

She snorted. 'As long as they've sold their grandmothers to be able to afford your billionaire rates.'

Romeo pursed his lips. His wealth wasn't the subject under discussion here.

The fact that she seemed to be a rare species, a mother who stood like a lioness in protection of her child, a child whom he'd yet to be certain without a shadow of a doubt shared his DNA, should take precedence.

'You know who I am now. You'll also know from your previous career that information can be discovered if one digs deep enough. My business associates dug deep enough and they found you and my son.'

'My son.'

The sudden urge to snarl *our child* took him by surprise. He stared down at the picture, clutching at the fraying edges of his control when he began to feel off balance again. '*Per favore.* Please. Tell me his name.'

Her gaze went to the picture and her features softened immediately.

The look was one he'd witnessed before, in that hotel room five years ago. It was a look that had set so many alarm bells ringing inside his head that he'd withdrawn swiftly and decisively from it. He looked away because just as he'd had no room to accommodate *feelings* then, he had no room for them now.

'His name is Gianlucca. Gianlucca O'Connell.'

An irrational surge of displeasure threatened to floor him. *'O'Connell?'*

Again that challenging arch of her eyebrow. Back in Palermo he'd seen her passion, her fire, but that had been directed to the bedroom, and what they'd done to each other in bed. Seeing it in a different light didn't make it any less sexy. Yet the punch of heat to his libido took him by surprise. He'd grown so jaded by the overabundance of willing women that lately he'd lost interest in the chase. For the past three months, work had become his mistress, the only thing that fired his blood in any meaningful way.

'That *is* my name. Or did you expect me to call him Gianlucca Romeo?'

He gritted his teeth. 'Did you even make an effort to find me when you knew you carried my child?'

A look crossed her face, a mixture of pride and anger, and she raised her chin. 'Did you want to be found?' she fired back.

Knowing how well he'd covered his tracks, a wave of heat crawled up his neck. He'd succeeded more than in his wildest dreams. He'd walked away, having effectively smashed down any residual feelings of rejection, or the idea that he could be worthy of something more than the brain and brawn that had seen him through his harrowing childhood into the man he was today.

The hours of imagined softness, of imagined affection, had been an illusion brought on by his mother's passing. An illusion he'd almost given in to. An emotion he'd vowed then never to entertain even the merest hint of again.

'We'll address the subject of his surname at another time. But now we've established who I am, I'd like to know more about him. Please,' he added when her stance remained intransigent.

'All I know is your surname. I don't even know how old you are, never mind what sort of man you are.'

Romeo rounded the desk and watched her back away, but looking into her eyes he saw no sign of fear. Only stubbornness. Satisfied that she didn't fear him, he moved closer, watched her pupils dilate as a different sort of chemistry filled the air. Her sudden erratic breathing told him everything he needed to know.

'I'm thirty-five. And five years ago, you gave yourself to me without knowing anything more about me besides my first name.' He watched a blush wash up her throat into her face with more than a little fascination. 'You were in a foreign place, with a strange man, and yet you trusted your instinct enough to enter my hotel suite and stay for a whole night. And right now, even though your heart is racing, you don't fear me. Or you would've screamed for help by now.' He reached out and touched the pulse beating at her throat. Her soft, silky skin glided beneath his fingertips and blazing heat lanced his groin again. Curbing the feeling, he dropped his hand and stepped back. 'I don't mean you or the boy harm. I just wish to see him. I deal in facts and figures. I need visual evidence that he exists, and as accommodating as I'm willing to be, I won't be giving you a choice in the matter.'

She swallowed, her eyes boldly meeting and staying on his. 'Just so you know, I don't respond well to threats.'

'It wasn't a threat, *gattina*.' They both froze at the term that had unwittingly dropped from his lips. From the look on her face, Romeo knew she was remembering the first time he'd said it. Her nails had been embedded in his back, her claws transmitting the depth of her arousal as he'd sunk deep inside her. His little wildcat had been as crazy for him as he'd been for her. But that was then, a moment in time never to be repeated. 'I'm merely stating a fact.'

She opened her mouth to reply, then stopped as voices filled the restaurant. 'I have to go. This is our busiest afternoon slot. I can't leave Lacey on her own.'

Romeo told himself to be calm. 'I need an answer, Maisie.'

She stared at him for a long moment before her gaze dropped to the picture he held. She looked as if she wanted to snatch it from him but he held on tight. She finally looked back up. 'He goes to playgroup from eleven to three o'clock. I take him to the park afterwards if the weather's good.'

'Did you have plans to do that today?'

She slowly nodded. 'Yes.'

Blood rushed into his ears, nearly deafening him. He forced himself to think, to plot the best way he knew how. Because rushing blood and racing hearts were for fools. Fools who let emotion rule their existence.

'What park?' he rasped.

'Ranelagh Gardens. It's—'

'I will find it.'

She paled and her hands flew out in a bracing stance. 'You can't... Don't you think we need to discuss this a little more?'

Romeo carefully set down the picture, then took out his phone and captured an image of it. He stared down at his son's face on his phone screen, and the decision concreted in his mind. 'No, Maisie. There's nothing more to discuss. If he's mine, truly mine, then I intend to claim him.'

Maisie slowly sank into the chair after Romeo made a dramatic exit, taking all the oxygen and bristling vitality of the day with him. She raised her hand to her face and realised her fingers were shaking. Whether it was from the shock of seeing him again after convincing herself she would never set eyes on him again, or the indomitability of that last statement, she wasn't certain.

She sat there, her hand on her clammy forehead, her gaze

in the middle distance as she played back every word, every gesture, on a loop in her mind.

The sound of laughter finally broke through her racing thoughts. She really needed to walk the floor, make sure her customers were all right. But she found herself clicking on her laptop, typing in his name on her search engine.

The images that confronted her made her breath catch all over again. Whereas she hadn't given herself permission to linger on anywhere but Romeo's face while they'd been in her office, she leaned in close and perused each image. And there were plenty, it seemed. Pictures of him dressed in impeccable handmade suits, posing for a profile piece in some glossy business magazine; pictures of him opening his world-renowned resorts in Dubai and Bali; and many, many pictures of him with different women, all drop-dead gorgeous, all smiling at him as if he was their world, their every dream come true.

But the ones that caught Maisie's attention, the ones that made her heart lurch wildly, were of Romeo on a yacht with another man—the caption named him as Zaccheo Giordano—and a woman with two children. The children were Gianlucca's age, possibly a little older, and the pictures were a little grainy, most likely taken with a telephoto lens from a long distance.

He sat apart from the family, his expression as remote as an arctic floe. That lone-wolf look, the one that said approach with caution, froze her heart as she saw it replicated in each rigid, brooding picture that followed. Even when he smiled at the children, there was a distance that spoke of his unease.

Trembling, Maisie sat back from the desk, the large part of her that had been agitated at the thought of agreeing to a meeting between Romeo and her son escalating to alarming proportions.

She might not know how he felt about children generally, but if the pictures could be believed, Romeo Brunetti wasn't the warm and cuddly type.

Maisie gulped in the breath she hadn't been able to fully access while Romeo had been in the room and tried to think rationally. She'd tried to find Romeo five years ago to tell him that they'd created a child together. It was true that at the time she'd been reeling from her parents' further disappointment in her, and in hindsight she'd probably been seeking some sort of connection with her life suddenly in chaotic free fall. But even then, deep down, she'd known she couldn't keep the news to herself or abandon her baby to the care of strangers as her parents had wanted.

So in a way, this meeting had always been on the cards, albeit to be scheduled at a time of her choosing and without so much…pulse-destroying drama.

Or being confronted with the evidence that made her mothering instincts screech with the possibility that the father of her child might want him for reasons other than to cement a love-at-first-sight bond that would last a lifetime.

She clicked back to the information page and was in the middle of Romeo's worryingly brief biography when a knock announced Lacey's entrance.

'I need you, Maisie! A group of five just walked in. They don't have a booking but I don't think they'll take no for an answer.'

Maisie suppressed a sigh and closed her laptop with a guilty sense of relief that she didn't have to deal with Romeo's last words just yet.

'Okay, let's go and see what we can do, shall we?'

She pinned a smile on her face that felt a mile from genuine and left her office. For the next three hours, she pushed the fast-approaching father-and-son meeting to the back of her mind and immersed herself in the smooth running of the lunchtime service.

* * *

The walk to Gianlucca's nursery took less than ten minutes, but with her mind free of work issues, her heart began to race again at the impending meeting.

Every cell in her body urged her to snatch her son and take him far away.

But she'd never been the type to run, or bury her head in the sand.

She'd give Romeo the chance to spell out what he wished for, and if his parting remarks were anything to go by he would be demanding a presence in her son's life. She would hear him out, but nothing would make her accommodate visitation with her son until she was absolutely sure he would be safe with Romeo.

Her heart lurched at the thought that she'd have to part from him for a few hours maybe once or twice a week. Maybe a full weekend when he grew older. Her breath shuddered out, and she shook her head. She was getting ahead of herself. For all she knew, Romeo would take one look at Lucca, satisfy himself that he was his and ring-fence himself with money-grubbing lawyers to prevent any imagined claims.

But then, if that was what he intended, would he have taken the time to seek them out?

Whatever happened, her priority would remain ensuring her son's happiness. She stopped before the nursery door, unclenched her agitated fists and blinked eyes prickling with tears.

From the moment he'd been born, it'd been just the two of them. After the search for Romeo had proved futile, she'd settled into the idea that it would always be just the two of them.

The threat to that twosome made her insides quiver.

She brushed her tears away. By the time she was buzzed in, Maisie had composed herself.

'Mummy!' Gianlucca raced towards her, an effervescent bundle of energy that pulled a laugh from Maisie.

Enfolding him in her arms, she breathed his warm, toddler scent until he wriggled impatiently.

'Are we going to the park to see the ducks?' he asked eagerly, his striking hazel eyes—so like his father's it was uncanny—widened expectantly.

'Yes, I even brought some food for them,' she replied and smiled wider when he whooped and dashed off towards the door.

She spotted the limo the moment they turned into the square. Black and ominous, it sat outside the north entrance in front of an equally ominous SUV, both engines idling. Beside the limo, two men dressed in black and wearing shades stood, their watchful stance evidence that they were bodyguards.

Maisie tried not to let her imagination careen out of control. Romeo Brunetti was a billionaire and she'd dealt with enough unscrupulous characters during her stint as a lawyer to know the rich were often targets for greedy, sometimes dangerous criminals.

All the same, she clutched Gianlucca's hand tighter as they passed the car and entered the park. Gianlucca darted off for the duck pond, his favourite feature in the park, as soon as she handed him the bread she'd taken from the restaurant.

He was no more than a dozen paces away when a tingle danced on her nape. She glanced over her shoulder and watched Romeo enter the park, his gaze passing cursorily over her before it swung to Gianlucca.

Maisie's heart lurched, then thundered at the emotions that washed over his face. Wonder. Shock. Anxiety. And a fierce possessiveness that sent a huge dart of alarm through her.

But the most important emotion—love—was missing.

It didn't matter that it was perhaps irrational for her to

demand it of him, but the absence of that powerful emotion terrified her.

Enough to galvanise her into action when he walked forward, reached her and carried on going.

'Romeo!' She caught his arm when she sensed his intention.

'What?' He paused, but his gaze didn't waver from Gianlucca's excited form.

'Wait. Please,' she whispered fiercely when he strained against her hold.

He whirled to her, his nostrils flaring as he fought to control himself. 'Maisie.' His tone held a note of barely leashed warning.

Swallowing, she stood her ground. 'I know you want to meet him, but you can't just barge in looking like…' She stopped and bit her lip.

'Looking like what?'

'Like a charging bull on steroids. You'll frighten him.'

His face hardened and he breathed deep before spiking a hand through his hair. After another long glance at Gianlucca, he faced her. '*Bene*, what do you suggest?'

Maisie reached into her bag. 'Here, I brought one of these for you.'

He eyed her offering and his eyebrows shot up. 'A bag of dried bread?'

'He's feeding the ducks. It's his favourite thing to do. I thought you could…approach him that way.'

Romeo's eyes darkened to a burnished gold. Slowly, he reached out and took the offering. *'Grazie,'* he muttered with tight aloofness.

She held on when he started to turn away, silently admonishing herself for experiencing a tiny thrill of pleasure when his arm flexed beneath her fingers. 'Also, I'd prefer it if you didn't tell him who you are. We can have a longer discussion about where we go from here before anything happens.'

A dark look gleamed in his eyes, but he nodded. 'If that is what you wish.'

'It is.'

He nodded, then tensed as a trio of kids flew by on their way to the pond. 'I agree, perhaps this isn't the most appropriate venue for an introduction.'

A tight knot eased in Maisie's stomach and she realised a part of her had feared Romeo would only want to see his son from afar and decide he didn't want to know him. She had yet to decipher his true motives, but she would allow this brief meeting.

'Thank you.'

He merely inclined his head before his gaze swung back to Gianlucca. Knowing she couldn't postpone the meeting any longer, she fell into step beside Romeo.

Gianlucca threw the last of his bread into the waiting melee of ducks and swans and broke into a delighted laugh as they fought over the scraps. His laughter turned into a pout when the ducks swam off to greet the bread-throwing trio of kids. 'Mummy, more bread!' When Maisie remained silent, he turned and raced towards them. 'Please?' he added.

She glanced at Romeo and watched the frozen fascination on his face as Gianlucca reached them. She caught him before he barrelled into her and crouched in front of him. 'Wait a moment, Lucca. There's someone I want you to meet. This…this is Romeo Brunetti.'

Lucca tilted his head up and eyed the towering man before him. 'Are you Mummy's friend?'

Romeo's head bobbed once. 'Yes. Nice to meet you, Gianlucca.'

Gianlucca immediately slipped his hand into Romeo's and pumped with all his might. A visible tremble went through Romeo's body, and he made a strangled sound. Gianlucca heard it and stilled, his eyes darting from the giant man to his mother.

The overprotective mother in her wanted to scoop him up and cuddle him close, but Maisie forced herself to remain still. Her breath caught as Romeo sank into a crouch, still holding his son's hand, his eyes glistening with questions.

'I look forward to getting to know you, Gianlucca.'

Lucca nodded, then gasped as he saw what Romeo held in his other hand. 'Did you come to feed the ducks, too?'

Romeo nodded. '*Sì*...yes,' he amended and started to rise. His body bristled with a restlessness that made Maisie's pulse jump. 'That was my intention, but I'm not an expert, like you.'

'It's easy! Come on.' He tugged at Romeo's hand, his excitement at having another go at his favourite pastime vibrating through his little body.

Maisie stayed crouched, the residual apprehension clinging to her despite the sudden, throat-clogging tears. As meetings between father and son went, it had gone much easier than she could've hoped for. And yet, she couldn't move from where she crouched. Because, she realised, through all the scenarios she'd played in her mind, she'd never really thought beyond this moment. Oh, she'd loftily imagined dictating visitation terms and having them readily agreed to, and then going about raising her son with minimal interference.

But looking at Romeo as he gazed down at his son with an intense proprietary light in his eyes, Maisie realised she really had no clue what the future held. Her breath shuddered out as Romeo's words once again flashed through her brain.

There's nothing more to discuss. If he's mine, truly mine, then I intend to claim him.

She slowly rose and looked over her shoulder. Sure enough, the two black-clad bodyguards prowled a short distance away. About to turn away, Maisie froze as she spotted two more by the south gate. Two more guarded the west side of the park.

Heart in her throat, she approached the duck pond, where Romeo was throwing a piece of bread under her son's strict instruction.

His head swung towards her and his expression altered at whatever he read on her face. 'Something wrong?'

'I think I should be asking you that,' she hissed so Gianlucca wouldn't overhear, but she placed a protective hand on his tiny shoulder, ready to lay down her life for him if she needed to. 'Do you want to tell me why you have *six* bodyguards watching this park?' Her voice vibrated with the sudden fear and anger she couldn't disguise.

His face hardened and the arm he'd raised to throw another bite into the pond slowly lowered to his side. 'I think it's time to continue this conversation elsewhere.'

CHAPTER FOUR

ROMEO WATCHED SEVERAL expressions chase over her face.

'What does that mean?' she asked, her blue eyes narrowing before she cast another alarmed glance at the burly men guarding the park.

He followed her apprehensive gaze and indicated sharply at his men when he saw that other parents were beginning to notice their presence. The men melted into the shadows, but the look didn't dissipate from Maisie's face. When her hand tightened imperceptibly on Gianlucca's shoulder, Romeo's insides tightened.

'My hotel is ten minutes away. We'll talk there.' He tried not to let the irony of his statement cloud the occasion. He'd said similar words to her five years ago, an invitation that had ended with him reeling from the encounter.

That invitation had now brought him to this place, to his son. He had no doubt in his mind that the child was his. Just as he had no doubt that he would claim him, and protect him from whatever schemes Lorenzo had up his sleeves. Beyond that, he had no clue what his next move was. He didn't doubt, though, that he would find a way to triumph. He'd dragged himself from the tough streets of Palermo to the man he was today. He didn't intend to let anything stand in the way of what he desired.

He focused to find her shaking her head. 'I can't.'

Romeo's eyes narrowed as a hitherto thought occurred to him. 'You can't? Why not?' He realised then how careless he'd been. Because Lorenzo's pictures had shown only Maisie with his son, Romeo had concluded that she was unattached. But those pictures were four years old. A lot could have happened in that time. She could've taken another lover, a man who had perhaps become important enough to see himself as Gianlucca's father.

The very idea made him see red for one instant. 'Is there someone in your life?' He searched her fingers. They were ringless. But that didn't mean anything these days. 'A *lover*, perhaps?' The word shot from his mouth like a bullet.

Her eyes widened and she glanced down at Gianlucca, but he was engrossed in feeding the last of the bread to the ducks. 'I don't have a lover or a husband, or whatever the *au fait* term is nowadays.'

Romeo attributed the relief that poured through him to not having to deal with another tangent in this already fraught, woefully ill-planned situation. 'In that case there shouldn't be a problem in discussing this further at my hotel.'

'That wasn't why I refused to come with you. I have a life to get on with, Romeo. And Lucca has a schedule that I try to keep to so his day isn't disrupted, otherwise he gets cranky. I need to fix his dinner in half an hour and put him to bed so I can get back to the restaurant.'

He stiffened. 'You go to work after he's asleep?'

Her mouth compressed. 'Not every night, but yes. I live above the restaurant and my assistant manager lives in the flat next door. She looks after him on the nights I work.'

'That is unacceptable.'

Her eyes widened with outrage. 'Excuse me?' she hissed.

'From now on you will not leave him in the care of strangers.'

Hurt indignation slid across her face. 'If you knew me at all, you'd know leaving my son with some faceless stranger is the last thing I'd do! Bronagh isn't a stranger. She's my friend as well as my assistant. And how dare you tell me how to raise my son?'

He caught her shoulders and tugged her close so they wouldn't be overheard. 'He is *our* son,' he rasped into her ear. 'His safety and well-being have now become my concern as much as yours, *gattina*.' The endearment slipped out again, but he deemed it appropriate, so he didn't allow the tingle that accompanied the term to disturb him too much. 'Put your claws away and let's take him back to your flat. You'll feed him and put him to bed and then we'll talk, *si*?'

He pulled back and looked down at her, noting her hectic colour and experiencing that same punch to his libido that had occurred earlier.

Dio, he needed this added complication like a bullet in the head.

He dropped his hand once she gave a grudging nod.

'Lucca, it's time to go,' she called out.

'One more minute!' came his son's belligerent reply.

A tight, reluctant smile curved Maisie's lips, drawing Romeo's attention to their pink plumpness. 'He has zero concept of time and yet that's his stock answer every time you try to get him away from something he loves doing.'

'I'll bear that in mind,' he answered.

He glanced at his son and that sucker-punch feeling slammed into him again. It'd first happened when Gianlucca had slid his hand into his. Romeo had no term for it. But it was alive within him, and swelling by the minute.

Unthinking questions crowded his mind. Like when had Gianlucca taken his first step? What had been his first word?

What was his favourite thing to do besides feeding greedy ducks?

He stood, stock-still, as a plan began to formulate at the back of his mind. A plan that was uncharacteristically outlandish.

But wasn't this whole situation outlandish in the extreme?

And hadn't he learned that sometimes it was better to fight fire with fire?

The idea took firmer root, embedding itself as the only

viable course available to him if he was to thwart the schemes of Lorenzo Carmine and Agostino Fattore.

The more Romeo thought about the plans the old men, in their bid to hang on to their fast-crumbling empire, had dared to lay out for him, the more rage threatened to overcome him. He'd tempered that rage with caution, not forgetting that a wounded animal was a dangerous animal. Fattore's lieutenant might be old, and his power weakened, but Romeo knew that some power was better than no power to people like Lorenzo. And they would hang on to it by every ruthless means available.

Romeo didn't intend to lower his guard where Lorenzo's wily nature was concerned. His newly discovered son's safety was paramount. But even if Lorenzo and the shadows of Romeo's past hadn't been hanging over him, he would still proceed with the plan now fully formed in his mind.

He followed Maisie as she approached and caught up Gianlucca's hand. 'Time to go, precious.' The moment he started to protest, she continued, 'Which do you prefer for your tea, fish fingers or spaghetti and meatballs?'

'Spaghetti balls,' the boy responded immediately, his mind adeptly steered in the direction of food, just as his mother had intended. He danced between them until they reached the gate.

Romeo noticed his men had slipped into the security SUV parked behind his limo and nodded at the driver who held the door open. He turned to help his son into the car and saw Maisie's frown.

'Do you happen to have a car seat in there?' she asked.

Romeo cursed silently. 'No.'

'In that case, we'll meet you back at the restaurant.' She turned and started walking down the street.

He shut the door and fell into step beside her. 'I'll walk back with you.'

She opened her mouth to protest but stopped when he

took his son's hand. The feel of the small palm against his tilted Romeo's world.

He hadn't known or expected this reality-changing situation when he'd walked into that mansion in Palermo yesterday. But Romeo was nothing if not a quick study. His ability to harness a situation to his advantage had saved his life more times on the street than he could recount. He wasn't in a fight-to-the-death match right now, but he still intended to emerge a winner.

Maisie's first priority when she'd decorated her flat was homey comfort, with soft furnishings and pleasant colours to make the place a safe and snug home for her son. But as she opened the door and walked through the short hallway that connected to the living room she couldn't help but see it through Romeo's eyes. The carpet was a little worn, one cushion stained with Lucca's hand paint. And suddenly, the yellow polka-dot curtains seemed a little too bright, like something a *girlie* girl would choose, instead of the sophisticated women Romeo Brunetti probably dated.

What did it matter?

She turned, prepared to show her pride in her home, and found him frozen in front of the framed picture collage above her TV stand. Twelve pictures documented various key stages of Lucca's life so far, from his scrunched-up hours-old face to his first Easter egg hunt two months ago.

Romeo stared at each one with an intensity that bordered on the fanatic. Then he reached out and traced his fingers over Lucca's first picture, the tremor in his hand hard to miss.

'I have digital copies…if you'd like them,' she ventured.

He turned. The naked emotion in his eyes momentarily stopped her breath.

'*Grazie*, but I don't think that would be necessary.'

Her heart stopped as the fear she hadn't wanted to fully

explore bloomed before her eyes. 'What does that mean?' she asked, although she risked him further exploiting the rejection he'd just handed her.

'It means there are more important things to discuss than which pictures of my son I would like copies of.'

Lucca chose that moment to announce his hunger.

Maisie glanced at Romeo, questions warring with anger inside her.

She didn't want to leave her son now that she knew Romeo was preparing to back away. Especially since there was also the outside threat evidenced by the bodyguards in the SUV that had crawled behind them as they'd walked back. He travelled with too much security for a garden-variety billionaire.

That knowledge struck fear into her heart that she couldn't dismiss.

'Go and make his meal, Maisie,' Romeo said.

The taut command in his voice jerked her spine straight.

'I'd rather take him into the kitchen with me.'

'Is that your normal routine?' he queried with narrowed eyes.

'No, normally he likes to watch his favourite children's TV show while I cook.'

Romeo gave a brisk nod. 'Go, then. I'll find a way of entertaining him,' he replied.

'What do you know about entertaining children?' she demanded fiercely.

His jaw clenched. 'Even rocket science has been mastered. Besides, you'll be in the next room. What could go wrong?'

Everything.

The word blasted through her head. She opened her mouth to say as much but saw Lucca staring with keen interest at them. The last thing she wanted was for her son to pick up the dangerous undercurrents in the room.

Romeo watched her for a minute, clench-jawed. 'Are there any other exits in the flat, besides the front door?'

Maisie frowned. 'There's a fire escape outside my bedroom.'

'Is it locked?'

'Yes.'

'Okay.' He strode out and she followed him into the hallway. She watched him lock and take out the key and return to her. 'Now you can be assured that I won't run off with him while your back is turned. I'll also keep conversation to a minimum so I don't inadvertently verbally abuse him. Are you satisfied?'

Her fingers curled around the key, and she refused to be intimidated. 'That works. I won't be long. The meatballs are already done... I just need to cook the pasta.'

Romeo nodded and looked to where Lucca knelt on the floor surrounded by a sea of Lego. He shrugged off his overcoat and draped it over the sofa. Maisie watched him advance towards Lucca, his steps slow and non-threatening, to crouch next to him.

Lucca looked up, smiled and immediately scooped up a handful of Lego and held it out to him.

Maisie backed out, fighting the tearing emotions rampaging through her. Admonishing herself to get her emotions under control, she rushed into the kitchen and set about boiling water for the spaghetti, all the while trying to dissect what the presence of the bodyguards meant.

Surely if Romeo was in some sort of trouble the Internet search would've picked it out? Or was she blowing things out of proportion? Was she wrong about billionaires travelling with that much security? She frowned at the total excess of it. And what about Romeo's explanation that his business associates had found Lucca? From her time as a lawyer, Maisie knew deep background checks had become par for the course during business deals, but from Romeo's expression in the park, she couldn't help feeling there was more.

Her heart hammered as horrific possibilities tumbled through her mind. The world was a dangerous place. Even in a picturesque haven like Ranelagh, she couldn't guarantee that she would always be able to keep Lucca safe.

She froze at the sink. Had she invited danger in by letting Romeo Brunetti through her front door? Or had he been right when he'd told her she'd instinctively trusted him in Palermo or she'd never have gone up to his suite that day?

She must have on some level, surely, or she'd never have given him her virginity so easily.

Stop!

The only way to find out what was going on was to talk to Romeo. That wouldn't happen unless she stopped dawdling and got on with it.

She fixed Lucca's meal and set it up in the dining nook attached to her kitchen. Seeing Romeo sprawled on his side on the living-room floor stopped her in her tracks. Between father and son, they'd built a giant castle and were debating where to station the knights, with Lucca in favour of ground sentry duty and Romeo advocating turret guards.

He sensed her watching and looked up. Again Maisie was struck by the determination on his face.

And again, he shuttered the look and handed the knight to Lucca.

Maisie cleared her throat before she could speak. 'Lucca, your food's ready.'

'One more minute!'

Romeo lifted an eyebrow and gave a mock shudder. 'Do you enjoy cold spaghetti, Gianlucca?'

Lucca shook his head. 'No, it tastes yucky.'

'Then I think you should eat yours now before it turns yucky, *sì*?'

'See what?' Lucca asked, his eyes wide and enquiring.

Romeo reached out and hesitantly touched his son's hair. '*Sì* means yes in Italian,' he said gruffly.

'Are you Ita…Itayan? Mummy said I'm half Itayan.'

Romeo's eyes flicked to Maisie for a moment, then returned to his son. 'Yes, she's right. She's also waiting for you to go eat your dinner.' A quiet, firm reminder that brought Lucca to his feet.

He whizzed past her and climbed into his seat at the small dining table. He barely waited for Maisie to tuck his bib into place before he was tearing into his spaghetti.

Romeo leaned against the doorjamb, a peculiar look on his face as he absorbed Lucca's every action.

Then he turned and looked at her, and her heart caught. Nothing could keep down the geyser of apprehension that exploded through her at what that absorbed look on Romeo's face meant for her and her son.

In that moment, Maisie knew that nothing she said or did would stop what was unravelling before her eyes. It didn't matter whether Romeo loved his son or not, he would do exactly as he'd said in her office this morning.

Romeo Brunetti had every intention of claiming his son.

Maisie entered the living room and paused to watch Romeo's broad frame as he looked out of the window at the street below. With the endless horrific thoughts that had been tumbling through her mind for the past three hours, she wondered if he was just pavement-watching or if there was some unseen danger lurking out there.

He turned and her breath caught at the intensity in his face, the dangerous vibe surrounding his body. Wanting to get this over with quickly, she walked further into the living room.

'He's out like a light. When he's worn out like that, he won't wake until morning.' Maisie wondered why she'd been dropping little morsels like this all evening. Then she realised it was because Romeo voraciously lapped up each titbit about his son.

Because a part of her hoped that, by doing so, she could get him to rethink whatever he was plotting for Lucca's future? Did she really think she could turn Romeo's fascination with their son into love?

Love couldn't be forced. Either it was there or it wasn't. Her parents had been incapable of it. They'd cared only for their academic pursuits and peer accolades. None of that love had spilled to her.

She balled her fists. She would rather Romeo absented himself completely than dangle fatherhood in front of her son, only to reject him later. 'You wanted to talk?' she ventured. The earlier they laid things out in the open, the quicker she could get back to the status quo.

Romeo nodded in that solemn way he sometimes did, then remained silent and still, his hands thrust into his pockets. He continued to watch her, dark hazel eyes tracking her as she straightened the cushions and packed away the toys.

Too soon she was done. Silence filled the room and her breath emerged in short pants as she became painfully aware that they were alone, that zing of awareness spreading wider in the room.

She realised she was fidgeting with her fingers and resolutely pulled them apart. 'I don't mean to hurry this along, but can we just get it over—'

'Sit down, Maisie.'

She wanted to refuse. Just on principle because she wouldn't be ordered about in her own home, but something in his face warned her she needed to sit for what was coming.

Heart slamming into her ribcage, she perched on the edge of the sofa. He took the other end, his large body turned towards her so their knees almost touched. Again awareness of just how big, how powerfully built he was, crowded her senses. Her gaze dropped to his hands, large with sleek fingers. She recalled how they'd made her feel, how the light dusting of hair on the back had triggered delicious shivers in her once upon a time.

A different tremble powered up her spine.

Maisie gave herself a silent shake. This wasn't the time to be falling into a pool of lust. She'd been there, done that, with this man. And look where it had got her.

Look where she was now, about to be given news she instinctively knew would be life-changing.

She glanced up at him. His hazel eyes probed, then raked her face, and his nostrils flared slightly, as if he, too, was finding it difficult to be seated so close to her without re-membering what they'd done to each other on a hot September night in Palermo five years ago. His gaze dropped to her throat, her breasts, and she heard his short intake of breath.

'Romeo…'

He balled his fists on top of his thighs and his chest ex-panded in a long inhalation. 'You're right about the body-guards. I normally only travel with two members of my security team.'

Her stomach hollowed out. 'Why…why the increase?'

'It's just a precaution at this stage.'

'What does that mean?' she demanded. 'Precaution against what?'

'It means neither you nor Gianlucca are in danger at the moment.'

'But you're expecting us to be at some point?' Her voice had risen with her escalating fear and the shaking had taken on a firmer hold.

He shook his head. 'You don't need to panic—'

'Oh, really? You tell me my son could be in danger and then tell me not to panic?' she blurted, all the different sce-narios she'd talked herself out of tumbling back again. She brushed her hands over her arms as cold dread drowned her.

'I meant, there was no need to panic because I'll ensure your safety,' he said.

'Safety from what?' When he remained silent, she jumped to her feet and paced the small living room. 'I think you should start from the beginning, Romeo. Who are these people and what do they want with you? With our son?'

She froze. 'Are you involved in…in criminal activity?' she whispered in horror.

His mouth compressed and his face set into harsh, determined lines. 'No, I am not.'

The scathing force of the words prompted her to believe him. But the fear didn't dissipate. 'Please tell me what's going on.'

He rose, too, and paced opposite her. When his fists clenched and unclenched a few times, she approached. At the touch of her hand on his arm, he jerked, as if he'd been elsewhere.

As he stared down at her, his mouth compressed. 'My past isn't what you'd call a white-picket-fence fairy tale,' he said obliquely.

Maisie attempted a smile. 'Only the books I read to Lucca contain those. Real life is rarely that way.'

A grim smile crossed his lips. 'Unfortunately, mine was a little more dire than that.'

She kept quiet, mostly because she didn't know how to respond.

'The man whose blood runs through my veins was the head of a Sicilian organised crime family.'

She gasped, then stepped back as the import of the words sank in. 'You're a member of a Mafia gang?'

'No, I'm not.' Again that scathing denial.

'But your…your father is?'

'He wasn't my father. We just share the same DNA,' he bit out in a harsh tone that spoke of anger, bitterness and harrowing pain.

Maisie's eyes widened. As if aware of how he'd sounded, Romeo breathed deeply and slid his fingers through his hair. 'The abbreviated story is that I met him twice. Both times ended…badly. What I didn't know until yesterday was that he'd kept tabs on me all my life.'

'Why?' she demanded.

Romeo shrugged. 'Since I didn't know the man, I can

only guess it was some sort of power-trip thing to watch whether I failed or succeeded. Or it may have been for other reasons. I care very little about what his motives were.'

Maisie frowned. 'You talked about him in the past tense…because…'

'He and his family died in a yacht explosion a year ago.'

The rush of blood from her head made her light-headed. 'Was it an accident?' she asked, her lips numb.

His mouth pursed for a few seconds before he answered, 'Officially. But probably not.'

Her gasp brought his head up. Cursing under his breath, he strode to her and grasped her arms. 'I'm only going by what my gut tells me, Maisie. I don't have hard evidence to the contrary.'

'And your gut tells you he was assassinated?'

He nodded.

A million more questions crowded her brain, but she forced a nod. 'Go on.'

His hands moved to her shoulders, a firm glide that left a trail of awareness over her skin. 'I received a letter from his lawyers a month ago, summoning me to Palermo, which I ignored. I received a few more after that. The last one told me he'd left me something I needed to collect in person.' His mouth twisted. 'My curiosity got the better of me.'

'What was it?'

'His monstrosity of a mansion. Along with his plans for my future.'

Ice slithered down her spine. 'What plans?'

One hand moved to her neck and cupped her nape. The familiarity of that gesture thawed the ice a little, replacing her terror with a wave of warm awareness.

'He never had a son…not a legitimate one anyway. I think somewhere along the line he intended to contact me, bring me into the *family business*. He just never got the chance to. But he told his second in command about it. He was the one who asked the lawyers to contact me.'

'What does he want from you?'

'The *famiglia* is falling apart. They need a new injection of young blood, and an even greater need for an injection of financial support.'

'You have both.'

'But I intend to give them neither.'

Maisie stared at his granite-hard face, the deep grooves bracketing his mouth and the dark gold of his eyes, and the pennies finally tumbled into place. 'But if you don't intend to… Oh, my God. You think they mean to use Lucca to make you do what they want?' she rasped in a terror-stricken voice.

His grip tightened and one finger caught her chin and raised her face to his spear-sharp gaze. Her stomach knotted at the savage determination on his face. 'They will *never* get their hands on you or our son. You have my word on this, Maisie.'

She shook her head, her insides growing colder by the second. 'But you can't guarantee that, can you? Or you wouldn't be here with *six* bodyguards in tow.'

'There's one way to ensure your safety,' he said, his gaze raking her face as if he wanted to pull the answer from her even before he'd asked the question.

'What's that?' she murmured.

'You will marry me. Then you and our son will know the protection of my name.'

CHAPTER FIVE

SHE WENT HOT, then cold, then colder. Until she felt as brittle as chilled glass. Dumbly, she stared into those burnished gold eyes, sure she'd misheard him.

'What did you say?'

'The *famiglia* isn't as powerful as it once was, but I'm not willing to dismiss them out of hand, either. Marrying me will grant you and Lucca protection, which you could be vulnerable without.'

'No way. I can't…I can't just *marry* you! We know next to nothing about each other.'

A look curled through his eyes. 'Our circumstances aren't commonplace. Besides, we've already done things a little out of sequence, don't you think?'

She laughed, but the sound was more painful than she wanted it to be. 'This is far from a quaint little romantic caper.'

He nodded. '*Sì*, which is why I want to ensure I have all the bases covered for your protection.'

'Oh, God!'

'Maisie—'

'No.' She pulled out of his hold and backed away. 'This is preposterous. You have to find another way to protect Lucca.'

Golden eyes bored into hers. 'There's no other way. There's an unspoken code, *gattina*. They may be thugs, but they respect family. Marrying me means you and Lucca become off limits.'

'But it still won't be a cast-iron guarantee, will it?'

He shrugged. 'Nothing in life is guaranteed. I have no

intention of involving myself in that life, but there may be resistance. A temporary marriage is our best option.'

The cold pronunciation chilled her to the bone. She kept backing away until her shoulders nudged the window. Unrelenting, he prowled towards her.

'No way. I can't do it, Romeo. I just… I can't just fold up my life and uproot my son to live goodness knows where, looking over my shoulder every day!'

'Look!' He reached her, grasped her shoulders and turned her around, directing her gaze to the street, where his men maintained a watchful guard. 'Is this how you want Lucca to live? Surrounded by men in black carrying guns? Can you honestly say that you'll experience a moment of peace in the park, knowing that his life could be in danger from unknown elements at each second of the day?'

She shuddered. 'That's not fair, Romeo.'

His bitter laugh scoured her skin. 'Life's *never* fair, *gattina*,' he whispered in her ear. 'Believe me, I have firsthand experience in just how unfair life can be. That's why I want this for our son. He will bear my name, legitimately, and my protection.'

'But you *cannot* guarantee that, can you? Can't you just go to the authorities and tell them about this?'

He levelled a deep sigh. '*Sì*, I can. My lawyers have been apprised of what's going on. But, technically, Lorenzo hasn't committed a crime yet, just issued veiled threats. Even when he does, the wheels of justice don't always move fast, Maisie. You of all people should know that.'

Sadly, she knew that all too well. Nevertheless, she couldn't give what he was suggesting any room to grow. That a part of her wanted to let it grow deeply unnerved her. 'We can still—'

'We can do a lot of things.' He reached for her again, pinning her arms to her sides. 'None would be as effective as what I'm proposing. At the very least, it'll buy time until I can find another solution.'

She pulled away. She thought of her parents, of the frosty existence she'd lived with. Her parents' lack of warmth hadn't just been directed at her. They'd been equally frosty to each other. As she'd grown up, she'd realised that the only reason they'd married and stayed married had been because of her. A shiver of horror raked her from head to toe at the thought of placing herself in a similar arrangement. Lucca was sharp. It would be a matter of time before he sensed that his parents didn't love one another. The thought of what it would do to him made her recoil.

'Maisie—'

'No!' she cried. The part of her that hadn't been freaking out completely threw up its arms and buckled beneath the part that was exploding with hysteria. 'I won't do it! I won't—'

She gasped as strong arms clamped around her and she was hauled into his body.

'*Basta!* There's no need to get hysterical.'

She fought to free herself, but his arms tightened their hold on her. 'I'm not getting hysterical,' she lied. Inside, she was going out of her mind with information overload. And being this close to Romeo, feeling his taut, warm body against hers, wasn't helping, either. Planting her hands on his chest, she pushed. 'Let me go, Romeo!'

'Calm down, then I will.'

She stilled, then made the mistake of glancing up at him.

His eyes were molten, his lips parted slightly as he stared down at her. The look on his face morphed to replicate the dangerous sensations climbing through her.

'No…' she whispered.

'No,' he agreed roughly. And yet his head started to descend, his arms gathering her even closer until her breasts were pressed against his chest.

A second later, his hot, sensual mouth slanted over hers, and she was tumbled headlong into a different quagmire.

Only, this one contained no fear, no horror. Only an electrifying sizzle that rocked her from head to toe.

His tongue breached her mouth, his teeth biting along the way. Maisie whimpered as sensation engulfed her. She opened her mouth wider, her tongue darting out to meet his.

He groaned and pulled her closer. One hand fisted her hair, angled her head for a deeper penetration, while the other slid down her back to cup her bottom. He squeezed and yanked her into his hardening groin. As if a torch paper had been lit between them, Maisie scoured her hands over him, trailing his shoulders, his back, the trim hardness of his waist before her fingers dug into the tightness of his buttocks.

A rough sound exploded from his lips as he rocked against her pelvis, imprinting his erection against her belly in a clear demand that made her moan. Hunger she'd taught herself to bury suddenly reared up, urgent and demanding. When his hand cupped her breast and toyed with her nipple, Maisie wanted to scream, *Take me!*

But even that sound would have taken too much effort, drugged as she was by the power of his kisses. Her fingers trailed back up, curled into his hair as she gave herself over to the sensation drowning her.

'*Gattina*…my little wildcat,' he groaned once he'd lifted his head to trail kisses along her jaw.

Maisie moaned as he bit her earlobe. 'Romeo.' Her speech was slurred and the secret place between her legs lit on fire from wanting him. From wanting her hunger assuaged.

He recaptured her mouth and Maisie was certain she would die just from the pleasure overload.

'Mummy!'

They exploded apart, their breaths erratic and ragged as they stared at each other across the space between them.

Romeo looked dazed, hectic colour scouring his cheekbones, his golden eyes hot and brooding and alive with arousal. She suspected she wore the same look, if not worse.

'Mummy!'

She lurched, still dazed, towards the door leading out into the hallway.

'Gattina.'

She didn't want to hear that term, didn't want to be reminded that she'd behaved like a horny little hellcat with her son asleep two doors away. But she turned anyway, met that torrid, golden gaze.

'Fix your shirt,' he rasped throatily.

Maisie looked down at the gaping shirt exposing her chest. The buttons had come undone without her having the vaguest idea when it'd happened. Flushing, she shakily secured them and hurried to her son's room.

He sat up in bed, rubbing his eyes, his lower lip pouting. She sat and scooped him into her lap and hugged him close.

'Hey, precious. Did you have a bad dream?'

'Yes. It was the bad goblins.' His lip trembled and he tucked his head into her shoulder.

'It's okay now, baby. Mummy's here. I'll slay the silly goblins so they can't get you.'

He gave a sleepy little giggle and wriggled deeper into her embrace.

She sat there, minutes ticking by as she crooned to him, until he fell back asleep. Planting a gentle kiss on his forehead, she caught movement from the corner of her eye and looked up to see Romeo framed in the doorway.

With her emotions nowhere near calm, Maisie couldn't form a coherent thought, never mind form actual words, so she watched in silence as he came and crouched at the side of the bed, his hand trailing gently down Lucca's back.

When his eyes met hers, her breath strangled at the fierce determination brimming in the hazel depths.

'You will slay his imaginary goblins. But what about his real ones?' he murmured, his voice low and intense.

'Romeo—'

'*I* will take care of those. All you have to do is accept my name.'

The implications of what he was asking was no less daunting, no less grave than it'd been half an hour ago when he'd dropped the bombshell. While she'd never given much thought to a future beyond being a mother and owner of a business she loved, she'd also not written it off. But what Romeo was asking… The idea was too huge to even comprehend.

'It's not as monumental an undertaking as you think,' he said, reading her thoughts with an accuracy that terrified her. 'Think of it as a time-buying exercise.'

His gaze fell to Lucca's sleeping form. His hand moved, as if to touch him, but he placed it back down on the bed.

The telling gesture made Maisie's breath strangle in her chest. 'You care about him, don't you?' she murmured.

A look crossed his face, which he quickly blanked. 'I didn't know he existed until twenty-four hours ago. But he's mine, and I take care of what's mine.'

He looked up, the clear, deadly promise blazing for her to see. It shook her to the soul, seeing the promise she'd made to her son the moment he'd drawn breath visible on another person's face.

She opened her mouth to say yes, then felt a cold finger of dread. As much as she wanted to protect her son, she couldn't live with herself if she risked swapping Lucca's physical well-being for his emotional one.

His eyes narrowed, and she was sure he was reading her thoughts again. He gently scooped up Lucca and placed him back in bed, pulling the Lego-themed coverlet over his little body before he straightened.

'Let's finish this talk. Now.' His voice vibrated with low, commanding intensity.

His heavy, dominating presence crowded her as they re-entered the living room. Knowing what she had to say, she turned to face him.

'What's the problem?' he asked.

She threw out her arms. 'Where do you want me to start? Even if I wanted to say yes to what you're proposing, what happens with us?'

A dark frown clamped his forehead. 'Us?'

'Yes, us. You and me. We're virtual strangers. What makes you think we'd last a day under the same roof?'

He shrugged. 'I'm inclined to think if we both know what's at stake, we can make it work.'

And what was at stake was her son's welfare. This was all for Lucca. She was merely the extra passenger along for the ride. The current situation had only made the claiming more urgent. The kiss that had happened was just residual hormones from their last time. Nothing more.

Lucca was the reason Romeo was here in the first place. She didn't think for a second that saying no would send Romeo packing. Regardless of the *Mafia code* or a marriage of convenience, the man in front of her would claim his son. She knew it with a bone-deep certainty.

'Maisie.' Another hard command. She was beginning to recognise how he'd risen to his powerful status so quickly. He packed more imperious presence in his little finger than most men packed in their whole bodies.

'I don't know what to say…'

He waited.

'Before I agree, I need your assurance that you'll resolve this as quickly as possible.'

His nostrils flared, but he nodded. *'Sì.'*

'That you'll tell me if anything changes where protecting Lucca is concerned.'

'You have my word.'

She sucked in a breath, but the enormity of what she was contemplating weighed on her with crushing force. 'Okay… then I'll marry you.'

A golden light flared in his eyes, and he nodded once.

'I'll take care of the details. You don't need to worry about anything.'

With that, he strode to where he'd draped his coat over the sofa and shrugged into it. Surprise scythed through her.

'You're leaving?'

'I have a few phone calls to make. I'll be back in the morning.'

Maisie was still reeling from his words and from what she'd committed herself to hours later when she realised that sleep would remain elusive.

She was still awake at 6:00 a.m. when firm knuckles hammered on her door.

'Is there a particular reason you feel inclined to break down my door at the crack of dawn?'

Romeo raised an eyebrow at the scowl that greeted him from beneath the cloud of auburn hair.

'I would've called, but I didn't want the phone to wake Lucca.' He also hadn't wanted to give her a chance to back out of what he'd convinced her to agree to yesterday.

Nothing would get in the way of him claiming his son. Attempting to give the child who was a part of himself the one thing that was denied him—a chance to choose his own path, free from the stain of illegitimacy.

Romeo might not know or even believe in love. But he could grant Gianlucca the acceptance and security that was never given him.

And Maisie O'Connell wouldn't stand in his way.

But she could, and continued to, glare at him. 'I suppose I should thank you for that consideration.'

'You're not a morning person, I see.'

'Great observation.' She eyed the coffee and croissants in his hand before slicing him with those bright blue eyes again. 'Is one of those for me?' she asked in a gruff, sleep-husky voice.

It was then he noticed the shadows under her eyes. Perhaps he should've waited a little while longer before arriving. But he'd grown tired of pacing his hotel suite. And he hadn't been certain that her *yes* had been from a place of belief that they were doing the right thing. The more he'd paced, the more he'd been sure she would change her mind given any more thinking room.

Romeo intended to give her none.

It had become clear very early on that her devotion to Lucca was absolute. It had been the only thing that had made him leave last night.

That and the need to push his investigators harder to find something concrete he could use against Lorenzo.

'Is that a no?'

He focused to see Maisie sliding a hairband from her wrist. She caught it in her teeth, then gathered her heavy silky hair into a bunch at the back of her head. The action drew up her nightshirt, showing off her shapely thighs and legs. Heat trickled through him as his gaze trailed up to linger on her heavy, pert breasts, thrown into relief by the act of securing her hair.

She seemed to notice the thick layer of awareness that had fired up, and her eyes darkened a touch.

Reining in his libido and burying the recollection of how those breasts had felt in his hands last night, he held out the coffee. There would be no repeat of last night's lust-fuelled encounter. Romeo had no intention of letting sex clutter up his plans.

He of all people knew one moment of madness could destroy a life. It was the reason he existed. It was the reason his mother had spent years blaming him for destroying her life.

It's the reason your son's here.

He accepted that sound analysis, just as he'd accepted that now he knew of Lucca's existence, he would safeguard his upbringing with everything he possessed. He'd witnessed too many people fall through the cracks to leave his son's fate to miracles and chance.

His own existence had been proof that miracles didn't exist.

'Thank you,' Maisie murmured huskily, taking the proffered beverage before stepping back to let him in. He handed her the pastry and followed her into the kitchen. She placed the croissants on a plate but didn't make a move to touch them. 'It's a little too early for me.'

Again he experienced a tiny bout of guilt, then told himself there would be plenty of time for her to rest once he got them away from here.

Her gaze flicked to him, then darted away. But in that look Romeo caught the hesitation he'd been dreading. He gritted his teeth.

He didn't want to resort to plan B, but he would if necessary. 'Second thoughts are natural. As long as you keep your eye on the big picture.'

She bit her lip. 'I can't believe this is happening.'

'It's happening, *gattina*. We'll tell Lucca when he wakes up. Is there anyone else you wish to inform? Your parents?' He vaguely recalled her mentioning them in the intermittent burst of chatter that had preceded him inviting her to his suite that night in Palermo.

Her expression shuttered and she took a large gulp of coffee. 'My parents are no longer in the picture.' A bleak note of hurt threaded her voice. 'And even if they were, this wouldn't be the ideal scenario to present to them, would it? Their only child marrying the father of her child because the Mafia were issuing threats?' Her mouth twisted in mocking bitterness.

His eyes narrowed at the odd note in her voice. 'They wouldn't want you to do what is necessary to safeguard their grandson?'

Her gaze remained lowered and she crossed her arms around her middle in a gesture of self-preservation. 'I wouldn't know. Besides the odd birthday and Christmas card, I haven't spoken to them in four years.'

Four years. The same length of time as his son had been alive. Certain there was more to the story, he opened his mouth to ask. But her head snapped up and she flashed him a pursed-lip smile.

'How much time do I have to get my things in order? I'll need a few days at least to talk to… You're shaking your head. Why?' she enquired curtly.

'We're leaving this morning.'

'That's impossible. I have to pack and make sure I get the right person to look after the restaurant until…' She stopped and frowned. 'Will I be able to return any time soon?' Wide blue eyes stared at him with a mixture of resignation and sadness.

'Not for a while.'

'How long is a while?'

'A few weeks, a few months? It's probably best that you forget about this place for the time being.'

The sadness was replaced with a flash of anger. 'That's easy for you to say. You haven't spent the better part of two years working night and day to get a business off the ground.'

He allowed himself a small smile. 'I know a little bit about the hard work it takes to establish a business.'

She grimaced. 'But you don't know how it feels to do it on your own with no support from anyone else. The fear that comes from knowing that one failure could mean you have nothing to help you look after your child.' She shook her head, as if realising how much she'd revealed.

Romeo chose not to enlighten her about his personal relationship with fear and failure—of the rough, terrifying nights he'd spent on the streets when he was barely into his teens; of the desperate need for acceptance that had led him to contemplate, for a blessedly brief moment, whether he was truly his father's son.

He'd rejected and stumbled away from the gang initiation rites and earned himself a bullseye on his back for a while. But it hadn't stopped the fermenting thought that perhaps the life of a *Mafioso* was blueprinted in his blood.

That was a part of him he intended would never see the light of day.

But it was a thought he had never been able to shake off.

He downed the espresso and watched her struggle to get her emotions under control. 'Tell me what you need to do to expedite things.' He had spent most of the night putting things in place to remove her and Lucca as quickly as possible, but he had the feeling telling her that right now wouldn't go down well.

'I have to speak to Bronagh about assuming a full-time managerial position for starters. Then make sure the staff are taken care of.' She started to slide her hands through her hair, realised she'd caught it in a ponytail and switched to sliding the long tail through her fingers. 'I can't just up and leave.'

The need to get her and Lucca away from here, as quickly as possible, smashed through the civilised barrier he'd placed on himself so far. 'A Michelin-star chef will be here at nine to take over the day-to-day running of the restaurant. Once Lucca is awake, I have a team of movers waiting outside to pack your things. You can keep the apartment or I can arrange for it to be sold, that's your choice. We'll stop over in London, where we will be married at four this afternoon. After that we'll fly straight from London to my island in Hawaii.'

She'd stilled as he spoke, her eyes growing wider with each plan he laid out. 'But…we can't get married that quickly,' she blurted. 'We need a special licence and that takes—'

'It's taken care of.'

She shook her head. 'This is going too fast, Romeo.'

He folded his arms. 'The sooner this layer of protection

is in place, the sooner I can concentrate on dealing with Lorenzo.'

Apprehension crept into her eyes and he cursed under his breath.

She abandoned her coffee and folded her arms. Romeo willed his gaze to remain above her neckline, not to watch the tail of hair trail across her breasts with each breath she took. 'Do we at least have time to discuss what sort of marriage we're going to have?'

He tensed. 'Excuse me?'

'Well, this isn't going to be a traditional marriage, is it? As you said, we're only doing this to ensure Lucca's safety, so I presume the physical side of things won't be part of the marriage.'

Despite having told himself precisely the same thing after his control slipped last night, something moved through his belly that felt very much like rejection. He gritted his teeth.

'If that is what you wish, then it will be so.'

Her lashes swept down. 'Yes, that's what I want. I think you'll agree, sex tends to cause unnecessary confusion.' A flush crept up her neck and Romeo was struck by how innocent she looked.

'*Sì*, Lucca is the most important thing in all this.' Why did the words feel so hard to get out?

She gave a brisk nod. 'I'll go and get changed. He'll be waking up any minute now.' She started to walk towards the door, then stopped and turned with a grace that hinted at balletic training.

Romeo frowned. He knew next to nothing about the mother of his child. All he had were the basic facts produced by his private investigators. He'd been so focused on his son that he'd only requested information from Maisie's pregnancy to date.

He hadn't really paid attention to their random conversations five years ago. He'd gone seeking oblivion of the carnal nature and had fallen head first into a maelstrom of emotions he still had a hard time reliving. He'd tried afterwards to explain it away as his grief talking, but that hadn't quite rung true.

The idea that he'd been burying a lonely yearning that had chosen his mother's death to emerge had shaken him to the core.

It wasn't a place he wanted to visit ever again.

He mentally shrugged. He didn't *need* to know any more about Maisie, other than that she would continue to remain devoted and invested in keeping their son safe.

'I'd like to keep Bronagh as assistant manager. She's been a huge support and I don't want this new manager tossing her out after I'm gone, okay?'

'If that's what you need to put your mind at rest, then it will be done.'

She opened her mouth, as if she wanted to say more, but nodded and left.

His phone vibrated in his pocket. He pulled it out before it started to ring. Anger throbbed to life when he saw the familiar area code. Strolling out of the kitchen, he answered it.

'You may be used to not taking no for an answer, but if you want to have any dealings with me, you'll listen when I say I'll be in touch when I'm good and ready.'

'You have the benefit of youth on your side, Brunetti, but I'm reduced to counting the minutes.'

'Perhaps you should remember that before you test me any further,' he grated out.

Lorenzo gave a barking laugh. 'You think I don't know what you're up to? You may secure your *figlio* a layer of protection, but your legacy will still need to be claimed.'

Romeo's rage built. 'My legacy doesn't involve indulging a handful of geriatric old men, desperate to hang on to the old ways. I'm better at this game than you give me credit for. Being forced to live in the gutter has a way of bringing out a man's survival instincts.'

For the first time, Lorenzo seemed to falter. 'Brunetti…'

'Do not call me again. I'll be in touch when I'm ready.'
He hung up and turned at the sound of his son's laughter.

The sound moved through him, and he froze in place for a second.

Gianlucca was his legacy. One he intended to guard with his life, if necessary.

He swallowed and got himself under control just as his son burst excitedly into the living room.

'Mummy says we're going on a plane today!'

'Yes, you're coming to live with me for a little while.'

'Do you have a big house?'

The corner of Romeo's mouth lifted. 'It's big enough for my needs, yes.'

Lucca's head tilted pensively. 'Does it have a duck pond?'

'Not yet,' he replied, then gave in to the compulsion to offer more; to make a little boy happy. 'But I will build one for you.'

His eyes rounded. 'My very own duck pond?' he whispered in awe.

A peculiar stone lodged in Romeo's throat, making it difficult to swallow. '*Sì*…yes. Your very own.'

A giant smile broke over his son's face. 'Wow! Can I also have a bouncy castle?'

Romeo opened his mouth, but Maisie shook her head. 'We'll discuss it later.'

Lucca continued to beam. 'It's going to be the best adventure ever!'

Unable to speak on account of all the tectonic plates of his reality shifting inside him, Romeo could only nod.

CHAPTER SIX

MAISIE FOUND OUT just how much of an adventure when she was ushered into an exclusive Mayfair boutique five hours later with a team of stylists. As per Romeo's imperious request, the shop had been shut so the attendants could focus solely on her. He sat in the large reception room, flipping through a document while keeping an eye on Lucca, who was getting his own special outfit for the wedding.

Wedding...

She was getting married. To the father of her child. The man she'd thought she'd never set eyes on again after waking up alone in a hotel room in Palermo. The dizzying turn of events threatened to flatten her. But as she'd taken to reminding herself in case any fanciful thoughts took over, all this was happening for the sake of her son.

This was a wedding in name only; it would *be* a marriage in name only. And once this whole business with Romeo's dark past was over with, she would resume her life.

All the same, she couldn't stop a bewildering shiver as the wedding dress she'd chosen was slipped over her head.

Made entirely of cream silk, the calf-length dress had the scoop-neck design both in the front and back, and lace sleeves covering her to the elbow. The material hugged her from bodice to thigh, with a slit at the back for ease of movement. It was simple, elegant and businesslike enough to not portray any of those fanciful thoughts that fleeted through her mind every time she so much as dropped her guard. Dress on, she slipped her feet into matching cream heels and moved to where a hair and make-up expert had been set up.

Maisie had lost the ability to keep up with how fast Romeo had moved once things were set in motion. There'd been no time to get sentimental once she'd summoned the staff, especially with Romeo's overwhelming presence at her side reassuring them that nothing would change in the running of the restaurant.

Her staff knew and respected Bronagh. It was that alone that had made temporarily stepping away from the place she'd poured her heart and muscle into bearable.

And then Romeo had floored her by inviting Bronagh to London to act as witness at their wedding.

The surprises had kept coming, with her first, brief trip in a private jet, hammering home to her just how powerful and influential the man she would be marrying shortly really was.

'There, I think you're set.'

Maisie refocused and examined the chic pinned-up hairstyle and subtle, immaculate make-up, and forced a smile. As much as she'd told herself this marriage wasn't real, she couldn't halt the horde of butterflies beating frantically in her belly. 'Thank you.'

'And I hope you don't mind, but we sent out for a bouquet. It seems a little wrong that a bride should get married without one, you know?' The owner of the boutique, an elegant, fortyish woman, said. 'Especially when you're marrying Romeo Brunetti.' The clear envy in her eyes and the awe in her voice echoed through Maisie.

She was saved from answering when the door opened and Bronagh entered holding a stunning cream-and-lilac rose arrangement bound with crystal-studded ribbon. 'I'd say this bouquet is the most gorgeous thing I've ever seen, but I think you take the prize for that, Maisie,' she said, her soft brown eyes widening as Maisie rose and she looked her over. 'You're going to knock that man of yours dead.' There was a faintly querying note in her voice, but the reason Maisie had become fast friends with Bronagh Davis was because she'd offered friendship without prying just when Maisie had needed that. And although the other woman had probably guessed that Romeo was Lucca's father—the similarities between them seemed to grow with each passing second—she hadn't questioned Maisie.

'You win all the points for flattery,' Maisie replied, surreptitiously rubbing her palms together to keep them from getting any more damp.

Bronagh smiled and handed over the bouquet. 'You can award me the points later. Your men are getting impatient, and from the way the older one is pacing, I wouldn't be surprised if he storms in here and claims you.'

The butterflies' wings flapped harder. Maisie swallowed down her absurd nervousness and any lingering sadness that indicated she wished this were real, that she were marrying a man she'd taken the time to meet, fall in love and ultimately join her life with.

That was a pipe dream she'd long ago abandoned, even before she'd been faced with an unplanned pregnancy and the sheer dedication she'd needed to take care of her child. She'd been exposed too many times to the ruthless indifference inherent in loveless relationships to believe that she would be the exception to the rule. The love she'd felt for Lucca the moment he was born had been a miraculous gift she intended to guard with everything she held dear. So she'd driven her energy into providing a home for her child, despite her parents' icy disapproval.

Maisie reminded herself that this situation wasn't in her control, that even in this she was putting Lucca's needs first.

Her needs didn't matter.

That particular thought took a steep dive when she emerged from the changing room and was confronted with Romeo Brunetti in a three-piece suit. Immaculate, imposingly masculine and utterly breathtaking, he was impossible to ignore. From the top of his neatly combed, wavy black hair, to the polished toes of his handmade shoes, he reeked irrefutable power and enough sexual magnetism to make kings quake and women swoon in his presence. And that look in his eyes…that brooding, almost formidable intensity that had made her tingle from head to toe the first time she'd seen him…

Yes. Maisie was reminded then how very needful she could be. And how some needs were impossible to suppress even with an iron will. She stared. Tried to pull her gaze away. Failed. And stared some more. At the back of her mind, a tiny voice said it was okay to stare because he was doing the same to her.

The look in his eyes was riveting, as if he were seeing her for the first time. A part of her thrilled at that look, the way it made her feel sexy and desirable…until she reminded herself that nothing would come of it. Nothing could.

Her attention was mercifully pulled away when Lucca rushed towards her. 'You look beautiful, Mummy!'

Her smile wobbled when she saw his own attire—a miniature one of his father's, right down to the buttoned-up waistcoat. 'So do you, my precious.'

Romeo seemed to unfreeze then from his stance. 'Come, the car's waiting.'

Everyone snapped to attention. Two guards appeared at the shop door and nodded. They exited and slid into the back of the limo and were driving the short distance to the register office at Marylebone when he reached into his jacket, pulled out a long, velvet box and handed it to her.

'What's this?' she blurted.

One corner of his mouth lifted. 'I thought your absence of jewellery should be addressed.'

Her hand went to her bare throat. 'I…I didn't think it was necessary.' Which, in hindsight, sounded a little foolish. She was marrying one of the world's richest men. Whether the marriage was real or not, she was about to be thrust into the limelight the proportions of which she was too afraid to imagine. The women Romeo had dated before were all raving beauties compared to her.

A flush rose in her face when his eyebrow quirked. 'You may not, but we don't wish to attract unnecessary gossip,' he murmured, his voice deep but low enough to keep Bronagh and Lucca, who sat on the far side of the limo, from overhearing. 'Open it.'

Fingers shaking, she prised the box open and gasped. The three-layered collar necklace contained over two dozen diamonds in different cuts and sizes, the largest, teardrop gem placed in the middle. The stunning jewels, along with a pair of equally breathtaking earrings, sparkled in her trembling hand. Maisie realised her mouth was still open when Romeo plucked the necklace off its velvet bed and held it out.

'Turn around.'

Still stunned, she complied and suppressed a tremble when his warm fingers brushed her nape. She turned towards him to thank him and froze when he leaned forward to adjust the necklace so the large stone was resting just above her cleavage. The touch of those fingers…there… sent her blood pounding through her veins. She looked up and met dark hazel eyes. The knowing and hungry look reflecting back at her stopped whatever breath she'd been about to take. They stared at each other, that intense connection that seemed to fuse them together whenever they were close sizzling between them.

'Wow, that's stunning.'

Maisie jerked guiltily at Bronagh's awed compliment. Another blush crept into her face when she realised she'd momentarily forgotten that her friend and son were in the car. To cover up her embarrassment, she hastily reached for the earrings and clipped them on. Then exhaled in a rush when Romeo produced another ominous-sized box.

'Romeo…'

His eyes flashed a warning and she swallowed her objection. This time he opened it. The large diamond-and-ruby engagement ring defied description. And probably defied any attempt to place a value on it. Silently, Maisie held out her left hand, absurdly bemused to take in the fact that between one heartbeat and the next she'd been draped in jewels that cost more than she would earn in a lifetime.

She smiled through further gasps from Bronagh and just willed herself to breathe. She might not have fully absorbed what she was letting herself in for publicly by agreeing to marry Romeo Brunetti the billionaire, instead of Romeo Brunetti, father of her child, but she'd faced tougher challenges and triumphed. She could do this.

The marriage ceremony itself was shockingly brief.

Whatever strings Romeo had pulled to secure a special licence had pressed home his importance. They were ushered into an oak-panelled room that reeked history and brevity. The registrar read out their commitments in a deep but hushed voice and announced that they were man and wife within twenty minutes of their arrival.

Romeo's kiss on her lips was swift and chaste, his hands dropping from her shoulders almost immediately. She told herself the wrench in her stomach was nerves as she followed him to the desk where their signatures formalised their union.

As she signed her name, Maisie reaffirmed that she was taking the necessary steps to keep her son safe. It was what kept her going through the lavish Mayfair meal with Bronagh, after which Bronagh was driven to the airport to catch a flight back to Dublin, and they were driven straight to a private airport south of London.

Unable to stand the thick silence in the car now that Lucca had fallen asleep, she cleared her throat.

'I didn't know Italians could marry in London without jumping through bureaucratic hoops.'

Romeo switched from looking out of the window. The brooding glance he sent her made her wish for a moment she'd let the silence continue. 'I've lived in London for over ten years. Other than two days ago, the last time I was in Italy was when you and I met.'

Surprise lifted her brows. 'I thought you were a resident. You seemed to know your way about where...where you were staying.'

His mouth twisted. 'I was, once upon a time. But in a much more inhospitable part.'

'Inhospitable?' she echoed.

That brooding gaze intensified. 'I wasn't always affluent, *gattina*. I can probably go as far as to say I'm the definition of *nouveau riche*. I know the streets where we met well because I used to walk there at night in the hope that I would find leftover food in bins or a tourist who was willing to part with a few euros for a quick shoe shine. Barring that, I would find an alleyway to sleep in for a night, but only for a night because inevitably I would be sent packing by the *polizia* and threatened with jail should I return.'

Maisie wasn't sure which was more unnerving—the harrowing account of his childhood or the cold, unfeeling way in which he recounted it. Either way, the stone-cold horror that had wedged in her stomach grew, until she was sure her insides were frozen with pain at imagining what he'd been through.

'You said you only met your father twice,' she murmured, unable to erase the bleak picture he drew in her mind, 'but what about your mother?'

Lucca stirred in his sleep, and Romeo's eyes shifted to his son before returning to hers. 'My mother is a subject I don't wish to discuss, especially on my wedding day.' His smile mocked the significance of the day.

But Maisie couldn't dismiss the subject as easily. 'And child services? Surely there was some support you could've sought?'

He blinked, his nostrils flaring slightly before he shrugged. 'The support is the same in Italy as it is in England. Some fall through the cracks. And if one tried hard enough to evade the clutches of a system that was inherently flawed, one could succeed.'

Despite catching his meaning, Maisie couldn't fathom why he would choose to live on the streets. 'How long did you sleep rough for?' she asked, her heart bleeding at the thought.

His mouth compressed in a cruel line. 'Two years until the authorities got fed up with hauling me away every other night. A do-gooder policewoman thought I would be better off in the foster system.' He gave a harsh, self-deprecating laugh. 'Unfortunately, she couldn't have been more wrong. Because then it was really driven home that my kind wouldn't be welcome in a normal, well-adjusted home.'

'Your kind?'

'The bastard children of violent criminals.'

Her hand flew to her mouth. 'Oh, God!'

Romeo's eyes once again flicked to his sleeping son and he shook his head. 'Don't worry, *gattina*. I got out the second I could. Now look at me.' He spread his hands in mock preen. And although his voice was even, Maisie saw the shadows of dark memory that blanketed his eyes and hardened his mouth. 'According to the media, I'm every woman's dream and every parent's ideal suitor for their wholesome daughter. Consider yourself lucky for bagging me.' His teeth barred in a mirthless smile.

'Romeo—'

He lunged close so quickly, filled every inch of her vision so spectacularly, her breath snagged in her chest. His fingers pressed against her mouth, forcibly rejecting any words she'd been about to utter. 'No, *gattina*. Save your warm-hearted sympathy and soft words for our son,' he rasped jaggedly. 'You be there for him when he scrapes his knee and when the goblins frighten him at night. I require no sympathy. I learnt to do without it long before I could walk.'

He sat back and for a full minute remained frozen. Then

his chest rose and fell in a single deep exhalation before he pressed a button next to his armrest. A laptop slid from a side compartment and flickered on. Strong fingers tapped the keys, flicking through pages of data with calm efficiency.

As if he hadn't just torn open his chest and shown her the raw wounds scarring his heart.

Romeo tapped another random key, stared unseeing at the stream of words and numbers filling the screen.

What in the name of heaven had he been thinking?

Had he not sworn only last night to keep his past locked in the vault where it belonged? Through all the voracious media attention that had exploded in his life once his first resort had achieved platinum-star status, he'd kept his past safely under wraps. Besides Zaccheo Giordano, the only man he considered a friend, and his wife, Eva, no one else knew about the desperately traumatising childhood he'd suffered. Many had tried to dig, only to accept the illusion that his secret past made him alluringly mysterious, and left it at that. Romeo had been more than glad to leave things at that.

So why had he just spilled his guts to Maisie O'Connell? And not only spilled his guts, but ripped off the emotion-free bandage he'd bound his memories with in the process?

He tried to think through it rationally; to decipher just what it was about this woman who let all the volatile, raw emotions overrun him.

Their meeting hadn't been accompanied by thunder and lightning. There'd been nothing remotely spectacular about it. To the contrary, he'd walked past her that night at the waterfront café in Palermo with every intention of continuing his solitary walk.

Lost in thoughts of bewildering grief and hoping the night air would clear his head, he'd walked for miles from the cemetery where Ariana Brunetti had found her last resting place. He'd barely taken in where he was headed, the need to put distance between the mother whose only interest had been for herself and how much she could get for selling her body, a visceral need.

When he'd finally reached the stone wall overlooking the water, he'd stood lost and seriously contemplated scaling the wall and swimming away from the city that bore only harrowing memories. The sound of tourists drinking away the night had finally impinged, and he'd had the brilliant idea of drowning his sorrows with whisky.

He'd walked past her, barely noticing her.

It was only as he'd ordered his third whisky that he'd caught her staring. Even then, he'd dismissed her. He was used to women staring at him. Women coming onto him since he'd been old enough to shave.

But he'd caught her furtive glances, those bright blue eyes darting his way when she thought he wasn't looking. Romeo wasn't sure why he'd talked to her that night. Perhaps it'd been that lost look she'd been trying so hard to disguise. Or the fact that a group of male tourists had noticed her and were placing bets on who would buy her the next drink. Or the fact that his mother's last words to him had left him raw, feeling as if his very skin had been peeled off.

You're just like him...just like him...

In the hours and days that had followed, he'd been able to stop those words ringing in his head.

Having that drink in that café had been a last, desperate attempt to drown out the words.

He'd raised his glass to her in a silent toast. She'd smiled shyly and asked what he was toasting. He'd made some smart remark or other he couldn't recall. He'd kicked out the seat opposite in brusque invitation and she'd joined him.

Midnight had arrived and they'd walked to his hotel, both of them very much aware of what would happen next.

He'd walked away the next day, even more exposed than he'd ever been in his life.

But he'd pulled himself together, refusing to be the needy

shadow of a man who'd yearned for a kind word from the mother who'd rejected him all his life. And he'd succeeded.

Nothing should've prompted this puzzling and clever way Maisie had managed to slip under his guard not once, but twice. It was a weakness he couldn't, *wouldn't* abide.

He stole a glance from the corner of his eye and saw that she was gazing at the passing scenery, her fingers toying with her new rings.

He breathed a little easier, confident that moment of madness was behind him. That she was taking his advice and letting the temporary aberration pass.

'I'm sorry I dredged up bad memories for you,' she said suddenly.

Romeo shut the laptop with studied care, resisting the urge to rip the gadget out of its housing and throw it out of the window.

'Maisie—' he growled warningly.

'I know you don't want to talk about it now and I respect that. But I just wanted you to know, should you ever feel the need to talk, I'm here.'

For one shocking, ground-shaking moment, his black soul lifted at those words. He allowed himself to glimpse a day when he would unburden himself and feel whole, clean. The picture was so laughable, he shook his head in wonder at his own gall.

He was the son of a whore and a vicious thug. He'd contemplated hurting another human being just so he could join a gang…to gain respect through violence. Walking away, sick to his stomach, hadn't absolved him of the three days he'd worn the probation leathers and trawled the dark streets of Palermo, looking for a victim. He would never be clean, never be washed free of that stain. He hadn't bothered to try up until now. He never would.

'*Grazie*, but I can assure you that day will never come.'

CHAPTER SEVEN

THE BRUNETTI INTERNATIONAL RESORT MAUI was a tropical oasis that had been created with heaven itself in mind. Or at least that was what the brochure stated.

Maisie had silently rolled her eyes when she read the claim.

Looking around her as they alighted from the seaplane, she accepted the statement hadn't been an exaggeration. A long, sugar-sanded beach stretched for a half mile before it curved around an outcrop of rock that looked perfect for diving.

From the beach, the land rose gently, swaying palm trees blending with the increasingly denser vegetation Maisie had spotted from the plane before they'd landed.

She knew the resort housed six koa-wood-and-stone mansions, each large and luxurious enough to cater to the most demanding guest, with the largest, a twelve-bedroom sprawling architect's dream, sitting on top of a hill in the centre of the island.

From the brochure she'd read she also knew that the mansion had been booked for the next three years and that guests paid a king's ransom for the privilege.

She had been admiring the stunning architecture of the resort when her eyes had grown heavy. Jerking awake, she'd found her shoes had been taken off, her seat reclined and a pillow tucked under her head. She'd looked up from the soft cashmere throw keeping her warm to find Lucca and Romeo at the dining table, tucking into a meal. Or rather, Lucca had been eating and chattering away, with his father watching him with that silent intensity and awe that had struck a peculiar ache in Maisie's chest.

Romeo had looked up then, locked gazes with her before being diverted by their son. Unlike in the car when his emotions had bubbled just beneath his skin, he'd looked cool and remote, very much the powerful, in-control billionaire. He'd looked untouchable, and Maisie believed he meant for the moment in the car never to happen again. Whatever had prompted him to reveal a horrific chapter of his past had been resealed in an impenetrable fortress, never to be revisited again.

She'd berated herself for feeling mournful, for experiencing his pain as acutely as if it were her own. She had no right to it, no right to pry or feel strangely bereft when he'd shut her out and refocused his attention on Lucca.

Her parents had tried to drill into her that her brain was her most valuable asset, but Maisie had known that wasn't true. With the birth of her child, she'd known love was the greatest gift she could give, and receive. Same as she knew that Romeo, like her parents, didn't have a need for it. He believed in protecting his son, much as her own parents had provided a roof over her head and put clothes on her back. But, like them, he had nothing more to give.

And while she couldn't turn her compassion off at will, she needed to guard against overexposure of the emotion that had drawn her to Romeo in the first place. His grief and misery that night had been like a beacon. She'd wanted to comfort him, grant him reprieve from the shackles that bound him.

The result had been waking up alone, and returning home weeks later, pregnant. She would do well to remember that.

'Are you coming?'

She jumped at Romeo's prompt and realised she'd stopped at the bottom of the stone steps leading up from the beach.

'Yes, of course.' She smiled at the six white-uniformed staff ready to unload their luggage and followed Romeo up to the buggy parked on the pavement. He lowered an excited Lucca onto the seat and fastened his seat belt before turning to her.

'Would you like a quick tour now or later?' he asked coolly.

'Now would be great, thanks.'

He nodded and started the buggy. When Lucca wriggled excitedly, Romeo slowed down and touched his son's arm. 'Sit still, *bambino*, or you'll have to walk all the way back to the house.'

Lucca looked round. 'Where's the house?' he asked.

Romeo pointed up the hill to a large villa whose glass cathedral-like dome dominated the hilltop. 'All the way up there.'

Lucca immediately stilled, his eyes rounding as he stared up at Romeo. 'I'll be still.'

Romeo looked over at her, a small smile playing on his lips before he tentatively ruffled Lucca's hair. *'Bene*…that means good in Italian.'

'Bene,' Lucca repeated, intoning the syllables in near perfect match of his father's accent.

Maisie looked around and realised two things. That the brochure hadn't done enough justice to the description of Hana Island. And also that only two of the mansions that Romeo drove past looked occupied.

'But I thought this place was fully booked for years in advance?'

'It was…until yesterday when I cancelled half of the bookings.'

'Why?'

'Because I wanted to guarantee our privacy. The two families who are staying here have been fully vetted and have signed confidentiality agreements. The others were a little more testy, so I compensated them for their trouble and sent them to another resort. Complimentary, of course.'

Maisie looked around as they headed up the hill. The whole place was the very epitome of paradise. But then paradise had contained a poisonous snake.

'Surely you don't think…'

He sent her a warning look. She bit her lip and waited until he'd stopped the buggy in front of a large set of double doors made of polished koa wood and released Lucca's seat belt. When Lucca scampered off towards the house, he turned to her.

'No, I don't think we'll have any trouble here, but I took the necessary precautions nevertheless.'

She looked around the lush paradise. 'But we can't stay here for ever, Romeo.'

His jaw flexed. 'We'll remain here until I find a way to fix this. Besides, the world thinks we're on our honeymoon, so why not enjoy the time off?' He glanced over to where Lucca was examining a spray of giant bright orange flowers. 'I can't imagine you've had any downtime since he was born.'

Maisie smiled reluctantly. 'I don't imagine I'll be getting any until he's at least eighteen.'

He watched her with a quizzical look. 'But it will be a relief not to be burdened with him 24/7, *sì*?' There was a hard bite to his tone that set her nerves on edge.

She frowned. 'I don't consider him a burden,' she retorted.

'Was he the reason you switched careers?' he enquired.

'Well…yes, but—'

'Pursuing a career in criminal law to operating a restaurant in a quaint little village is quite a change.'

'It was a choice I made both for Lucca and myself.'

He nodded. 'You've proved you're capable of adapting. So adjusting to our new situation shouldn't be a big problem.'

She looked around. 'I'm not built to lie about sipping cocktails. I need a challenge, even with Lucca around.'

'Then we will find other challenges for you.'

'Thank you. Now, is this interview of my mothering skills and commitment over? I'd like to get out of these travelling clothes.'

He continued to stare at her in that direct, invasive way of his, as if trying to see beneath her words to any truth she was hiding.

After several minutes he nodded and alighted from the buggy.

Double doors swung open and two women came forward, one an older Tongan native and a younger girl who approached Lucca with a smile. Maisie noticed she walked with a slight limp.

'This is Emily. She'll be helping you look after Lucca. And Mahina is our housekeeper.

Maisie managed to keep a smile on her face throughout the introductions and the tour of Romeo's mansion. She even managed to make the right noises when she saw the Olympic-sized pool and the hot tub, and the man-made cave that opened up into a private waterfall complete with pool at the back of the property.

She smiled through giving Lucca a quick wash, with a helpful Emily unpacking his clothes. When the girl offered to take him away for a glass of juice, Maisie forced a nod, welcoming the opportunity to find Romeo and give him a piece of her mind.

After searching fruitlessly upstairs and knocking on over a dozen doors, she finally found him in a large, airy room converted to a study, with rows of books covering one wall, and an imposing desk and chair fronting a floor-to-ceiling glass window.

She shut the door behind her after his imperious directive to come in and stalked to where he sat, master and commander of his empire.

'How dare you hire a nanny without consulting me,' she fired at him when he looked up from the document he was perusing.

His brows clamped for a second before he rose and rounded the desk. Maisie forced herself not to step back from the broad-shouldered magnificence of his physique. He'd also changed from the suit he wore to travel, into a turquoise polo shirt and a pair of white linen trousers, into which he shoved his hands. 'I didn't think you would object.'

'Why? Because I'm so eager to be lightened of the *burden* of caring for my son?'

'Because I'm told every mother needs a break every now and then.'

'And who, pray tell, enlightened you of this fact? It can't have been your mother, since I'm guessing she wasn't a contender for mother of the year?'

His cold tensing confirmed she'd gone too far. 'We seem to be straying away from the issue under discussion. You slept for less than an hour on the plane and I'm sure you didn't have much sleep the night before. The jet lag will kick in very hard shortly.' He shrugged. 'I thought you would welcome the help.'

She told herself not to soften at his consideration. 'Is that all she is—temporary help?' she pressed.

'No. She helps around the resort when needed, but she's the only one with childcare training.'

She shook her head. 'Romeo—'

Narrowed eyes studied her closely. 'What exactly is the problem here?'

'The problem is you made a decision about Lucca's care without consulting me.'

He exhaled with a rush of irritation. 'This is an adjustment for all of us, Lucca included. Some decisions will have to be made with or without your input.'

'No, I don't accept that. Not when it comes to my son.'

He shrugged. 'Okay, you can use Emily when you see

fit, or not at all. I'll leave that decision up to you. But you can't control every moment of his life, Maisie.'

Cold anger robbed her of breath for a moment. Then the words came tumbling out. 'You've known him for what, two days? And you dare to say that to me?'

His eyes turned a burnished gold. 'Is it my fault that I didn't know of his existence before then?'

'Well, it's not mine! Had you bothered to stick around the morning after—'

'For what purpose? Exchange false promises of hooking up again? Or perhaps you wanted compliments on what a great night we shared?'

An angry flush replaced the cold rage. 'I don't know why you're being so vile! And pardon me if I didn't know the right etiquette for the morning after one-night stands. That was my first and last experience. But I certainly didn't think I'd wake up alone with no trace of the man I'd spent the night with. Or that you'd instruct the concierge not to divulge any information as to your identity. If you want to be angry at anyone, be angry at yourself, because despite that deplorable behaviour, despite you leaving me there to do the walk of shame on my own, I still went back to look for you when I found out I was pregnant.'

His face froze in a mask of surprise. 'You did what?'

'I went back. I used savings I would've been better off investing for my unborn child to pay for a two-week stay in that exorbitant hotel. I walked the streets of Palermo every day and visited every café I could find for a fortnight.' She laughed. 'I drank enough decaf lattes to float a cruise ship, all in the hope that I might find you. Do you know how many hits there are for *Romeo of Palermo* on the Internet?'

He shook his head slowly, as if in a daze.

'Well, I won't bore you with figures. Let's just say tracking every one of them down would've taken me years. I didn't speak the language, so either I was laughed off or every enquiry was met with a blank look. So, yes, I gave up after two weeks and decided my time would be better spent planning a safe and comfortable future for my son. So don't you dare tell me I won't be consulted about each and every decision where he's concerned. And don't you dare make me feel bad about the consequences of something that we both did *consensually*.'

A red flush scoured his cheekbones before he inhaled deeply. Whirling about, he strode to the window and gazed out at the spectacular view.

When she was convinced the silence would stretch for ever, she approached and stood next to him. 'Are you going to say something?' she ventured in a quieter voice once several more minutes had passed.

He slanted a glance at her. 'It is not often I'm surprised. But you have surprised me, *gattina*,' he rasped.

'Because I've shown that underneath that auburn hair I have a temper?' she half joked.

A flicker of a smile ghosted over his lips. 'That wasn't a surprise. I'm very much aware of the depths of your passion.'

She reddened and glanced away before she was tempted to read a different meaning to his words. 'What, then?'

'What you did…' He paused and shook his head. 'No other person I know would've done that. And you're right. After the way I left, you had every right to write me off. And I did make sure that I would not be easy to find.'

'That's an understatement. Do you do that often? Erase your presence so thoroughly your conquests can never find you?' she asked before she could stop herself.

'Not in such direct terms. There is usually an understanding of the transient nature of my liaisons.'

'Oh…right.' That told her.

'That night was different for me, too, in many ways.'

She wanted to ask, but that bleak, haunted look was back in his eyes again, along with that do-not-disturb force field that told her she would risk emotional electrocution if she so much as raised an eyebrow in inquiry. To her surprise, he continued.

'It had been a trying day, one I didn't wish to face even though I knew it was coming.'

'Yeah, we all have days like that.'

He looked at her, his gaze brushing her face, her throat, her body, before turning his attention to the window again. 'But you came back, despite feeling the sting of rejection and perhaps a lot aggrieved?' he asked.

'I put myself in my child's shoes and knew that I needed to give him a chance to know his father. But I guess a part of me was terrified that I couldn't do this on my own and was in some way looking for support.' She shrugged. 'The moment I got back to Dublin, I accepted that I was in this alone. Then Lucca was born, and with each day that passed the fear receded. I was no longer alone. I had him.'

His stare returned, stayed longer this time. 'You're no longer alone where his care is concerned.'

She raised her eyebrows. 'But you don't agree that I should be consulted on all things?'

A steely look entered his eyes. 'I'll grant you a healthy debate about the major issues that concern him. And you can attempt to tear me to pieces on the minor ones.'

'So in other words, we'll argue about everything?'

The corner of his mouth lifted. 'Only because you seem to thrive on arguments.'

Her mouth curved in answer. 'Be warned, I never stop until I get my way.'

His eyes dropped to her mouth, and a heated channel forged between them. Her breath shallowed, her heart racing as she read the look loud and clear.

Desire thickened in her veins, her core throbbing until she yearned to squeeze her thighs together to alleviate the ache.

'Perhaps I will let you win on occasion,' he murmured,

his voice husky and deep. When his gaze dropped to linger on her breasts, a light tremble went through her.

She was thinking it was wise to move away before she did something foolish, like rise on tiptoe and taste his mouth, when a knock sounded on the door.

'Yes?' he answered, his eyes still on her.

Emily entered with Lucca, who smiled broadly when he saw her. 'Lucca wants to go for a swim. I wanted to check with you that it was all right to take him,' Emily said.

Romeo eyed Maisie with one brow quirked.

She lifted her chin. 'I'll take him,' she answered. When his eyes narrowed, she sighed. 'We'll *both* take him?' she amended.

The corner of his mouth twitched. *'Grazie,'* he murmured.

Maisie nodded. 'Okay. I'll go and change.'

Romeo strode forward and caught Lucca up in his arms. 'We'll meet you by the pool.'

In her room, Maisie fingered her sensible one-piece suit, replaying the conversation with Romeo in her mind. He'd been surprised that she'd returned to look for him, more than surprised, in fact. Stunned. That she would want to do the right thing.

Again she found herself wondering just how damaging his relationship with his mother had been. He'd called her a whore in the car. Had he meant that *literally*? She shuddered. Why else would a child call his mother by such a derogatory term?

It was clear that Romeo Brunetti had huge skeletons in his closet. And she was treading on dangerous ground in being so interested in uncovering them. That he'd taken such drastic steps to disconnect himself from her after their single night together should warn her that he didn't want any entanglements that didn't involve his son. She would do well to remember that. Along with remembering that theirs would in no way be a physical merger. No matter

how heatedly he looked at her. No matter how much her
blood thrilled to insane sexual possibilities each time he
was within touching distance.

There would come a time when she'd have to walk away
with her son after all this was done.

She would be better off if she made sure to walk away
with her heart intact.

Romeo noticed her cooler demeanour the moment she came
down the terrace steps and walked through the leafy arch-
way dividing the extensive barbecue and entertainment area
from the pool. And it had nothing to do with the military-
issue swimming suit she wore, or the tight knot she'd pulled
her hair into at the top of her head.

Her gaze, when it skated over him, was wary. As if between the time they'd spoken in his study and her changing, she'd withdrawn into herself.

Had she somehow guessed at his true intention towards
his son when this problem with Lorenzo was over?

No, there was no way she could know. He quashed the
voice in his head that prompted him to recall Maisie's uncanny intuitiveness. She'd known just how to delve beneath
his skin and burrow to the heart of his need that night five
years ago.

She'd given him passion and compassion in abundance,
two emotions that had been seriously lacking in his life up
till then. She'd made him *believe* and *hope*, for a few blissful hours, until dawn and reality had come crashing in. For
a while he'd resented her for those feelings. Until he'd realised the fault wasn't hers. It was him, daring to believe
in mirages and miracles.

He watched her drop her sunglasses on the table and
walk to the edge of the pool, her smile guarded as she ob-
served Lucca's antics. For the first time in his life, Romeo
experienced the need to enquire as to a woman's feelings.
The unsettled feelings that had slashed through him in the

car returned and grew as he watched her swim to the other end of the pool and stay there.

Normally, when the women he dated began exhibiting contrary attitudes, it was a prelude to them asking for *more*. Of his time. Of a commitment. It was the reason he'd drastically reduced his dating span from a few weeks to the odd weekend.

He had nothing more to offer a woman besides a good time in bed and a very generous parting gift come Monday morning.

So what did Maisie's attitude mean?

She had his ring on her finger. Albeit temporarily, and for the sake of their son. But she also had him here, far from civilisation should they choose, and as exclusive as resorts came. And if and when she chose to alter the terms of their non-physical relationship to a physical one, he was more than willing to negotiate.

So what was wrong?

'Faster, faster!' Lucca urged as he rode on Romeo's back. 'Mummy, let's race.' He held out his arms to his mother. Maisie smiled and swam towards them, but she still avoided Romeo's gaze. And kept a conspicuous distance between them as they splashed from one end of the pool to the other.

Eventually, he took a tired and protesting Lucca out of the water. Maisie followed them out and dried him, before taking him indoors. When she returned and perched on her lounger with that same air of withdrawal, he narrowed his eyes.

'I don't like mixed signals,' he snapped.

Her head jerked towards him. 'What?'

'You were fine when you left the study. Something has obviously happened between then and now. What is it?'

'Nothing. I just took a little time to think, that's all.'

Something tightened in his chest, but he forced out the question. 'And what did thinking produce?'

She flashed a bright, false smile. 'I concluded that you're

right. Lucca and I have never had a holiday. This will be good for him…for all of us. As long as I can find something to keep me busy at times, I won't stand in your way about the small things.'

He heard the words and processed them as the half-truth they were. Then sat back and formulated how to get the full truth out of her.

CHAPTER EIGHT

'WE'RE HEADING OUT to choose a venue for a duck pond. You said you'd join us.' Romeo used a tone that made it clear his request wasn't up for debate. His annoyance the past few days had grown into a simmering anger. Albeit that anger was directed more at himself for the unaccustomed feeling of *caring* so much.

But some of it was directed at the woman who raised her head from her video conversation with her friend in Dublin and looked at him with a blank stare.

He'd been on the receiving end of that stare every time he walked into a room, just as every time he came within touching distance she found a way to move away. He'd thought she would be happy when he'd arranged for her to work with the chef at the resort restaurant a few hours each day to keep her skills sharp. She'd been pleased and his chef had sung her praises, but Maisie continued to be aloof.

Enough was enough. He wanted that distance gone.

The voice that suggested he might live to regret closing that distance was ruthlessly suppressed. He strolled further into the room and stopped in front of her, arms folded. 'Our son is waiting.'

Satisfaction burst through him when her eyes lit up with rebellious fire.

'Um…sorry, Bronagh, I have to go. I'll be in touch again at the end of the week.' She smiled and signed off, then glared up at him. 'Was there any need to be so rude?'

'Perhaps you should ask yourself the same question.'

A frown marred the light, golden hue of her skin, the result of enjoying the Hawaiian sun. 'What on earth are you talking about?'

'You've called your friend three times since we got here. You don't think she'd be offended that you're micromanaging her from a distance?'

Her eyes widened. 'Of course not, we discussed me calling her before I left Dublin.'

'Every other day?'

'Maybe not, but—'

'What percentage of your call involved discussing the restaurant?'

She bit her lip and flushed bright red. 'That still doesn't excuse your rudely interrupting me.'

'I'm only doing what you asked, *gattina*, and reminding you that you said you'd come with us to view the site. If you've changed your mind, all you have to do is say so. Lucca would be disappointed, of course, but...' Romeo shrugged.

She frowned and checked the clock on the laptop. 'I haven't changed my mind. I just didn't realise what the time was, that's all.' She looked at him and her gaze swung away almost immediately. 'I...I'll be right there.'

He narrowed his eyes when she remained seated. 'Is there a problem I should know about?' he grated, realising he was reaching the end of a hitherto unknown rope of patience.

'No.' Her lower lip protruded in an annoyed action so reminiscent of their son that he almost laughed. But his annoyance was far greater than his mirth. And it grew the longer she remained seated.

'Do I need to eject you from that chair?' he asked softly.

Her loose, waist-length hair slid over her shoulders as she swivelled her chair sideways. 'I only meant that I'd meet you outside after I get changed.'

He assessed her blue vest top. 'There's nothing wrong with what you're wearing.'

Her colour rose higher. 'Not the top maybe, but the shorts aren't appropriate for going outside.'

Romeo's legs moved of their own accord, skirting the desk to where she sat. 'Stand up.'

She threw him another of those highly annoyed looks but reluctantly stood.

He nearly swallowed his tongue.

The bright pink hot pants moulded her hips like a second skin and ended a scant inch below where the material met between her thighs. Instant arousal like nothing he'd ever experienced before battered him so hard, he was sure his insides had been rearranged in the process.

'*Che diavolo,*' he managed to squeeze out when he dragged his gaze from that triangle of temptation between her thighs and the silky smooth length of her shapely legs to her bare feet and up again.

'Don't blame me,' she muttered with husky accusation. 'It's not my fault your personal shoppers got my size wrong. If you'd let me go with them like I suggested, none of this would've happened.'

He met her impossibly blue eyes with a stunned exhalation. 'Are you telling me *all* your clothes are too small?'

He'd had a new wardrobe organised for Maisie and Lucca when it had become apparent that she'd packed clothes suitable for an Irish summer, not the tropical Hawaiian heat. And he for one had been tired of Maisie's ugly swimsuit after seeing it a second time.

She lifted her hand to fiddle with her hair and a glimpse of her toned midriff sent his temperature soaring another thousand degrees. 'They're a size smaller than I'd normally prefer.'

'And you didn't say something because?' He was aware his voice was uneven, hell, *strangled*, and that continuing to stand this close to her while she was dressed like a naughty cheerleader was an immensely bad idea, but his feet refused to move anywhere but closer, the need to slide his fingers between her legs, test the heat of those hot pants, almost overpowering.

'Would I have sounded anything but a diva if I'd demanded they send everything back?'

Since he knew every single one of the women he'd dated before would've made exactly that demand, and more, he allowed himself a smile. 'You're my wife. You're well within your rights to demand anything you want, as often as you want.'

She seemed to grow unsteady, her hand reaching out blindly for the sturdiness of the desk. But her gaze didn't move from his, an action for which he felt almost elated. Romeo couldn't take in how much he'd missed looking into her eyes until that moment. Which was absurd, but unshakeably true.

'It's okay, it's not a big deal. I can get away with most of the tops and dresses, and I'd planned to only wear the shorts indoors.' She licked her lips and laughed a touch nervously. 'Besides, I can stand to lose a pound or ten.'

'*Nothing* about your body requires adjustment,' he growled.

She was perfect. And she was blushing in the full-bodied way again that was pure combustion to his libido.

His eyes dropped to where she was winding one leg around the other, her toes brushing her opposite insole. Hunger clawed through him.

Madre di Dio!

'Go. Change if you must. We'll be waiting out front,' he forced out before the unbearable need pounding through him overcame his better judgement and he bent her over the desk.

She nodded and backed away, turning to hurry out of the door. When he was sure she was out of earshot, he let out a thick, frustrated groan, the sight of her delicious backside seeming to tattoo itself in his mind.

He was nowhere near calm when she emerged in a strapless lilac sundress and flip-flops. Luckily for him, his son's presence served as enough of a deterrent for his out-of-control libido.

Ten minutes later, it became clear she'd gone back to not fully engaging with him, busying herself with fussing over Lucca and avoiding his eyes when he looked her way.

Gritting his teeth, he focused on delivering them to the first duck-pond scouting location.

They toured three sites before arriving at the perfect place for a duck pond. Well within sight of the villa, the area was flat and clear of trees, within full view of the beach. Not that Lucca would ever be alone, but Romeo was satisfied the security posted at various points around the island would have a perfect view of where Maisie and his son were at all times.

The head of the three-man construction crew he'd hired spread out the blueprint on a portable table and began discussing design and schedules, with Lucca merrily pointing out where he wanted his rocks and fountain situated.

Leaving them to it, Romeo strolled to where Maisie stood several feet away, her gaze on the beach a quarter of a mile below.

Her head jerked up as he neared, and she inhaled sharply at the force of his stare, her eyes widening before she attempted to avert her head. He caught her chin and held her still.

'You want to tell me what's going on?'

That blank stare again. 'Sorry, I don't know what you mean.'

'I thought we agreed to make this work,' he rasped.

'We are.'

'You call *this* making it work?' he blazed under his breath.

'Romeo, why are you annoyed with me?'

His low mocking laughter grated. 'I suppose I should be gratified that you've noticed that I am annoyed.'

She pulled her chin from his hand. 'If it's about me for-getting about the time of the duck-pond visit—'

'Don't do that, *gattina*. It's beneath you,' he cut across her.

'I don't know what you want me to do. I'm here for Lucca. Isn't that what we both ultimately want?' Her voice pulsed with something he couldn't put his finger on.

No, he wanted to say. *I want you to stop shutting me out.*

He stepped closer and her delicate apple shampoo and sunflower perfume washed over his senses. 'What he needs is parents who exchange more than a greeting and a "pass the salt" when they're in the same room. I may not know enough about little boys yet, but I know he'll pick up the tension between us if we don't clear the air.'

She shook her head. 'But there *is* nothing to clear.'

He begged to differ. About to demand the truth, he looked deeper into her eyes and finally got *why* the atmo-sphere between them had altered so drastically.

'*Dio,* how could I have missed this?' he muttered almost to himself.

Panic flared in her eyes, darkening the striking blue to an alluring navy. He allowed himself a smile, a little less unsettled now he knew the root cause of her frostiness.

'We'll take this up again tonight, when Lucca is in bed.'

'I have nothing to take up with you,' she blurted.

'Then you can enjoy your meal and listen to me talk.'

Enjoying the heated suspicion in her eyes, he turned and strode back to join the group. The final design of the pond was agreed, an ecstatic Lucca skipping back to the buggy.

Back at the villa, he watched Maisie rush away with an excuse of rustling up a snack for their son. Romeo curbed a smile, satisfied now that he knew what the problem was of fixing it. He was pussyfooting his way through the un-familiar landscape of being a father. The tension between him and Maisie stood to jeopardise that. The unnecessary argument in his study this afternoon had proved that. It needed to be resolved. And by midnight, the situation between them *would* be rectified, with results he was sure would please them both.

He picked up his son and hurled him in the air, his heart tumbling over when he received a shriek of delight in return.

'Again!' Lucca urged.

Romeo's smile widened and he complied.

He'd never relied on luck to achieve his goals, but with a tiny bit of luck he'd get his son's mother shrieking those same words to him by the time he was done with her.

Maisie inspected the multitude of new dresses in her wardrobe and finally selected a bronze-coloured cotton shift with a crossover bodice tie. She knew she was risking being late, but ever since her conversation with Romeo earlier she'd been dreading the seven-thirty dinner he'd asked Mahina to prepare.

To say she was terrified of that sudden light that had dawned in his eyes after he'd demanded to know what was going on would be an understatement. And that self-assured smile he'd worn from then on had been an even more ominous sign that whatever he intended to discuss with her tonight would be something she might not be able to deny him.

She tied the knot beneath the bodice of the dress and shakily clipped her hair into a loose knot at her nape. The sleeveless design of the dress would ensure she remained cool in the sometimes sultry evening heat.

And if all hell broke loose, there was also the swimming pool to jump into. She gave a short hysterical giggle and slipped her feet into open-toed platform heels.

Knowing she couldn't linger any longer, she hurried to Lucca's room and checked on him, smiling at Emily, who was folding laundry in the walk-in closet, before making her way to the terrace.

The light from fat candles giving off evocative scents blended with solar lamps dotted around the garden and pool.

Next to the table set out for two, a tall silver ice bucket held a bottle of champagne. Romeo was nowhere in sight.

Before she could breathe a sigh of relief from the nerves churning her stomach, she sensed him behind her and turned.

He was dressed in black trousers and a fitted black shirt, his sleeves rolled back to reveal bronzed forearms and a sleek watch. With a few buttons opened at his throat, it was impossible to miss the light wisps of hair or the strong neck and the rugged jaw thrown into relief by all that black. That image of a dark lord, master of all he surveyed, sprang into her mind again.

Maisie swallowed and willed her hormones to stop careening through her bloodstream. But even at this early stage in the night, she knew it would be an uphill battle to continue fighting the need that whistled through her with the ominous sound of a pressure cooker reaching explosion point.

'There you are,' he murmured in a deep, hypnotic voice. 'I was beginning to think I'd been stood up.'

'I wasn't aware this was a date,' she replied feebly. The setting sun, the soft Hawaiian music playing from hidden speakers…the way he looked at her, all pointed to this being all about the two of them and nothing to do with their son.

She took a tiny step back as he came towards her, all dark and brooding. His eyes told her he knew what she was fighting. And the calculating gleam told her he intended to make sure she would lose.

'Come, sit down.'

He walked past her, trailing an earthy scent of spicy sandalwood and his own potent musk that drew her like a supercharged bee to pollen, and pulled out a chair.

With a feeling of walking towards her doom, Maisie approached and took her seat, then gasped when his fingers trailed the back of her neck.

'You must be more careful in the sun, *gattina*. You have mild sunburn right here.'

She shivered and touched the slightly sore spot, berating herself for being disappointed because his touch had been for an impersonal reason. 'September in Palermo was the hottest weather I'd encountered before Hawaii. I think I might need a stronger sunscreen.'

He sat opposite her, his gaze thoughtful as it rested on her face.

As Mahina served their first course, she held her breath, knowing questions were coming from Romeo.

As soon as the housekeeper left, he asked, 'You never took holidays abroad when you were younger?'

She shook her head. 'There was never time for holidays. Or any free time for that matter. Dedication to my studies seven days a week from kindergarten till I graduated from law school saw to that.'

His eyes narrowed. 'Your parents demanded this of you?'

'Yes.'

When she didn't elaborate further, he pressed. 'Tell me about them.'

'I thought our pasts were out of bounds?'

Reaching for the chilling bottle, he poured her a drink before serving himself. 'They are, but I seem to have shared a lot of mine with you without meaning to. I think it's time we address the imbalance.'

Looking away from him for a moment, she contemplated the last of the lingering orange-and-purple sunset and the stars already beginning to make an appearance.

She didn't want to talk about her parents, or the single-minded ambition that drove them and had made her child-hood an endless drudge of trying, and failing, to please them.

And yet, she found herself nodding.

CHAPTER NINE

SHE PICKED UP her fork and tasted the exotic fruit and prawn salad, and busied herself with chewing while pushing her food around on her plate as she struggled to find the right words.

'My parents knew very early on that I wasn't academically gifted as they were—they're both Fulbright scholars and prize academic excellence above everything else.'

'Including you?' he asked astutely.

She swallowed and answered without looking up. 'Including me. I was an accident, who turned even more burdensome when I was unable to fulfil my full potential in their eyes.' When he didn't respond, she risked a glance.

His face was set in a carefully blank expression, but she glimpsed a look in his eyes, a *kinship*, that made her throat clog.

Clearing it, she continued. 'To say they were stunned their genius hadn't been replicated in me was an understatement. I was five when they made me take my first IQ test. They refused to believe the result. I took one every year until I was fifteen, when they finally accepted that I wouldn't be anything more than slightly above average.'

She sipped her champagne, let it wash away the bitter knowledge that she would always be a disappointment in her parents' eyes.

'Did they stop pushing you at this point?' he enquired sharply after helping himself to the last morsel on his plate.

Her mouth twisted. 'On the contrary. They pushed me harder with the belief that as long as they continued to polish me I would turn into the diamond they wanted instead of the unacceptable cubic zirconia.'

'I disagree with that description of yourself, and the assessment that you're average, but go on,' he encouraged, lounging back, all drop-dead-gorgeous danger, to nurse his drink as their first course was cleared away.

She shrugged. 'There's nothing much to add to that. They were indifferent to everything in my life besides my academic achievements, such as they were. When I told them I wanted to be a lawyer, they grudgingly accepted my decision, then immediately started pulling strings for me to be hired by one of the Magic Circle law firms in the country. When I told them I was taking three months off and then returning to take a position at a firm in Dublin, our relationship strained even more.'

'But you didn't back down?'

She laughed bitterly. 'It's hard being an average child of two geniuses, who hadn't wanted a child in the first place. I guess I'd reached a point where I'd had enough.' She'd wanted to lash out, rebel against the oppressive weight of her parents' indifference. Palermo had been her moment of rebellion. And while she would never regret having Lucca, she was beginning to be afraid that the one man she'd rebelled with had set a benchmark for all other men to come. And that each and every one of them would be found wanting.

She drank some more, felt the bubbles buzz through her veins and loosen her tongue. She even managed a less strained smile when Mahina delivered their second course.

'I presume that three-month vacation included your stop in Palermo?' he asked when they were alone again.

With the unburdening of her past came an unexpected increase in appetite. Or it could've been the alcohol.

Shrugging inwardly, Maisie tucked into the grilled mahi mahi and gave an appreciative moan. 'Yes. I'd always been fascinated with all things Italian.' She paused, glanced at him and saw the mildly mocking brow he lifted in her direction. Flushing, she returned her attention to her plate. 'I had some money saved from when I worked part-time at uni, and toured the whole of Italy. Palermo was my third stop.'

'And did your relationship improve once you resumed your career?' he asked. His questions weren't prying, as she supposed hers had been. He seemed to be interested in her life, her past, and not just as a means of passing time at the dinner table.

So she found herself recounting the one painful event in her life she'd sworn never to revisit again. 'Not once they found out I was pregnant by a man whose last name I didn't even know. Both my mother and father came from broken homes. They were estranged from their parents by the time I grew up. I know they hadn't planned on getting married, but they did because my mother fell pregnant with me. When I in turn got pregnant, the confirmation that the apple truly didn't fall far from the tree was too much for them to stomach.' The words fell from her lips in sharp bursts, the pain she'd smothered away in her heart rising to stab her once again.

She chanced a glance at Romeo and saw that he had frozen, his face a taut, forbidding mask.

'So they severed ties with you?' he asked in a chilling voice.

'Not exactly. But they had views on how to bring up Lucca that I didn't welcome.'

'What views?'

'They wanted me to put him in the care of nannies to start, and then boarding school when he was four—'

Romeo's curse stemmed the flow of her narrative. 'So he wouldn't get in the way of your career?' he bit out.

'Yes,' she replied, her throat painful with the admission that no matter what she achieved, she wouldn't be worthy in her parents' eyes.

His breath hissed out in pure rage. *'Madonna mia,'* he sliced out, his nostrils flaring as he struggled to control himself. 'Did you consider it?' he asked with a narrow-eyed stare.

'No. I gave up my job, enrolled in a gourmet cooking course, then moved to Ranelagh to open the restaurant.'

A morose silence fell over the table, their half-eaten meal growing cold as the sharp cries of cicadas pierced the night.

'This wasn't how I planned this evening unfolding,' Romeo said several minutes later after he'd refilled her glass.

Maisie laughed self-deprecatingly, that buzz in her veins somehow making the pain throbbing in her chest sharper. She was sure it was light-headedness that made her enquire breezily, 'So how had you planned this evening going, then?'

He didn't answer for a long time. Then he stood, tall, imposing, breathtaking. 'Come, we'll walk on the beach for a while.' He grabbed his glass and the half-finished bottle in one hand and held out his other. 'Let the night air wash away unpalatable memories.'

Maisie knew she ought to refuse, that the alcohol swirling through her bloodstream would inhibit any rational decisions she needed to make.

And yet she found herself sliding her hand into his, rising to her feet and discarding her shoes when he instructed her to.

The walk to the beach was lazy, the sultry night air and soft ukulele-threaded music emerging from hidden speakers seeming to slow everything down to a heavy, sensual, irresistible tempo.

He let go of her hand when they reached the sand, filled their glasses with the last of the champagne, then walked a few feet away to dispose of the bottle.

Toes curling in the warm sand, she strolled to the water's edge, laughing softly when the cool water splashed over her feet.

For a single moment, Maisie dared to wonder how it

would be to be in this place with the man of her dreams under different circumstances; if she'd been on a real honeymoon, not a desperate attempt to thwart a wizened old thug's threats.

The path her parents had set her on as a child hadn't left much room for dreaming. She'd been too busy trying to earn their love, to make herself worthy of their acceptance, to entertain such flights of fancy.

But she was a grown woman now, and surely there was nothing wrong with letting her imagination run wild for a few minutes, in letting her senses be overwhelmed by this beautiful place, this breathtaking man beside her?

She drained her second glass and didn't protest when Romeo took it away, then returned to stand behind her. Her breath shuddered out when he slid his hands over her shoulders and started a gentle massage of the tension-knotted muscles.

'What are you doing, Romeo?' she asked shakily after several minutes, when she started to melt beneath the warm kneading.

'You're tense. Why?'

'Probably because you're touching me.'

'You were tense before I touched you. Did I do something to make you this way?'

She released a single bark of laughter. 'The whole world doesn't revolve around you, Romeo.'

'Perhaps not, but if there's a problem going on with you it needs to be addressed, do you not agree?' He turned her around, looked into her face and frowned. 'Are you bored? Do you require more challenges?'

'No, I'm finding the lessons with Chef Sylvain illuminating and Mahina is teaching me a few Tongan recipes that will come in handy when I return to Ranelagh.'

His mouth compressed but he nodded. 'But you're not happy. Don't deny it.'

She tried to step out of his hypnotising sphere, but he held her by the elbows.

'This afternoon you thought you knew what ailed me.'

His gaze sharpened, then he gave a wry smile. 'Maybe it was my own need talking.'

'What…what need?'

'The need that claws beneath my skin, threatens to eat me alive…'

She made a barely audible sound when he pulled the clip from her hair and the heavy knot tumbled over her shoulders. Strong fingers slid through her hair in slow, sensual caresses. Maisie realised her dream was sliding dangerously into a yearning for reality that would be hard to push back in a bottle should she set it free.

But still she stayed, moaning softly when his mouth brushed the sensitive and tender spot below her ear. Light kisses traced along her jaw, down her neck to the pulse hammering at her throat. Desire pounded her, making her limbs heavy and the need to maintain that distance she'd been struggling to achieve melt away.

He spun her into his arms, and she gasped at the voracious hunger stamped on his face.

'Romeo…'

His kiss stopped whatever feeble attempt she'd been scrambling for to save herself from the unstoppable freight train of sexual fury that hurtled towards her. But as he took control of her mouth, control of her body, Maisie knew she would welcome being taken over, being flattened by the sheer force of his hunger, as long as it satisfied hers.

And it would.

From searing memory, she knew Romeo was an unselfish lover. If anything, he achieved a deeper level of arousal by piling on her pleasure, taking her to the very brink of sexual release and burning with her as they both fell.

He would give her everything her body desperately craved. And more.

But what happened next? What of tomorrow?

The questions began like small, icy kernels at the back of her mind. Then loomed, snowballed, until she pushed at his chest, desperate to free herself of this illusion.

'Stop!'

He raised his head immediately but didn't release her. 'You want me. Don't bother denying it,' he lashed out at her, his body vibrating with the tension that would surely explode at any moment.

His gaze dropped to her lips when she licked them, savouring the taste of him to pathetically add to her collection of memories.

'Yes, I do. But I won't let you use me to scratch an itch that only stems out of being thrown together more than anything else.'

He cursed under his breath. 'What's that supposed to mean?'

'It means we have a thing for each other, I won't deny that. But it's meaningless. Just a brand of chemistry that will probably go away if we ignore it. I'm not going to experiment on something cheap and tawdry just because we both happen to have time on our hands. I have more self-worth than that.'

He dropped his hands and took a single step back, but his dark gold eyes stayed on her. Accusing. Condemning. 'We took marriage vows. I think that elevates anything that happens between us well above cheap and tawdry.'

'Please don't do that. Don't rewrite the script on what the end goal is here. We only got married because of Lucca. And we agreed there would be no physical manifestation of those vows. Don't change the terms now.'

He laughed mockingly. 'You talk to me about changing the terms when you can't be in the same room as me or have a simple conversation without your pulse jumping all over the place?'

Heat suffused her face, along with anger. 'So you thought

you'd take pity on your sexually frustrated wife and do something about it?' she threw at him. 'How very stoic of you.'

'If I recall, leaving the physical side out of the marriage was your decision. I merely agreed because you seemed strongly wedded to the idea, pun intended. There's no shame in requesting a renegotiation.'

'I'm not requesting anything! All this…' she waved her hand at the sandy beach, the jaw-droppingly gorgeous moonlight and the discarded champagne bottle and glasses '…was your doing. Some sort of attempt at seduction, perhaps?'

He fisted his hair and then released it with a Latin flourish that made her belly quiver against her will.

'Only because I thought it wise to tackle the situation before one of us exploded,' he growled, his cheekbones hollowing out as he glared at her.

'Well, consider it tackled. I'll endeavour to keep my *desires* under better control from now on.'

The tension in his body was so palpable, she could almost reach out and touch it.

'You do realise there are millions of married couples who actually have sex with each other? Why not us?'

A shiver went through her, but she still managed to lift her chin and face that challenge head-on. 'Because I'm not built to have emotionless sex,' she flamed at him, at the end of her tether. 'And I'm damn sure you know that, Romeo. So stop. Please…just stop!'

Burnished gold eyes gleamed with such intensity, Maisie feared she might have poked the lion one too many times. For several seconds he just stared at her, hands on hips, his gaze probing to her very soul.

A heavy sigh depressed his chest, then he nodded solemnly. 'I will stop if you want me to. But I think we both know it won't be that easy, *gattina*. Come and find me when you change your mind.'

CHAPTER TEN

SHE MADE IT through the next seven days. Even went as far as to pat herself on the back for her stellar performance. Even when her body threatened resistance and advocated surrender at every turn, Maisie ground her teeth and sallied forth.

She looked into Romeo's eyes when he addressed her; didn't move away when he approached to discuss whatever was on his mind, or dance away as she normally would've when they took turns teaching Lucca to swim.

Even when she began to suspect that Romeo was deliberately testing her resolve by standing too close when they watched a particularly stunning sunset, or when his fingers lingered a touch too long when he passed her a plate of fruit at the breakfast table.

In those times she forced herself to remember how transient this situation was. And that the end might come sooner rather than later. He'd opened up when she'd heard him having a heated phone call two nights after their escapade on the beach.

Lorenzo had finally come out and demanded a cash settlement to restore the *famiglia's* dwindling power. Romeo had flatly refused.

The old man had retreated.

Whether that was merely a distraction tactic was something Romeo was investigating, but so far they had nothing concrete to indict him with. But if it proved not to be, then Lucca could be well out of danger before his fourth birthday next week. They hadn't discussed what would happen afterwards and she'd presumed Romeo would want access to his son, but Maisie couldn't see the man who'd been labelled the Weekend Lover, the same man who'd walked away from her so definitely five years ago, wanting to remain tied down through a marriage licence.

Her heart lurched painfully and she turned from watching Romeo and Lucca splashing on the other side of the pool. She thought of her little flat in Ranelagh and immediately hated herself for thinking it would be dull and dreary compared to this brilliant paradise. Compared to living under the same roof as Romeo.

Ranelagh was her home. One she was proud of.

She'd survived putting Romeo behind her five years ago. As painful as it'd been, she'd survived walking away from parents who would never love her the way she knew parents should love their child.

She would get through this when the time came.

'Is this your new way of attempting to tune me out? Staring out to sea and hoping you'll be turned into a mermaid?' His low voice seared along her nerve endings, starting that infernal flame that would only build the longer he stayed close.

She looked around and saw Emily walking off with a tired Lucca. Once they'd settled into a routine, Maisie had come round to the idea of letting Emily help with Lucca. They got on well, and Maisie could indulge in honing her culinary skills without guilt.

Bracing herself, she met Romeo's dark hazel eyes, the blazing sexual fire he no longer attempted to hide evident in his return stare.

'How very arrogant of you to assume my every thought revolves around you,' she replied coolly, although cool was the last thing she felt when he was this close, his arms braced on either side of the pool wall, caging her in.

'When I'm with you, like this, I guarantee that every one of mine revolves around you,' he supplied in a whispered breath.

Maisie suppressed a shiver. 'If you're trying to get me to crawl into your bed like a pathetic little sex slave, forget it.'

'There's nothing remotely pathetic about you, *gattina*. When you *do* crawl into my bed, I imagine you'll be a fierce little warrior woman.' He moved closer, his warm, chiselled torso sliding against her back in the water. 'Don't make me wait too long, though.'

Her fingers clung to the edge of the pool, her knuckles turning white with the effort. 'Or what?' she whispered fiercely. Daringly.

'Or your wildcat ways will be met with a much more predatory force than would be wise for either of us,' he breathed.

'Romeo, don't.'

It was then she felt the barely leashed dominance of his whole body. His powerful erection nudged her bottom, its hard and thick promise making her shut her eyes and bite back the helpless, hungry moan that rose to her lips.

'You think sex between us will be emotionless?' he queried in a harsh whisper.

She shook her head. 'What else can it be?'

'It wasn't five years ago. You had enough passion for both of us, and more. And I gave you what you needed. This time, we're husband and wife. You can let it count for something or you can let the transient nature of our situation stop you from demanding what you want. What we both want. Think about that, Maisie.'

The next second, he was swimming away, hauling himself out of the water like an arrogant god. He didn't look her way again as he towelled off and entered the villa.

Maisie stayed put, fighting the need to surrender with every last atom in her body, fiercely resisting the knowledge that the uphill battle with herself where Romeo was concerned was only just starting. And that this time, she risked losing more than just her dignity.

* * *

As Romeo had instructed all week, they dined outside, between sunset and when the stars came out. She kept the conversation on safe topics, determined to stay away from the bombshell he'd placed between them at the pool.

We're husband and wife.

The yearning those words triggered in her was something she didn't want to dwell on.

'The builders assure me the work will be done by the weekend. Which is just as well because I think our son has reached the point where we'll wake up one morning and find him down there finishing the pond with his own two hands.' The words were delivered with a bracing amount of amused dread.

Maisie laughed. 'I think poor Emily's at her wits' end, too, with reassuring him the pond will be ready by his birthday. If he decides to finish it on his own, I think she might help him, just for the sake of achieving some peace.'

Romeo smiled, and his face was transformed from brooding sexiness to heart-stopping so fast her heart took a dizzy dive. 'I suppose it's a blessing then he's managed to twist her around his fingers so soon. I can foresee a time when she adores him as much as we do.'

He froze suddenly and his breath caught. The eyes that met hers held stunned shock and when he reached for his red wine, she saw how his hand trembled.

She laid her hand over his as a lump rose in her throat. 'It's okay to admit you love your son, Romeo,' she said gently. 'In fact, I think it's time you told him as much, and that you're his father.'

The shock dissipated, replaced by the customary brooding. He eyed her with a mildly disparaging look. 'So was this some sort of test?'

She jerked her hand away. 'Excuse me?'

'To see how I fared in the fatherhood stakes before offering your permission to let him know I'm his father?' he tagged on.

'Of course not,' she replied, the barb stinging deep and painfully. 'You really think so little of me? Or of yourself?' she added, because she sensed some of that pointed remark was directed at himself.

A fleeting expression flashed across his face, almost like regret. Then his features tightened. 'Why would you think any more of me or my fathering skills? You know enough about my background to know I have no experience in this. That my own childhood has left scars I'll never be able to erase. Scars that could manifest in unpredictable ways somewhere down the line.'

She frowned. 'What do you mean?'

His mouth pursed for so long she thought he wouldn't answer. 'You know I lived on the streets. What you don't know is that I joined a gang a few years after that. One that even the authorities feared to tackle.'

Unease climbed into her throat. 'Why?'

'Because I wanted to fit in, *somewhere*.'

The raw vulnerability caught at her heart. 'And did you?'

He exhaled harshly. 'Not after I refused to perform the initiation rites.'

'Which were?'

Her heart froze as he enunciated what he'd been asked to do. Silence settled over their table, until he raised his head.

'You see why fatherhood isn't a job I'm to be trusted to settle into easily.'

Maisie's heart squeezed at the pain in his voice. 'But you walked away. You chose to walk away instead of hurting another human being.'

'That doesn't mean I'm equipped to handle this!'

'You're fighting Lorenzo instead of giving in to threats and extortion. You swore to protect Lucca within hours of meeting him. You've done nothing but care for him since we got here. Doesn't that tell you something? Love makes you vulnerable sometimes, but it doesn't make you weak.'

His mouth twisted, but the pain in his eyes dissipated a little. 'I wouldn't know. Lucca's young now, adorable and easy to handle. Who's to say what will come later, and how well we'll handle it?' His voice was thin and a touch bleak, holding echoes of his past.

Her hands clenched on the pristine white tablecloth. 'Stop borrowing trouble, Romeo. You've done well so far. Let's just take it one day at a time. And if you're not ready to tell Lucca that you're his father, then we'll wait.'

A muscle flexed in this jaw. 'I wanted to tell him who I was the first moment I knew he was mine.'

The touch of frost inside her melted. 'Fine. Tomorrow, then, or the day after. Whenever you're ready.'

His mouth compressed for several seconds. Then he nodded. *'Bene.'*

Maisie swallowed and nodded in return. She started to reach for her water glass, but he caught her hand in his.

'I'm sorry for not handling this better.'

The remaining frost was replaced by dizzying warmth. 'It's okay. I muddle through motherhood every day.' She smiled.

He raised her hand to his lips and kissed the soft skin. 'You've done an admirable job, *gattina.*'

Heat unfurled in her stomach, wending its way through her body when he continued to caress her with his mouth.

She cleared her throat and forced herself to say something before she crumbled beneath the smouldering onslaught. 'And you've had more experience than I think you're letting on.'

His eyebrows rose.

'There was a picture of you in the paper, on a yacht with two little boys,' she pried gently.

A look crossed his face, a facsimile of the one he wore whenever he interacted with his son. 'Rafa and Carlo are

Zaccheo's twin sons, and my godsons.' He shrugged. 'At least that's what it says on paper. I don't really have much interaction with them.'

'Zaccheo is your ex-business partner?'

He hesitated for a moment, then nodded. '*Sì*, but he is more than that.'

'In what way?'

Hazel eyes darkened a touch. 'Our pasts were intertwined for a brief time during which we formed an unlikely bond.' His tone suggested he wouldn't elaborate, but as she had before, Maisie couldn't help but pry, her need to know this man inside and out a yearning that wouldn't go away.

'Before or after you lived on the streets?'

'Before. Zaccheo's parents took me in for a while, but that situation could never be anything but temporary because my presence in their lives was not their choice.'

He turned her hand over, his fingers tracing her palm in slow, lazy circles. It wasn't a sensual move, even though there was plenty of that arcing between them. It was a grounding touch that sought, and received, a connection.

'Are you ever going to tell me what happened with your mother?' she murmured.

He froze immediately. 'I don't consider the subject suitable dinner conversation.'

She sighed. 'Then I guess, since dinner is over, I should retire to bed.'

'So you can tuck yourself into your cool sheets and congratulate yourself for escaping this needless torture you insist on putting us both through?' he grated at her, a different, more dangerous brooding taking over his face. She also detected a vulnerability that made her wonder whether there was something more going on here than she was aware of.

She slowly pulled her hand away. 'It's not needless.'

His mouth twisted. 'I suppose it's something that you don't deny it's torturous.' He caught up his glass and drained the last of his wine. The precision with which he set down the exquisite crystal made her think he would very much like to launch it across the terrace floor and watch it shatter in a million pieces.

He shoved his chair back and stood. 'Perhaps I'll take a leaf out of your book and live in denial for a while. I'm sure there's an urgent business decision I need to make somewhere in my company. Sleep well, *gattina*,' he said mockingly, before striding off in the direction of his study.

She knew the mocking command would have the opposite effect even before she undressed and slid into bed two hours later after giving up the pretence of reading.

Tossing and turning, Maisie tried rationalising and re-affirming her decisions. When by the thousandth time her own reasoning sounded mockingly hollow, she gave up. Frustrated, she yanked back the sheets and sat up. The hot-pink silk negligee she wore felt sticky on her skin, but the warm night air was inviting, a great way to empty her thoughts of the disturbing feeling that her resistance was crumbling.

Tugging the silk over her head, she went into her dressing room and rummaged through the drawer containing her new selection of swimwear. When her fingers closed over an as-yet-unworn set, she pulled out the string bikini she'd looked at and immediately discarded when her wardrobe had arrived. Of all the swimwear that had been delivered, this was the most daring. The cups of the top part of the black-and-orange set barely covered half her breasts and the matching panties were made of nothing more than three pieces of string, leaving very little to the imagination.

Making a face, she set it aside. Then glanced back at it. The little thrill of naughtiness surged higher the longer she eyed the garment.

She was tired of being sensible. Especially at one o'clock in the morning. Deciding to add a little bit of spice to her illicit swim, she quickly donned the bikini and threw a white linen tunic over it.

The villa was quiet, and she breathed a sigh of relief as she passed Romeo's empty study.

The path to the waterfall was softly lit by garden lamps. Snagging a towel from the stack near the swimming pool, she skirted the villa and hurried through the short tunnel and cave that opened into the stunning rock pool. Disrobing, Maisie dived into the pool, submerging for several seconds, hoping the heavenly cool water would wash away her turbulent thoughts.

The strong compulsion to make the most of what she had *now* before it was taken away from her wouldn't dissipate. On the contrary it grew stronger the harder she willed it away, the harder she swam from one end of the pool to the other.

Finally, wrung out emotionally and physically, she perched on the rock beneath the waterfall, leaning her head back to catch the edge of the cascading water, and sighed at the delicious sting of the warm water on her face.

'You insist you have no illusions of pursuing a life as a mermaid, and yet here you are again.'

She jerked at the sound of Romeo's voice and nearly fell into the water. Righting herself, she stared at his imposing, braced-legged stance at the opposite end of the pool. And swallowed hard.

He was dressed, like her, for swimming, his trunks hugging thick, hair-dusted thighs. But whereas she'd worn a tunic, he only wore a towel around his neck. Her breath strangled and died in her lungs, her pulse racing at the sheer magnificence of him.

She was doomed.

She knew it even before he dropped into the pool and swam lazily towards her. Halfway, he ducked under the water, struck out in a powerful crawl and emerged at her feet. Hands braced on either side of her thighs, he stared wordlessly at her, his gaze intense, broodingly ravenous. Maisie stared down at his breathtaking face, the droplets of water glistening on his skin in the moonlight like tiny diamonds.

Raw sexual energy leapt where their skin connected, firing arousal so strong she could almost touch it.

'Did sleep elude you, as it did me, *gattina*?' he enquired with a husky rasp after an endless throb of silence.

She nodded dumbly, her fingers reaching out of their own accord to trace his eyebrow, his cheekbones. His jaw.

'Have you grown tired of fighting the inevitable?' he pressed.

Her blood roared in her ears, drowning out her every resistant thought. 'I've grown tired of fighting you.'

The gleam in his eyes dimmed for a moment. 'It's not me you've been fighting, but yourself. If nothing else, be true to yourself about that, before this goes any further,' he growled, his stare telling her he wouldn't accept anything but her agreement.

And he was right.

She had been fighting this purely for her own self-preservation. How could she not? The consequences should he reject her a second time would be even more devastating than before. She knew it deep in her soul. With the passage of time her feelings towards him were changing, morphing into something deeper, stronger, that she couldn't seem to control.

The movement of the water jerked him a tiny fraction. The result was a slide of her fingers across his hot, beautiful skin, bringing her to the here and now, to the almighty need pounding through her blood.

'I'm tired of fighting,' she whispered raggedly.

'Then surrender,' he urged thickly. 'Just let this be.' His hands moved, sliding over her thighs to capture her knees. Tugging them open, he surged closer, his eyes so fierce and intense they seemed aflame from within. 'I can't stand another night of wanting you and being denied. Of imagining the many ways of having you, without going out of my mind. Surrender, *gattina*. Surrender now.'

Desire, wild and unfettered, wrenched through her, rendering the last of her resistance useless. Her fingers speared into his wet hair, using her hold to tilt his face up to hers.

Bending, she took his mouth in a greedy kiss, intent on gorging herself on a feast she'd stalwartly denied herself but couldn't resist another moment longer.

Somewhere down the line the devastation would be great. When she was back in her role of single mother far away in Ranelagh, her shredded emotions would have time to mourn, to berate her for her choices.

But here…now, in this heavenly place with this man who put the very gods to shame, she would live in the moment. She would just…*live*. As she had that night in Palermo, she would give as much of herself as she could and take what Romeo offered.

She groaned when he moved her closer to the edge of the rock and deepened the kiss, taking over her surrender with the terrifyingly intoxicating thrust of his tongue and the thrilling power of his body.

The waterfall pounded with elemental force behind her, but it was nothing compared to the demanding power of Romeo's kiss. He kissed her as if he'd hungered for her for aeons. As if he couldn't get enough of her.

Being wanted like that was like a drug to her senses. After years of bleak, icy indifference, it was a drug she craved more of with each passing second.

So she protested with a loud whimper when he pulled away. Before she could reach for him, he planted a hand on her belly, pressed her back till she was flat on the rock. He picked up her legs and swung them onto the rock before surging out of the water to join her.

For a long, taut moment, he stared down at her, his gaze

sizzling over her from top to toe. Then he prowled over her, his hands braced on either side of her head.

'I've often imagined you like this, spread over this rock like a pagan sacrifice for me to feast on, to pleasure until neither of us can move. Now here you are, wearing this wisp of clothing meant to tempt even the holiest of saints,' he breathed, triumph blazing through his golden eyes.

'It's a good thing you're not a saint, then, isn't it?' she managed, then watched a wicked smile curl his lips.

'*Sì*, it's a very good thing. Because no saint should be allowed to see you like this. Or allowed to do this.' He flicked his tongue over the wet material of her bikini top, then, with a deep groan, he shoved the material aside with his teeth and repeated the action several times, before pulling her nipple into his mouth.

Her back arched off the rock with a cry that was indeed pagan, thick arousal firing straight between her legs. He suckled long and hard, his groans matching hers as sensation cascaded through her.

'*Dio mio,*' he muttered when he lifted his head. He speared her with an almost shocked expression before he looked down at her exposed breasts. '*Dio mio, gattina*, you're intoxicating. I want to devour every inch of you.' Impatiently, he tugged at the bikini strings, pulling them away to bare her body to him.

A drop of water splashed onto her neglected nipple. With another wicked smile, he licked at it, then trailed his hot mouth down her torso to the line of her bikini bottom. Unable to keep her hands at her sides, Maisie speared her fingers in his hair, holding him to her quivering belly when he nipped her flesh in tiny, erotic bites.

By the time he released the ties and pulled away her meagre covering, she'd skated into pure delirium, compelled by a force beyond her control. She raised her head and met his gaze a second before he tasted the centre of her.

'Oh, God!' The force of her need jerked through her, then

set in motion a series of undulations he was only too glad to follow. When her eyes started to roll shut, he pulled away.

'No, watch me, *gattina*. Watch me enjoy you the way I've been dying to do.'

The eroticism of the request pushed her closer to the edge. Panting, she nodded and kept her gaze on him as he lapped at her, his tongue executing wicked circles that cracked open a previously untapped well of pleasure.

'Romeo,' she groaned raggedly, the rush of feeling almost too much to bear. 'Please…I can't take any more.'

'You can.' Opening her wider, he altered the pressure of his tongue, his hypnotic gaze telling her she was under his control, to do with as he pleased.

When she began to thrash, he simply laid a hand on her belly and continued his assault. And with each kiss, he grew just as possessed with the red-hot fire consuming them.

'Now, Maisie,' he growled against her swollen flesh an eternity later.

With an agonised cry, she let go, her whole body convulsing with a release so powerful, she lost all sense of space and time.

CHAPTER ELEVEN

She opened her eyes to find him sprawled next to her, his fingers tracing her mouth as he stared down at her, a peculiar expression simmering in his eyes.

'What?'

He kissed her, her earthy taste on his lips and the reason for it making her blush. When he raised his head, that look still lingered.

'You returned home from Palermo pregnant.' His hand trailed from her neck to her belly and stayed there while his eyes held her prisoner.

'Is there a pointed question in there somewhere?' she murmured, her heartbeat still thundering loud enough to compete with the sound of the waterfall. 'I'm on the Pill now if that's what you're asking. It helps regulate my period.'

'It's not, but that's good to know.' His hand continued to wreak havoc on her. 'You changed careers and forged another life for yourself all alone. Did you at any point seek another man's bed to alleviate your loneliness?' he asked thickly.

She knew how weak and pathetic responding in the positive would make her look. But she couldn't lie. Not when she'd just experienced an incredible earth-moving event.

She threaded her fingers through his wet hair. 'I was alone, not lonely. But no, Romeo. You were the last man I slept with.'

His chest moved in a deep inhalation and his eyes filled once again with that primitive, razor-sharp hunger that threatened to obliterate her.

The hand on her belly trailed to her thighs, his fingers

digging into her skin in an urgent caress as his head dropped to hers once more. Falling into the kiss, Maisie gladly let sensation take over again, moaning when her hand trailed over taut muscle and bone to finally close on his steely length.

She caressed him as he'd once hoarsely instructed her to, a thrill coursing through her when he groaned brokenly against her lips.

All too soon, he was rolling on the condom he'd plucked from his trunks. Bearing her back, he parted her thighs and hooked his arms under her knees.

He stared deep into her eyes and thrust home in one smooth lunge.

'Oh!'

His growl of male satisfaction reverberated to her very soul. Her fingers speared into his hair as he began to pleasure her with long, slow strokes, each one pulling a groan from her that only seemed to turn him on harder.

He kissed her mouth, her throat, her nipples, with a hunger that grew with each penetration, until she was sure he wouldn't stop until she was completely ravished.

'You're mine. Say it,' he demanded gutturally, when her world began to fracture.

'Romeo…'

'I want to hear it, Maisie.' He slid deep and stopped, the harsh, primitive request demanding a response.

Something shifted inside her, a deep and profound knowledge sliding home that once she admitted this there would be no going back. That she would be giving herself over to him completely, body and soul.

He angled his hips, the move a blatant demonstration that he had all the power, that he controlled every fibre of her being.

'I…' She groaned when he moved again, delivering that subtle thrust that sent her to the very edge of consciousness.

'Tell me!'

'I'm yours…yours. Please…' Her nails dug into his back, and she surged up to take his mouth with hers. 'Please, Romeo. I'm yours…take me,' she whispered brokenly.

Romeo moved, his senses roaring from the words, from her tight and wet heat, from the touch of her hands on his skin. He couldn't get enough. He wanted more. All of her, holding absolutely nothing back. He reared back so he could look into her eyes, to see for himself that she meant it, that she belonged to him completely.

Her eyes met his, the raw pleasure coursing through her shining in the stunning blue depths. There was no fight, no holding back, just a beautiful surrender that cracked something hard and heavy in his chest, bringing in the light and abating the tortured, weighted-down bitterness for the first time in his life.

The sense that he could fly free, that he could find even deeper and truer oblivion in her arms than he had their first time in Palermo, slashed across his consciousness, making his thrusts less measured, the need to achieve that transcendental plane a call to his very soul.

He looked down at her, saw her eyes grow dazed and dark as her bliss encroached. Letting go of her legs, he speared his fingers into her hair and kissed her.

'Now, *gattina mia*,' he croaked, knowing he was at the edge of surrender himself.

'Yes, oh, yes,' she replied. Then she was thrashing beneath him, her sex clamping around his in a series of convulsions that sent him over the edge.

With a loud roar, Romeo flew, barely able to keep from crushing her as he found a release so powerful, had he believed in heaven he would've been certain he'd truly found it in that moment.

He came back down to the touch of her hands trailing up and down his back, her mouth moving against his throat in a benediction of soft kisses.

Again another blaze of memory slashed across his mind,

a sense of déjà vu throwing him back five years, to his hotel suite in Palermo. The feeling that he was raw and exposed, that the woman beneath him wasn't one he could bed and discard, pounding through him. Romeo was certain it was why he'd left as he had the next morning, ensuring he left no trace of himself behind.

Because after mere hours with her, he'd instinctively known that Maisie O'Connell had the power to burrow under his skin, unearth tortured truths and hidden desires he wanted no man or woman to unveil. He'd listened abstractedly as she'd spilled her hopes and dreams and had wanted nothing more than to tell her he'd arrived in Palermo the week before, hoping that for once in his life the woman who'd given birth to him would look at him with any feeling other than hate. That he'd spent a week by his mother's bedside, hoping for a morsel of affection, or regret for the way she'd callously discarded him.

He'd somehow managed to keep his tortured thoughts to himself, but he could tell she'd sensed them, and she'd soothed his soul with the same soft kisses and caresses she gifted him with now.

Then, as now, she'd given herself completely, despite not knowing any more than his first name.

The need to unburden completely powered through him now, but he held himself back. She knew about his father partly through the need to furnish her with information about Lorenzo's plans and partly because he'd let down his guard. But his mother was a different story.

The secret shame that clawed through him had never abated, despite the years he'd spent in bitterness. After he'd buried his mother, he'd bricked away the pain, secure in the knowledge that she no longer had the power to hurt him with her rejection. He'd only ever felt those foundations crumble with Maisie. And her power over him wasn't one he felt comfortable with. It spoke to a weakness he wasn't ready to face.

Shoving his unsettling thoughts back in the vault, he stared down and allowed himself to bask in her soft smile. The sex he could more than deal with, even if it came with a brief exposure of his soul. The benefits were worth it. More rewarding than securing the best business deal.

'Should I be afraid of that smug smile you're wearing right now?' she asked, her voice slightly dazed and heavy with spent bliss.

Arousal spiked again, the magic of her body transporting him into pleasure with blinding speed. Replacing the condom, he expertly reversed their positions, lying back to take in her goddess-like beauty.

With her long, wet hair plastered to her golden skin, she truly looked like a wanton mermaid.

'*Sì*, you're about to make another of my fantasies come true.' He cupped her heavy breasts, played his thumbs over the stiff peaks and felt her body quicken to his touch. He grew harder, need lashing through him as he watched her accept, then revel in, her new position.

She tested the rhythm, quickly found one pleasing to them both and commenced a dance that had them gasping and groaning within minutes.

He reached between them and found her heated centre. Playing his fingers expertly over her, he watched her throw back her head, her nails digging into his chest as she screamed her release.

He followed gladly, eager to experience that piece of heaven again. Eager to leave behind hopes and yearnings that would never be fulfilled. He'd refused to wish after seeing each fragile desire turn to dust before his eyes as a child.

But Maisie in his arms, in his bed, was an achievable goal. One he intended to hang on to for as long as he could.

Maisie awoke slowly, her senses grappling with the strange bed she slept in and the warm, solid body tangled around hers. Vague memories of being carried from the waterfall slid through her mind. She stirred and the heaviness of satiation moved through her limbs, bringing back wild and more vivid memories of last night.

Opening her eyes to brilliant sunshine, she forced herself not to panic as the full realisation of what had happened reared up like a giant billboard in front of her.

She'd given herself to Romeo. Not just her body, but her heart, her soul. She'd known right from the start that giving herself to him this time round would be her undoing. Heck, she'd told him as much!

Just as she'd suspected when she'd promised she was his, she'd been making a declaration that went beyond sex. Each decision she'd taken when it came to her child and his father had been made from her heart. She just hadn't been brave enough to admit it to herself. But now she knew.

She was in love with Romeo Brunetti.

Had probably fallen in love with him the moment she'd sat down across from him that day in Palermo.

Her stomach clenched even as her heart accepted the deep, abiding truth. He was the reason she'd never paid another man any attention, had embraced motherhood without much of a thought for finding a father figure for her son. Deep down she'd known no one could come close to Romeo so she hadn't even tried to replace him.

And now… She breathed deep as her eyes fell on her wedding rings. Now, she could do nothing but brace herself for the agony to come. And it would come. Loving Romeo was her greatest risk and would bring the greatest consequence. Of that, she was certain.

'Buon giorno, gattina.' Strong fingers brushed her hair from her face and drew her back against the warm sheets. 'What troubles you so much that you wake me with the power of your thoughts?' he asked, his eyes probing hers with the sharpness of a scalpel.

'Everything and nothing,' she replied obliquely, desperately hoping to buy more time to compose herself.

'An answer guaranteed to send a man into fits of puzzlement. Or the nearest jewellery store.'

'Is that how you usually placate your other women?' she asked, a sensation moving through her that she deciphered as deep jealousy.

Intense eyes narrowed. 'I wasn't aware you needed placating. Perhaps you should tell me where I've misstepped?'

She glanced away. 'I don't. You haven't. Sorry, I was prying again.'

Warm fingers captured her chin, a thoughtful look in his eyes. 'I guess it's only fair, since I questioned you about past liaisons.'

She shook her head, perversely wanting to know, but also desperate to live in denial. If only for a while longer. She chose the latter. 'I don't need a biography of your past conquests. I know enough to get that you have a healthy sexual appetite.' A blush suffused her face and he slanted her a wicked grin.

'Is that what concerns you?'

She shook her head, but she couldn't tell him, of course. Because that would be tantamount to shoving her heart underneath the wheels of a Sherman tank. So she went for the next best thing. 'Why did you bring me to your bedroom? I wasn't expecting to wake up here.'

The smile left his face and that dark brooding look returned. 'Why do you think?' His voice pulsed with an emotion she couldn't name.

She pulled her lower lip into her mouth. 'I thought last night was just…' She paused. 'I meant it when I said I don't want this to get complicated.'

Too late.

But that didn't mean she couldn't salvage a little bit of dignity from the dire situation. Guard her heart from more pulverising down the road.

'So *your* itch has been scratched and you're ready to put

it all behind you?' he queried in a dark, dangerous voice, throwing her own words back in her face.

'I didn't expect it to last beyond last night. Isn't that your record?'

'I see we're back to past conquests again.'

'Romeo—'

'No, you listen. Last night barely dented the depth of my need. And if you're truthful, you'll admit the same. I brought you to my bed because this is where you belong. You can protest as much as you want and we can go back to circling each other until we drive each other insane, or you can choose to admit your feelings and take what you want.'

She opened her mouth, intent on denying everything he'd said. On doing *the right thing*. Getting up, walking back to her own room. To her painfully lonely bed. And more nights filled with the vicious ache of wanting him.

But the words died in her throat. Denying herself suddenly felt like the opposite of *the right thing*. As if saying the words out loud would be like slicing a knife into her arms and opening her veins. Sure, there was a life of desolation waiting for her once she walked away from him, but there was no need to start the torture *now*.

She stared up at him, at the vitality of the body caging hers, the need blazing in his eyes, and resolved to just *be* for now.

'Will you stay?' he pressed.

Slowly, she nodded. 'Yes, I will.'

He proceeded to show her the true meaning of good morning. And she gave herself over to the incandescent sensation.

She was still smiling four mornings later, even as she studiously ignored the tiny voice that called her ten kinds of a fool.

They rose, showered together, their hands and lips revelling in the newness of just being together without tension. Oh, the sexual tension was ever-present. It barely left them alone and Maisie was beginning to doubt it ever would. But there was an ease between them that tugged at her heart when Romeo smiled at her and walked her to her room so she could get dressed.

He lounged in the doorway of her dressing room, his eyes wickedly intent on her body as she pulled on panties and a bra, and slid her white shift dress over her head.

After slipping her feet into heeled sandals, she took his outstretched hand and they left the room.

'Are you sure?' she asked him.

He nodded, although his throat moved in a hard swallow. 'Yes, it's time to tell him.'

As they reached the stairs, she glanced at him and was shocked to see that, for the first time since she'd known him, Romeo looked nervous. Vulnerable.

'Are you okay?' she asked as they descended the stairs and headed towards the kitchen, where Lucca could be heard chattering away to Mahina and Emily.

Romeo gave a strangled laugh. 'It's not every day I tell an almost-four-year-old boy I'm his *papà*.'

Her hand closed on his and drew him to a stop. Standing on tiptoe, she offered what she'd intended to be a supportive kiss.

His hands locked on her hips, and he slammed her back against the wall to deepen the kiss. He kissed her as if trying to draw sustenance from her. By the time they pulled apart several minutes later, they were both breathing hard. His eyes were needy pools, searching and a little lost.

She placed her hand on his cheek, her heart melting when he cupped it and pressed it deeper into his skin. 'You'll be fine. He adores you as much as you do him.'

His head dipped as if he wasn't quite sure how to deal with the alien feeling of being the object of a child's adoration. *'Grazie,'* he finally murmured. When he raised his head, the confident, virile man had slid back. 'Let's do this.'

He tugged her after him, and they entered the kitchen together.

Ten minutes later, in the privacy of Romeo's study, Lucca stared at his father from the safety of his perch on his mother's lap. Then his gaze moved to her face and back to Romeo's, his eyes wide, hazel saucers. 'You're my daddy?' he asked in hushed awe.

Romeo's throat moved several times before he could speak. '*Sì*, I am your *papà*,' he intoned in a deep, moving voice.

Lucca tilted his head to one side, then shook his head. 'Not *papà…daddy*. I want you to be a *daddy*.'

A telltale sheen covered Romeo's eyes and he blinked rapidly before he nodded. '*Va bene*, I will be a daddy.'

Lucca launched himself off her lap and threw his arms around his father. Romeo's strong arms gathered the chubby body to him, his eyes closing on a depth of feeling that made Maisie's eyes fill with helpless tears. Father and son stayed locked for an eternity. Or as much as a toddler could stand until impatience set in.

When he was lowered to his feet, Lucca stared up at his father. 'Can I tell Emily?'

Romeo nodded. 'You can tell whomever you wish.'

Lucca started to race out of the door but then stopped suddenly. 'I wished very, very hard for a daddy,' he said solemnly. 'And it came true!'

Romeo looked stricken for several long seconds. Then he shook his head, as if denying whatever thought had crossed his mind. 'I'm glad for you, *bel bambino*.'

After watching Lucca run off, Romeo turned to her and pulled her to her feet. Seeing her tears, he gently wiped them away and planted a soft kiss on her lips. '*Grazie, il mio dolce.*'

Swallowing the lump in her throat, she smiled. 'I told you it'd be a piece of cake,' she said.

His blinding answering smile lit her up from the inside,

starting a shaky weakness that made her lower her gaze in case he read the depth of emotions moving through her. 'Perhaps I should listen to you more,' he suggested with a quirked brow.

'Perhaps I should get that in writing,' she answered.

He was still chuckling when they trailed their son. The announcement turned into an impromptu celebration with pancakes and juice, after which they got down to the urgent business of planning Lucca's heavily duck-pond-themed birthday party.

Finding out that the Giordano family would be joining them on the island in two days, along with the guests staying at the villas, and that Romeo was expected to host a dinner party, Maisie felt a rush of panic.

The only party she'd thrown so far had involved a cake, sandwiches and screaming kids in a playgroup's ball pit.

She was nowhere near sophisticated enough to handle a houseful of billionaires. She tried to pin a smile on her face as Romeo's eyes narrowed at her from across the kitchen island.

'What's wrong?' he asked as soon as they were alone.

'Nothing...' she started to say, then blurted, 'I've never thrown a dinner party before. Or a birthday party for a billionaire's son for that matter.'

He frowned. 'He's still the son you raised from birth. As for the party, everything's taken care of. I have caterers flying in from Honolulu to assist the chefs who cater for the island guests.'

Somehow her anxiety only escalated. 'Oh, so you don't really need me at all, do you?'

His frown deepened. 'Of course I need you. What's this really about?'

On some level, Maisie knew she was reacting to a deeper anxiety, one that stemmed from the knowledge that Romeo's life was so smoothly coordinated, aside from her role in his bed, he didn't need her for much else. Even Lucca would be extremely well taken care of by Emily and Mahina, should Maisie suddenly find herself rubbed out of the picture.

'Maisie?' he growled warningly.

She shrugged. 'I guess I'm feeling a little surplus to requirements.' Not to mention suddenly aware of her precarious position of temporary wife. 'I barely do anything for Lucca any more besides eat breakfast and sometimes lunch with him. Other times, he'd rather play with Emily or hang out with you.'

He took her by the arms. 'You've had him to yourself for almost four years. It's understandable the small separation on occasion would feel strange. And that separation was probably more pronounced because you were avoiding *me*,' he pointed out. 'But if you want me to prove that you're not surplus to requirements, just say the word, and I'll oblige you.'

She looked into eyes darkening into burnished gold and a blaze sparked through her. But alongside it rose a wave of desolation. Sex with Romeo was out of this world. Each experience felt as if she were touching the stars. But it was *just sex* for him. It would never be anything more.

So when he gathered her close and kissed her, she responded with a lingering taste of sadness that made tears brim behind her closed eyes.

His phone rang just when she thought the tears would spill and betray her, and she breathed a sigh of relief. He pulled it from his pocket and checked the screen. Frowning, he looked at her. 'Sorry, it's Zaccheo. I have to take it.'

Waving him away, she hurriedly escaped the sunlit living room. Her first thought was to find Lucca. She found him in the playroom and pulled him into a close embrace. When he demanded she read his favourite story, she obliged.

She was on the fifth read when Romeo entered the room.

She jerked upright at the volcanic fury on his face. 'What's wrong?'

'Zaccheo and Eva are arriving tomorrow.'

A day earlier than planned. 'Why?'

'Because they've been pulled into this insane situation in Palermo. It's time to end this before it gets out of hand.'

CHAPTER TWELVE

HER FIRST IMPRESSION of Zaccheo Giordano drove home the understanding of why the two powerful men were friends.

He carried himself with the same ruthless energy as Romeo, albeit with a little less brooding intensity. That energy was exhibited clearly when he stepped from the buggy and clasped Romeo's hand in an unsmiling, yet moving greeting.

His intensity lessened dramatically when he helped his heavily pregnant wife up the short steps into the wide villa entranceway.

Eva Giordano was gorgeous in a pocket-Venus, burst-of-energy way that drew interested eyes to her wild tumble of blonde hair and sharply contrasting dark eyebrows and darkly ringed green eyes.

Despite the strong evidence of love between them, Maisie sensed a tension between her and Zaccheo, which was explained once introductions had been made and Romeo was hugging Eva.

'I'm sorry we had to descend on you prematurely, but it was either *we all* came here or *we all* went to Palermo.' She cast an irritated look at her husband. 'The vote was eventually unanimous that we come here, since I refused to be left behind while Caveman over here went off to tackle Carmelo and Lorenzo on his own.'

Zaccheo muttered under his breath about intransigent women and helped corral his twin sons when they escaped their nanny and started fighting over who was better suited to drive the buggy.

Eva turned from greeting Romeo and her gaze fell on

Lucca. 'Oh, hello there, beautiful boy.' Her wide smile seemed to enchant her husband, who lost his growly look and came to stand beside her, one hand gently caressing her swollen belly.

The look of pure, blazing love that passed between them caused Maisie's heart to drop in misery into her belly. But she managed a smile and coaxed a shy Lucca from behind her. Within minutes he and the Giordano boys were exploring the new toy room Romeo had installed for him.

Mahina served drinks on the terrace and the tension mounted again the moment she left.

'What exactly did Carmelo want from you?' Romeo asked tersely, once Zaccheo had apprised them of the threat from Palermo's other crime lord.

'His ridiculous demands are the same as Lorenzo's to you. They're both terrified one would attain more power than the other. But he had the nerve to threaten my family. I cannot allow that to stand.'

Eva rolled her eyes. 'You realise how much like a bad gangster movie actor you sound?' When his eyes narrowed, she continued, completely unfazed. 'You have a veritable army guarding me and the boys when you're not around, and Carmelo's claims of you owing him allegiance because your father was a one-time lieutenant of his before he switched sides to Romeo's father is flimsy at best. How do we even know that's true?' She looked at Romeo. 'Besides, I know you two have enough dirt on the man to send him to jail for a long time.'

Romeo shook his head. 'I've talked to the lawyers about it. It's all circumstantial without hard evidence. I only witnessed Zaccheo's father being beaten.' He sent his friend a look of grim-faced sympathy, to which Zaccheo nodded. 'He was still alive when I was thrown out of Fattore's mansion. We need irrefutable evidence of blood on Lorenzo's hands.'

'So, what's the alternative?' Eva exclaimed. 'A duel at dawn beneath Mount Etna?'

Romeo's jaw clenched but he didn't refute Eva's outlandish claim. Maisie's stomach hollowed out, both at the news Romeo had just delivered and his intent expression.

'You're not thinking of going back to Palermo, are you?' she demanded in a shocked whisper.

His eyes when they met hers were hard, implacable, with no trace of the gentleness they'd held yesterday before Zaccheo's phone call. 'It's the only option. I won't entertain the idea of my son living in fear.'

Zaccheo nodded in grim agreement and captured his wife's hand when she began to protest.

Maisie struggled not to feel excluded and even more miserable as Romeo proceeded to converse to the couple, switching to Italian when the debate got heated.

Once or twice, she spotted Eva's probing glance and fixed a smile on her face, answering her questions about the island and the villa when she switched back to English.

When Eva yawned loudly and started to droop, Zaccheo stood and ushered her inside.

Knowing she wouldn't be able to sit and make small talk while her insides were shredding with the knowledge that Romeo had room in his heart only for his son, and not her, she jumped to her feet.

'I'll go see if the boys are okay.'

He caught her hand and stopped her. 'You're upset because I intend to confront Lorenzo?'

'Does my opinion matter enough for you to change your mind? I thought you were pursuing a different route other than direct confrontation.'

His jaw flexed. 'I suspected his mellowed stance was all a bluff. Just as I suspect, this is nothing more than an extortion scheme, probably concocted between him and Carmelo. The timing is a little too synchronised. Whatever it is, I need to end it once and for all.'

She tried to pull away but he held on. 'Since your mind's made up, there's no need for my opinion, is there?'

'Gattina—'

'Don't call me that.' The blurted plea rushed out before she could stop it.

He gave a hiss of frustration. 'You suddenly have a problem with the name?'

'No, only your use of it when you're trying to put me back in your little box marked *Handled*.'

His mouth twisted. 'Even if such a box existed, the physical and psychological scratch marks you leave on me would point to an abject failure in my task.'

She tugged at her hand again until he freed her. 'And you'll continue to fail. Because I won't be put in a box and labelled as to what I need to be. Never again.'

A new tension stilled his body. 'You think that's what I've been doing to you?'

'What have you been doing, if not knocking down my every objection in a bid to get your way since you found out about Lucca?' she threw back.

'He's my son. There was never a doubt that I would claim him. You knew that. Did you think I wouldn't do everything in my power to give him everything that had been denied me?' he demanded.

'No, but what sort of mother would I have been if I'd wilfully turned my back on the one thing you led me to believe would save our son.'

His nostrils flared. 'You believe that's no longer true?'

'I went along with this marriage because it would protect us while you found a *business* solution to this problem. Now you tell me you're planning some sort of vendetta-settling and I'm left asking myself whether this marriage was worth the aggravation I put myself through in the first place if the outcome is going to be a different one! Would I not have been better off in Ranelagh, alone with my son while you carelessly diced with death?'

A searing wave of shock washed over his face before his eyes, mouth and jaw hardened in a look of pure bitterness.

'So you regret this marriage?' he demanded in a low, icy voice.

'Tell me the truth, Romeo. Was marrying me really necessary?'

His jaw clenched for a long time before he bit out, 'Yes.'

'To save Lucca from Lorenzo or to give him your name?'

Her heart threatened to beat itself out of existence, and her limbs felt frozen and useless as she stared at him.

'At the time, the two weren't mutually exclusive.'

'So you didn't exaggerate one to get the other?'

He jerked upright and strode to the edge of the terrace, his movements erratic. For several minutes he said nothing, and slowly his balled fists loosened.

Then he turned. 'You're right. I should've thought this through a little longer, given myself better options.'

Maisie's agonised gasp was barely audible, but it seemed to open a new set of floodgates, bringing fresh waves of pain. She knew she was a fool then for expecting him to tell her their marriage wasn't a mistake. That it was more than just a means to ensure Lucca's safety. That however it'd started out, it was worth holding on to, worth salvaging.

Hearing his words brought home to her just how foolish she'd been to hope. Just like five years ago, Romeo had made a mistake with her. One he regretted. Only this time, he'd told her so to her face rather than let his absence speak for him.

Footsteps preceded Zaccheo's reappearance on the terrace and brought a jagged but final end to the conversation. Catching the other man's narrow-eyed, assessing glance, she pinned a smile on her face. 'I'm going to check on the boys.'

She stumbled blindly indoors, operating on automatic rather than with any sense of purpose, as she headed for the toy room. Reaching the doorway, she saw that Emily and the Giordano nanny had readied the boys for bed.

Forcing her feet to move, she went to her son and brushed her fingers over his hair. He looked up for a moment, his deep hazel eyes connecting with hers in a wide, loving look before he was distracted by one of his new best friends.

Feeling lost, cast adrift in a merciless ocean, Maisie wandered back out, trying hard not to buckle under the realisation that she'd sped up her exit from Romeo's life with that last tirade. Because surely telling the man who'd married you for the sake of his son that you'd rather not be married to him was a request to be freed the moment the necessity became obsolete?

Pain ripped through her heart as she entered her bedroom. How could it look so bleak and lonely after just a few short nights spent away from it? How could her heart shred so badly at the thought that she wouldn't spend another night in Romeo's bed?

A broken moan, much like a manifestation of grief, poured out of her throat as she sank onto the side of her bed.

Her shame at the knowledge that she would shed her dignity for another night in Romeo's bed bit deep as she lay back and sobbed into her pillow. She would go back on her word, on the promise she'd made after distancing herself from her parents' continued disapproval never to contort herself into another's expectations of her. She would put herself in a box labelled *desperate and willing to beg for Romeo's love* if she had the faintest glimpse that he returned a sliver of what she felt for him.

The sickening feeling of how far she would go triggered harder sobs, until her head throbbed and her body was wrung out. Still the pain came, washing over her in waves as the sun slid low and she knew she had to get up and dress for dinner.

Over and over as she showered, she saw his face, felt his silence like a final, doomed slash across her heart and wondered how she would face him across the dinner table. For a moment she wished for the man who had brushed her feelings aside and taken control. But she shook her head.

They'd gone past that this afternoon. There was no hiding from the glaring knowledge that Romeo didn't love her and never would. That his only interest was for his son.

Her only choice was to muddle through the next few days, and leave the island when Romeo did. If he was intent on having his son guarded by a security detail, he could do so in Ranelagh. She wouldn't be able to bear staying here, cocooned in a fool's paradise. She would confront reality head-on, put one foot in front of the other until she learned to live with the pain.

Shutting off the shower, she dressed in an ensemble appropriate for entertainment, applied enough make-up to disguise the puffiness under her eyes and left her room.

She encountered Eva emerging from her own suite and pinned a smile on her face.

'Oh, good, were you going to check on Lucca? We can share story time and be done in half the time,' Eva said with an engaging grin.

They entered the large guest suite where the children had been relocated after Lucca refused to be parted from his new friends and took turns reading until all three fell asleep.

In the living room, they found the men sipping whiskies. Romeo crossed to the drinks cabinet and returned with a mineral water for Eva and a glass of champagne for her, which he handed over with a rigidly blank look on his face.

Her breath caught painfully and she looked away as Eva smiled and patted the bump covered by her stunning jade-green gown. 'Sorry I conked out on you earlier. These two kept me up during the flight with their incessant kicking.'

Maisie's eyes widened. 'You're having another set of twins?'

Eva grinned. 'Turns out twins run in both our families. My great-grandmother was a twin, and Zaccheo's mother told him his grandfather was a twin, too. Something to be thankful for, since he's determined to not stop knocking me up until he has a full football team. That means I get to do this *only* half a dozen times.'

Zaccheo broke off his muffled conversation with Romeo and strolled over to his wife. 'You know you love carrying my children, *dolcezza*.'

'Yeah, keep telling yourself that, champ. After these two I'm taking an extended leave of absence from getting pregnant.'

Zaccheo lifted a brow. 'As long as it's merely a leave and not a resignation.'

Eva rolled her eyes but curled into his side when he sat down next to her.

The conversation turned to children. Romeo maintained brooding silence throughout, and only offered brusque opinions when Eva forced him into the conversation. Zaccheo seemed perfectly at ease with Romeo's mood, but Maisie couldn't help her breath catching whenever Romeo slid her an icy glance.

The tense atmosphere continued through dinner, the men chatting about business and Eva attempting to engage Maisie in general conversation. She couldn't remember because she was concentrating on keeping the sob at the back of her throat whenever she looked at Romeo.

And how pathetic was that? To know she'd been nothing more than a plaything in his bed while he got to know his son, and yet still feel as if her world were caving in on itself every time she remembered that in a handful of days she would walk away from him for ever.

'Oh, for goodness' sake. Can we sort this thing out once and for all? Can't you see how distressed this is all making Maisie?'

Her head jerked up at Eva's sharp retort to find the other woman glaring at her husband.

Zaccheo turned to her with one brow tilted. 'Don't get yourself worked up, *dolcezza*. Everything's under control.'

Eva snorted. 'God, you men can be so blind at times! Can't you see we're tearing ourselves apart here? Tell them, Maisie.'

Both sets of male eyes turned towards her, one grimly amused and the other as icily brooding as they'd been all evening.

Painfully pulling her gaze from Romeo's, she pursed her lips. 'Sorry, it seems I no longer have a vote.' Not that she ever did. Or ever would.

Eva sighed heavily and pulled her fingers through her wild, curly blonde hair. 'What do we have to do to get through to you two?' she demanded, exasperated.

'Eva, *mia*, I won't have you this distressed,' Zaccheo all but growled.

'Then stop this stupid cavemen course of action.' She threw her napkin down, winced when her babies also made their thoughts known about the effect her distress was having on them. Zaccheo started to rise, but she waved him away. 'I'm fine. I think Maisie and I will go for a walk, leave you two to ponder the wisdom of your ideas.'

The excuse to be out of Romeo's oppressive presence was too great to turn down. Rising, she took the arm Eva held out after kicking off her shoes. Following her, Maisie kicked off her shoes, too, and they headed outside.

'I hear there's a stunning waterfall here somewhere. I'd love to see it.'

Maisie stumbled to a halt. 'Um…do you mind if we don't?' she pleaded raggedly, unable to bear the thought of returning to where she and Romeo had made love. She knew she'd given herself away when Eva's eyes widened.

'Of course,' she murmured softly. 'We'll go down to the beach instead.'

They walked in silence for a while, taking in the lush vegetation gleaming under strung-out lights, and the view of a night-lit Maui in the distance, before Eva glanced at her. 'You'll have to take the bull by the horns at some point, you know. Men are obtusely blind sometimes—even the cleverest, billion-dollar-empire-commanding ones can fail to see what's right in front of their faces.'

Maisie shook her head. 'It's not like that between Romeo and me,' she painfully explained.

'Maybe not, but the pain you are feeling right now, I've been there. It took weeks before I came to my senses, and I didn't have a toddler to contend with during that time. You and Romeo—there's something there.' She stopped Maisie when she opened her mouth to deny it. 'You had his child four years ago, and he married you within two days of seeing you again.'

'Because of Lucca.'

Eva pursed her lips. 'I married Zaccheo because I thought I didn't have a choice. But deep down, I knew I did. Things happen for a reason, but it's the endgame that matters. Fighting for what you want even when you think everything's hopeless.'

'I don't *think* it's hopeless. I know it is,' she stressed.

Eva looked as if she wanted to argue the point, but her lashes swept over her lovely green eyes and she nodded. 'Okay. I'm sorry for prying. I'll let the matter drop, except to say I've never seen Romeo like this before. Sure, he has that sexy brooding thing going on most of the time, but never like this, not even five years ago, when his mo—' She stopped, visibly pursing her lips to prevent her indiscretion.

Maisie's chest tightened. 'Something bad happened to bring him to Palermo then, didn't it?' It went to show how much she didn't know about Romeo.

'I can only say a bad chapter of his life came to an end. But he wasn't as affected as he is now.'

Maisie shook her head. 'This is all about Lucca,' she insisted as they reached the beach.

Eva nodded, a sage smile curving her lips, before she pulled up the skirt to her elegant gown. 'Okay. Now I'm probably going to ruin my dress, but since my husband refuses to allow me to swim in the ocean until our sons are born, but he happens to be annoying me a lot right now, I'm damn well going for a quick dip.'

Maisie gave a smile that barely lifted the corners of her mouth. 'You know he can see you from the villa, right?'

Eva gave a stubborn, cheeky smile. 'I'll be out before he gets here.'

Maisie didn't think it was wise to stand in her way. The waters weren't especially deep for half a mile or so, but she kept an eye on her, trying not to think about what Eva had said.

Because it wasn't a subject worth pursuing. Romeo had made himself more than clear. And if he'd looked shocked, it was because he probably hadn't thought she would confront him about it.

After a few minutes, tired of the agony replaying through her soul, Maisie adjusted her clothing and waded into the warm, inviting water.

CHAPTER THIRTEEN

ROMEO DIDN'T LOOK UP from the fireplace when his friend joined him, but he accepted the glass containing a double shot of whisky Zaccheo held out to him.

'Tell me your wife drives you half as crazy as mine does me,' Zaccheo growled.

Romeo downed half the glass's content and stared into the remaining amber liquid. 'She's not my wife,' he growled.

'That ring on your finger and the misery on your face tell a different story, *mio fratello*,' Zaccheo challenged with a grim chuckle.

Romeo's chest squeezed at the term. Although he'd only connected with Zaccheo for a brief month when they were children, he'd never forgotten the boy whose life had touched his. Rediscovering that bond of brotherhood as an adult had made Romeo believe he wasn't truly alone in this world. But lately, he'd discovered there were various forms of loneliness.

A loneliness of the heart, for instance…

Zaccheo's hand of friendship might have conquered a small part of his soul, but he was finding out, much to his emerging horror, that it would never be enough. Not like what he'd been secretly hoping for a few weeks.

'The ring is meaningless. She doesn't want to be married to me,' he snapped and downed the rest of the drink. A replacement arrived seconds later, and he took it, his fingers tightening around the cold glass. The platinum-and-gold wedding ring in question caught the light, winking mockingly, and a deep urge to smash the glass moved through him.

Before he could give in to it, Zaccheo replied, 'Before you tear the place to pieces, perhaps you should listen to what your woman has to say.'

'She's already said her piece. And I heard her loud and clear.' Although he wished he hadn't. He wished he hadn't stopped her on the terrace in the first place, that he'd postponed the moment of complete rejection for a while longer.

Why? So he could continue to live in this fool's paradise?

'I've learned to my cost that there's a difference between listening and hearing.'

Romeo's mouth twisted. 'You sound like a damn agony-aunt talk-show host. A very bad one.'

'Mock all you want. You'll learn the difference soon enough.'

Used to Zaccheo providing solid, formidable opinions when needed, Romeo wondered whether his friend was going soft in the head. A glance at him as he strolled to the window to look down at the beach where his wife and Maisie had headed proved otherwise. The ruthless man was behind those strong features.

Zaccheo turned towards him. 'What are we going to do about Palermo? We need to resolve it soon before my wife decides she doesn't want to be married to me any more, either.' The mocking tone belied the brutal intent in his face.

Romeo shook his head. 'Fattore's absurd demands started all of this. Eva's right. You need to be with her and the boys in New York. I'll handle Lorenzo and Carmelo.'

The old man was what had set all this in motion. And while he was grateful for having his son in his life, he couldn't let the nuisance carry on any longer.

The need to teach Fattore's ex-lieutenant a salutary lesson charged through him and he rolled his tense shoulders. 'I should've gone with my instincts and cut Lorenzo off at the knees much sooner, instead of entertaining his foolishness.'

'You needed time to find out what he was capable of.'

'And now I have.'

His phone buzzed and he looked at the screen. Speak of the devil.

'Lorenzo.' His blood boiled as he put his phone on speaker. 'You've saved me the trouble of a phone call.'

'*Bene.* You have good news for me, I hope.'

'I don't deal in hope, old man. Never have,' Romeo snarled.

Zaccheo gave a grim smile and sipped his whisky.

'Whether you like it or not, you have blood ties to this family. Your father left it to you. You can't just turn your back on it.'

Romeo exhaled through the need to punch something. He managed to suppress his rage and frustration and glanced at Zaccheo.

The man he considered his only friend also wore an expression of quiet rage. Romeo knew Zaccheo had learned a thing or two about seeking retribution from his wrongful imprisonment several years ago. Just as he knew the threat against his sons would need to be answered.

But he also knew getting dragged into a Mafia war wasn't what either of them wanted. What he wanted was to be done with this in a single, definitive way.

He hardened his voice so there would be no mistaking his intent.

'You've insisted on shoving my parentage down my throat every chance you got to suit your needs. Well, you got your wish. I'll be in Palermo in seventy-two hours. I promise, you won't like the news I deliver.'

He ended the call and threw the phone on the sofa. About to down his drink, he noticed Zaccheo's rising tension as he stared at the beach far below. In a split second, his friend's disbelieving expression turned into bewilderment. '*Madre di Dio*, is that…? Are they…?'

Romeo followed his gaze, and horror swept through him. 'Yes, they're swimming in the ocean,' he supplied grimly.

And Maisie was further out, almost at the point where the ocean floor dipped dangerously.

'*Porca miseria*, only my wife would decide to swim in the Pacific Ocean fully clothed and at five months pregnant with twins.' He sprinted towards the door with Romeo fast on his heels.

They reached the beach in minutes, with Zaccheo a few feet ahead of him, just as Eva waded ashore. Romeo didn't have to guess that she was exhausted, despite the sheer exhilaration on her face.

Exhilaration that turned into wary apprehension when she spotted her husband's thunderous look. She put out her hands. 'Zaccheo—'

'Not a single word, *dolcezza*, if you know what's good for you,' he sliced at her, before scooping her into his arms and striding off the beach.

Romeo rushed past them, toeing off his socks and shoes. He'd discarded his jacket and shirt as they raced from the villa. He dived into the water, striking out for the lone figure a quarter of a mile away.

He reached Maisie in minutes. And she had the audacity to look at him with a puzzled expression.

'What are you doing out here? Is Eva all right?' she asked.

'What the hell do you think you're doing?' he snapped.

'I thought it was obvious.' She searched the beach, her face turning anxious. 'Is—'

'*Sì*, Eva is fine,' he reassured impatiently. 'Although I've no idea what she was thinking, going for a swim in her condition.'

'She's a strong swimmer, and I was right beside her until she decided to head back. Then I made sure I kept an eye on her.'

'From here, close to where the currents swirl dangerously?' he accused. He couldn't see below the water, but he could see the neckline of her gown and knew how long her dress was, and how hopelessly inept she would've been at saving herself had she been caught in a rip current.

Her mouth twisted as she treaded water. 'Did I not mention I was regional champion swimmer? It was one of the many *almost* talents my parents tried and failed to turn me into. Sadly, I never made it to nationals. One of my many, *many* failures, I guess.' The bitterness in her voice caught him in the raw, threatened to rip open a place he didn't want touched. Especially not since her declaration this afternoon.

'So you thought you'd add one more tick to this imaginary quota by wearing a dress that adds at least twenty pounds to your body weight when it's soaking wet?' he snarled, all the alien feelings that had been bubbling through him since their conversation on the terrace this afternoon rising to the edge.

She looked away from him, and he could've sworn she blushed before her face tightened with deep unhappiness. 'Not exactly.'

He caught hold of her shoulders and pointed her towards the beach. 'Swim back now.'

Her chin rose mutinously. 'Or what?'

Despite the dark emotions swirling through him…the searing agony of knowing that ultimately this woman didn't want him, the knife-edge of arousal lanced him at the fire in her eyes. 'You swim back under your own steam or I drag you back. Those are the only two choices available to you.'

'Romeo—'

'Now,' he interrupted her, unable to believe how like heaven and how very much like hell it felt to hear his name on her lips. 'You may be in a hurry to end this marriage, but it won't be through you carelessly drowning yourself.'

Her mouth dropped open in stunned shock, and he wanted to believe tears filled her eyes, but she turned abruptly and struck out towards shore before he could be certain, her strokes surprisingly swift and strong considering what she wore. He waited until she was a few dozen feet away before he followed.

She was wading waist deep by the time he passed her a few metres from shore. Heading for the cabana where fresh supplies of towels were stocked, he grabbed two and stalked back.

'You had no right to say that to me!'

Romeo looked up and stopped dead. 'What the hell are you wearing? Where's the rest of your dress? And I had no right to say what?' he tagged on abstractedly, unable to tear his eyes away from her body.

'To say that I'd deliberately drown myself.'

'I didn't say you'd do it deliberately, but I didn't think you'd be that careless, either. Although from the look of you, I was wrong in my assumption.'

The bottom part of her dress was missing, leaving her clad in a scrap of wet white lace that brought a growl straining from his chest. And with the top part wet and plastered to her skin, Romeo wondered how long he would last on his own two feet before the strength of need pounding through him buckled his knees.

Under the lights strung out between the palm trees, he watched heat crawl up her face. Although it was a fraction of the fire lighting through his veins. 'Care to tell me what happened to the rest of your dress?' he asked, his voice thick and alien to his own ears.

She waved at the sand near the steps. 'The skirt's over there. The top and bottom are joined by a zip,' she supplied. 'See, I wasn't as stupid as you imagined,' she added bitterly. 'Nor did I plan on risking drowning, either accidentally or deliberately. Amongst other things, I love my son too much to do that.'

Romeo wanted to ask what those other things were, whether it could include him, but for the first time in his life he stepped back from the need to know, his mind clasping on the fact that she hadn't corrected him on the need to end their marriage. Weariness moved through him, parts of him he didn't want to acknowledge feeling brutalised, as if he'd gone ten rounds with an unseen opponent and emerged the loser.

'Are you going to stand there all night or will you hand me one of those towels?' she asked in a low, tense voice.

He started to hand it to her, then stopped. Moving closer, he stared into her eyes, darker now with whatever emotions swirled through her. 'You're not a failure.'

'What?' she croaked, her face raised to his.

'In the water, you said you'd failed at many things.'

'Oh.' Her eyes darkened further and tears brimmed her eyes. 'I have. I failed to get my parents to love me, for instance.'

Her naked pain slashed him hard, despite thinking he'd steeled himself adequately against further unsettling emotion. 'That is *their* fault, not yours. I've learned the hard way that, with the best will in the world, you can't get someone to love you if they're incapable of it.'

Her eyes widened, questions swimming in her eyes. Questions he felt too raw to answer right then. He shook his head and briskly rubbed the towel in her hair. 'You're a huge success at the things you're passionate about.'

Her eyelids swept down, hiding her expression from him. Her laugh was hollow as she tried to take the towel from him. 'I wish I could agree, but sadly the evidence states otherwise. For one thing, you insist on calling what we have a marriage, but has it really been? Or have I just been the body to warm your bed while you burrow your way into your son's life? The woman you didn't trust enough to let her know how much legitimising your son means to you.'

His arms dropped. 'Maisie—'

'Don't, Romeo. I don't want to hear your slick excuses. The moment you found out about Lucca, you wanted him, regardless of who stood in your way. You scooped me up for the ride because that was the easiest option for you.'

He stepped behind her, and his gaze was dragged help-lessly over her body, down the enticing line of her spine to the twin dimples at the top of her buttocks, and the allur-ing globes below, perfectly framed by the wet lace caress-ing her skin.

'Easy? You think any of this has been easy?' He shook his head in self-disgust. 'I'm stumbling round in the dark, pretending I've got my head screwed on straight when the reality is that I'm terrified I'll irrevocably mess up a four-year-old boy's life. And, believe me, I'm perfectly equipped to do it. Whereas you know the answer to every question he asks. You know what he wants before he does. So yes, I exploited your devotion to him to help me get to know my flesh and blood. Condemn me for that, but believe me, *none* of this has been easy for me,' he rasped.

Her head fell forward with a defeated sigh. He told him-self to remember that she intended to walk away, take away the only thing resembling a true family he'd ever known. She was the reason he couldn't take a full breath without wondering if his organs were functioning properly. Some-how, she'd taught him to hope again, to dare to dream. And she'd smashed that dream with a handful of words.

Romeo *tried* to remember that.

But he couldn't help it. He lowered his head and brushed his lips against the top of her spine, where the wet hair had parted to reveal her creamy skin.

She made a sound, part arousal, part wary animal, but he was too far gone to heed the latter. The thought of her leaving, of never being able to do this again, scattered his thoughts to a million pieces, until only one thing mattered.

Here and now.

'Maisie.' He heard the rough plea in his voice. He dropped the towel and trailed his mouth over her shoul-ders, down her back, anxiety hurrying his movements. She shuddered under his touch.

'Romeo, please...'

He dropped to his knees and spun her around. '*Tesoro mio*, don't deny me this. Don't deny *us* this.' He wanted to say more, bare himself with words that were locked deep, but it was as if the language he needed to express himself was suddenly alien to him. But he could show her. He *would* show her.

He held her hips and kissed her soft belly, where his son had nestled, warm and loved. She gave a soft moan. Empowered, he deepened the caress, his tongue tasting her intoxicating skin. When she swayed and her hands clutched his shoulders, he groaned.

Roughly pulling her panties to one side, he fastened his mouth to her sex, caressing her with his tongue as he lapped at her.

'Romeo!'

He drowned beneath the heady sensation, of his wildcat digging her fingers into his skin. He dared to entertain the thought that there might be a way through this landmine that threatened to destabilise his world. He went harder, desperate to bring her pleasure, unashamed to hope it brought him something *more*, something lasting.

She gave another cry and shattered in his arms, her head dropping forward as she shuddered. Rising, he caught her in his arms, saw the dazed but almost resigned look in her eyes, and his stomach hollowed.

Ignoring the look, he carried her to the steps and helped her with the skirt. Then, covering her top half with the towel, he swung her into his arms and headed for the villa.

'I can walk, Romeo,' she said in a small, tight voice.

'I believe I'm living up to my caveman reputation.'

'You're performing to the wrong audience. You don't need to prove anything to me.'

He glanced down at her tear-stained face and his chest tightened. 'Do I not?'

She shook her head, but her eyes refused to meet his. 'I think we understand each other perfectly.'

He wanted to rail at her that he didn't understand; that he'd thought their moment at the waterfall, *before* they'd made love, had started something they could build on. Her mutinous expression stopped him.

Besides, he was beginning to think they communicated much better using a different language.

Entering the villa, he headed for the stairs and his bedroom. The moment she raised her head and looked around, she scrambled from his arms.

Romeo set her down and shut the door.

'Why have you brought me here?' she demanded.

The accusation in her eyes ripped through him but he forced himself not to react to it. Reaching for the towel, he tugged it from her, then he pulled her close.

'Answer me, Romeo…'

'Shh, *gattina*, just let this be.' Another rough plea he was unashamed of, even though it threw him back to another time, another place, pleading in a much younger but equally desperate voice.

It was the night his mother had packed his meagre belongings in a tattered bag and told him she was sending him to his thug of a father.

Disturbed by the memories that seemed intent on flooding in, he sealed his mouth to Maisie's, searching for her unique balm that soothed his soul.

His heart leapt when she didn't push him away, but then she wasn't responding, either. Groaning in frustration, he pushed his fingers into her hair, desperate to stem the alarm rising through him that he was fighting a losing battle.

Eventually, she tore her mouth away. 'Please stop. I don't want this.'

He raised his head, the landmine seeming to spread like an ocean before him. 'This?' he intoned starkly.

Her eyes slid past his, to a point beyond his shoulder. 'You. I don't want you.'

Acrid bitterness filled him, along with the sharp barbs

of memory, but still he pushed. 'That's a lie. I proved it once, I can prove it again and as many times as you need to face the truth.'

She shook her head wearily. 'That was just the sex talking. Nothing more.'

'So you mean you don't want me, the man?' Why did that feel so damn agonising to say?

Her gaze remained averted for another minute before meeting his eyes. 'You're an amazing father, and I'm sure you'll offer Lucca support and opportunities in life I can only dream of. But I can't stay with you. After our guests leave, I'm returning to Ireland with Lucca. I'm sorry, but this…this was a mistake.'

She started to take her rings off. He lunged for her hands, stopped the action before he fully realised he'd moved. 'You will not take off your ring!' The snarled command stemmed from deep within his soul.

Her blue eyes reflected pain, enough to hammer home just how much being here, being with him, was costing her. How could he not have seen that? How could he have entertained the idea that they could attempt a proper marriage?

'I can't…'

'I know my opinion matters very little to you, but think of our son. It's his birthday tomorrow. Are you this determined to throw a shadow over the occasion?'

Her face lost a trace of colour. 'Of course not.'

'Then wait. For his sake.'

Her head dipped and she pushed the rings slowly back on her finger. He forced himself to drop her hands, move away.

'I'll see you in the morning,' she murmured.

He didn't respond. He was struggling to find even the simplest explanation of what was going on inside him. He heard the door shut and paced to the window. In the reflection behind him, he saw the bed they'd risen from this morning and wondered at how much he hated the idea of sleeping in it now.

Undressing, he entered the shower and let the water beat over his head. It wouldn't drown out her words, her face.

I can't stay with you.

His bitter laughter rose above the pounding cascade.

At least those words had been less harsh than the ones his mother had thrown at him before she'd left him on Agostino Fattore's doorstep.

At least this time he wouldn't starve. Or live rough.

And yet he found himself bypassing the bed when he left the bathroom, and collapsing onto the sofa in his private living room. And when he was still awake when the orange streaked the horizon, he'd almost convinced himself the pain ripping through him wasn't worse than it'd been when he was a child.

The performance Maisie gave the next day was award-worthy. At some point while she was smiling and taking pictures of her son at what had been dubbed *The Best Birthday Party Ever*, she half hysterically toyed with contacting her parents and telling them they should've tried enrolling her into acting school.

Because she was able to stand next to Romeo as he helped an ecstatic Lucca cut the ribbon that officially unveiled his duck pond. Then look into his eyes and smile as they helped their son release the fifty balloons tied to the sturdy bridge in the middle of the pond. She even managed a laugh as two necking swans were immediately named Maisie and Romeo. She didn't crumble into a pain-ravaged heap when Lucca insisted his father kiss his mother to celebrate the naming.

And she certainly aced the small talk with the grown-ups while the kids took turns at the duck-feed dispenser.

Once the birthday-cake candles had been blown, the cake devoured, the children tucked in bed, she retired to her suite, showered and got ready for the dinner party.

She stood by Romeo's side as they greeted the two couples Romeo had trusted to remain on the island. Then calling on her skills as a restaurant owner, she supervised the caterers, made sure each guest was looked after, while avoiding being too close to Romeo for longer than a few minutes.

Luckily, Eva, and the phenomenon of carrying a second set of twins, quickly became the centre of attention and, seeming to have made up with her husband, engaged everyone with her effervescent personality.

As soon as the last guest left, Maisie headed for the door.

Romeo blocked her path. She stopped, her heart pounding.

'Well done on the dinner party,' he muttered.

She tried to avert her gaze, to stop absorbing every expression and contour of his face. But she couldn't look away.

'Thank you,' she replied.

He stared at her for another long moment, then he stepped away. 'Goodnight.'

She couldn't respond because her heart had lodged itself in her throat. Hurrying away, she gave in to the insane urge to glance over her shoulder. Romeo was watching her.

She tried to tell herself she didn't yearn for him to follow. By the time she got to her room and shut the door behind her, she knew she was lying to herself.

CHAPTER FOURTEEN

THEY LEFT THE ISLAND two days later, with a distraught Lucca heartbroken at having to leave his beloved ducks. Although he was slightly appeased at the thought of returning to his old pond at Ranelagh Gardens, Maisie knew there would be more tears when he found out his father wouldn't be staying.

The thought troubled her as she played with Lucca during the long flight. A couple of times, she'd attempted to start a conversation with Romeo about scheduling visits, but he'd given her a stony look and a crisp, 'We'll discuss it later,' after which he'd promptly returned to his endless phone calls.

That he was returning to Palermo had become clear during a particularly heated conversation.

Her heart flipped over hard at the thought of him returning to the place that had given him such a rough start in life.

He looked up then, and their eyes connected. For a moment, she thought she saw a flare of pain mingled with hope. But his expression hardened and his gaze veered away. This time, her heart bypassed the somersault stage and went straight for cracking right down the middle.

She was still trying to hold herself together when he took a break to eat and play with Lucca. He stopped by her armchair on the way back to where he'd set up his office and looked down at her.

'I have a team childproofing my London apartment and another scouting for a place in Dublin. Emily will be flying out to help take care of Lucca when he's with me. Is that acceptable to you?'

As she stared up at his grim face, her heart broke all over

again. Slowly, she nodded. 'I won't keep him away from you. I just need a reasonable heads-up when you're coming to see him, so I can arrange it with the playgroup.'

His mouth compressed and he nodded. '*Bene*, it will be done.' He walked away to the far side of the plane and didn't speak to her again until they landed.

As predicted, Lucca turned hysterical at the idea of his father leaving. Maisie watched, a stone lodged in her throat, as Romeo hugged him on the tarmac and reassured him that his absence wouldn't be a long one. After several minutes, Lucca calmed down and Romeo strode to where she stood.

He handed Lucca over, his hand lingering on his son before his jaw clenched. 'I'll be in touch in the next few days, a week at the most, to arrange a time to see him. And I'll call him tonight.'

'Um…sure.'

With another look at his son, Romeo turned and walked back into his plane.

Maisie stood frozen, her mind reeling at the thought that her marriage was ending right then and there, on a painfully bright summer's day in Dublin.

She clutched Lucca closer as he whimpered at his departing father. Romeo disappeared, and Lucca began to weep.

Forcing herself to move, she strapped him into his seat in the sleek car waiting for them, then buckled herself in next to him.

The sun was still shining when they pulled up outside her restaurant despite it being evening. Unable to face going in, she waved at a gawping Lacey and went straight up to her apartment. Her heart sank when a knock came at the door less than an hour later.

She opened it to Bronagh, who was trying hard to pretend she wasn't shocked to see her.

'I've just put Lucca down for the night. Do you want to come in for a cup of tea?' Maisie offered.

'Tea is great, but *you* look like you need something stronger.' Bronagh held out a bottle of red wine, the concern she was trying to hide finally breaking through.

By her third glass, Maisie had broken down and spilled every last pathetically needy feeling.

'So…what are you going to do?' Bronagh asked when Maisie stopped to toss back another fortifying gulp of wine.

Maisie looked up. 'Oh, please don't worry that I'm going to take over again at the restaurant. To be honest, I could do with the break.'

Bronagh shook her head. 'That wasn't what I meant. What are you going to do about Romeo?'

Maisie frowned. 'What do you mean? It's over.'

'You really think so? From what you said he didn't *have* to marry you. This is the twenty-first century and he's rich enough to afford a dozen armies to protect you and Lucca if he wanted to without putting a ring on your finger.' She nodded to Maisie's hand. 'And you're still wearing your wedding rings. Is he still wearing his?'

Maisie nodded abstractedly and frowned at the sparkling rings. 'What are you saying?'

Bronagh shrugged. 'That things seem awfully *unresolved* for two people hell-bent on chucking in the towel so quickly.'

'I'm not…I wasn't… He only wants sex.' She blushed and drank some more wine.

'Of course he does. Sex is the easiest way to hide deeper emotion, that's why it's called angry sex, rebound sex, make-up sex…need I go on?'

Miserably, Maisie shook her head.

Bronagh laid a gentle hand on her arm. 'You haven't known a lot of love in your life, but then neither has he. One of you has to be brave enough to scratch beneath the surface.'

'Why do I have to do the scratching?' Maisie blurted. 'Just because he thinks I'm a wildcat in bed doesn't mean… *God!* I can't believe I just said that.'

Bronagh laughed and rose. 'I think the jet lag and wine are doing their job. Get some sleep. I'll take the monitor with me when I go downstairs in case Lucca wakes up.'

Maisie hugged her friend, her thoughts rioting as she prepared for bed. When she lay wide awake three hours later, she wasn't surprised.

Bronagh's words raced through her mind.

While she didn't think she'd misinterpreted her conversations with Romeo, was it possible she'd blinded herself to a different possibility?

Could she guide Romeo into loving her? He might have been devoid of love before he'd arrived on her doorstep three weeks ago, but Maisie had seen what he felt for his son. And Romeo hadn't rejected the love that poured from Lucca. Surely he couldn't rule it out of his life for ever?

Turning over, she exhaled slowly, careful not to let too much hope take root.

When Romeo arrived on Saturday, she would try to broach the subject, see if there was a glimmer of anything worth pursuing.

Except Romeo didn't come on Saturday. He sent Emily and a team of bodyguards after calling with his apologies. He'd established a routine with Lucca where they video-called for half an hour in the morning and half an hour in the evening. His greetings to Maisie when she connected his calls were cool and courteous. Any attempt at a conversation was quickly curbed with a demand for his son.

By the time he cancelled on Saturday, she knew, once again, she'd been foolish to hope. Yet she couldn't bring herself to take off her wedding rings. Nor could she find the strength to tell Lucca that, no, Mummy and Daddy would never live together again.

Admitting to herself that she was burying her head in the sand didn't stop her from doing exactly that. She helped out in the restaurant when she could, but even there she knew she wasn't on her full game, so she kept her presence to a minimum.

And then Romeo stopped calling.

For the first two days, she didn't have time to worry because she had her hands full controlling Lucca's misery-fuelled tantrums.

By the third day she was debating whether to call him. She talked herself out of it for half a day before dialling his number. It went straight to voicemail. Leaving a garbled message guaranteed to make her sound like a lunatic, she sat back, her stomach churning.

When he hadn't called by evening, she marched downstairs and strode across the road to where one of his guards was stationed.

'Have you heard from your boss?'

The thickset man frowned. 'My boss is across the road.' He indicated another heavily muscled man wearing wrap-around shades.

She sighed, exasperated. 'I mean your boss's boss. Mr Brunetti.'

'Oh. Sorry, miss, I don't have his number.'

'It's not miss, it's Mrs…Brunetti.' She waved her rings, unnecessarily, then cringed inside. 'I need to speak to Mr Brunetti.'

The man snapped to attention, then quickly strode over to his boss. The hushed conversation ensued and Wraparound Shades approached.

'I'm sorry, Mrs Brunetti, but Mr Brunetti requested that his whereabouts not be disclosed.'

Panic flared through her belly. 'Why?'

A shrug. 'He didn't say. I'm sorry.'

Maisie raced back upstairs, her heart crashing wildly against her ribs. She tried Emily's number and got a message to say she was on sabbatical in Hawaii.

She spent the night pacing her living room, alternating

between leaving a message and hitting Romeo's video-call button. Both went unanswered.

By mid-morning she was frantic. And angry. And miserable. For herself and for her son. But mostly, she was angry with Romeo.

Yanking her front door open, she faced the head bodyguard, arms folded. 'I'm about to buy a round-the-world plane ticket and drag my four-year-old to go and look for his missing father. I'm assuming your job includes accompanying us on trips abroad?'

He nodded warily.

'Good, then consider this your heads-up. We're leaving in an hour. I intend on starting in…oh, I don't know… Outer Mongolia?'

His eyes widened.

'Or perhaps you can save us all a wasted journey and tell me what country I should start in.'

The man swallowed, shifted from foot to foot. Maisie glared harder. 'You should start in Italy.'

The relief she'd expected never materialised. If Romeo was in Italy, then… 'Specifically in Palermo?'

Another wary nod.

She raced back to her flat and opened her laptop. The restaurant was closed today, and Bronagh had issued a standing babysitting assistance.

After debating whether to take Lucca with her, she decided against it, called Bronagh to tell her to pick up Lucca from nursery and booked a solo ticket.

Until she knew where Romeo was and the reason for his silence, she wasn't risking taking their son to Palermo.

After flying in Romeo's private jet, her cramped economy seat felt like torture. She emerged from the flight hot, sweaty and filled with even more panic when she realised she had no idea where to start looking for Romeo.

The last time she'd done this she hadn't been in possession of a last name.

This time the last name was one that held such power and prestige that, in her state of dishevelled hair and worn jeans, she would probably achieve the same results as last time. Laughter and ridicule.

Hailing a taxi to a three-star hotel, she quickly texted Bronagh to say she'd arrived, then showered, changed into a blue cotton dress and clipped her hair at her nape. Smoothing on lip gloss, she froze for a second when she realised it was the same dress she'd worn the night she'd met Romeo.

Hand shaking, she capped the tube and grabbed her bag.

The weather was much hotter in July than it had been the last time she was here, and a sheen of sweat covered her arms by the time she made it to Giuseppe's.

Heart thumping, she sat at a table and ordered a *limoncello*. Sipping the cool drink more for something to do than anything else, she tried to think through what she'd say to the only person who could give her answers as to Romeo's whereabouts—Lorenzo Carmine.

Whether the old man would actually answer her questions was a bridge she'd cross when she came to it. According to the article she'd found online, Lorenzo lived in a mansion once belonging to Agostino Fattore, a man whose picture bore a strong resemblance to Romeo, once you dragged your gaze from the skin-crawling cruelty in his eyes.

Her fingers curled around her glass, her stomach churning in horror at what the man she loved had suffered. Was probably still suffering…

Shutting her eyes, she dropped her head into her hands and breathed in deep. She wouldn't think the worst. She would get her chance to tell Romeo exactly how she felt.

All of it. With nothing held back.

Firming her jaw, she opened her eyes and jerked upright in shock.

He was pulling back the chair at the adjacent table. Sunglasses obscured his eyes and the direction of his gaze suggested he wasn't looking at her, but Maisie knew Romeo had seen her.

Her body's sizzling awareness was too strong to be anything but a reaction to his direct scrutiny.

A judder shook its way up from her toes as she stared at him, relief pounding through her to see him in one piece. Hungrily her eyes roved over him. His cheekbones looked a little more prominent, and his mouth a lot grimmer, but there was no mistaking the powerful aura emanating from him or his masculine grace when he curled elegant fingers around the tiny espresso cup the waiter slid onto his table a few minutes later.

He picked up the beverage, knocked it back in one greedy gulp, then stood, extracted a ten-euro note from his pocket and placed it on the table.

She sat poised in her chair unable to believe he would just leave without speaking to her.

Then his arrogant head turned her way. Heat sizzled over her skin, far hotter than the sun's rays as she stared back at him. His hands clenched into fists, then released.

Without a word, he strode onto the pavement leading away from the waterfront.

Maisie grabbed her handbag and raced after him. Everything about his quick strides and tense shoulders suggested he didn't want to be disturbed. But she hadn't come all this way to be turned away.

He turned into a vaguely familiar street five minutes later. When she recognised it, she froze, her pulse tripling its beat as she read the name of the hotel.

She jerked into motion when Romeo disappeared inside. By the time she entered the jaw-dropping interior of the marble-floored atrium, he was gone. She bit her lip and looked around the plush surroundings, wondering whether she would receive the same humiliating reception as she had last time.

'Signora Brunetti!' A sharply dressed man hurried towards her, his hand proffered in greeting.

'Um, yes?'

'I was asked this morning to look out for you and inform you that the room you seek is Penthouse One.'

'Ah…thank you.'

'*Prego.* If you'll come with me, I'll personally access the private lift for you.'

He escorted her to the lift, inserted the key and pressed the button, before stepping back with a respectful bow.

Clutching her bag against her chest, Maisie willed her pulse to stop racing. But it was no use. Now that she'd seen that Romeo was unharmed, every ounce of adrenaline was churning towards the emotional undertaking she was about to perform.

Should that fail…

Her knees buckled and she sagged against the gilt-edged mirrored walls as the lift doors opened. Sucking in a deep breath, she forced one foot in front of the other. The pristine white doors and gold-encrusted knobs loomed large and imposing in front of her.

Lifting a hand, she knocked.

CHAPTER FIFTEEN

HE OPENED THE DOOR after the third round of knocking. And said nothing. Bleak hazel eyes drilled into hers, seething emotions vibrating in the thick silence.

Maisie cleared her throat.

'You haven't called in four d-days. Our son is miserable without you,' she stammered when she eventually found her brain.

Romeo's face twisted with agonised bitterness and regret, before it resettled into stark blankness. 'I'll make it up to him. My business in Palermo took longer than I thought. I have a month-long business commitment in London starting next week. Once I'm settled, Emily will resume coordinating with you on visiting schedules. I'll also have my team provide you with useful numbers including my pilot's so you don't have to rely on commercial travel. There's a car waiting for you downstairs right now. My plane will take you back home. Have a safe trip back. *Arrivederci.*'

He shut the door in her face.

Her mouth dropped open in shock for several seconds before, temper flaring, she slapped her open palm repeatedly on the door. When he yanked it open, his face was a mask that covered a multitude of emotions. Emotions he was hell-bent on keeping from her.

'I came all this way and that's all you have to say to me?'

He shoved his hands deep into his pockets. 'What more is there to say? You've made it more than clear our son is the only subject on the table when it comes to you and me.'

'That's not true,' she replied.

His jaw worked. 'Dammit, what the hell do you want from me, Maisie?' he demanded gutturally.

'For starters, why did you tell the concierge my name with the instructions to let me up when I arrived?'

'Because you're the mother of my child, and still my wife—at least until one of us decides to do something about it. And also because I have security watching over you and Lucca twenty-four hours a day. I was told the moment you bought a plane ticket to Sicily. I thought I'd save you the trouble of an awkward enquiry at the front desk when you eventually got here.' The thinly veiled mockery made her skin sting.

Nervously, she shifted on her feet. 'Well…okay. I'm here. So are you going to let me in?' she asked with a fast-dwindling bravado.

He raised an eyebrow. 'Are you sure you want to come in? Surely this room holds bad memories for you.'

She looked over his shoulder and caught sight of the mixture of opulent and beautiful antique and modern furniture, some of which they'd appreciated up close and personal with their naked bodies. 'They weren't all bad,' she murmured huskily. 'In fact, the night before the morning after was quite spectacular. One of the best nights of my life.'

He froze, his hazel eyes flaring a bright gold before a cloud descended on his face. 'What a shame it is then that your worst was finding yourself married to me.' His voice leaked a gravel roughness coated with pain and her heart squeezed.

'Don't put words in my mouth, Romeo. I said I didn't want to be married to you. I didn't say it was because I hated the idea. Or you.'

Tension filled his body. 'What did you mean?' he asked raggedly.

'Are you going to let me in?'

He jerked backwards, his hand rigid around the doorknob. His warmth seemed to reach out to her as she passed him, his scent filling her starving senses so headily, she almost broke down and plastered herself against him.

The suite was just as she remembered. The luxurious gold-and-cream-striped sofa stood in the same place she'd first made love with Romeo. She dropped her handbag on it, her fingers helplessly trailing over the exquisite design as memories flooded her.

Unable to resist, she touched the glass-topped console table set between two floor-to-ceiling windows, then the entertainment centre, where Romeo had played *Pagliacci's* mournful theme tunes while he'd feasted on her.

'Do you wish me to leave you alone to reminisce?' he enquired tightly.

She turned to find him frozen against the closed door, his arms folded. He wasn't as calm as he appeared, a muscle flicking in his jaw as he watched her.

'Why are you standing over there, Romeo? Are you afraid of me?' she challenged, even though her heart banged hard against her ribs.

A harsh laugh barked from him, then his face seemed to crumple before he sliced his fingers through his hair. '*Sì*, I'm afraid. I'm terrified of what I feel when I'm around you. And even more terrified of my emotions when I'm not.'

The naked vulnerability in that announcement strangled her breath. The room took on a brightness that made her blink hard. Then she realised the brightness was her heart lifting from the gloom, hope rising fast and hard, against her will.

'What are you saying, Romeo?' She couldn't allow room for misinterpretation. The stakes were higher than ever this time.

He exhaled. Deep and long and shakily, his massive chest quaking beneath his black shirt. 'I mean, I love you, Maisie. Of course, I could be mistaken because I really don't know what love is. But I feel a ravaging emptiness every second of every day that I have to survive without you. I thought I knew what it felt to contemplate a hopeless future until the day you told me you regretted marrying me.' He shook his head and surged away from the door.

Striding to the window, he stared down into the street. 'I haven't been able to function since that moment. You're all I think about, all I crave…' Another juddering breath. 'Is that love? This feeling of desperate hopelessness?' he intoned bleakly.

Maisie moved until she was a few feet from him, desperate to touch him. 'I don't know, Romeo. Do you feel the same ache when you imagine us being together instead of apart? Or is it different, better?' she whispered.

His head dropped forward, his forehead resting against the cool glass as a tremble moved through his body. '*Per favore*…please, *gattina*, why are you doing this?' he groaned roughly. 'Why are you here?'

Maisie swallowed. 'I needed to see that you're all right. That Lorenzo—'

'Lorenzo is no longer an issue. The *famiglia* are abandoning his sinking ship. We have a witness who'll testify to what happened to Zaccheo's father after my father threw me out that night. Lorenzo is now facing a murder charge. Our combined testimony will put him away for good.'

She gasped. 'Why did he attack Zaccheo's father?'

'Paolo Giordano had the task of disposing of me after my mother left me on my father's doorstep. My father didn't want me, so Paolo took me home. Unfortunately, his wife was less than enthusiastic about having another mouth to feed. Paolo had the audacity to offend my father by trying to return me to him after a month. My father set Lorenzo on him.' He stopped, distant memories glazing his eyes before he shook them off. 'I made a statement to the chief of police two days ago. He issued warrants for Lorenzo's arrest. The case may collapse or it may not. Either way, Lorenzo is going to spend some time in prison before the case goes to trial. He'll know better than to come after me or mine again.'

'So, that was how you ended up on the streets? Because your mother didn't want you?'

'She was a high-class prostitute. Getting pregnant with me put a huge obstacle in her chosen career. When I became too much for her, she drove me to a house I'd never visited before, told me it was my father's house and drove away.'

'Did you see her again?'

He closed his eyes for a split second. 'Not until I stayed with her for a week, here in Palermo, five years ago.'

'The week we met?'

He nodded. 'She called, finally. After years of silence, she called me. I'd kept tabs on her over the years and knew when she fell on particularly hard times. I found ways to send her money without her knowing it came from me. I didn't want her contacting me because I was rich. I wanted her to do it because I was her son and she wanted to see me.' He shook his head, bitterness and pain warring over his face. 'The week before she died, she finally called. I was elated.'

'What happened?'

'She wanted the use of my credit card. She wasn't interested in who I was or whether I could afford it. She had a fast-growing brain tumour and didn't have long to live. She wanted to die in style. I checked her into the presidential suite at the Four Seasons. And I stayed with her, hoping that she'd show me, in some small way, that she'd regretted giving me away. She didn't. I held her hand until she passed away and all she did was curse me for looking like my father.

'So, you see, I don't know if this living, breathing thing inside me is love, or if it's a twisted need to cling to something that's damaged because I've touched it.'

The words wrenched at her soul. 'Please don't say that.'

He turned to face her, and his eyes were deep dark pools of pain. 'That day we met was the first time I accepted that hope was a useless emotion. That love didn't exist. Not for people like me.'

'Romeo…'

'It's okay, *gattina*. I know you don't love me.' His shoulders drooped in weary, agonised defeat. 'I'll make sure the divorce is fast and the settlement more than generous.'

Her breath shook. 'I don't want a divorce or your money, Romeo.'

A sound of a wounded animal seared from his throat. She took the final step and placed her left hand on his chest. 'If I did, I would've taken off my wedding ring the moment we left Hawaii.'

His gaze fell on her ring and his eyes flared bright, and then dimmed almost immediately. As if a light had gone off inside.

'We can't stay married simply for the sake of Lucca. I won't be responsible for bringing unhappiness to your life.'

'Then bring happiness. Love me. Be with me.'

His eyes slowly rose, connected with hers. 'But on the island, you said—'

'I said I didn't want to be married because I couldn't bear the thought of loving you and not having you love me back.'

His eyes widened and he jerked upright, his strong arms closing on her shoulders. *'Che cosa?'*

Tears brimmed her eyes. 'I love you, Romeo. I've loved you since the night we spent in this room. I've been miserable without you and I really don't want a divorce, if you don't mind,' she pleaded in a wobbly voice.

'I don't mind,' he responded, his face and voice dazed. 'If you let me, I intend to not mind for at least a dozen lifetimes.'

That bright light ripped through her senses once again. This time she embraced it. Revelled in its warmth. 'Good, because that's how long it'll take for me to show you how much you mean to me, too.'

'*Dio mio, gattina...*' His voice held humble worship, a touching vulnerability that made her cup his face.

'Hold me, Romeo. Kiss me. I've missed you so much.'

With a groan, he sealed his lips to hers.

Three hours later, she dragged her head from his chest and the soothing sound of his heartbeat. 'Are you ready to video-call with Lucca?'

Romeo raised his head and kissed her mouth. 'Hmm, I think I've finally come up with something that'll make him forgive me for not being in touch these past few days.'

'Oh, what's that?'

'A promise of a brother or sister.'

Maisie's heart leapt. She planted a kiss of her own on his willing lips. 'I think you just elevated yourself to *Best Father Ever* status.'

Romeo laughed and set up his laptop after Maisie alerted Bronagh to the incoming call.

Seconds later, the screen filled with their son's beautiful face. 'Mummy! Daddy, when are you coming home?' he demanded plaintively.

Romeo exchanged glances with her. 'We will be there by the time you wake up tomorrow, *bel raggazo*.'

'Okay! I've been learning some Itayan words, Daddy.' He gazed keenly into the screen.

Romeo's hand found hers, and he pressed it to his chest. 'Tell me,' he invited softly.

'*Ti amo, Papà,*' he said haltingly, then his face widened in a proud smile. 'It means, I love you, Daddy.'

Beneath her hand, Romeo's heart lurched, then raced wildly. His throat worked for several moments, before he spoke. 'That is exactly right, and I...' His eyes connected with hers, and tears brimming in hers, she nodded in encouragement. 'I love you, too.'

They rang off several minutes later, and Romeo took her in his arms and just held her. Somewhere in the suite, a mournful opera started.

'Why do you listen to those things? They're so sad.'

He hugged her closer. 'It was a reminder that hope was a futile emotion, that everything dies in the end. But now it'll be a reminder that even in the bleakest moments, the voices of heaven can still be heard.'

She raised her head and stared deep into his soul, her heart turning over. 'I love you, Romeo.'

He kissed her, accepting her love.

He hadn't said he loved her after that first time. But she didn't mind, because she felt it in every touch, every look, and knew he would get around to saying it again eventually, when their world grew less shaky with the depth of emotion rocking them.

When he raised his head, his eyes shone with a brightness that seared her with happiness, right to her very fingertips.

'I see you got away with not being taken to task by Lucca.'

He laughed. 'But I still intend to keep my promise to him and provide him with a brother or sister. Soon,' he stated with serious intent.

She traced his mouth with her fingers. 'Soon. I can think of nothing I want more than another baby with you.'

He gently turned her around and caressed her belly with both hands. Then his strong arms slid around her, swaying her to the sound of angels' voices.

'You're my beginning and my end, *il mio cuore*. My everything.'

EPILOGUE

Three years later

'WHO CAME UP with the brilliant idea that it'd be fun to pack seven hyperactive kids and two overachieving fathers onto a yacht for a vacation?' Eva grumbled as she chased after her ten-month-old daughter crawling at top speed towards the boat's chrome railing. Baby Donatella Giordano immediately screeched in protest at her thwarted bid for freedom.

Maisie grinned, raising her face to the dazzling Mediterranean sunshine. 'You think there would've been any stopping Romeo or Zaccheo once they co-bought the super-yacht they'd been drooling over for a year?'

Eva walked across the wide marble-tiled second-floor deck of the stunning vessel to join Maisie, her white bikini accentuating her tanned skin beautifully. Sitting down, she bounced Donatella on her lap until she quieted. 'It's a beautiful boat, but I haven't been able to sleep a wink from worrying that one of the boys will throw themselves overboard just for the sheer hell of it.'

'Romeo assures me that's impossible. Trust me, I grilled him for hours on that very subject before I agreed to bring Lucca and Marcelo.'

Two-year-old Marcelo glanced up at the mention of his name and grinned from where he splashed in the shallow pool with the second set of Giordano twins, Gianni and Angelo.

Eva kissed the top of her baby's head and sighed happily.

'It's good to see them relax, though, isn't it? I just wish they wouldn't relax so...*vigorously.*'

Maisie laughed and glanced to the side as two power-ful Jet Skis whizzed by, trailed by excited cheers and urges to *go faster.*

Romeo's jet carried Lucca and Zaccheo's his oldest sons.

As they made a final turn past the boat, Romeo's gaze met hers. The contact was brief, but the love blazing in his eyes snagged Maisie's breath. Her heart raced as the over-whelming love, which incredibly grew stronger every day, pounded through her blood. She reached up and touched lips that still tingled from when they'd made love hours ago. Then her hand drifted down to her flat belly, and the surprise that would bring another smile of joy to her hus-band's face.

'Since Romeo hasn't crowed about it, I'm guessing he doesn't know yet?' Eva asked, glancing pointedly at Maisie's stomach.

Maisie gasped. 'No, he doesn't, but how...?'

'Please. You've been positively glowing since you stepped aboard the *Dolcezza Gattina* yesterday. I'm guess-ing you didn't get a chance to tell him because Zaccheo mo-nopolised his attention until the early hours?'

Maisie snorted. 'He didn't come to bed until five this morning.' Whereupon he'd woken her and made love to her until she'd been too exhausted to move. By the time she'd woken again, he'd been up with their children. 'I'll tell him tonight.'

'Tell me what, *amore mio*?'

Maisie jumped guiltily at the deep voice that heralded her husband's arrival.

Romeo climbed the last step and headed straight for her. This close, his tight, lean physique, damp from the ocean's spray, was even more arresting. 'If I told you now, it wouldn't be a surprise, would it?' she finally said when she could speak past the wondrous reality that this gorgeous, incredible man belonged to her.

After kissing his younger son, he lowered his body onto her lounger and braced his hands on either side of her hips, caging her in. Outside the unique cocoon that wrapped itself around them whenever they were this close, Maisie peripherally saw Zaccheo greet his wife with a kiss; heard the staff attend to the children.

But she only had eyes for the man who stared down at her with an intensity that hadn't abated since the first moment they'd set eyes on each other.

'Is there any reason it needs to wait till tonight?' he asked with a thick rasp that spoke of other urgent desires.

She scrambled for a sound reason, but in the end couldn't find one. 'No.'

'Bene.' He stood and held out his hand. 'Come.'

Her excitement ratcheted another notch, but she paused as she stood. 'The children…'

His fingers tightened around hers. 'Emily has everything in hand.'

Romeo led his wife to the master suite and shut the door behind them.

Surprise or not, he would've found a way to bring her here at the first opportunity. Because he couldn't get enough of her. Of her love, her devotion to him, to their family. Of everything.

He pulled her bikini-clad body close now and exhaled with happiness when her arms slid around his neck.

'I love you.' She sighed against him.

He shuddered hard, those three words never ceasing to move him. *'Ti amo anch'io,'* he replied gruffly. 'I'm so thankful you made that journey to Palermo three years ago.'

'So am I, but I'd like to think you would've found your way to me sooner or later. You just needed to put your ghosts to rest.'

He nodded. The ghosts *had* finally been slain. Lorenzo Carmine had been found guilty of murder and jailed, never to breathe free air again. The rest of the *famiglia* had scattered to the wind, bringing an end to Agostino Fattore's poisoned legacy.

Romeo had resisted the urge to raze the Fattore mansion to the ground, instead renovating it with Maisie's help and donating it to the local orphanage.

From the trauma of his childhood and the bleak landscape he'd anticipated his future being, he was now submerged in love and happiness so profound, it scared him sometimes. Not enough that he would fail to hang on to it with both hands.

He pulled his wife closer. 'So, about my surprise?' he pressed as he tugged at the strings of her bikini.

Breathtaking blue eyes met his as she captured his hand, kissed his palm, then laid it gently over her stomach.

His heart stopped, then raced with pure bliss. 'Another baby?' he murmured in awe.

Maisie nodded, tears filling her eyes.

Dropping to his knees, he kissed her belly, and the miracle nestled within. *'Ciao, bella bambina,'* he whispered.

She smiled. 'You're so sure it's a girl this time?'

'I'm certain. She'll be as beautiful as her mother. And she will go a little way to balancing out the testosterone you find so challenging.'

She laughed as he scooped her up and tumbled her into bed.

Laughter ceased, and desire took over. They expressed their love in the gentle kisses and furnace-hot lovemaking.

A few hours later, they dressed and joined their children and the Giordanos around the large dinner table.

Their news was greeted with hugs and kisses, after which Zaccheo raised his glass.

'To family,' he toasted, glancing at every face around the table until finally resting lovingly on his wife. 'And to love.'

'*Sì*, to family,' Romeo echoed. Then his gaze found Maisie's. 'To my for ever,' he murmured for her ears alone.

* * * * *

CLAIMING THE
ROYAL INNOCENT

JENNIFER HAYWARD

This one is for my brother, Andrew, and his unfailing belief in me in following my dream. It's true – dreams aren't too expensive to keep! xx

CHAPTER ONE

"The Count and Countess of Agiero."

A soldier in ceremonial uniform announced the exquisitely dressed couple queued in front of Aleksandra Dimitriou in the foyer of the Akathinian royal palace ballroom, his booming voice with its perfect elocution sending her heart plunging to the marble floor. She had hoped arriving late for Princess Stella's twenty-fifth birthday party would mean the introductions would have been long concluded.

But then again, what did she know? She had never attended a high society party before, let alone an official royal function. The blue silk gown she wore was rented from one of those designer dress services that mailed the couture creation to you in exchange for an exorbitant amount of money, her shoes were those of her fashionable friend Kira, her jewelry unearthed in a knockoff boutique in the city. In fact, not even the invitation belonged to her. She had *stolen* it with the intent of slipping in unnoticed.

The furor in her head, gathering momentum by the minute, suggested her ploy was about to be revealed to the hundreds of people gathered to celebrate the princess's birthday. Not to mention the dozens of paparazzi who stood poised like a flock of vultures behind the stanchioned-off red carpet waiting for a money shot.

Her palms went sweaty. A shot of *her* in handcuffs, a *royal intruder* caught red-handed during a time of high security for the country, would be great fodder for them. She could just see the residents of her small, sleepy coastal village waking up to her face splashed across the front page of the daily newspaper. Picture them doing a double take, their bemusement quickly turning to horror...

Her heart pounded madly against her ribs. There was no way she was going to pull this off. She should turn around and go back to Stygos and forget she'd ever had this stupid, foolish need to know a piece of herself. To right a wrong that had long since been undoable.

But it was too late to back out now. The palace official was reaching for her blue and gold-embossed invitation, an expectant smile on his face. She handed it to him with frozen fingers. He checked his list. Frowned. Ran his finger over the names again, then looked up at her. "*Lypamai, despoinis,* but your name doesn't seem to be on the list."

Alex swallowed hard. Summoned composure from a place deep inside her she hadn't even known existed. "I originally had to decline the invitation," she said smoothly. "When I found out I would be in the country, I sent another note accepting."

He procured another list, scanned it, consulted someone by radio, then nodded. "*Kala.* It's fine. You're on the original list." He passed the invitation to the soldier with the booming voice and nodded for her to proceed. "Enjoy your evening."

She pinned a smile on her lips, picked up the hem of her gown and moved toward the entrance to the ballroom.

"*Kara Nicholson,*" the soldier announced, his deep baritone seeming to hang on the air forever. Alex's step faltered, a thin layer of perspiration breaking out on her brow as she waited for someone to point out that she was *not* Kara Nicholson. That she was a *fraud.*

The din of the crowd remained unchanged. The soldier gave her a curious look. Exhaling the breath she'd been holding, she propelled herself forward on legs that shook so badly it was hard to put one foot in front of the other.

The powder room was her first priority. There, she restored her outward composure with her makeup compact. Inner composure, however, was somewhat more elusive.

That she and Kara, the American heiress who'd stayed in her family's tourist hotel a few weeks ago, were both slim with dark hair and blue eyes had just saved her from certain disaster. It was Kara's discarded invitation she'd picked out of the trash can to gain admittance to the party. Kara's identity she'd assumed. But resembling the beautiful socialite and being in any way prepared to do what she'd come here to do, to mingle with the exclusive crowd Kara frequented, were two entirely different things.

You just have to fake it long enough to get this done. Jaw set, shoulders back, she made her way into the elegantly clad crowd that filled the magnificent sweeping ballroom, champagne flutes in their hands. The upper echelons of Akathinian society were in attendance to celebrate the princess's birthday—assorted celebrities and a smattering of royalty from across Europe. The kind of people she checked into her hotel for a quiet, idyllic week where they wouldn't be bothered, the best view in all of Akathinia offered from their seaside window. Not those she socialized with.

She plucked a glass of champagne off a waiter's tray and moved deeper into the thick crowd, searching for a spot to locate her target. Taking a long sip of the delicious, clearly outrageously expensive bubbly, she swallowed, the champagne fizzling its way down to her stomach, where it spread a slow warmth through her. Exactly what she needed.

Securing a quiet corner from which she could survey the room, she tucked herself against a pillar and drank in her spectacular surroundings. Lit in the same blue and gold tones as the invitation, the richly appointed ballroom was a feast for the eye. The Akathinian royal crest was projected onto black marble floors, which looked as if they were threaded through with real gold vein. Massive antique chandeliers glittered from the ceiling, serving as a brilliant counterpoint for the dark accents in the room, while precious, larger-than-life paintings adorned walls that soared to impressive thirty-foot heights.

Her head spun at the opulence of it all. None of it seemed real. But then again, nothing *had* seemed real since her mother, a former lady-in-waiting to the elder Queen Amara, had broken a twenty-five-year silence with a bombshell that had blown her life apart.

Her father had not been an Akathinian businessman who had died before her birth. He was King Gregorios, the former monarch of this country, with whom her mother had carried out an extended affair before the queen discovered her betrayal and fired her.

Her hand trembled as she downed another swallow of champagne. That her mother, whom she'd considered above reproach, whose strength and courage symbolized everything that was good in the world, had indulged in a dangerous, illicit affair with the king, a married man, then manufactured a series of elaborate stories to paint a rosy view of her childhood, for whatever altruistic reasons she cared to offer, seemed inconceivable. *Unimaginable.*

And yet it was the truth. She had a father she'd never known. The siblings she'd longed for as a child, all of whom would have been lost to her if her mother hadn't broken down and told her the truth.

A bright burst of laughter drew her gaze. Princess Stella, *her half sister*, clad in a dazzling silver gown, held court in the center of the room, a handful of handsome men arranged around her, vying for her attention. She looked every inch the Grecian goddess with her slim figure and sleek blond hair caught up in an elaborate twist. Every inch a princess.

How different would her life have been had her mother told her the truth? Would she have become a princess, glittering alongside her sophisticated elder sister? Would she never have known her quiet, idyllic life in Stygos?

A fist tightened in her chest. How her half siblings would receive her was yet to be determined. Her priority, however, was her father's ill health, which had made tonight's subterfuge necessary. A heart attack had sent King Gregorios back to the hospital, his absence tonight marked. She needed to meet him before he died. It was the only thing that *had* been clear in the confusion of the past few months.

She scanned the room, locating the young, strikingly handsome King Nikandros mingling with a group of guests, his wife, Sofía, by his side. *Her brother.*

Nikandros had ascended to the throne after his father's initial heart attack during a difficult time for Akathinia, with its aggressive sister island Carnelia threatening to annex Akathinia back into the Catharian island group to which it had once belonged. Many feared the seventy-year-old Carnelian King Idas might finally have lost his mind, his recent mobilization of the Carnelian military suggesting a war might be on its way.

Thus the reason she had chosen tonight as her avenue to speak to the king. Securing an audience with him under any other circumstances would have been nearly impossible given the security that surrounded him and the demands on his time.

So tonight it was. She set her flute down on a waiter's tray with a determined *clink* of crystal. Took another. The expensive vintage was boosting her confidence by the minute, easing the tightness in her chest as it filled her with its insidious warmth. After this glass, she'd work up the courage to do what she needed to do. To rock the royal family with a scandal at a time when it needed it the least.

* * *

Aristos Nicolades leaned against a column in the packed ballroom, watching the stunning brunette in the sexy blue gown toss back her second glass of champagne with a speed that suggested she needed courage of some sort.

For what? he wondered idly, studying the play of shimmering light as it highlighted every dip and curve of her petite, shapely figure. Considering she'd lied about who she was to gain admittance to the party, he'd thought it best to keep an eye on her.

He'd been behind her in the lineup to the ballroom, his flight from the United States delayed, making him almost an hour late for the party. His every desire had been to skip the event, go home, take a long, hot shower and sleep after a grueling week abroad. But considering the king had finally granted him a license to build the jewel in his crown, a new casino on the sparkling, glitterati-strewn Mediterranean island of Akathinia, giving the occasion a miss had not been an option.

Bemused when the blue-gowned angel had swanned up to the doors of the ballroom and announced herself as Kara Nicholson, he thought he'd been hallucinating after almost thirty-six hours without sleep. The Kara Nicholson he'd divested of her clothes before he'd taken her in a long, hot encounter in Vegas six months ago, the Kara Nicholson known to travel in Stella's circles, was *not* the brunette standing in front of him.

With her near-angelic look—all big blue eyes and long, satiny dark hair—she hardly seemed the type to be one of Carnelia's spies or, God forbid, worse. But nothing could be discounted in this time of tension—spies had been pinpointed; separatist factions had emerged—and considering that a satellite company of his was in charge of security tonight, he wasn't taking any chances.

He studied the nerves the beautiful brunette was clearly

fighting despite her attempt at outward composure. She had come alone, hadn't attempted to talk to anyone, clearly knew no one here. The only person she had shown an interest in, other than the fleeting glances she'd been sending his way as an immediate attraction had sparked between them, had been the king. She had been inordinately interested in his whereabouts ever since she'd arrived.

It was possible she was simply one of those women who couldn't seem to accept that King Nikandros was happily married. There were enough of them around. Perhaps a jilted ex-lover? It would fit with the lost look she had at the moment...the inherent aura of vulnerability that surrounded her.

She sensed his perusal. Turned her chin to meet his gaze. The confusion, the anxiety in her beautiful blue eyes, stoked his curiosity higher. Confusion that quickly morphed into the unmistakable interest he'd seen there before. He held her gaze. Sustained the connection. Electricity arced between them, a rosy pink staining her cheeks.

Dipping her chin, she broke the contact first in one of those shy gestures that didn't seem to fit with the sexy image. A plus B plus C wasn't adding up.

His curiosity got the better of him. Downing his last swallow of scotch, he set the glass on a table and headed toward her. He'd played games he'd enjoyed far less than the one he was playing now. *This* could prove highly enjoyable.

Thee mou. He was headed over here.

Alex swallowed hard, wondering what on earth she was doing. She was here to talk to her father, to know him before he died, not flirt with the most strikingly good-looking male she'd ever seen, in a tuxedo or out of one. Yet *he* had been staring at her, making no effort to hide his interest. Difficult to ignore, particularly since every time she worked up the courage to speak to King Nikandros, he had moved on to another group.

Meanwhile, doubts were piling up about whether it had been an extremely bad idea to choose this party as the venue for her mission as the king glittered as an untouchable force. Would her father even want to see her? Would he even care she existed? Would he toss her out without acknowledging her?

Her ruminations were interrupted by the scent of expensive aftershave, followed by the man who wore it. He was tall, well over six feet, his height backed up by the lean, hard-packed muscle that covered every inch of him. With his dark-as-sin eyes and designer stubble, he made every other man in the room look effeminate in comparison.

Undeniably intimidating. Insanely attractive.

"I was standing over there wondering why a beautiful woman finds herself alone throwing back champagne like water." The rich, velvety undertone to his voice stoked every nerve ending to full attention. "Rather than allow my imagination to conjure up all sorts of creative possibilities, I thought I would simply come over and ask."

Her eyes slid to her empty glass. "It's only my second."

"In rapid succession." He swept his dark gaze over her in a perusal that scorched her skin. "To provide courage perhaps?"

She tossed her hair over her shoulders. "Why would I need courage?"

His eyes glittered with amusement. "You tell me. You are here alone. Perhaps that makes you feel uncomfortable?"

Very. She lifted a shoulder in what she hoped was a nonchalant gesture. "I have business to attend to. It's not so much a social occasion for me."

"Business at a birthday party? How distasteful."

"A personal matter."

He inclined his head. "Perhaps you could combine your

personal matter with a little…*pleasure*. I find myself at loose ends."

She suspected this man hadn't spent one second of his life at loose ends, but his sexy drawl had the intended effect, tangling her up inside.

"You look quite comfortable at loose ends."

"I prefer to find a…*diversion*. And you," he said, holding her gaze, "are the most beautiful woman in the room."

Her stomach flip-flopped, a wave of betraying heat rising from her chest to fill her cheeks. "Hardly true. The princess is hosting, after all."

"She has a layer of ice that surrounds her. You do not."

Alex swallowed past the sudden dryness in her throat, finding herself unable to pull her gaze away from his smoky, sexy one. "I'm afraid I'm not available as a diversion."

"Because you are here for someone else?"

"Because I really must see who I need to see, then go."

"One dance." He held out a lean-fingered, bronzed hand. "Then you can get on with your business."

He made it seem rude, *impolite* to refuse. Over his shoulder, she could see the king and queen still immersed in conversation. Perhaps it *would* be better to say yes to a dance rather than stand around at loose ends looking painfully out of place as she clearly had been.

"All right," she said, placing her palm in his much larger one. "I would love to."

He wrapped his fingers around hers. "Aristos," he drawled. "And you are…?"

Her brain froze, her clear thinking not aided by the two glasses of champagne she'd consumed. "Kara," she said after a pause. Better to continue the facade.

Not that it was easy to keep anything straight in her head with the energy that pulsed between them, moving from his fingers through her body until she was buzzing with the intensity of it.

His tall, impressive physique parted the crowds easily as he led her toward the dance floor, where a live band was playing a slow, sexy jazz number.

Aristos laced his fingers through hers, slid his arm around her waist and pulled her into a close hold that had her pulse racing. His smooth, skillful steps as he directed her around the packed space surprised her for such a solidly built male.

"So," he said, leveling his gaze on her face, "how do you know the princess?"

Her stomach seized. *A natural question*, she told herself. *Relax.*

"We're friends," she said, repeating what Kara had told her. "We're on a few of the same charitable boards."

He inclined his head. "And what do you do when you aren't tending to these…*charitable endeavors*?"

She blinked. Thought furiously. But a few scattered conversations with Kara hadn't provided that depth of information. "Mostly that," she murmured awkwardly. "My father has a large philanthropic portfolio. He needs the help."

"And where is home?"

"Texas," she said faintly, as if that would make up for her lack of a drawl.

"Funny, you don't *sound* like a Southerner."

Her mouth went even drier. *Diavole*, but this had been a bad idea. "I think I've lost my accent," she prevaricated. "I travel so much I've become somewhat…international."

His mouth twisted. "I get that one hundred percent. It's the same with me." His hand tightened around hers as he spun her in a smooth circle. "Texas is a big state. Which part?"

She had no idea. "Dallas," she said, guessing.

"The home of J.R. Ewing…"

She smiled a tight smile. "The very same. And you?"

she asked, attempting to regain control of the conversation. "How do you know Stella?"

"I'm a business partner of the king."

Oh, no. Not good. Swallowing her panic, she lifted her gaze to his. "What business would that be?"

"Hotels and casinos. A bit of this, a bit of that."

She thought that fit perfectly with his dark, edgy vibe. "That must be a very…*interesting* world."

His mouth quirked. "You don't sound so sure about that."

She lifted a shoulder. "I'm not a gambler. It seems to me you prey on the vulnerable. Take unsuspecting people's money."

"Those who walk into a casino do so of their own volition."

"Yes," she agreed, "but do they always know their limits?"

"They should. I find there is an epidemic of late of people who have no sense of personal responsibility. We are all responsible for our own actions."

Yes, she agreed silently, hysteria biting at the edges of her composure. That concept was top of mind at the moment.

"Perhaps true," she conceded. "Although I'm not sure it's a fair comparison. I'm an idealist. I think we all need to be looking out for the greater good."

"A dying breed," he said softly, his dark gaze resting on her face. "Idealists…"

He left it at that. She shut up before she said something she shouldn't. She should have protested when he tugged her closer so his tall, muscular body brushed against hers, his chin resting atop her head. But when there was no talking involved, there was no danger in exposing herself.

She couldn't resist allowing herself to melt into all that strength, just for a moment, of course, until the dance was over. It felt hedonistically good, frankly exciting to be in his arms, and when would she ever have another chance to meet a man like him? Stunning-looking members of the opposite sex were a precious commodity in Stygos. She'd known all of them since childhood.

The plaintive, haunting notes of the saxophone were beautiful. The champagne had kicked in full force now, leaving in its wake a heady buzzing feeling that instilled a confidence in her she hadn't had before. It made the dangerous attraction she felt toward the man holding her even more powerful. Made her even more aware of the strong column of his thighs as they pressed against her, driving home how powerfully built he was. How the spicy scent of his cologne mixed with the heady male musk of him was doing crazy things to her insides…

The warmth of his hand splayed at her waist burned her skin like a brand through the thin silk of her dress. It made her wonder what it would be like to be touched by him. *Truly* touched by him.

Her champagne-clouded brain was floating in a sea of pheromones when the song came to an end. She moved to extract her fingers from his, but he tightened his hold. "One more."

She should have ended it right there. But it was far too tempting to say yes. A glance over his shoulder revealed the king still deep in conversation. How harmful was one more dance?

He pulled her closer, their bodies perfectly aligning as they moved to the sultry notes of the song. It was an inappropriate hold, she knew, the heat of him moving through her like the most potent of caresses, his hand drifting lower to lie against the small of her back. But her sensible side seemed to have deserted her. He was the dark, mysterious hero of her favorite novels come to life, with a dangerous, presumptive twist that was impossible to resist.

A couple more minutes and she'd go.

She thought maybe a third song had come and gone when she finally pulled her head from where it was nestled under his chin and realized they had gradually worked their way from the couples dancing along the edge of the ballroom to the shadows of the small terrace that led off it.

She looked up into the mesmerizing heat of his black gaze, suddenly aware of exactly where this was going. "I told you I'm not interested in being a diversion," she reminded him a little too breathlessly.

"No?" he said derisively, bending his head toward her. "Your signals are saying the contrary." Sliding his fingers around her jaw, he captured her lips in a kiss unlike any she'd had before. Cajoling and demanding her acquiescence all at the same time, it was sensual, playful and masterful, enticing her to respond to his seductive expertise.

Her lips clung to his, helpless to resist his slow, intoxicating kisses. She swayed closer to him, her hand settling on his waist. He drew her into his warmth, the proximity of their bodies sending a shiver through her.

He lifted his lips from hers, their breath mingling. "Open your mouth, angel."

She hadn't been aware she was denying him anything. Obeying his command, she allowed his firm, beautiful mouth to part hers in a hot, languorous exploration she felt right down to her toes.

Her sigh split the air. He moved his hands down to her hips and shaped her buttocks, drawing her even closer to him until their bodies were molded together without a centimeter between them. She could feel the hard heat of him burning against the juncture of her thighs, as impressive as the rest of him. It made her knees weak.

"Aristos," she gasped, pulling her mouth from his. "Stop."

Satisfaction laced his gaze as she stared up at him, the supreme control she found there snapping her out of her haze. She put a palm against his chest to put some distance between them, but the hand he held at the small of her back kept her where she was. He slid it down over her buttock to wrap around her thigh.

"What *are* you doing?" she demanded, pushing harder against the rock-solid wall of his chest to no avail.

"Checking for weapons."

"Weapons?" Her brain struggled to compute. "Why would I be carrying weapons?"

He ran his palm over her other buttock and down the back of her thigh in a leisurely exploration that brought a heated wave to her cheeks. "Maybe you should tell me, *Kara*."

The edge to his voice made the hairs on the back of her neck stand up. *He knows. Had known all this time.*

She pushed a hand against his chest and this time he released her, setting her away from him. She bit down into her lip. *Hard.* "You know I'm not Kara."

He raked his gaze over her face. "Correct, angel. So maybe you'd care to tell me what you're doing here. And why you impersonated Kara Nicholson to get in."

A buzzing sound filled her ears. "How did you know?"

"Well, let's see… Your accent, for starters. Second, Kara is from *Houston*, not Dallas. And finally, I happen to know Kara. *Intimately.* And *you* are not her."

Thee mou. She closed her eyes, cheeks flaming. He and Kara Nicholson were lovers. How could she have ever thought she'd get away with this?

She opened her eyes. "You were behind me in line. Why didn't you call me out then?"

"I wanted to see what your intentions were."

"What did you *think* I was doing?"

"We have a country trying to draw us into a war, in case you hadn't noticed."

Disbelief sank through her. "You think I'm a spy? An *assassin*?"

"I think when anyone enters an official royal engagement under false pretenses, it needs to be investigated."

"So you thought you'd appoint yourself investigator? *Maul me* while you're at it? Make a game of it?"

"I wouldn't call it mauling. You were as into that as I was. And as for my *interest* in you, it's my security team the palace is using tonight. A side business of mine, angel, along with my *big, bad* casinos. I wasn't about to set you loose with the king in the room."

She clenched her hands at her sides, her gaze fixed on his. "You are going to regret this."

An amused glimmer filled his eyes. "Really? Do tell. My guess from the way you've been eyeing the king is that you're an ex-lover. A jilted one, perhaps… You don't seem—how should I put it?—*off your rocker*, so I'm assuming you've come with some misguided belief he'll take a lover. I hate to break it to you, but he's madly in love with his wife. It isn't going to happen."

A jilted lover? She gaped at him. "Are you out of your mind?"

He lifted a shoulder. "I've seen the women who throw themselves at the king. They crash parties to meet him. They go to ridiculous lengths to get his attention. So even though you," he said, stripping the clothes from her with a look that singed her skin, "are undoubtedly every man's type, *this* was a wasted escapade."

Fury swelled up inside her. "I came tonight because I need to speak to the king about a personal matter. Just like I said earlier."

"Why do it under false pretenses?"

"It's complicated."

"Complicated *how*?"

"That's my business."

"I'm afraid it's mine if you don't want me to have you handcuffed and hauled out of here right now."

"You wouldn't."

"Try me."

Her heart surged painfully against her chest. Pressing her hands to her face, she paced to the other side of the terrace. "I can't tell you why. I admit my methods for getting here were unconventional, but they were necessary given the security surrounding the king. I would never have gotten an audience."

"That security is in place for a good reason."

"Yes," she said, turning around. "It is." She took a deep breath. Fixed him with an imploring look. "I promise you it's imperative I speak to the king. In fact, if you would just take me to him right now, I would highly appreciate it."

"Not happening until you tell me who you are and what your business is."

"I can't."

"Kala." He spun on his heel and stalked toward the door.

"Aristos, stop."

He turned around. "No one knows this," she said. "You can't say anything to anyone."

"Spit it out," he growled.

She lifted her chin. "My name is Aleksandra Dimitriou. The king is my half brother."

CHAPTER TWO

ARISTOS'S MOUTH WENT SLACK. *Nikandros's half sister*. He couldn't have heard her correctly.

"Can you please," he said deliberately, "repeat that?"

Aleksandra, *if that was even her right name*, rubbed a hand against her temple. "My mother, Melaina, was Queen Amara's lady-in-waiting. She had an affair with King Gregorios during her tenure at the palace. The queen knew about her husband's indiscretions, but when she discovered the affair with my mother, it was one step too far. She fired her. No one knew my mother was pregnant. She went home to her village and raised me by herself."

He blinked. "Why keep it a secret? By Akathinian law, you would have been a royal."

"My mother knew I would be taken away from her if anyone found out. She didn't want that life for me. She told everyone, including me, that my father was an Akathinian businessman she'd met while she worked at the palace who was killed in a car accident before I was born. It wasn't until the king had his heart attack that I learned the truth."

Thee mou. His head spun. The queen's lady-in-waiting. *The ultimate betrayal.*

It was well-known that King Gregorios had indulged in countless affairs. But a child kept secret this long? Born to the queen's most trusted aide? If true, it was a scandal that would put all before it to shame.

He scrutinized the woman in front of him. Was she telling the truth? Her skin was pale beneath her olive-toned complexion, the vulnerability that emanated from her a quality he didn't think could be manufactured. Nor did he think she was a threat to anyone. She was not a practiced liar, that was clear. But he had learned long ago never to trust first impressions. Particularly when it came to a woman—the most deceptive creature on the face of the earth. One who wanted an audience with the king.

It hit him then, that same feeling of familiarity he'd experienced from the first moment he'd seen her. *Those eyes...* That particular shade of blue belonged to only one bloodline he knew. They were Constantinides blue. It was like looking at Nikandros and Stella.

His blood ran cold. She was telling the truth.

Aleksandra pressed her lips together. "I told you you were going to regret doing *that*."

He closed his eyes. For once in his life, he did. He and the king had just gotten their relationship on a solid footing after an adversarial start. *This* he didn't need.

"Just because you have the Constantinides eyes, as rare as they are, doesn't mean your story is true," he said roughly. "It will need to be verified, as I'm sure you will appreciate. You can understand my suspicions."

Her eyes flashed. "Your suspicions, yes, but not your tactics."

"Like I said, it took two to make *that* kiss."

That shut her up. He paced to the edge of the terrace, his brain working furiously. They were smack in the middle of a royal function with every paparazzo camera, gossip and royal watcher in the country in their midst. This could not get out before it was verified and the ramifications considered. But that was the king's job—not his.

He closed the distance between them. "What were your intentions coming here tonight? What do you want from the king?"

"I want to see my father. Talk to him. That's all."

He studied her for a long moment. Cursed under his breath and pulled his mobile phone from the inside pocket of his jacket. A phone call to the man in charge of security brought a detail in a dark suit out to the terrace.

"This is how this is going to go," he said to Aleksandra. "*You* are going to stay here with him. You do not move from here, you do not talk to anyone and if you do, he will restrain you. Understood?"

Her eyes widened, skin paling. "Yes."

She looked as if a good gust of wind might blow her over. Intensely vulnerable. His heart contracted despite his effort to stay distanced from the explosive situation unfolding in front of him. It had taken an immense amount of courage for her to come here and do what she'd done. He could only imagine how terrified she felt.

Closing the gap between them, he slid his fingers under her chin and brought her gaze up to his. "The king is a good man. You have nothing to fear."

He, on the other hand, did, if she spilled what had just happened to Nikandros.

Alex's heart thudded painfully beneath her ribs as her rather ominous-looking security detail nodded at her to precede him into the room. She stepped inside the palace library, its elegant chandeliers and wall sconces illuminating shelf upon shelf of precious volumes.

With her voracious passion for literature, the shelves might have stolen her attention had it not been fixed on the man who stood at the far end of the room looking out the windows, hands buried in his pockets.

She stood there, fingers biting into her tiny silk clutch as the king turned around and studied her, his expression intent. His eyes widened imperceptibly, then that perfectly controlled countenance that made him vastly intimidating resumed its tenure.

He turned to Aristos. *"Efharisto."*

Aristos nodded and headed for the door. She fought the crazy urge to beg him to stay—he who had threatened to put her in handcuffs and have her tossed out—but after a long glance at her that seemed to say *keep your head up, you can do this*, he left, the door clicking quietly shut behind him.

The king nodded at the two leather chairs beside the window. "Please. Sit."

She obeyed, her weak knees only too happy to find a resting place. The king sat down opposite her. All at once, she was struck by how much they looked alike. The bright blue eyes, high cheekbones, dark ebony hair her brother wore short and cropped.

"You are Melaina's daughter."

"Yes." She cleared her throat as the response came out faint, raspy. "You knew her?"

"I was only eight when she left, but yes, I remember her. My mother and she were very close."

Until my mother had an affair with your father and was thrown out of the palace.

"Aristos has filled me in on your conversation. On your claim that my father is your father."

She lifted her chin. "It isn't a claim. He is."

"Forgive me," he said bluntly, "if I cannot accept that as fact. For over two decades your mother has kept you a secret, but now when my father is nearly in his grave, she's seen fit to speak out. *Why?*"

"She was afraid I would be taken from her. She didn't want my life marked by her mistake. She thought I would be better off with her, rather than carry the stain of my illegitimacy. But your father's heart attack hit her hard. I think she realized she had made a mistake in denying me my birthright."

He raked a hand through his hair. "So you came here tonight to…"

"Know my father. To know you and Stella. I—" Her gaze held his vivid blue one. "I don't have any siblings. I don't want anything else. I have a life in Stygos that I love."

He narrowed his gaze. "You can't be so naive as to think everything will stay the same if it's confirmed you are a Constantinides. You will be of royal blood. Third in line to the throne."

She shook her head. "I don't want any of that. I am not so *naive* as to think I would be welcomed into this family given the nature of my birth."

The king's eyes flickered. "There is a…*complexity* to the situation. But if you are telling the truth, the blood that runs through your veins cannot be denied. It must be dealt with. Acknowledged. But that is dependent upon us having the facts. A DNA test will need to be performed."

She nodded. Had assumed as much would be required. Knew she couldn't have expected more. So why did her insides sting so much?

The king stood up. "I must get back to my guests. You'll understand, given the need for security at the moment, if I have you escorted to a suite where you will remain for the evening. In the morning, we will address this."

"Of course." She got to her feet.

The beautifully appointed suite she was shown to at the back of the palace overlooked the formal gardens. It was done in gold and a soft moss green, the shimmery, wispy fabrics of the sweeping brocade curtains and the romantic overlay of the big canopy bed like something straight out of one of the fairy tales she'd devoured as a child.

When a maid showed up minutes later with a beautiful silk nightgown and inquired if she needed anything else, Alex fought back the hot tears that gathered in her eyes.

She'd accomplished what she'd come here to do. She *would* see her father. But what she wanted in this moment was for her brother to have believed her.

She assured the maid she had everything she needed. Unable to sleep, she wandered out onto the terrace. The band, whose lazy serenade had been drifting through the open windows of the ballroom, stopped playing. Then there was only the buzz of the cicadas as she contemplated row after row of perfectly tended, riotous blooms in the floodlit gardens.

A quiet knock reached her from inside the suite. Frowning, wondering who it could be at this late hour, she padded inside and inched the door open. Standing in the dimly lit corridor stood the princess, still clad in her silver gown.

"I had to come."

Alex stared at her sister. The princess's startling blue eyes were counterbalanced by a wide mouth and the high cheekbones that were a signature of her mother's aristocratic haughtiness. Arresting rather than classically beautiful, Stella stared back at her, all of her earlier poise stripped away, her carefully applied dramatic makeup standing out in stark contrast against the pallor of her skin.

Her quick intake of breath was audible. "*Thee mou*, but you two look alike."

"Who?"

"You and Nik."

Alex swallowed hard, a tightness gripping her chest. Her legs felt unsteady, consumed by the emotion of the day, as if one more blow would fell them. She forced herself to move past it, stepping back to allow her sister in.

Stella slipped inside and shut the door. "The party just finished. I hope I didn't wake you."

"I couldn't sleep."

"I expect not."

They regarded each other in silence, wariness and shock

filling the air between them. She searched her sister's gaze for the mistrust her brother had displayed, finding only bemusement and curiosity in return.

"The king told you I was here?"

"Of course not." The princess's lips curved in a wry smile. "At least not willingly. Nik is too protective for that. I overheard him and Aristos talking."

Her lashes lowered. "He is suspicious of me."

"My brother has to be cautious. He has a million grenades being lobbed at him every day with King Idas's descent into lunacy."

Alex bit her lip, chewing uncertainly on flesh she'd already made raw. "You don't doubt my story?"

"When you look more like Nik's sister than I do?" The princess shook her head. "My father's affair with your mother was common knowledge. I think we've all lived with the possibility that something like this might result from his indiscretions. Although for it to happen now is a bit...*startling*."

"I didn't know. I only found out a few weeks ago."

"Nik told me." The princess regarded her silently. "I hope you are not disappointed. My father is an imperfect man. A great king, but an imperfect man. Manage your expectations. Do not expect him to be warm and fuzzy."

"I thought my father was dead," Alex said quietly. "I'm not sure *what* I'm expecting."

The princess's golden-tipped lashes fanned her cheeks. "I can't imagine how you must feel. To find this out now."

Alex exhaled an unsteady breath. "Confused. Bewildered. I'm angry my mother lied to me. I feel...betrayed. And yet I know she did it for the right reasons. She wanted to protect me. How can I be angry about that?"

"Easily." Stella waved a hand around them. "She denied you this. Your birthright."

"Is it?" A vision of her beautiful, serene village filled her head. "I love my life in Stygos."

"You are a royal," Stella countered. "A Constantinides. You could have had the world at your fingertips. Instead she took that away from you."

Had she? Or had her mother given her the safe, loved existence she'd always known?

"Perhaps it's about destiny," Alex said. "Maybe mine was to live the life I have."

"Perhaps." A glimmer filled the princess's eyes. "The life of a royal has its challenges. I will be the first to admit that."

The reticence in her sister's voice stirred her curiosity. "But the benefits outweigh the challenges?"

"I'm not sure that's an analysis I can make." Stella's lips firmed. "Do I think it's my destiny to be where I am? Yes. Would I have chosen it if given the choice? That is the million-dollar question."

It certainly was. The cicadas buzzed their musical song as a silence stretched between them. Stella set a probing gaze on her. "I saw you dancing with Aristos."

Heat rose to stain her cheeks. She had been hoping *that* part of the evening would go unnoticed. Her inappropriate behavior had been uncharacteristic for her, foolish, particularly damning in light of her mother's scandalous reputation.

"It was a mistake," she said quietly. "I was nervous. I'd had a couple of glasses of champagne…"

"Aristos has that effect on women." The princess's mouth twisted. "A word of warning. He takes what he wants until you are too blind to see the danger. Before you know it, you're hooked. Then he turns you loose."

She was clearly speaking from experience. Alex set her jaw resolutely. "It's never happening again. After I talk to my father, I'm going home."

The princess regarded her silently. "I just met my sister," she said softly. "I find I quite like the idea of having one. It would be a shame to lose her so quickly."

A throb consumed her chest. It grew with every breath, threatening to bubble over into an emotion too big to contain. Stella seemed to sense it, the thread that was close to breaking inside her. She stepped toward the door. "It's late. We can talk in the morning. Better you get some sleep so you have a clear head as all of this unfolds."

And then she was gone, her exotic perfume wafting through the air. Alex's mouth trembled as she shut the door. She stood, leaning against it, every muscle, fiber, of her body shredded, spent.

As all of this unfolds. She was terribly afraid of the chain of events she had set into play tonight. A force she couldn't retrieve. That in needing to know her father, by taking a risk that was so totally outside of her nature, she had not only stepped outside her safe little world in Stygos, but entered one that could consume her. A world her mother had done everything she could to protect her from.

CHAPTER THREE

Two DAYS PASSED, and with them Alex's premonition came true. As the blood test undertaken by the royal physician was rushed through the requisite channels, rumors of her presence spread through the palace in a flurry of gossip only a royal household could induce.

By the time the results of the test were delivered to the palace, confirming that Alex was indeed King Gregorios's daughter, the gossip had spilled to the press, who were demanding confirmation.

Nikandros made it clear they could not wait long in issuing a statement from the press office confirming her as a Constantinides. The longer they waited, the more time the press had to speculate on the story, something the family didn't need as the country fretted about a coming confrontation with its sister island.

It was with this daunting scenario in place that Alex met her father for the first time. Accompanied by Stella to his suite in the west wing of the palace where the king was convalescing, they were told Queen Amara was out for the day. Alex had the distinct impression she was avoiding her as the scandal she was.

Propped up against a pile of pillows, his leathery olive skin lined and craggy from almost four decades of rule, her father was pale beneath his swarthy complexion, his abundant shock of white hair looking out of place on a man who was clearly fighting what might be his last battle.

Stella left. Frozen with indecision, Alex stood in the

center of the room. The king opened his eyes, directing a brilliant beam of Constantinides blue at her. "Come. Sit."

She forced herself to move, perching on the chair drawn up beside the bed. Ruthless, arrogantly sure of his rule, beloved by his people, perhaps one of the last of an impenetrably powerful group of monarchs, her father was vastly intimidating.

He scoured her face. "You look like your mother."

She nodded. Cleared her constricted throat. "We are very much alike. In looks and disposition."

"How is she?"

"She is fine. We run a hotel, my family. It does well."

The king nodded. Contemplated her silently. "You are a Constantinides. As Nikandros will have told you, that gives you royal status. A place in this family."

"Yes." She drew a deep breath. "That's not why I'm here. I came to see you. To know my brother and sister. Not to cause upheaval."

His eyes darkened, a hint of emotion entering his gaze for the first time. "Upheaval there will be. Many mistakes have been made on all sides." He lifted a hand. "I am not long for this world, as you can see, so it will not be up to me to right my wrongs. My wife will come to terms with this. It is *you*, Aleksandra, who must step up and claim your rightful place in this family."

Her hands, clasped together in her lap, tightened their grip, nails digging into her flesh. No outpouring of warmth from this man. No declarations of love for his own flesh and blood. No regret he hadn't been there for her…

Stella had been right. She shouldn't have gotten her hopes up. And yet she had.

Knowing her father was alive had instilled a sense of longing in her. To have that illusion her mother had painted for her, that of a father who'd be excited at the thought of her. Perhaps not the one who would have taken her fishing, who would have taught her about boys, because that was not who this man was to her. Perhaps one with whom she could have forged a more mature bond. One who would have considered her a gift he'd never known he had.

It knocked the wind out of her, the hope. A dull, dead throb pushed its way through her.

"Did you love her?" she rasped, needing to know if her mother's feelings had ever been returned. Needing to salvage *something* from this.

The king fixed her with that steely blue gaze. "I cared about your mother, but no, I did not love her. A king's priority is to the state. There is no room for anything else."

She could have begged to differ, because clearly her brother was very much in love with his wife, but the frozen feeling invading her, siphoning off the emotion that threatened to corrode her insides, made it impossible to speak. Buffered her from more pain.

She had come for answers and she had gotten them. Perhaps not the ones she'd wanted, but answers nonetheless.

Alex spent the rest of the day attempting to wrap her head around the decision she had to make, the media circus going on outside the palace walls making her imminent decision a necessary one.

The decision should have been easy, because she'd never wanted to be a princess. Her visit with her father had been desperately disappointing. Her loyalty lay with the promise she'd made to her mother and the hotel they ran. No one could *force* her to become a royal, but the fact that she was third in line to the throne wasn't a minor detail she could ignore.

What played a larger role in her decision-making were her brother and sister. Now that she'd met her siblings, it was hard to think of walking away from them. But what did she know of being a royal? A princess? It was perhaps the most important question of all, one only Stella could answer.

She pulled her sister aside before dinner and picked her brain. Was life as a princess the endless round of royal engagements and charitable commitments that it looked from the outside, or was there more to it? Would she have any freedom to chart her course, or would it all be decided for her?

Stella answered honestly, which seemed to be her default setting. Yes, it was much as she'd described. But there was an opportunity to own the role, as she herself had proven.

Armed with the full scope of Stella's perspective, not that it cleared her confusion much, she and her sister joined her family for a predinner drink. Nik and Sofía were already enjoying a cocktail, minus two-month-old Theo, their infant son, who was with his nanny. Queen Amara walked into the salon just as the butler handed Alex a glass of wine. All eyes focused on the elder queen as she made her way toward Alex. Breath stalling in her throat, she dropped into a quick curtsy, entirely forgetting Stella's instruction that it wasn't necessary.

The elder queen waved it off with a flick of her hand. "You are a member of this family now."

Am I? I haven't made that decision yet. Her brain rifled through safe things to say. "It's an honor to meet you, Your Majesty."

The queen inclined her head. "Amara will be fine."

The cocktail hour seemed stilted and forced compared with the previous night. When they sat down to dinner, Alex was thrilled to have a knife and fork to devote her attention to.

"When will you be announced as princess?" Queen Amara directed her cool green gaze at Alex. "I would expect soon, given the throngs of media driving us all mad."

"I—" Alex put down her fork and knife. "I haven't actually decided yet what I'm going to do."

Queen Amara lifted a brow. "What do you mean, *decide*? You are third in line to the throne."

"I have a life." Alex lifted her chin. "My mother and I run a hotel together."

"You are a royal. There is no *decision* to be made. Duty says you take your place as an heir to this country."

Her mouth tightened. "My *duty*," she said, "is to my mother and the business we have built together."

Silence fell over the table. "This is all a great deal for Aleksandra to take in," Nik interjected smoothly. "Of course we hope she stays. She is family."

Her stomach tightened at the warmth in her brother's gaze. It was as if he'd been withholding emotion until it was safe to express it. It unraveled something inside her, an almost unbearably bittersweet swell consuming her chest. She picked up her water glass and drank, giving in to the impossibility of eating.

By the time the meal mercifully came to an end, she felt raw in her skin.

Nik headed off to a meeting in his palace office, Sofía upstairs to bathe Theo, Stella out for a drink with a friend. After a call home, an emotional conversation in which her infinitely wise mother told her she needed to do what was right for her, her voice breaking as she did, Alex curled up in the library to think. Process.

But when even that peaceful setting felt too stifling to think, she headed for the magnificent palace gardens instead. If she was going to find a clear head, it would be there.

Aristos emerged from his second visit to the palace in under a week with a strong sense of foreboding that Akathinia had yet to see its most trying times. The king had requested the unusual after-dinner meeting to inform him he'd called all his troops up for active duty after Carnelia had summoned its own reservists, signaling a possible imminent aggression by Akathinia's sister island.

Nikandros had requested he release the rest of the financial commitment he had made to the armed forces to enable the country to protect itself, to which he had agreed.

His head mired in what this would mean for his casino, a potentially devastating delay in breaking ground next month looming, he headed for the front doors of the palace. He was almost there when he saw an undeniably eye-catching female in a white dress headed across the foyer in the opposite direction. *Aleksandra.* He would have recognized that sweet derriere anywhere.

He couldn't deny he'd been wondering how she was. The apprehension in her eyes when he'd walked out of the library the night of the ball had been playing on his mind. Why that was, why he felt in any way protective toward her, was a mystery to him. Out of sight, out of mind wasn't a cliché in his world; it was how he lived his life.

If you didn't invest in people, it was impossible for them to disappoint you. For *you* to disappoint them.

His step faltered on the gleaming marble floor. *Don't do it, Aristos. You already crossed the line with her once. You have far too much on your plate already.* If the $2.5 billion Akathinian hotel and casino didn't get off the ground, his personal investment went down the drain with it, a loss that could threaten his company's existence.

Why he then found himself changing direction and heading toward the back of the palace was anyone's guess. Aleksandra had been headed toward the gardens. He chose the path toward the spectacular fountains and pool at the center of the sprawling botanical extravaganza and found her perched on the wide lip of the fountain, looking like something out of an Impressionist painting.

Wearing a simple white summer dress that left her tanned legs bare, her silky dark hair caught up in a high ponytail, her full mouth pursed as she contemplated what appeared to be a significant issue, she looked good enough to eat. Undeniably edible to his far-too-jaded palate. And yes, this, he decided, had been a big mistake.

Too late, however, as she looked up at him, blue eyes widening. "Aristos."

"Sit," he said as she scrambled to her feet, brushing off the back of her dress. Dumping his jacket on the edge of the fountain, he sat down beside her. Noted the distance she put between them as she returned to her perch with an amused pull of his mouth.

She slid him a wary look from beneath dark lashes. "Overseeing your security again?"

"Meeting with the king. I saw you on the way out. I thought I'd check to see how you're doing."

"You who hunted me down, seduced me to find out what I was up to, then threatened to put me in handcuffs?"

His amusement intensified. She was embarrassed about what had happened between them. About the undeniable chemistry they shared...

"Let's get one thing straight," he drawled. "I *kissed* you because you are one hundred percent my type, angel. Petite brunettes with insane curves do it for me. *Seducing* you would have required more privacy than we had. Although I am not against a bit of voyeurism to add some spice to a sexual encounter, a palace party would *not* have been the occasion I'd have chosen."

Her mouth went slack. "You would not have had the chance, regardless."

He raked his gaze over her pink cheeks, ramrod-straight spine, the faint dip of cleavage the neckline of her dress revealed. The flush staining her chest. The thin material did little to hide the peaks of her breasts thrusting against the material, hard delectable buttons he knew would be a rosy slice of heaven. All signs of a very obvious sexual attraction between them.

"No?" he challenged silkily. "When was the last time you let a man put his hands on you like that?"

She shut her mouth and kept it shut this time. He reached out and ran the pad of his thumb down her cheek, her silky soft skin hot to the touch. "Just for the record, I *am* disappointed, Princess. Your little bombshell that's rocking the country has put you on the endangered species list. Not to be touched under any circumstance. Unfortunate, when that kiss proved just how spectacular we would be together."

Alex hauled in a breath, her insides collapsing into a pool of molten heat. She knew she should be saying something smart back to this unholy man who appeared to say and do anything he deigned, but she was too busy imagining what it would be like to be seduced by him in the true sense of the word. *Hot, forbidden, unbearably exciting.*

He was insufferable, had done a job on her sister, who refused to admit it, and still, she couldn't deny she was disappointed, too.

She pulled her gaze away from the dark vortex it was sinking into. Lifted her chin. "Stella isn't petite and curvy."

His gaze narrowed. "Exchanging notes, you two?"

"She saw us."

"We were like oil and water." He lifted a shoulder. "It was a mutual decision."

She gave him a long look. "Is there a woman on earth you haven't taken to bed?"

"Dozens," he drawled. "Too bad you'll be one of them."

She blinked. "*Wow.* Just wow."

He threw her the most charming of smiles. "I *did* come out here to see how the meeting with your father went."

She considered him. He looked sincere. "It was…fine."

"Fine?"

"I wasn't expecting an outpouring of affection."

"So what did you get?"

She hesitated, unsure if she should be sharing this with him. He spread his hands wide. "The king trusts me with his military secrets…"

"He was aloof," she said. "Abrupt. He said he cared for my mother but never loved her. That there is no room for love when you are married to the state."

"It's a tough job," Aristos offered. "Your life can't be your own."

She was sure that was true. "My mother painted me a rosy picture," she said in response to his continued study. "She led me to believe she and my father were very much in love, to protect me I know, but I think I would have preferred the truth."

"Love is a concept we've all been trained to believe in. It gives us false expectations of our relationships, convinces us monogamy, a lifelong, eternal love, is the norm, when in fact it isn't. Human biology, the study of other animals, tells us that. And yet we continue to aspire to it because we think it's the right thing to do. The golden ideal."

She absorbed the depth of his cynicism. "So you don't believe love exists?"

"No, I don't. I think love is actually sexual attraction disguised as something deeper. When that fades, as it always does as evolutionary history has proven, people drift apart."

She didn't want to believe that was true. Didn't want to let go of her idealism so easily. For if the king of England was willing to abdicate for Wallis Simpson, didn't true love have to exist? If Scarlett and Rhett's passion could survive a civil war and two marriages, wasn't a once-in-a-lifetime bond possible? If it wasn't, if it was only the stuff of fiction, then all her daydreaming during her stolen moments with a book had been an exercise in foolish fantasy.

She wasn't letting *him* burst yet another bubble, she decided. Not at this particular moment when she needed some illusions to hang on to.

"So what happens now?" he prompted.

"I have to decide whether I want to be a princess."

"There's a decision there? I thought every woman wanted to be a princess."

"Not me. I love my life in Stygos."

"So you're going to spend the rest of your life living in a tiny coastal village when you could be exploring the world?"

"Lots of people would give their right hand to live in Stygos." She couldn't help the defensive note in her voice. "What's wrong with a quiet life?"

"Nothing if you're fifty. What do you *do* there?"

"I run my family's hotel with my mother."

"And when you're not working?"

"I see friends or I…read." Her chin rose at his mocking look. "The hotel business is a 24/7 occupation."

"I know that, Alex. I run several of them. I also know what hard work it is if you own a small property and have to do everything yourself. You could leave that behind. Hire someone to work with your mother."

She shook her head. "My mother and I made a pact when my uncle turned the hotel over to her to run. We promised we would always be a team, that we would do this together. To leave her seems like a betrayal."

"But these are extraordinary circumstances. Are there other family members who can help?"

"My cousin, yes. Much of my extended family is involved in the business."

"Then you shouldn't worry about it."

"But I *love* it. I love getting to know people. I love making them happy for a week or two out of their year. I love being busy. If a person has a calling, this is mine."

"Because you don't know any differently." He eyed her. "I think it's wonderful you and your mother are so close. But someday you're going to have to break free of that bond."

She bit her lip. "You think it's a crutch for me?"

"Your words… What I'm saying is that life is about living. Having the freedom to live. When was the last time you went out on a date?"

A long time.

"That long, huh?"

"A year. Since my boyfriend and I broke up."

"And he was?"

"Sebastien Soukis. He's the butcher from the next village."

An amused glint entered his eyes. "Don't tell me… He knows how to *handle* a woman."

Her mouth tightened. "It's a very respectable profession. Whereas yours is questionable."

"Right." He nodded. "I steal unsuspecting people's money."

"I didn't quite put it like that."

"Yes, you did. So what happened between you and Soukis?"

"I—" She waved a hand at him. "We decided to split."

"You were bored."

"He asked me to marry him."

"And you said no because?"

"It didn't seem right. I couldn't…envision it."

"Because it would have been too limited a life for you. You are young, Aleksandra. If you accept this opportunity, you'll have a life, experiences few people will ever have. A life most people would give their right arm for. What's the hesitation?"

"The fear of the unknown." The anxiety that had been

plaguing her all day tipped over into an honesty she couldn't contain. "I'm happy with my life. What if I do this and I'm terrible at it? What if I give up everything and find out it was a big mistake?"

"Then you go home," he said softly. "But don't shy away from this opportunity because you're scared. It's harder to run from your fears than face them. Trust me."

She took in his ultra-confident, ever-so-self-assured persona. "That's easy for you to say."

"Why? Because I'm a powerful man? It wasn't always that way. I've had my own conflicts. Two different roads I could have taken. It would have been easy for me to take the simpler one, the one I was drifting toward at the time, but it wouldn't have been the right one. Taking yourself out of your comfort zone is the most powerful thing you can do."

That intrigued her. "What were they? The two roads?"

"Ancient history." He tucked a wayward curl behind her ear. "My point is you should take the jump, Princess. Privilege is a powerful thing. Use it wisely and it'll be worth the reward."

His touch sent an electric impulse firing through her. She sank her teeth into her bottom lip as a shiver of reaction chased up her spine. If she'd been hoping her visceral response to him was a product of the champagne that night, she'd been sadly mistaken. She hadn't touched but two sips of her wine before dinner, and still she was so aware of him she wanted to jump out of her skin.

His dark, sinful gaze commanded hers. Dragging his thumb along her lower lip, he nudged the tender flesh free of the bruising grip her teeth had taken of it. "Stop fretting," he murmured, "and make the decision."

She got all tangled up in him. In the intimate claim he was staking on her mouth, the pad of his thumb stroking the vulnerable curve of her lower lip. Her stomach went into free fall as heat built between them, wrapped itself around her like an invisible force she was helpless to resist.

Her mouth went dry, anticipating, *willing* the kiss she knew would be worth the insanity of allowing it.

He brought his lips to her ear, his warm breath playing across her skin like an intimate caress. "That would be breaking the rules. I have a great deal of incentive not to do that, angel."

Rolling to his feet, he picked up his jacket. She hauled in a breath, attempting to corral her racing pulse.

He tossed his jacket over his shoulder, his gaze on her. "The woman who sashayed her way into the royal ball insisting on speaking to the king would see this for the opportunity it is. Guess you have to decide which one you are."

Turning on his heel, he sauntered off into the night. She watched him go, head spinning. Inhaling a long, steadying breath, she digested the encounter. Attempted to determine the veracity of what he'd said.

Had she been missing out on the world in Stygos? Would she regret it if she stayed there? It had been easy to work most of her waking hours, to devote herself to the family business in the pursuit of a better life for her and her mother. To satisfy her need to know the world by burying her nose in a book, lost to the adventures she'd found there. *Safe.*

She thought about everything that had happened since her mother revealed her shocking news. How it had seemed as if the world had shifted beneath her feet. How everything she'd thought she'd known seemed like an illusion, and everything she hadn't, her earth-shattering new reality.

She had a choice. To take back control of her life or have it control her. Because one thing was for sure; Nik had been right. Her life would never be the same no matter what she decided. She was a royal. A princess.

Perhaps it was not duty that would inform her decision, but a desire to truly know herself. To expose herself to the world and see what it reflected back at her. To stop living her life on the pages of a book and instead experience it for real.

Did she have the courage to take another huge leap? To leave everything she knew behind? If she did, what would she find when she got there?

CHAPTER FOUR

"How does it feel to be a princess, Aleksandra?"

Terrifying. Bewildering. Like I have no idea what I am doing.

Alex swallowed hard, her knees knocking together as she looked out at the sea of reporters crowding the palace gardens for the official announcement of her appointment as Her Royal Highness, Aleksandra, Princess of Akathinia. Packed into the center of the labyrinth of neatly trimmed hedges in the Versailles-style gardens, there were hundreds of them toting cameras of all varieties, the buzz in the air palpable as they waited to grill the new royal.

It was the largest showing of a press contingent since the king and queen's wedding the year before, a showing Alex had been well prepped for since making her decision to take her place as a Constantinides. And still her tongue was cleaved to the roof of her mouth, a rivulet of perspiration running down her back under the handpicked designer dress she wore.

Stella gave her an encouraging look from her position beside her, Nikandros flanking her other side. Taking a deep breath, Alex addressed the reporter in the front row.

"I'm still getting my feet wet. Perhaps you can ask me that again in a few months and I'll have a better idea."

"What is your role going to be?" the reporter followed up. "Do you have any causes you currently support?"

She was still trying to figure that out. It was her number

one point of anxiety, in fact, since getting the hotel in the black had been her "cause" to date.

"I'm working through that," she said. "More to come."

"Why hasn't the world known about you before now, Aleksandra?" another reporter called out. "Is it true your mother kept your birthright a secret?"

"That's a personal matter I won't comment on."

"What about your father's affairs? Is it possible there are more of you out there?"

"Again," she said, "I won't comment on my family's personal affairs."

"How do you anticipate handling the glare of the spotlight?"

"Day by day. Like any new job, I will have to learn my role. Luckily," she added, nodding at her siblings, "I have my brother and sister by my side."

A reporter directed a question at Stella about her new sister. Alex took the opportunity to breathe. A tall figure leaning against a tree behind the reporter claimed her attention. *Aristos.*

Clad in another of his bespoke suits, he sent her pulse scattering. *What was he doing here?*

"Aleksandra." The reporter turned her attention back to her. "Overnight you have become one of the country's most eligible women. Are you single or in a relationship?"

"I'm single."

"What are you looking for in a potential husband?"

"I'm not looking," she countered. "I have enough on my plate at the moment. But if I were, integrity, intelligence and kindness would be high on the list."

Aristos's mouth kicked up at the corners. Heat flamed her chest, rising to her face. *Diavole,* but why was he here?

"It's rumored the duke of Catharia is quite taken with you. Perhaps there's potential for a romance there?"

Her eyes widened. The duke had been seated beside

her at an official dinner two nights ago. He was charming and attentive, and she'd enjoyed his company, but since she'd been told to keep a low profile considering today's announcement, she hadn't given him any encouragement. Perhaps also because her head had kept going back to her encounter with Aristos in the gardens. Charming as he might be, proper like the duke, he was not.

"The duke is lovely," she said, lifting her chin. "But nothing to report there."

The press flung a dozen more questions at her, covering everything from her life in Stygos to her favorite color. When they had exhausted anything that could be considered remotely interesting, a reporter in the middle of the pack directed a question at Nikandros.

"What do you make of the fact that Carnelia has called its reservists up to active duty?"

Her heart jumped. *It had?* Nikandros moved to the mike. "I think we're doing everything we need to be doing to ensure Akathinia's safety, now and in the future.

"Are you anticipating an invasion by Carnelia?"

"We hope it won't come to that."

The media peppered the king with a series of questions on the Carnelian situation. Alex kept her gaze on the press corps rather than on the man making her feel utterly conspicuous. *Naive* and conspicuous.

The press conference thankfully came to an end. The PR liaison appeared to usher them back into the palace. Stella stopped to talk to a reporter she knew, while Alex continued on with her minder, anxious to get away from the frenzy.

Aristos appeared at her side, his long strides easily gaining him even with her as she walked toward the palace. "Well done," he murmured. "You took the leap."

His designer stubble was thicker than usual, giving him a wicked, pirate-like appearance. It kicked her insides into high gear despite her better sense. She gave him her best haughty princess look. "Surely you didn't come just to laugh at me?"

"You've been busy," he noted. "Taking my advice. A duke already… And no, angel, I didn't come to see your performance. I have a meeting with the king."

Oh. Her stomach dropped. And why was that? She needed to be staying away from him, not courting his attention.

"There is no duke. He was seated beside me at dinner. That's all."

"And you flashed those baby blues at him and he didn't stand a chance."

She turned to face him. "I was *not* flirting."

"You don't have to. You're a natural." He gave her a pained look. "But kindness, integrity and intelligence? Really, Alex? You might as well have posted a neon sign inviting all the Sebastiens of the world to come running. That was *not* what I meant when I said expand your horizons."

She narrowed her gaze. "That is just…*rude*. Any woman would be lucky to have Sebastien."

"Except you," he pointed out. "You're far too hot-blooded for that, Princess."

"Oof." She stuck her hands on her hips. "I tell you what. The next time I need dating advice I *won't* come to you and your heartless reputation. I'll figure it out myself."

"Ouch." He pressed a hand to his chest. "Heartless. That hurts."

"I'm sure you are withering away inside." Noting that Stella was directly behind them, she pressed her lips together and flung him a cool look. "Enjoy your meeting, Mr. Nicolades. Good afternoon."

She turned on her heel and swished her way through the palace doors. Stella caught up with her in the hall. "What was *that*?"

"Nothing." Absolutely *nothing*.

Alex headed to her meeting with her cultural adviser. A familiar anxiety worked its way through her as she sat through two hours of princess training. How was she ever going to get this all right? It all seemed unnecessarily complex and...*antiquated*.

She reminded herself why she was doing this. Stella and Nik were amazing. She hadn't been able to resist the chance to get to know them better. And perhaps because Aristos had been right. She had been playing her life safe with a whole world out there to explore.

Which didn't mean she had to pay attention to *him* and his condescending, provocative comments. If she was going to master this princess thing, she couldn't allow Aristos Nicolades to distract her at every turn.

Firming her mouth, she gave her adviser her undivided attention.

Aristos was still smiling over his confrontation with the feisty Aleksandra when he walked into the king's office. Nikandros's personal aide ushered him into the inner sanctum without delay.

"Thank you for coming," the king said, gesturing for him to take a seat in the sitting area by the windows. "I need a favor."

Aristos's always-opportunistic side perked up. The more goodwill he could bank with the king, the better. Construction on the casino on the shores of the Akathinian harbor would mean surprises—rude, *expensive* surprises a royal influence could help smooth out. Accelerate solutions for.

"Always," he said, crossing one long leg over the other and sitting back in the chair. "What can I do?"

Nik sat down opposite him. "My sources say Idas may make a move on this country as soon as his armed forces are at full strength. As such, we need to shift to a high alert."

His stomach plummeted. It was the worst-case scenario he'd hoped would not come to pass. What would his investors think of such an uncertain environment? A war that could destabilize the region? Would they jump ship? Let their nerves get the better of them?

A knot formed in his gut. He had doubled down on this one. Put the better part of his personal fortune up to back this casino. If it failed, *he* failed.

Your ambition will be the thing that fells you, Aristos, unless you learn to control it.

"Aristos?" Nik was frowning at him.

He shook his mentor's words out of his head. "Sorry, yes?"

"I want both princesses off the island. Stella has a good friend she can stay with in Athens. I need you to take Aleksandra to Larikos."

He blinked. The king wanted him to take his stunningly beautiful, unwittingly sexy, *very* innocent half sister to his private island in the Aegean Sea for safekeeping?

"Of course I'm happy to do whatever you require," he said carefully, "but of all people, Nik, you must know *I* am not a babysitter."

The king fixed his laser-sharp blue gaze on him. "I'm not asking you to babysit Aleksandra. I'm asking you to provide a safe place for an heir to the throne until this is settled. The security on Larikos is impenetrable."

Because he had a casino there where some of the richest men in the world came to play...in a few weeks, actually. "She would be better off with Stella," he suggested. "Wouldn't that be more reassuring for her?"

"Akathinian law says I can't have two heirs to the throne, however distant, together in a situation like this."

He firmed his mouth. "I'm not the man for the job, Nik.

I am scheduled to be all over the globe the next few weeks. I'll ask friends to host her."

Nik pinned his gaze on him. "That you are precisely *not* the man for the job is exactly why I want her with you. It's the last place anyone would think to look for her."

It was not a request. It was a command if he valued the casino license he'd spent the past five years chasing.

"All right. When?"

"Friday."

"Friday?"

"Friday," the king said firmly. "And, Aristos?" Nikandros shot him a deadly look. "I don't think I have to say that Aleksandra is off-limits."

Aristos absorbed the underlying message. The insinuation he wasn't good enough to fraternize with a royal. It had been this way, too, when rumors of his and Stella's brief liaison were circulating. He would have hoped with all the respect he and Nik had gained for each other over the past year working together, the king's opinion of him might have changed. Yet clearly, Nikandros still considered him beneath his family's blue blood.

His jaw hardened, his fingers tightening around the arms of the chair. He'd made an art of not caring what anyone thought of him. It had been a necessity in the life he'd led, in the business he operated in, with the checkered past he carried with him that was always in danger of resurfacing. The tightness in his chest suggested he hadn't quite perfected it.

"Consider it done," he said curtly, rolling to his feet. He had bigger fish to fry than a princess, including a flock of investors whose hands needed holding. A plan B to execute he'd hoped he'd never have to use.

His ambition wasn't the problem. It was the universe and how it was unfolding that was messing him up. Fortunately, he'd never met a calamity he couldn't conquer.

This casino *would* happen. His business would not fail. He was never going back to where he'd come from. *Ever.*

Alex and Stella were summoned to Nik's office after dinner, an unusual request given that the king had been burying himself there of late, forbidding interruptions. Alex rose from her chair, darting a look at Stella. "Do you know what this is about?"

Stella shook her head. "No idea. Could be Carnelia."

The worried look in her sister's eyes had *her* worrying. She followed Stella down the hall to Nik's office, where her brother waved them into chairs.

"You heard the speculation today about Carnelia calling up its reservists," he began, without preamble. "We have confirmed this is true. We have no idea whether Idas is bluffing or planning to make a move on Akathinia."

Her heart dropped.

"He wouldn't dare," Stella exclaimed. "He knows the world is against him."

"I'm not sure he is in his right mind. Regardless, I think it's prudent to remove both of you from the island for the next little while until we can determine the situation."

"And Sofía and Theo?" Stella asked.

"They stay. Sofía refuses to leave."

"Then I'm staying, too," Stella said. "I'm not leaving you."

Nik's gaze softened. "I appreciate the show of solidarity, but I can't have the three heirs to the throne here. Nor do I have the energy to fight with you. My wife is making it hard enough."

"He won't do it," Stella said. "He's bluffing. Why doesn't Kostas talk some sense into his father? What is *wrong* with him?"

"The crown prince remains noticeably absent. Do what

I ask. *Please.* We are well defended, Stella. It's just a precaution."

Stella clamped her jaw shut. Nodded. "We can stay with Cynthia, then."

"You can. Aleksandra will stay on Larikos with Aristos. It is written in our laws the heirs must be separated in a time of war."

"Aristos?" The sisters said the word in unison. Stella's jaw dropped. "Why?"

"Because his casino is impenetrable. She'll be better protected there than anywhere else."

"I'll go home," Alex interjected.

"I'm afraid that's impossible. You would be too vulnerable there."

She bit her lip. "What about my family? I can't leave them unprotected."

"I will make sure they are looked after."

Her head spun. This was *madness.* "I really don't think this is a good idea."

"Why?" Nik threw the question at her with the look of a man who'd just about reached his limit.

She exchanged a meaningful look with Stella. "I just… don't."

Nik's gaze moved between the two of them. "If you have something to say, spit it out."

I can't be marooned with Aristos on his private island for Lord knows how long when I am clearly, inadvisably attracted to him.

Unfortunately, the next day, she was packing to do exactly that.

CHAPTER FIVE

LARIKOS, ARISTOS NICOLADES'S private island in the heart of the Aegean Sea, sat to the east of Greece. Surrounded by sparkling cerulean-blue water, it comprised seventy acres of priceless real estate upon which Aristos's much-buzzed-about, invitation-only high-roller casino was situated, as well as his private estate and guest residences.

"The famous Great House." Aristos's pilot pointed at a massive, sprawling thatch-roofed structure that sat perched on a hill overlooking the sea. He listed off names of celebrities, politicians and royals who'd stayed in the €10,000-a-night suites. "The villas," the pilot said, "for those who wish for more privacy, are the structures scattered down the hill."

Alex absorbed the spectacular aerial view, then sat back in her seat, fingers clutching the armrests. Having never been on a plane before in her life, let alone a helicopter, she had been torn between terror and exhilaration as they'd made the trip from Akathinia to the place she would call her home for the foreseeable future.

She had, of course, not been about to tell Nik about her disreputable behavior with Aristos the night of Stella's party, thus the inevitable conclusion of her conversation with the king. There had been time only to call her mother to assure her she would be taken care of before she and Stella were whisked away from the palace for safekeeping.

Safekeeping. Her stomach dropped as the helicopter dipped and made its way toward the landing pad near the

Great House. She was worried about her family. Worried about what Idas would do. Sure she should be there by their sides and not *here* hidden away with the man she'd practically thrown herself at the other night.

Being uprooted again, separated from everything she knew under the most worrying of circumstances when she'd only just begun to settle into her new life, had been disconcerting. Unnerving. As if she were frozen midjump.

She wanted to know she'd done the right thing in abandoning the life she'd loved, to know everything would fall into place. Instead she'd been handed complete uncertainty.

Her fingernails sank deeper into the leather as the pilot set the helicopter down on the landing pad. A tall, dark male stood waiting, his shorts and T-shirt whipping in the wind. *Aristos.* Her stomach did a flip-flop of a whole other kind. She'd thought maybe he'd send one of his staff to greet her, hadn't even known if he would be here. Just because he was hiding her away didn't mean he had to play host.

Aristos pulled the door of the helicopter open and greeted the pilot. It gave her an opportunity to inspect him in casual clothes during the short exchange that followed.

The show began with the close-fitting T-shirt that stretched taut over his broad shoulders and cut abs, not an excess centimeter of flesh in sight, and ended with the most impressive set of powerfully built thighs and calves she'd ever seen. Pure masculine perfection that hinted at the fact that the rest of him she *couldn't* see was just as mouthwatering as what was on display.

He eyed her as he lifted her down to the ground. "You okay? You look a bit green."

"Fine," she managed past a churning stomach. "I've never flown before. It was an adventure."

He kept his hands on her waist. He smelled like earthy sexy male today, with a hint of sandalwood as opposed to his usual spicy urbane sophistication. Little pinpricks of heat flared beneath her skin as he studied her face, multiplying with unnerving speed until she was drowning in her awareness of him.

"You mean you haven't flown in a *helicopter* before," he corrected.

"No. I haven't flown, period."

His eyes widened. "Surely you've been outside of Akathinia?"

"Only to the Greek islands. Perfectly accessible by boat and automobile."

He looked at her as if she were a creature from Mars. She stepped back, pressing her palms to her flaming cheeks. "There's been no opportunity. You said it yourself. Running a small business means you have no personal time. Every time we hired someone we thought was reliable enough to take part of the workload on, we found we couldn't trust them."

"Staff will always be your biggest headache and asset. Has your cousin stepped in to help your mother?"

She nodded, a throb filling her chest. *Taken her place* was how she saw it.

"How did your mother take the news?"

"Not well." Her mother had been trying to mask her feelings, but she knew she was devastated by her decision, feeling the loss of their bond as much as Alex was.

His gaze softened. "No one said taking the untraveled road was easy."

Brutally hard was more like it. She was getting the sense this new life of hers was going to be a one-challenge-a-day kind of affair.

Aristos picked up her suitcase and headed toward the Great House. She trotted along behind him, half running to keep up.

"I'll show you to your room. Get you settled. Yolande,

my manager, is going to give you a tour of the island this afternoon. She'll be your point person for anything you need while you're here."

Because she was a pain in the neck to him. Because having her here was a huge inconvenience, likely the last thing he needed with a potential war delaying his casino.

"Thank you for opening your home to me," she said, drawing alongside him. "But please, don't feel like you have to play host. I'm sure you have a million things to do."

His dark gaze glittered in the sun. "Unfortunately, you and I are stuck together, angel. I am your official babysitter for however long it takes Carnelia to realize Akathinia can't be taken."

She blinked. *That could be weeks. Months.* "Surely you have to travel… You can't stop doing business because of me."

"I'm going to do it from here. I'll do day trips if I need to."

"That's ridiculous. Your business is all over the world. I don't need a babysitter. I can take care of myself."

He stopped and looked down at her. The warmth in his gaze had vanished, replaced by a cold black stare. "The king has entrusted you to my care. You are a potential target in these games Carnelia is playing should they elect to make a point out of you. You are therefore my responsibility and will do what I say while you are on this island. Understood?"

An icy feeling invaded her. She wasn't sure if it was this vastly intimidating version of Aristos that did it, or the fact that he'd just marked her a kidnapping target.

She swallowed past the lump in her throat. "You don't really think Idas would come after me or Stella, do you?"

"No. I think it would be highly unwise of him. But taking chances would be equally foolhardy."

Right. She shut her brain down before her imagination

ran wild and considered, instead, Aristos's distinctly cool demeanor as she followed him up the steps of the sprawling, airy structure with its incomparable views of the sea. Gone was the incorrigible, devilish version of him she'd come to expect, replaced by the Aristos she'd met the night of the ball.

Apparently Aristos ran hot and cold. Too bad the last time he'd run hot she'd practically begged him to kiss her.

"You can pretend I'm not even here," she suggested. "Better yet, put me to work. I've managed a hotel. I'm sure there are things I can do."

"There are no guests here right now. And what," he tossed over his shoulder, "would the king think of me putting you to work?"

"He'd be happy that you've kept me occupied?"

"I don't think so, Princess. Not going to happen."

She and Aristos were alone on this island. Well, them and a few dozen staff, likely. She digested that fact as she followed him up to the third level.

"When do the next guests come?"

"I'm not hosting any groups while you're here for security reasons. With the exception of an invitation-only poker game in three weeks. Everyone attending is a personal acquaintance of mine, each one thoroughly screened with background checks."

Oh. Her heart plummeted as she stepped onto the third-floor landing. His gaze speared hers. "What's the matter, Princess? Afraid to be alone with me?"

Not in your current chilly state, no. She lifted her chin. "Why would I be?"

Their gazes clashed, black battling with blue. "Oh, that's right," he said silkily. "You're looking for 'integrity, intelligence and kindness.' You'd best go find your duke."

She pressed her lips together. "I already told you, there is no duke."

He turned and strode down the hall. She followed, staring at his broad back. What had she done to annoy him? Or maybe he was simply irritated with the situation?

Her confusion fell to the wayside as she stepped into the ridiculously large, high-ceilinged bedroom Aristos had entered at the end of the hall. Her suite at the palace had been straight out of a fairy tale, but *this*, this was something else. Paradise, perhaps.

The three walls that enclosed the room were a cream-colored canvas for the bright, beautiful island art that covered it. The final wall that faced the sea comprised floor-to-ceiling glass with sliding doors that opened onto a terrace, offering a spectacular view of the endless blue horizon.

With that jaw-dropping perspective as a backdrop, the suite descended into sumptuous, hedonistic heaven. Gauzy cream-colored curtains were drawn to either side of the dark wood canopy bed. A decadent-looking daybed enjoyed a perfect view of the sea, promising hours of reading pleasure.

"Aristos," she breathed. "This is incredible."

"Nothing too good for the princess in residence."

She ignored the gibe, too caught up in the magic of the ethereal room. "I love it. It's perfect."

"Good. My bedroom is there," he said, pointing to the terrace beside hers. "So I can keep an eye on you. My office is in the casino. Yolande will show it to you this afternoon so you know where to find me." He turned and gestured toward the writing desk tucked away in the corner of the room. "There's a secure phone and internet line. You're not to use your usual devices. Turn them off and keep them off."

She bit her lip. "Okay."

"As for meals," he continued, "the chef on the main level is at your disposal. As are any of the water sports and activities. The staff are available to accompany you. The only thing you will *not* do is swim unaccompanied. The undertow can be strong with the *meltemia*."

"I'm Akathinian, Aristos. I was born on the water."

"The rule still applies." He leaned against the wall. "A few things. You will notice armed guards posted on the island. They carry *big* guns. There's no reason to be alarmed—they're for the protection of the guests we host, many of whom are VIPs whose safety is a top priority. To that end, there is no way on or off this island without my personal knowledge and approval. There's a three-mile blackout around us, meaning no aircraft or boat crosses it without my team's knowledge."

Armed guards with big guns and a no-fly zone? What had she walked into?

"Is that really necessary?"

"Yes. More than one of my guests have been kidnapped and held for ransom. It won't happen here."

That word again. *Kidnapped.* She wiped a palm over her brow.

"I thought we could have dinner. Sometime around eight?"

She met his cool gaze with one of her own. "I meant what I said. You don't need to babysit me or keep me company. I'll be fine."

"I have time tonight." He headed toward the door. "Enjoy your tour."

She tried to. Yolande was lovely, and Larikos *was* paradise. Whereas Stygos relied on its wild, natural beauty to attract visitors, its way of life virtually unchanged from a hundred years ago except for the most necessary of modernizations, Larikos was sleek and sophisticated.

From its sensational tropical gardens to the world-class clay tennis courts to the Romanesque-inspired casino, the island sparkled with an opulence that was reflected in every detail. But all that sophistication only made her pine for home. For beaches that were just as beautiful, views just as spellbinding. Her mother, who must be terrified as to what was to come…

She would have given anything in that moment for everything to be back to normal, where life had made sense. But nothing was normal anymore—perhaps never would be again. Her world as she knew it had vaporized, and she felt completely, utterly adrift.

Aristos spent the afternoon in his office, immersed in conference calls to make up for where he was supposed to be had he not been babysitting a princess. Almost all of them were to pacify nervous investors about the Akathinian situation, including one of his biggest, Russian oligarch Dimitri Smirnov, who had seemed even more wily and elusive than ever, marking the Akathinian political situation as "worrying" and refusing to give him a firm commitment that he would stick with him.

He'd therefore put plan B into motion: using his shrouded-in-secrecy, much-anticipated, invitation-only annual poker game on Larikos to keep everyone happy.

He never messed with the sanctity of the game. Any of the business contacts he mixed with the pros were players who could hold their own, but this year, he had invited all his key financial backers, including a wild card in Dimitri, so he could keep a finger on the pulse of them all. He only hoped it wouldn't destroy the game.

Frustration swirled through him, singeing his skin. *Too many calls. Too many uncertainties.*

He slammed a fist on his desk. If he'd been in Moscow as he was *supposed* to be, he could have talked Dimitri into a commitment. Instead he was here, protecting a princess he was supposed to have dinner with in a few minutes. Entertain. He could only hope the Russian would take the bait and attend the game he'd long coveted a place in. It wasn't looking promising.

Noting the espresso he'd spilled in his tirade, now eating up the pages of a report on his desk, he uttered another choice word, grabbed some napkins from his drawer and started mopping it up. He refused to consider the graveyard of men who'd conquered Vegas and Atlantic City, only to end up destitute, consumed by their own greed.

That would never be *him*. He wadded up the napkins and threw them in the trash. His risk had been big but calculated. Bold but not foolhardy. He couldn't imagine a day when he forgot what it was like to wonder where his next meal was coming from, where he was going to sleep that night. It was the kind of desperate clawing existence that was burned into your brain forever, no matter how far your star shot up in the sky—no matter how distant a memory it became.

It was something every human being knew if they were reasonably self-aware. Everything you had could and would go away in the flash of a neon Sin City sign if you didn't keep your eye on the prize.

Just as his own life had once vaporized in the space of a head-poundingly hot Athens night in which heated accusations had been delivered, ultimatums issued and decisions made that could never be taken back.

He pulled himself out of his ruminations with a scowl. It was the thinking of a man who hadn't slept enough, who had subsisted on a diet of far too much coffee and too little food today, his hesitation in heading toward sustenance with only one name: Alex.

She'd had another of those lost, disoriented, utterly out-of-her-element looks on her face when she'd arrived. And why wouldn't she? She'd been ripped away from her family once again with a war looming in Akathinia, clearly no happier to be here with him than he was to be stuck with her.

He had been cold with her, yes, stifling what seemed to be his natural desire to comfort her, because it was the only way to manage the attraction between them.

The women he dated were sophisticated creatures with the benefit of a world of experience. Who knew the score with him. Who didn't complain about his lack of commitment because they'd known from the start it was never coming, and for the time they were together, he provided them with everything money could offer.

It had been that way since his early days in Vegas. Since he'd discovered that having money meant an endless supply of women who cared more about his wealth than the man behind it. Which had suited him just fine. After his parents' disastrous marriage that had seen his mother kick his father out after years of vicious fighting and his infidelity, he had no desire to ever enter into the illusionary institution of marriage.

Carin, his PA, stuck her head in his office and prompted him about dinner. He rolled to his feet, threw his laptop into his briefcase and headed toward trouble. Trouble he was going to neutralize. If Aleksandra's innocence wasn't enough of a deterrent for him to keep his hands off her— which quite honestly, he suspected it might not have been under different circumstances—the fact that the king had warned him off her was.

Which meant keeping Alex at a distance by whatever means necessary.

Showered, changed, dressed in jeans and a T-shirt, and still not entirely free of his filthy mood, Aristos found the princess waiting for him on the terrace of the Great House. The fragile image she cut against the dusky pink-and-red sky, a tiny figure versus the big, scary universe she'd been thrown into, tugged at his heart. He was, after all, partially responsible for encouraging her to embrace this brave new world.

"I should have told you the dress is casual here unless we're having a formal night."

She turned around, a wry smile curving her mouth. "And here I was just getting used to the training that's been drilled into my head. *Refined dress on all occasions, Aleksandra. Classy yet understated.*"

He could have told her that on her, with her perfect curves, anything looked sexy. That the very proper turquoise wrap dress she had on only made a man want to unwrap her as a most fortunate present. That her hair, plaited down her back, elicited the same urge. But since his mind was supposed to be out of the gutter when it came to Alex, he declined to go there.

He crossed to the wine bucket sitting on a table and began uncorking the bottle of sparkling white. "You aren't supposed to let them turn you into a robot."

"I'm not." She frowned. "It's just…there are rules. So many rules. Standards to uphold. It's all a bit much."

"Stella knows her own mind." He filled two glasses, waiting for the fizz to die down to top them up. "Use her as an example."

She took the glass he handed her, a contemplative look on her face. She was curious, he knew, about his relationship with Stella, but there was nothing to tell. They had been two consenting adults scratching an itch, whereas Alex was vulnerable, *emotional*.

He surveyed the dark circles that lined her eyes, their red-rimmed appearance. Her emotions were not his concern; her safety was. But the tug on his heart at her obvious misery was too strong.

"So," he drawled, "what's eating you? You've been off since you arrived."

Her eyes widened. She opened her mouth to say something, then clamped it shut. "I'm worried about my mother," she said quietly. "I feel like I should be there by her side, not here, as lovely as it is."

A twinge of guilt assailed him. He should have been more reassuring earlier rather than scaring the hell out of her. "There's no need to be concerned about the political situation in Akathinia. The minute Idas makes a move, which I still have doubts will ever happen, the world will respond. Akathinia is too important a symbol for its former colonial interests to watch its democracy be compromised."

She gave a doubtful nod. "I suppose you're right."

"I am," he said firmly. He lifted his glass. "To your leap. May it lead you to many fantastic adventures."

She lifted her glass to his. Remained pensive as she drank.

He cocked a brow. "What?"

"I feel like I've been ripped away midjump. I was just getting settled, trying to figure out what I'm going to do, and then all *this* happened." She pursed her lips. "I need to find my 'thing.' My cause to support. All I've learned so far is how to smash a bottle of champagne against a ship without maiming myself and how to cut a ribbon without making it fray. It's making me crazy."

He leaned against the railing, balancing his glass on the top. "Rome wasn't built in a day. Have you been given any direction? Perhaps Stella has some ideas."

"She took me on a tour of the new youth center the charity she represents is building. It's very impressive."

"Youth Compass?"

She nodded.

"I'm on the board of directors. It's a good organization."

She crossed her arms over her chest and tucked her glass beneath her chin. "What got you involved with them?"

"A percentage of the profits from each of my casinos is diverted to the homeless and youth organizations in the cities we operate in."

Her blue gaze turned assessing. "So the big bad casino mogul has a heart."

"Oh, I wouldn't go that far, Princess. Corporate social responsibility is smart business."

"And that explains the staff you've hired to work on Larikos who were living on the streets? Who had no particular skill when you hired them and now they're the head groundskeeper and the engineer who maintains your solar project?"

He must remember to tell Yolande to cut down on the personal anecdotes. "It's an issue society has to tackle."

She pointed her glass at him. "I need something like that."

"You need to be personally invested in it. What turns you on, Princess? Gets those creative juices of yours flowing?"

Her face went a rosy pink. He knew exactly where her head was, because it was where his was. Where it was every time they were within five feet of each other. *In bed, satisfying their intense sexual curiosity about each other...*

"Other than me, angel," he drawled. "We've already established that as a nonstarter."

Her eyes widened, a deep flush staining her chest to match the one in her cheeks. "You are insufferable sometimes, you know that? And just...*deluded.*"

His mouth curved. That was better. Feisty he could handle. The sad puppy-dog look, not so much.

"Insufferable, yes," he agreed. "Deluded, I'd argue. You were craving a follow-up to that kiss that night in the gardens as much as I was." He moved his gaze over her soft, pink, very consumable mouth. "You aren't exactly subtle with your signals."

Her mouth thinned. "Wanting something and acting on it are two different things. In actuality," she said, pinning her gaze on his, "the duke *is* much more my type than you. There is a civility about him I enjoy."

"Really?" The blatant lie, yet another slight from a Constantinides insinuating he was beneath their blue blood, evaporated his good humor. *His rules.*

"If I took that glass out of your hand right now," he said, holding her gaze, "picked you up and carried you upstairs to my bedroom to do exactly what we both want to do, you would *not* be complaining, Princess. You would be *begging* for me to finish it. And *that* is the truth."

She blinked. "That would never happen."

"You want to *try me*, angel?"

Color leached from her cheeks, leaving behind a pallor that told him he'd gone too far. And still the nerve she'd hit pulsed in his jaw, making it difficult to summon the self-control he knew he needed.

"Perhaps you're right," she acknowledged quietly. "But hormones don't have a lot to do with common sense, do they?"

She slayed him with that one simple line.

Alex almost turned on her heel and skipped dinner with Mr. Hot-and-Cold after that display. Her deeply ingrained good manners, however, wouldn't allow her to do it. Mr. Hot might be back, but she could manage him. Manage *this.* At least she thought she could.

What plagued her as Aristos seated her at the candlelit table for two on the edge of the large formal dining room, in the cooling breeze of the sea, was that she was afraid he was right. That if he'd done what he'd said, she might not have protested, might have been unbearably excited instead. And that was a head-scratcher, given what she knew of Aristos's reputation. Given the fact that Sebastien hadn't been able to persuade her into bed with him during their yearlong relationship, her boyfriend resorting to asking her to marry him in an attempt to get her there.

She wasn't sure what she'd been waiting for. Lizzie and Darcy's spark-strewn courtship? Gatsby's grand obsession with Daisy? Or perhaps the inescapable attraction she felt toward Aristos—as if a magnet kept pulling her toward him no matter how hard she tried to escape. Made worse by the fact that now she knew he had a heart. That the man behind the stunning good looks was one who cared enough to pluck two strangers off the street, one in Rio and one in Las Vegas, pay for their education and give them a job on Larikos, his most exclusive property. A second lease on life...

He liked to paint himself as the devil beyond redemption, but he was far more than that. It was dangerous to even let herself go there; she knew it as she lifted the glass Aristos had refilled and sipped her wine. But she couldn't seem to help herself.

"What about your reading?" he said, breaking the silence that had fallen between them with a return to their earlier discussion. "You said you love to read. Why not literacy as a cause? Youth illiteracy is a major issue. You could team up with Stella on activities..."

She thought about it. She had never thought of her reading that way, as a privilege, when in fact, it was. For her, a story that transported her to another world had always been a part of her life. Her mother had taught her English as a little girl, considering it an invaluable skill. The nook in her family's hotel where guests left their discarded books had become her gold mine. And yet not everyone had been granted that privilege, even for critical, life-sustaining purposes.

"I love that idea," she said quietly, recognizing it as the peace offering it was.

"Then use the time here to pick a short list of organizations you might like to work with."

She would. She attempted to focus on her salad as a

silence fell between them again. More peaceful this time. But she found her appetite had waned. Or was it just difficult to concentrate on anything with Aristos sitting across a candlelit table from her? When it looked as if he had been poured into the white T-shirt and dark blue jeans he had on, his current level of intensity only making him that much hotter.

"Enough about me," she said, offering a peace branch of her own. "What's been keeping *you* up at night?"

An amused expression crossed his face. He sat back in his chair, his wineglass cradled in his palm. "The list is too numerous to bore you with."

"You have to be worried about the casino."

"Yes, but much of that is out of my control. All I can do is try to convince my investors there is no need to worry."

"And is that working?"

"Most seem fine. One in particular, Dimitri Smirnov, a Russian oligarch, seems shaky. I've invited him to come to Larikos for the poker game, so I can firm him up."

Her stomach sank. "Which you could be doing now if you weren't babysitting me."

He shot her a reproving look. "We've had this conversation."

Yes, but she hated that she was standing in the way of something so important. "How does the game work?" she asked. "Who gets to come?"

"I thought you found my profession distasteful, Princess."

She sighed. "Hector Rigatos, my best friend's father, lost all his family's money gambling in Las Vegas. I know it's an extreme case, but that's why I have a problem with gambling. And could you *please* stop calling me Princess? You know very well I dislike it."

"There are some unfortunate cases like that," he acknowledged. "Most people, however, learn to enjoy responsibly.

As for calling you Princess," he drawled, "I like it. I find it reminds me *who* you are."

As if he'd forgotten for one second. She shook her head. "How long has the game been going on?"

"Five years. The players like it because it's private. They can let their hair down. What happens on Larikos stays on Larikos, so the saying goes. Social media, any type of reporting, is banned."

She could only imagine what happened when men, money, power and competition got together. "Do they get up to very naughty things?"

"Sometimes. Nothing that's fit for your ears."

"Please. How much is the opening ante?"

"One hundred thousand US dollars."

Thee mou. "And by the end of the game?"

"Last year it went as high as one point three million. We ended with twenty million worth of chips on the table. Which," he advised, "is not a public figure."

Her head spun. This was *beyond* fascinating. Unlike poor Hector Rigatos, these men knew what they were doing.

"You give a percentage to charity," she guessed.

"Yes."

"Do you play?"

"Sometimes."

She'd bet he'd be the most formidable of players…bet he looked smoking hot doing it.

She pursed her lips, regarding him thoughtfully. "So how do we get Dimitri Smirnov here?"

"You mean how do *I* get Dimitri here?"

"I can help. I can do some research… We've done some really great events at the hotel to draw in high-profile guests."

"I run a poker game, Princess, that's all. Dimitri's always wanted to play. We'll see if he bites."

She chewed on her lip. "Why the hesitation, then?"

"It's his wife's birthday that weekend. I already offered them an extended stay on Larikos to celebrate. If that doesn't do it, I'm not sure what will."

She couldn't imagine what woman in her right mind would turn down a week on Larikos. When they weren't in captivity, of course… But maybe, she thought, her brain percolating, there was more, something personal they could offer Dimitri Smirnov's wife as a birthday present. An experience she couldn't find anywhere else.

Her lips curved. Research was what was needed. Good thing Aristos had given her a laptop. If she just so happened to surf up some information on Mrs. Smirnov that might help, was that a crime?

Aristos eyed her. "No, Alex."

"No, what?" she countered innocently, spearing a tomato with her fork.

The conversation remained on neutral, innocuous topics after that, topics Aristos seemed to handpick to keep their interaction in a safe zone. She played along with it because she knew it was the smart thing to do.

After dinner, he walked her upstairs, likely to ensure she was ensconced in his heavily guarded fortress for the night. Each step along the long hallway, toward a bedroom, *another* foreign existence that was now hers for weeks, perhaps months, brought with it a low-grade anxiety. She didn't want to be alone. She didn't want to be *here*. She wanted her life back. Which one she wasn't sure.

"Can I get you anything?" Aristos asked as they reached her bedroom door.

It was the wrong question to ask. She bit her lip, hot tears burning the backs of her eyes. "No," she said huskily, blinking them back. "I'm fine."

He reached out and traced her cheek with the tip of his finger. "Alex—"

She flinched. Shut herself into her room with a murmured thanks and told herself to stay there before she did something really, really stupid.

Aristos stood outside Alex's room for a good minute, torn between the desire to go after her and comfort her and knowing exactly where it would be headed if he did. In the end, he turned and went to his own room, where he answered a few last emails from his overseas teams.

The storm rolled in about an hour later. One of those vicious assaults that came out of nowhere and packed the wrath of God. It brought with it a stunning display of thunder and lightning that seemed to shake the walls of the Great House, although in reality it was far too well-built for that.

He got up from his chair on the terrace, went inside and checked that the lightning strike detection system was activated. When he saw that it was, he poured himself a drink and went back outside to watch the show.

White and gold streaks of lightning arced across the inky black tropical sky, jagged, intricate fingers of pulsing light that dazzled the eye with their spectacular patterns. The thunder grew louder with every pass, its powerful roar shaking the floorboards beneath his feet. Faster and more frequent it came until there was virtually no pause between the cracks of thunder. It must be close. Almost directly overhead.

He wasn't sure what alerted him to Alex's presence on the terrace adjacent to his. The storm was too loud for him to have heard her. She stood, wrapped in the white silk robe the resort provided its guests, her arms wrapped around her. A bolt of lightning zigzagged through the sky, hitting the water not a hundred feet from them. It illuminated Alex's pinched white face. *She was terrified.*

Turning on her heel, she ran inside. He headed toward

her room, expecting the door to be locked. She must have forgotten to do it, because the handle turned and he walked into the room, colliding with a wall of frightened female.

"Whoa." He gathered her into his arms. "What's going on?"

"Th-that strike," she stuttered. "It was too close. It was—"

"We're fine." He ran a soothing hand down her back. "We get these storms all the time."

"So do we. I *h-hate* them."

"They sound worse than they are."

"What if it hits us?"

"We have sophisticated detection systems. We'd be on it in a minute."

A crack of thunder made her jump. She was shaking so hard her teeth were chattering. Uttering a curse, he set her away from him, walked to the bar and poured her a finger of cognac. Drawing her down on the sofa, he pulled her into his arms, her back nestled into his warmth.

"Drink," he said, pushing the tumbler into her hands.

He was staying for a few minutes until she calmed down. That was it.

She curled her fingers around the glass. Took a sip. "That's really strong."

"It'll calm your nerves."

She took another sip. He smoothed his palm over her hair, still bound in the tight plait. It made him hurt to look at it. "This *has* to be giving you a headache."

"My hair was a little wild. I'll take it out before I sleep."

He undid it for her, sliding the elastic from the bottom of the plait and methodically working the braid free with his fingers as the storm continued to roll over them. "Why are you so frightened? A bad experience with a storm?"

"My uncle Rasmus was hit by lightning when I was a little girl. He was a fisherman. He went out on his boat one morning, early, very early, when a storm like this rolled in. Luckily, one of his fellow fishermen saw it happen. They took him to the hospital, but his left side was paralyzed. He could never man a boat after that."

"That must have been frightening for a little girl."

She nodded. "I know the chances of it happening are one in a million, that it's an irrational fear, but you think if it can happen once, it can happen again."

He worked the last section of the braid free. Her hair fell around her shoulders, like warm silk under his hands. It was beautiful. She should never wear it up. If she were his, she never would.

The bizarre train of thought made him scowl. He never kept women around long enough for them to be "his." Where was *that* coming from?

The beats between thunderclaps lengthened, the bright bursts of lightning lessening in their intensity, becoming fewer and further in between. He moved his fingers to her scalp, his slow, easy massage meant to distract.

"Aristos…"

"Mmm?"

"Your two roads. What were they?"

His fingers paused in her hair. "Ancient history. Like I said."

She twisted around to look at him. "If it's ancient history, why won't you tell me?"

"Because it doesn't matter anymore."

"If it doesn't matter, why can't you tell me?"

Because it involved intimate details of his personal history. Because barely anyone knew the story. Because she *would know him if he did.*

And yet she'd had the courage to tell him her deepest fears. Had taken a massive leap few would ever have had the courage to take in leaving her life to become a princess.

Surely he could tell her a story that didn't matter anymore? That had nothing to do with the man he was now?

Or perhaps had everything to do with the man he was now...

He pulled her back against his chest, his hand returning to the satiny fall of her hair. "When I was sixteen, I was living on the streets in Athens. Running with a gang. I was distanced from my family for various reasons, bitter about the lot the world had handed me and headed down a very dark road. My mentor, David Tennyson, one of the men who revitalized Las Vegas, was visiting Athens. He was in front of a restaurant one night, smoking, when I attempted to relieve him of his wallet.

"He was too street savvy to let that happen. But instead of turning me in to the police, he wanted to know why I was on the street. I told him my story. He saw something in me, saw past the anger and the bitterness. He wanted to help me, he said, but only if I gave up my lawless ways. He handed me twenty one-hundred-dollar bills and a business card that night and told me if I wanted to learn the casino business to come to Las Vegas."

She twisted around to face him. "You went."

He nodded. "You only get a chance like that once in your life."

"Or never." She sank her teeth into her bottom lip, a habit he found himself once again wanting to correct. Only, he knew how he'd do it, and there wasn't anything innocent about the vision that filled his head. "That's quite a story."

"It wasn't a match made in heaven. Not in the beginning. I had a lot of baggage I had to work through...anger issues. David has a tough background himself. He wasn't about to put up with me breaking the rules. There were no easy shortcuts, I would come to realize. The path to success was a great deal of hard work."

"What's your relationship like with David now?"

He thought about it. "Like father and son, really."

"And your own family? Did you reconcile?"

"No."

"Why not?"

"Some paths you can never reconcile."

His tone was hard. Final. She opened her mouth, then closed it. "Does David come to your poker game?"

"Yes." He held her gaze. "That story is not for public consumption, Alex. David and I are the only ones who know the history, the only ones who ever will."

"I won't tell a soul," she said. "Thank you for telling me. I understand now about the choices you were speaking of. How difficult it must have been for you to choose. How we all have a choice."

He tucked a chunk of her hair behind her ear. "What were you upset about earlier?"

"I was homesick." She waved a hand at the sea. "It's so beautiful here. Your island is incredible. But it makes me think of Stygos. How much I miss it…"

"Did you call home?"

"Yes. It's just…I feel lost. I want to know I've made the right decision giving up my life. I *think* I have, then the doubts creep in."

"That's when you have to stay the course," he said firmly. "It gets harder before it gets easier, just as I said about my early days in Vegas. Once you've passed the point of no return, doubt is normal. It's what you do with that doubt, the strength of spirit you put behind it, that makes the difference."

Her lips curved in a heartbreakingly vulnerable smile. "You are wise, Aristos Nicolades."

"Along with being insufferable and rude?"

"Yes." Her smile grew. "Perhaps you are my David. Pushing me on the right course…"

He shook his head. "I identify with your struggle, that's

all. I know how hard it is to walk away from everything you know. To tell yourself you're doing the right thing even when it's terrifying. Even when you *know* it's right."

Her gaze darkened. Stayed on his. The moment hung, suspended between them. She was soft and warm against him, still within the circle of his arms, that brilliant blue gaze of hers eating him up.

"Alex," he growled, blood drumming in his ears. "We have rules."

"I know." She whispered the words even as she drifted closer. Her scent, a mix of jasmine and something he couldn't put a finger on, wound its way around him. To have all those curves within touching distance, that amazing mouth close enough to touch, *taste*, was playing havoc with his common sense. His rules.

She had drifted so close now, her lips were mere centimeters from his. He could have stopped the madness; he was still in possession of all his faculties, whereas Aleksandra was on the far side of vulnerable and clearly not. Perhaps because of that and not in spite of it, he didn't push her away. Didn't listen to the voice in his head asking him if he had a death wish.

She was seeking comfort. Surely he could keep it to a kiss? One kiss. Then he'd put her to bed, *alone*, and be on his way.

He could do that.

He let his breath mingle with hers. "What's the matter, angel? Don't have the guts to take it all the way?"

She brushed her mouth against his. He almost groaned out loud at the pillowy softness of it…how good she tasted.

The alpha in him couldn't leave it like that. Capturing her jaw in his fingers, he took control. Firmer, lusher, the kisses went until they had fully explored the texture and shape of each other. Then he slid his tongue into her mouth and rediscovered the intoxicating flavor of her. She tasted like peaches and pears from the wine she'd consumed, as heady as he remembered.

His blood heated, his body responding to the perfection of their connection. He should stop it now. Do what he'd said he'd do. But when he moved to disentangle them from each other, Alex protested and moved closer. "Soon," she murmured against his lips.

Soon? She was too tempting beneath his hands not to touch. Too tempting *to* touch. *A couple more minutes*, he told himself. Max.

Sinking his hands into her waist, he lifted her up so her knees came down on either side of his thighs. It gave him access to all of her. Perhaps not so smart.

Moving his lips to the smooth column of her throat, he satisfied a burning need to taste more of that silky smooth skin with lazy openmouthed kisses that revealed she tasted that good all over. *Christe mou.* Lust coiled low in his gut at the sweet, honeyed flavor of her. It made him wonder if she'd taste like that between her thighs…like some kind of forbidden ambrosia he'd never get to sample…but desperately wanted to.

He traced the pulse that raced at the base of her throat with his tongue, absorbing her indrawn breath.

"Aristos." His name on her lips sounded so sexy with the perfect roll of the *r*, all the blood in his body fled south.

"You are so perfect," he murmured, dipping lower to the hollow between her breasts. The plunging neckline of the robe gave him easy access to the beginning of those beautiful round curves. Succumbing to temptation, he slid his fingers beneath the silk, rasping his thumbs across the twin hard peaks. Alex gasped and arched into his touch, her breathy moan kicking him low in the gut.

He wanted to look at her, to wrap his mouth around her, to lavish his attention on her naked flesh. Instead he brought his lips back to hers in a kiss that flouted sanity, searched for it even as Alex buried her fingers in his hair, urging him on. Unable to resist those sexy moans, he rolled her nipples between his fingers, teased the aroused peaks even tauter, her answering groan heating his blood.

This is madness. Somewhere deep inside his brain the thought registered, finally clicked with unerring precision. Lifting his mouth from hers, he pulled the silk lapels of her robe together and set her away from him on the sofa. Alex stared at him, a stricken look on her face.

"*Soon* is over," he bit out. "*Soon* was a bad idea."

"Aristos—"

He got to his feet. Hardened his heart against the vulnerability that cloaked her like a second skin. "The storm has passed. Get some sleep."

Turning on his heel, he left before his common sense deserted him completely, his rules in tatters.

CHAPTER SIX

IT WAS NO USE.

Alex set her laptop on the table, swiped up her espresso and sat back in the plush lounge chair, drinking in the idyllic view of an endless blue horizon from her private terrace. Perhaps more caffeine might kick-start her brain into working order, because all it could focus on right now was *the kiss*. Well, not just the kiss. The way Aristos had taken intimate possession of her body *after* the kiss.

She closed her eyes as the memory singed her skin. How utterly and completely lost she'd been…how it had felt as if she were playing with fire but she hadn't cared… the knowledgeable rasp of his thumbs across the peaks of her breasts igniting a need she hadn't known existed…

Her blood pumped through her veins at the memory, warming her cheeks. In the cold light of day she recognized her actions as foolish, inspired by the loneliness enveloping her the night before, by the need to know if that kiss the night of the ball had really been *that* good, that that kind of passion existed off the pages of a book. And perhaps, most of all, because uncovering the Aristos who was so much more than the ruthless casino scion he was made out to be had proved undeniably fascinating. Lethally compelling.

She wondered at the strength of character he must have displayed to get where he was today. Wondered what could have happened in his family to drive him onto the streets. She wanted to feel special because he'd confided something to her he'd never confided to anyone else, but she knew that would be taking her foolishness to a whole other level.

She was sure the Aegean Sea was littered with the emotional corpses of countless women who had crashed and burned in their attempts to get to the bottom of Aristos. Who'd thought *they* would be the one. She would not be one of them. Not when he was the same kind of philanderer as the one who had broken her mother's heart. Stolen her dreams. Left her pining for a love that would never be hers.

That he was fast becoming an anchor for her, that Aristos Nicolades, notorious playboy and ruthless take-no-prisoners force of the business world, was serving as a fountain of wisdom on this new road she was traveling, seemed a rather bizarre development. But last night she'd seen he was far more than the image he presented to the world. She had a feeling it had been only the tip of the iceberg. So perhaps not so crazy after all...

Still, even if all that were true, even if she wanted to know that kind of passion for real in this new, more-daring version of herself, Aristos was the last man she should do it with. The way he'd dumped her on the sofa and left last night should be more than enough incentive to convince her of that. It had been vastly...*humiliating*.

She took another long draw on the espresso, attempting to drown her mortification in the dark eye-opening brew. She would be far better off doing what Aristos had suggested, working on her future, taking back control of her life in constructive ways, than fixating on a kiss.

She spent a couple of hours doing just that, looking at literacy organizations that not only appeared as if they were doing good work but also might benefit from her support as a spokeswoman. She jotted down the names of a couple of charities that looked interesting, then put her research aside for her more pressing task.

Typing in *Dimitri Smirnov* and *wife*, she searched

everything she could find on the oligarch's significant other, Galina Smirnov, a glamorous London-based socialite. The oligarch himself seemed to be of questionable reputation, some of his interests on the shadier side, it seemed. It made her wonder why Aristos did business with him, but that wasn't her mission here.

Working her way through the articles, she unearthed a profile from a glossy magazine. It was rife with information. Skimming her way through the stories of the Smirnovs' legendary soirees, weekend residences and politically notable connections, she found a paragraph about the hostess's not-to-be-missed London dinner parties.

Galina Smirnov entertains with a glamour that harkens back to a golden age, when the jazz greats dominated and the making of a superior cocktail was an art. Cocktail hour at the Smirnovs' is sacrosanct, vodka-based, of course, Galina's collection of the jazz masters incomparable, enjoyed by the guests on an antique gramophone.

Jazz music. Her lips curved. This she could work with. Her mother just so happened to be old friends with the retired jazz legend Nina Karvelas, who had once come to Stygos to sing for their guests at the hotel's grand reopening.

Could she convince Nina to come out of retirement to sing on Larikos as a birthday present for Galina Smirnov? Perhaps the singer would do it if a donation were made to one of the charities she'd spent her retirement working with.

Exhilaration flooding through her, Alex threw on shorts and a T-shirt and went in search of Aristos at his office. His PA, Carin, told her he was booked solid until nine that evening with conference calls. Cooling her heels with difficulty, she headed to the beach, read a classic, took a surfing lesson from the water sports instructor, Diego, then ate dinner by herself. Still no Aristos.

She rose the next day only to be told by Carin that Aristos was in Athens for meetings. *Diavole.* Was he avoiding her because of that kiss? Was he going to avoid her forever?

Humiliation dogging her footsteps, she buried her head in another book to fill the day. By the time dinner rolled around, the thought of consuming another meal by herself didn't appeal. She wasn't even hungry. It felt as though all she'd done was sit around and eat.

She went for a hike up into the cliffs instead, the early-evening air still hot and humid. Sitting on a rock at the top, she took her time enjoying the view, then walked back along the beach toward the Great House.

Passing the tiny little cove off the main resort, a slice of heaven with its pristine white sand crescent bounded by the walls of the cliffs, she was irresistibly tempted. What she wouldn't do for a swim right now, her body grimy and sweaty from the hike. But Diego was off for the evening, Aristos nowhere in sight, the helicopter pad empty. She couldn't even *swim* by herself.

Frustration coursed through her, tightening her fists by her sides. She was a prisoner…a damn prisoner on this island. In this fortress Aristos called paradise. She was an excellent swimmer, there was no risk.

Heat pushed through her, egging her on. She glanced around the deserted little cove. There was no one to see her…

Mouth set, she stripped off her T-shirt and shorts to the bathing suit she had underneath, waded into the heavenly water and sighed. It was perfect.

Aristos landed on Larikos just before nine, the resort sparkling with light against a sky full of stars. Retrieving his briefcase, he thanked the pilot, jumped to the ground and propelled his weary body toward the Great House.

It had been quite the day. Still no word from Dimitri, and a score of meetings with suppliers in Athens persuading them to hang tight, that the ground-breaking for the casino would not be delayed long.

His thoughts turned to Alex as he climbed the stairs toward his suite. He had been ignoring her ever since that kiss, hoping the cloud of vulnerability that surrounded her would fade along with his instinct to comfort her and spill pieces of his past while he was at it.

Kissing her was one thing, a mistake he never should have made, but revealing so much of himself had been worse. If he pretended his past had never happened, refused to acknowledge it, it held no power over him; others couldn't use it as a weapon against his undeniable success. Telling the story to Alex, however, had established it as fact. Brought it into his present. And even though he trusted her and knew it would go no further, it still felt like a chink in his armor.

He climbed the final set of stairs, mouth flattening. The problem was, now he felt guilty. Alex must be lonely. Perhaps she hadn't eaten? Perhaps they could have dinner together? Dinner was safe.

He dropped his things off in his room and knocked on her door. When there was no response, he knocked again. No answer. Turning the knob, he pushed the door open and called her name. Nothing. *Strange.* The dining room had looked empty on his way up.

He went downstairs and found Yolande. "Do you know where Alex is?"

"I haven't seen her since this morning. I thought she might be having a rest."

"She's not in her room. Could she be using the spa?"

His manager made a call. Frowned as she hung up. "She's not there."

Then where the hell is she? An uneasy feeling slid across his skin. Alex had mentioned the cliffs the other night, how she'd thought the view would be amazing. He'd told her the rocks could be treacherous, unstable; it was a hundred-foot drop to the water below; better to do it together sometime.

His unease intensified. Had she gone and done it anyway? Even if she had, it was a short hike; it wouldn't take hours.

"Go ask the staff," he told his manager curtly. "Find out who saw her last."

When Yolande reported back to say no one had seen Alex in hours, a web of apprehension snaked its way around him. His brain flipped to the Carnelians, a thought he immediately dismissed. The island's perimeter was unbreachable. But it remained in the back of his mind, eating away at him, as he called his head of security and ordered a search of the island.

The cliffs worrying him the most, he jumped into a Jeep and headed toward them, his progress hampered by the darkness and the rutted track. Had she fallen? Hurt herself? There were venomous snakes up there…scorpions that could incapacitate a person in seconds.

His brain spun in a million directions. If anything had happened to her…she was his responsibility…under his care.

He hit the gas and the Jeep jumped ahead. This was why he hadn't wanted her here. Why he never wanted to be responsible for anyone. Because every time he had been he'd failed, too caught up in himself to be there when the person he was responsible for needed him.

He had exhausted every possible scenario in his head, his insides in knots as he neared the cliffs, when his pilot called him. He had located Alex. Swimming. In the cove below the cliffs.

What he had strictly forbidden her to do.

He slammed on the brakes, a red mist descending over his vision. She would not have done that. She would *not*.

He sent his pilot home, pulled his security team in, turned the Jeep around and headed back along the track. By the time he reached the path to the cove he was beyond furious; he was apoplectic.

Pulling the vehicle to a screeching halt, he jumped out and headed down the path toward the beach. There, lying on her back, floating in the water, was Alex, illuminated by the light of the moon.

A choked sound alerted Alex to the fact that she was not alone. Flipping onto her front, she trod water, eyes widening when she saw Aristos in a designer suit standing on the shore. Her heart hammered in her chest as he headed toward the water. Surely he wasn't going to… *Thee mou.* Her hand flew to her mouth as he stalked into the sea, a lethally dangerous expression on his face.

She was in so much trouble.

Her tongue, cleaved to the roof of her mouth, could manage only a helpless "Aristos—"

He pushed through the water, sank his fingers into her waist, picked her up, slung her over his shoulder and headed for shore. She gasped, fingers grasping his jacket. "What are you *doing*? Put me down… You're ruining your suit."

He stalked up onto the shore and set her on her feet.

"While you were enjoying your swim, which I expressly forbade you to do, my search team, the entire island, has been looking for you."

"The entire island? Why?"

"You didn't show up for dinner. No one's seen you in

hours. You didn't deign to tell anyone where you were going."

Her heart sank. "I was on my way back. I was just going to be a few minutes more. It's—" she waved her arm around them "—it's so nice here. I told you I'm an excellent swimmer. Isn't this a bit of an overreaction?"

He stepped closer, his powerful body a wall of heat that bled into her skin, sending her heart racing in her chest. "You forget, you are a target, Princess. You are under *my* care. How do you think I'm going to react when you disappear? Do a whistling little stroll around the island calling your name like my dog's gone missing?" He raked his gaze over her face. "There are poisonous creatures on this island. A hundred-foot drop from that cliff. I was worried you'd fallen, were lying somewhere in need of help."

A tight band wrapped itself around her chest. She pressed her palms to her cheeks. "*Lypamai.* I'm sorry… I wasn't thinking right. I was so bored, I didn't—I didn't think to tell anyone."

"*Bored?*" His breath rasped across her cheek, the intimidating bulk of him pushing her heart rate from fast to furious. "I'll tell you who isn't bored. My pilot, who was finally settling down to dinner… My security team, who've already had a full day's work… Yolande, who is frantic about you."

Tears burned the backs of her eyes. "I said I was sorry. I'm just trying to explain."

"Why?" he demanded. "Why would you disobey my direct request not to swim?"

"I was…frustrated."

"About what?"

"About being here. I have nothing to do. You won't let me help."

His lip curled, wisps of pure fury coiling in his gaze. "You know what you need to do, Princess? *Grow up.* Stop whining about being here and thank your lucky stars people care enough about you to want you safe. Some don't have that luxury."

She flinched. Knew he was right, but the humiliation blanketing her lifted her chin. "What about you, Aristos? How grown-up are you being? We share one kiss and you go running for the hills."

"I was *working*, not running for the hills."

"And you couldn't spare five minutes to say hello?" She shook her head. "What are you afraid of? That I won't be able to keep my hands off you? That in my naive, vulnerable state of being, I can't resist you? Because I promise you, I know that kiss was a bad idea."

A smoky, sultry edge laced his furious expression. "Quite the opposite, Princess. I am afraid *I* won't have the discipline to walk away the next time you throw yourself at me. My next move after that kiss would have been to carry you to my bed, remove your clothes and explore every inch of your beautiful body with my hands and mouth to see if you tasted as sweet in all the places I'd fantasized about. And then where would we be?"

Thee mou. Heat uncoiled under her skin, a soft, sinuous unfurling of something molten that scalded her insides. Swallowing hard, she lifted her chin. Halted the insanity. "I know the kiss can't happen again. I would have told you that if you hadn't been avoiding me. As for tonight, I am truly, *truly* sorry for the mess I've caused. It was thoughtless of me."

"Hurricane Aleksandra," he murmured silkily, watching her with a hooded look. "Blows in and sweeps everything up with it."

Her lashes lowered. A shiver moved through her as the breeze swept over her wet skin. Aristos stripped off his jacket and draped it around her shoulders, the brush of his fingertips against her collarbones sending electric shocks of awareness through her. She clasped the lapels together, refusing to show how much he affected her.

"I did," she ventured carefully, "have something I wanted to discuss with you."

He lifted a brow.

"I did some research on Galina Smirnov."

The dark look reappeared on his face. "*No*, Alex."

"Hear me out. I read a profile piece on her. She's a big fan of jazz music."

"And this is relevant why?"

"My mother is old friends with Nina Karvelas."

"*The* Nina Karvelas?"

"Yes. She did a concert once for us at the hotel. She's retired now, but I was thinking she's heavily into her charitable causes. What if you threw a birthday bash for Galina? Nina sings, you donate a sum of money to her charity, everyone wins. It's an experience money can't buy. Exactly what might entice Galina to Larikos…"

His brows came together. "How do we even know Galina is that much of a fan of jazz? People say all sorts of things in profiles to look interesting."

"She has one of the most complete collections in the world. The interviewer was wowed by it."

He rubbed a palm against the stubble on his cheek. "We don't have parties, Alex. It's a poker game."

"So you have an opening night reception before you start playing. This is *Nina Karvelas*. If we could get her to say yes, it would be the coup to end all coups. How could Galina not come?"

"If her existing birthday plans can't be changed."

"So you find out. I could ask my mother to ask Nina in the meantime."

He pursed his lips. Stuck his hands into his pockets.

"Have you heard from Dimitri?"

"No." He gave her a long look. "I need to think about it. And you need to get some clothes on."

They walked back to the Jeep and drove back to the Great House. She changed when they got there, had dinner with Aristos, throughout which she kept her mouth shut, a low profile…until he walked her to her bedroom door that was, when she couldn't resist speaking up.

"What you told me the night before last," she said, looking up at him as he rested a palm against the frame of the door, "about your past…about that strength of character you needed to survive, *that's* what I took away from our conversation. Not the mistakes, not the dark parts, but the courage, the strength you must have had inside you to not only walk away from a life you knew was wrong, but to cross an ocean, to leave everything you knew behind to be something different." She shook her head. "*That* I think is amazing."

His gaze darkened. "So good at building fairy tales, Princess. You're a natural."

There he went again, deflecting praise, admiration. Anything that might be construed as good about him. Refusing to acknowledge who he was beneath the layers, because heaven forbid, someone might get close to him.

She was getting the impression Aristos didn't know how to be intimate in anything but the physical sense. He didn't believe in love, treated his relationships like transactions and preserved that protective shell around himself at all costs because he had been built that way, because whatever had happened in his early years to drive him onto the streets had scarred him badly. Impaired his emotional IQ.

"All right," he said, still striking that same indolent pose, palm against the door. "You win, because frankly, I need the carrot to dangle in front of Dimitri. Call your mother and see if Nina could make an appearance here. But don't make any promises."

A surge of satisfaction flooded through her. *Finally something to sink her teeth into.* Now she only hoped Nina would say yes.

Aristos's gaze narrowed. "This game is a well-oiled machine, Alex. It runs itself. You're making one phone call, that's all."

"Yes." She nodded her head vigorously.

"As for tonight," he said softly, straightening away from the door, "you've signed your warrant. You have now earned yourself a babysitter in the truest sense of the word."

A wary skitter went up her spine. "What does that mean?"

"It means you and I are going to be joined at the hip, angel. I intend on returning you to Nik in one piece."

She pressed her lips together. "That isn't necessary. I've learned my lesson. I won't take a step out of line."

"No, you won't, because I will be there to make sure you don't."

"Aristos…"

He sauntered off down the hall toward his room. "Start thinking of creative strategies to keep ourselves in line, Princess. I'm already off and running."

CHAPTER SEVEN

ALEX MADE THE call to her mother the following morning on a still, quiet Akathinian day in which the Carnelian military exercises continued on the waters bounding the two nations, the only sign anything was amiss. Having assured herself her mother was okay, she explained the situation Aristos faced and how Nina could help.

I owe Nina a call, her mother had said. *I'll see what I can do.*

Setting down the phone, Alex crossed everything. Her impulsive and admittedly recalcitrant behavior last night had had far-reaching consequences. If she could pull this off and Nina said yes, if the Smirnovs took the bait and came to Larikos, she could make amends for her thoughtlessness by planning this party for Aristos. Channel her frustration into something constructive.

True to his word, Aristos was on her like glue. He had lunch with her, dropped by her surfing lesson in the afternoon and joined her for dinner that evening. When he didn't have an eye on her, he had one of his dangerous-looking guards keep vigil. It was all getting a bit old by the next morning when her mother called to tell her Nina had said yes—the singer would consider doing the appearance on Larikos in exchange for the proposed donation to the charity of her choice.

She almost jumped out of her chair with glee, particularly when Nina's charity turned out to be a program that encouraged kids to learn to read through the power of song.

As the singer talked her through it in their follow-up call, Alex's excitement grew. It was exactly the type of work she wanted to get involved in with her love of reading, she'd told Nina. Something she could really make a difference with.

She practically flew over the beach to Aristos's office, one of his professional shadows hot on her heel.

"You've made your point," she said, stopping in front of his desk. "You can call the dogs off now."

"I don't think so," he drawled, sitting back in his chair, gaze lingering on the sweep of her legs in the shorts she wore. "I like having you on a leash, Princess. It gives me great peace of mind."

"Call them off," she said firmly, "or I will phone my mother back and tell her Nina's services aren't required. She said yes, by the way."

A slow smile curved his mouth. "Nicely done."

"I have been negotiating contracts for the hotel for years," she said crisply. "Do we have a deal?"

"Yes. But if you ever wander off like that again, there will be consequences, angel." He crossed his arms over his chest, that lethal gaze resting on her. "Don't let my imagination run wild."

Her lashes lowered, heat shimmering through her. She couldn't help but imagine what those consequences would be. She *should* be ignoring him. Instead she couldn't stop thinking about that fantasy he'd painted of her in his bed, kissing, *tasting* her all over...

"Still working on those creative strategies?" Aristos's taunting gibe brought her gaze up to his. "Looks like it's still a work in progress."

Diavole. She folded her arms. "How are yours coming? You seemed quite interested in my legs when I walked in."

He lifted a shoulder. "I'm a leg man, Alex. I'd have to be dead not to look at yours. Besides, I have strategies."

"Like what?"

"I drew up a list of dinner topics. Wait until you sit down—you won't believe how dry it's going to be. The weather, the spectacular meteor shower that's coming and the fascinating scientific phenomena behind it, what a charitable board member does in all its intricate, excruciating detail so you have your expectations set…" He waved a hand at her. "All guaranteed to have us dying for a good book."

All guaranteed to ensure they didn't have to engage in the intimate type of conversation he clearly preferred to avoid.

"How studious of you," she said. "*My* strategy is to get Galina to bite so I can plan this event and have something to do."

"*If* I let you plan the event."

"Oh, didn't I mention that?" She put her fingers to her mouth. "That's part of the deal."

He gave her a long look. Summoned her into a chair to go through the details. She sat, crossing her legs to give him maximum view, enjoying the power that surged through her when he took advantage of the opportunity to study the scenery with unabashed fascination.

"The exciting thing," she said, "is that Nina's new charity is about engaging youth in education through the power of song. She said we can talk when she comes, and if it seems like a good fit, we could work together."

He tore his gaze away from her legs. "A match made in heaven. That's good news. A happy princess might actually allow things to return to normal around here."

She made a face at him. "Do you want to hear the details? Nina has some requests."

"Go ahead." She went through the list of conditions the jazz singer had detailed. When Aristos approved them all, she left him to call Dimitri.

It was midafternoon, her surfing lesson about to begin, when he found her on the beach, a triumphant glitter in his eyes. "He said yes."

Her heart swelled, a buzz of excitement zigzagging through her. "Will you let me plan the party?"

"Yes." His gaze narrowed. "You own those two hours before the game. Work with Carin on the logistics. She'll have my security team do background checks on Galina's guests. But not another foot out of the box, Princess. You and this game are not mixing."

She gave him a salute. "Aye, aye, captain."

"Also, you are not supposed to be here. You will simply be Alex that weekend. Understood?"

She nodded.

He waved her off to join Diego. She turned and headed toward her instructor, a huge smile on her face.

"Alex?"

She swung around.

"Thank you."

A warm feeling spread through her. "Don't thank me yet. I still have a party to throw."

Alex took her mandate and ran with it. With the party only two and a half weeks away, there was a great deal to do in a short period of time. She created a menu for the party, a special bohemian decor for the bonfire setting and liaised with Nina on her requirements for the performance and her travel and with Galina on her guests and special requests for the evening.

Luckily, event planning was a skill she'd mastered at the hotel. She created a critical path of things to do and checked them off as the days slid by, working furiously to ensure that every detail of Nina's performance would be perfect, because impressing the Smirnovs was so critically important to Aristos.

Aristos continued to work day and night between his spot checks on her, his tension palpable as the poker game approached. He rose with the sun and worked late into the night, more driven than any human being she'd ever encountered.

Now she knew where that drive came from. He had known what it was like to have nothing, had built his business from the ground up, and that business was being threatened.

If the questions in her head grew ever more persistent—about the early experiences that had caused him to cut himself off emotionally from the world, what had happened to send him out onto the streets—she kept them to herself as they tiptoed around their perpetual awareness of each other.

She was finding her feet. It felt good to be contributing. Her mantra was to stay out of trouble, pull off a great party. Which meant keeping her attraction to Aristos buried deep.

CHAPTER EIGHT

HIS KEY INVESTORS locked down for the game, Aristos turned his attention to the rest of his business he'd been neglecting as he attempted to hold the Akathinian project together.

It was a daunting task. With thirty-three hotels in eleven countries, he relied on his property and country managers to handle issues in his absence and keep things afloat. Luckily, the team he'd handpicked was superior, and by the Thursday before his poker weekend, he'd caught up to a point where things were once again running like a well-oiled machine. His creative strategies for avoiding his attraction to his princess, however, could use some work.

With both of them on their best behavior and Alex immersed in the party planning, he would have thought the undercurrent between them would have faded. Instead it had grown stronger.

If he'd found her undeniably attractive before, Alex in her element, brimming with confidence, was even sexier. It was impossible not to respond to the vibrant, enthusiastic flip side to her vulnerability as she chatted about how the party was coming along at dinner and the ideas she had. It was like watching her potential surface, and it did something funny to his insides.

She was smart, creative and perceptive, her glass-half-full approach to life a fascinating, compelling foil for his jaded view of the world. Which subsequently rendered his list of strategies, his attempts at dry, safe dinner conversation, wholly ineffective. He, a creature who thrived on self-inflicted solitary confinement, looked *forward* to her company at dinner every night.

A buzz sounded from his desk. His gaze flicked to his mobile. *David.*

"Just checking to see if you're still alive," his mentor said drily. "You've gone deep underground."

Which in the past had not always been a good sign. When his darkness caught up with him… He got up to roam to the window, the moon a thin new slice in a dark sky. "Been busy pinning down investors for the game."

"Got everyone you need?"

"Now I have. Dimitri was being elusive."

There was a pause on the other end of the line. "You sure you trust him? I can try to line something else up here."

"I've got it," he said, his tone clipped. He wasn't about to let his mentor, a man who owned half of Las Vegas, rush to his rescue. Especially when David had made it clear he thought he'd pushed it too far this time.

"I appreciate the offer," he added in a more conciliatory tone. "But I'm good. I am looking forward to seeing you, though. Going to ditch those amateur bets you were making last year?"

"Going to get over the need to prove yourself? You've done it a hundred times over, Aristos."

And there it was, David's usual slice of advice delivered in a succinct left hook. He picked up the stress ball sitting on the windowsill and crushed it between his fingers. "Maybe when Akathinia's done."

Maybe when he felt he had the respect due to him that had never quite seemed to come. When his critics finally stopped finding reasons, trumped-up flaws in his visions, to leave him waiting in the wings while his competitors graced the covers of glossy magazines.

David bantered on for a few minutes, then signed off to go to bed. Aristos put the phone down, rested his palms on the sill and looked out at the perfection of a clear Larikos night.

The sense of accomplishment the rush of the week had provided faded in the silence of the darkened room, a bone weariness settling over him. *When are you going to get over trying to prove yourself?*

He was tired of fighting, he acknowledged. Exhausted from attempting to one-up the competition to get to the pinnacle—to be the name on everyone's lips in a fickle entertainment industry that changed on a dime. He thought maybe Akathinia had to be it. *The one.* Wasn't sure how much he had left in him.

He stared out at the clear, bright sky, littered with a sea of stars. What weighed on his mind, ate away at him when he allowed himself time to think, was what he would find when that day came—when he'd exorcised his demons, what he'd find underneath. He suspected it would be an empty shell—that he'd traded his soul for success.

It was why being in perpetual motion was the only way he knew how to operate. Pushing away from the window, he was about to return to his desk to finish up the report he'd been working on when a flash of white caught his eye, picked up by the floodlights on the beach. Alex, who'd stopped working hours ago with most of the details for the party wrapped, stopped under a palm tree, reached into her beach bag and pulled out a blanket. Shaking it out on the sand, she sat down, her eyes on the sky.

The meteor shower was tonight. He'd totally forgotten. In actual fact, despite his sarcasm, he found them fascinating and stunningly beautiful.

Like the woman who sat waiting for the show.

He should finish the report. Instead he found himself shutting off the lights and heading for the beach, his footsteps measured and purposeful. Just like that night in the palace gardens, it was clear to him he should be walking in the opposite direction from the one he was. But he was afraid he'd think too much in his own head, so he walked toward temptation instead.

He'd been resisting her for two weeks. Surely he had this down by now?

Alex looked up as he approached. "There are still front-row seats available."

"You remembered." His gaze touched her tanned, shapely thighs revealed by the modest hem of the shorts she wore, the kind of curves that stopped a man in the street. He didn't need to see more to know they were the perfect toned framework for the fantasies he'd had. Fantasies that involved him ordering her to wrap them around him as he demonstrated what steady-as-they-go Sebastien had clearly not had in his repertoire.

Hot, hard and memorable.

Color darkened her cheekbones. "Your scintillating, well-versed recap of the sight to be seen wouldn't allow me to stay away. I will, however, point out those types of looks are not within our rules."

"True," he agreed, settling himself down beside her on the blanket. "I, however, am in a bit of a mood. You want careful, Princess, you should send me on my way."

She stayed where she was, still as a statue. His excellent peripheral vision caught the big inhale that lifted her chest before she pulled her knees up to it and wrapped her arms around them.

"I thought you'd solved your biggest problem with Dimitri."

He settled himself back on his elbows. "I'm not getting a good vibe from him. I still have to convince him not to bolt."

"What happens if he does?"

"It leaves me one hundred million dollars short of financing. Not to mention the precedent that could set for other investors."

"That must be worrisome. But like you yourself said, you can only control what's within your power."

His mouth twisted. "A little difficult to tell yourself that when you have a half a billion dollars riding on a casino. But I'll give it my best shot, Princess."

She gave him a long look. Sat back on her elbows, mirroring his pose. "It should start soon. It said nine thirty on the web."

A silence fell between them. He studied the push and pull of the sea as it ate up the sand, inching its way forward in a steady, ancient rhythm. *Inescapable, unrelenting.*

Alex was right. He had shored up every weak link within his power. Dimitri was a wild card who played outside the usual rules—he'd known that from the start.

"It's so quiet here," she said after a while.

His gaze flicked to her. "Your village must be quiet. How many people live there?"

"A couple hundred, many of them my mother's family. And yes," she said, a wry note to her voice, "it's sleepy, caught in a past generation. Important announcements are still posted on the *platias* in the village, the fish truck still delivers the catch of the day and the farmers bring the milk to our door."

"How quaint."

"I like it. It's the best way to start my day. Sam, the farmer's son, and I always have the most interesting conversations."

He smiled. He'd bet it was the highlight of Sam's day, too.

"On Sundays we work a half day, let our weekend manager handle things. We have a big dinner with family, family being a loose term that usually encompasses everyone— neighbors, anyone who's around from the neighboring village. It's a big gossip fest, a chance to catch up. Someone handles the grill, someone's playing music, there are kids, dogs everywhere…all a little maniacal. When it's over, my head is usually buzzing so much I'll escape to my favorite little cove to read, center myself, before the week starts."

"It sounds wonderful." A hollow feeling invaded him. His cynical wasteland of an existence couldn't be more different from the reality Alex had lived, from the warmth and community she had been surrounded with. It would be like setting Alice in Wonderland down in the middle of Dante's Inferno…or perhaps Purgatory, he conceded, although he wasn't sure he'd rid himself of all his vices before he'd climbed out.

A throb unfurled low in his gut, wrapping itself around him and squeezing hard. It had never bothered him before, the emptiness of his existence, the connections he'd severed, the absence of affection he'd grown up with. But tonight it did.

A bitter regret assailed him, a sorrow that lingered just beyond the edges—for what he hadn't had, for the things he'd craved so deeply he'd had to let them go before they destroyed him. Guilt. Guilt for what he'd done. Guilt for what he *hadn't* done. Guilt for all of it.

He pinned his gaze on the sea. Fought against the emotion that seemed ever so close to the surface. Alex sat quietly beside him, giving him space in that intuitive way of hers she had. In that way she had of *knowing* him.

If he was pretty sure he'd forgotten how to connect with people—if he'd ever understood the concept—he'd never had that problem with this woman. Their connection had been real from that first night at the ball. Powerful. It had prompted him to reveal parts of himself he'd sworn he never would. If that wasn't enough to make him run, he wasn't sure what would.

Alex absorbed the turbulence of the man sitting beside her. He was clearly working through something in this dark mood he'd announced upon sitting down, as if he wanted to be here and didn't all at the same time.

"You were right," she said quietly, when she'd decided his brooding had gone on long enough. "What you said in the gardens at the palace. I told myself it was enough, my life in Stygos, and it *was* wonderful, I am blessed to have had it. But it was too safe. I needed to leave to find out who I am. I needed to step outside my comfort zone."

His mouth curved. "You've done that, all right. Still feel like it's the right decision?"

"Yes." She pressed her palms to her cheeks, marveling at everything that had happened since that night. "Identifying where I want to put my energy, planning this party, I feel like myself again, only better. Because I know I have all these amazing experiences out there waiting for me."

He blinked, his dark lashes shading his cheeks. "You will be a force to be reckoned with. I have no doubt about it, Princess."

Something unfolded inside her, a warmth, a yearning that was shocking in its intensity. Pressing her lips together, she lowered her gaze, attempting to wrestle her feelings under control. Her eyes slid over the dark purple tattoo half hidden by the sleeve of his T-shirt. Reaching up, she traced it with her fingertips. "What's this? I've seen some of the guards with it."

He pushed his T-shirt higher. "It's a man-of-war. It's the marking my gang members and I carried."

"You brought some of them with you here to Larikos?"

He nodded. "I knew I needed the best in protection for the clientele we would host. Knew I could trust them. Their allegiance is unquestionable, as is their ability to keep a man alive."

A shiver went through her. She traced the intricate detailing of the beautiful design. Done in varying shades of purple and black, it perfectly represented the dangerous creature that had inhabited the seas she'd grown up in, an animal she'd been warned away from as a child. Fascinating, but to be avoided if you knew what was good for you. Like Aristos himself.

She absorbed the corded, impressive muscle beneath her fingertips. It was intoxicating to touch him, to give herself permission to explore his beautiful body for a purely innocent reason. Except she wasn't sure it was so innocent, touching him, not when she lifted her gaze to his and found a banked heat there that made her insides simmer.

She let her fingers fall away from his skin. "What is the significance of the man-of-war?"

"They are deceptively beautiful. Deadly in numbers."

Her lashes arced over her cheeks. "Were you? Deadly?"

He eyed her. "What are you asking me, Princess? If I've ever killed a man?"

"Yes."

"No. My organization, the Men of War as we were known, thought of ourselves as revolutionaries. We were soldiers, taking from the haves to give to the have-nots, reclaiming what society had taken from us. There was a sense of justice to it. It was mostly petty thievery, some armed robberies. There were a few instances where things got out of hand, yes, people got hurt, but those were the hard-core personalities, not the majority."

She stared at him, fascinated. "What was the background of the members? What led them into it?"

"Poverty, violence at home, single-parent families in which the mother was left to cope. The gang provided the bonds we didn't have at home, leadership figures, brother figures…"

"And you?" she asked quietly, her heart in her throat. "What kind of a home did you come from?"

"A broken one. A poor one. My father was a mechanic,

an alcoholic, chronically unfaithful to my mother, often out of work. They fought constantly."

"Was that what drove you out of the house?"

"Partially. I got older, stronger. My father and I would go head-to-head. It was either that or let my rage get the better of me."

"How did they react, your parents, about you joining a gang?"

"My father was furious. He gave me an ultimatum— quit, get back in school or stay away."

"So you chose to stay away?"

"Yes."

"How old were you?"

"Fourteen."

Her chest tightened. *So young. Cast out of his home for reasons that should never have been in the first place.*

"What about your mother? Your brothers and sisters? It must have been difficult to leave them behind."

A silence followed, so long, so pronounced, it made her fear she'd crossed the line, gone too far in her need to know. His reply when it came was low, tight. "My anger was tearing me up. I was afraid of what would happen if I stayed, afraid of what would happen if I left."

The band around her chest tightened. "An impossible decision," she said softly.

"Yes."

"Do you know how they're doing, your family?"

"My mother kicked my father out the year after I joined the gang. She'd had enough. When I sold my first hotel, I went home and bought her a house, made sure she never had to work again. Beyond that, we've had very little contact with each other."

And therein lay the key to so much about this man. Alienated from the family he'd loved, damned if he did, damned if he didn't, he'd cut himself off from feeling, from *allowing* himself to feel because, she suspected, it hurt too much.

She bit the inside of her mouth. "Family is everything, Aristos. Family is the thing you have when everything else is gone. I know you said those ties have been severed, but surely nothing is irreparable?"

"This is."

"But—"

"Angel." The warning in his voice was clear, the glitter in his dark eyes sending a shiver down her spine. "I know you love where you come from. I know you like to idealize that paradise on earth you think it is, but not everyone gets to have that. Sometimes you get hell on earth instead. Sometimes wishing for things you'll never have is too expensive a proposition to keep."

She digested that stunning proclamation, her heart thudding painfully in her chest. She knew the feeling well. She'd spent her life wishing for a father who loved her, only to be served up with reality instead. But Aristos was talking about his *life*. About the love and care he'd never had, not until David Tennyson had picked him up off the street at sixteen, perhaps too late to ever heal the wounds inside him.

If she'd been living her life on the pages of a book, Aristos had been living his in a bitter existence no one should ever have to experience. Making choices no one should ever have to make.

Her head was still spinning when Aristos pointed at the sky. "There's one."

She looked up, watching a bright ball shoot horizontally across the inky black sky, a trail of light flaring behind it. Not far behind was another, then another, until the heavens were a stunning display of bursts, streams and flutters of light.

Spellbound, she drank it in. On and on it went in a symphony of color. When a particularly jaw-dropping explosion scorched the sky, she reached for Aristos's arm to point it out to him, but her hand landed on his thigh instead.

Tight, hard muscle coiled beneath her palm; his heat bleeding into her. An electrical current vibrated from where she touched him up through her arm to encompass her entire body. It tore her gaze from the sky and planted it solidly on that of the man beside her. If her heart hadn't been firmly secured in her chest, it would surely have jumped right out of it at the look on his face.

Jaw set, expression predatory, the fire in his eyes made the blood pound in her veins.

The world could have exploded around her in that moment and it wouldn't have stopped her from drifting toward him, toward the imminent collision she knew would be as explosive as the ones happening in the sky above. Eyes darkening with an emotion she couldn't read, Aristos pressed a palm to her chest, stopping her before she got there.

"*No*, angel."

Her brain didn't immediately compute. She stared at him, confused. He dropped his hands to her waist and rose, lifting her along with him and setting her down on her feet in the sand. Retrieving the blanket, he shook it out, threw it over his arm and propelled her toward the Great House, a hand at the small of her back.

Up the stairs they went, the silence surrounding them deafening. Humiliation heated her cheeks, dragged her every step. When they reached the door to her bedroom, she turned to look at him, leaning back against the frame. "Aristos—"

"Alex." He cut her off with a clipped voice. "That would not have been wise, and you know it."

She brought her back teeth together, corralling her emotions. "You're right," she bit out. "There I go again, throwing myself at you. My deepest apologies…"

Turning, she reached for the door handle. Aristos's fingers clamped around her biceps and spun her to face him. "Alex—"

"Forget it," she snapped furiously. "Let me go."

He backed her up against the wall instead, his palms flattening on either side of her. "Princess," he murmured huskily, pressing his forehead against hers, "I am not rejecting you, I am choosing *sanity*."

Wasn't it the same thing? She sucked in air, attempting to find some of that particular attribute because he was right. Perfectly right. This shouldn't be happening. Except wrong, because she didn't give a flip about sanity. She wanted *this*.

A second passed, two, three maybe, their heat spilling into each other. His mouth was a fraction from hers, so close she was breathing his air. His hard thighs, pressed against hers, broadcasted his arousal.

The oath he uttered then as he levered himself back to stare at her made her stomach clench. "I don't know what I'm doing with you anymore," he rasped, his gaze raking hers. "And tonight is not the night to figure it out. Trust me."

Cool air drifted over her as he stepped back, turned and walked down the hall to his room. Pulse racing, blood pounding in her ears, she watched him go, waiting for her knees to assure her they would function before she pivoted, reached for the doorknob and let herself in the room.

Would her mistakes with that man never end?

CHAPTER NINE

A PICTURE-PERFECT LARIKOS night had presented itself for Galina Smirnov's birthday party, at which the jazz legend Nina Karvelas would sing in public for the first time in over five years.

A blood-orange sky streaked with fingers of yellow marked the occasion, drawing a dressed and ready-to-go Alex out onto the terrace to drink it in as the day sank slowly into night as only a Mediterranean evening could, with its intoxicating blend of vivid colors that stoked the senses.

A flock of butterflies traced a looping path through her stomach. She'd double-, triple-checked that every detail was in place, and still she felt nervous. She wanted it to be perfect for Aristos. Perfect for Nina, with whom she'd met earlier in the day to discuss her charity, another reason for the overabundance of adrenaline running through her veins. It seemed a perfect fit. If Nik approved the choice, she would be off and running.

The butterflies in her stomach intensified. Now if only the tension between her and Aristos could be resolved. He hadn't spoken to her since he'd left her at her door two days before with that cryptic line.

I don't know what I'm doing with you anymore.

What did that even mean? He was conflicted, to be sure. About her, about his feelings for her. He was charged with protecting her, yes, but she suspected his walking away had more to do with how much he'd revealed to her...

the intimate conversation they'd shared…the connection between them neither could seem to control.

What he'd shared with her on the beach that night had been heartbreaking, had followed her around ever since. Had changed *everything*. She could no longer label him a heartless philanderer. Instead she had discovered a complex, wounded man behind those walls he liked to build, a man who'd never been given the tools to connect or love.

She felt empathy for him, yes, but also something far more dangerous: the belief that whatever was happening between them was real, different. That *she* was different to him.

What she'd felt that night when he'd stood there outside her door fighting his emotions hadn't changed. She wanted to be with him, to know that kind of passion. Of all the jumps she'd taken, this might be the biggest, most dangerous, because it involved her heart. Because if they explored what they had, Aristos might break it.

But wasn't that what her new life was all about? Taking the risks she'd always avoided?

Her watch told her it was time to make her way down to the beach. Stepping her feet into crystal-studded flip-flops, a prerequisite for the sandy white beach, she joined the staff as the first guests began to arrive.

The hiss and crackle of the roaring bonfire that licked almost six feet into the air was the star attraction, surrounded by the sultry sounds of Nina's jazz band. Sleek-looking serving staff handed out vibrantly hued cosmopolitans, Galina's favorite cocktail, to inspire a celebratory mood.

She stood surveying the scene as the beach filled up, a satisfied smile curving her lips. Not only were the Smirnovs and their guests here, but every single one of Aristos's poker players was, too, clearly anticipating the show. As long as nothing went wrong with the acoustics, which weren't a given with the tricky winds of late, the evening would be a smash success.

Her gaze shifted to Aristos, who stood speaking to the guests of honor, Dimitri Smirnov and his wife, Galina. Galina was as lovely as her superior hostess reputation had suggested; her husband, on the other hand, was another story. His reputation preceded him; first impressions hadn't improved it. He struck her as cocky, not entirely transparent and full of himself.

Aristos, meanwhile, had a very different impact on her. Elegant in a silver-gray shirt and black pants, his short-cropped dark hair pushed back from his face in a ruffled, spiky look, he oozed intensity. He reminded her of the fire dancing and crackling behind him: beautiful, imminently combustible, undeniably dangerous, a dozen layers deep, each one a darker, more complex version than the last.

Her stomach dipped, a wave of heat shimmering through her. What would it be like to have that single-minded intensity focused on you and you alone? She'd had a taste of it. It had been enough to convince her it would be worth every heart-stopping second.

He looked at her then, before she had a chance to wipe the evidence from her face. Moved that intense gaze over the sophisticated French twist she'd engineered, down over her face, where ebony eyes tangled with blue for a long, suspended moment, then over the sleek black dress that skimmed her curves, cataloging every inch, every centimeter as he went.

She sucked in a breath, heat bleeding into her skin as if he'd physically touched her. It shook her in her shoes, vibrating every inch of her skin, as if for a moment, he'd forgotten to marshal his defenses, that impressive control of his, and all she could see was the truth. The hunger.

He didn't want to want her, but he did.

He moved his gaze back to her face. Tension thickened

the air between them. Held her frozen. Then rationality, in precious little quantity of late, thankfully kicked in. She wasn't letting Mr. Hot-and-Cold take her on an emotional roller-coaster ride tonight. Not when so much was riding on the success of this party, for her and for him.

Turning her back on his stare, she made her way into the crowd.

Aristos absorbed the princess's turned back with a blink and then another, noting, of course, her amazing behind in the formfitting black dress, because she had the best one he'd ever seen.

Was that just a kiss-off look? He thought it might have been… He'd never actually had one to compare it to.

It stirred an animalistic desire to wipe it off her face even though he knew exactly why she'd directed it at him. That he deserved it. This time he *had* been running for the hills. Sharing your life story with a woman you were clearly developing feelings for did that to a man. Well, that, and he'd been completely focused on the game, on clearing the decks so he could devote his attention to his investors tonight.

It ate away at him, that look. Festered as he found himself watching Alex rather than Nina's performance, as spectacular as it was, wondering what he was doing with her. He'd walked away from her the other night because Nik had told him in no uncertain terms that she wasn't to be his—that hadn't changed. Yet every time he came within a foot of her, those good intentions flew out the window, clouded by a complex set of emotions and lust he couldn't seem to make head nor tail of.

The lust he could handle, decipher. The other feelings Alex aroused in him, not so much. That he had cared for her from the start was clear if you shone a light on his behavior. What he felt for her now was more complex.

She was getting under his skin, making him feel things, question things, *want* things he couldn't have. He couldn't turn her off like a switch as he did with his other women.

That was the heart of the issue. The source of his problem. But he thought maybe he could have handled it better.

He pulled her aside after the performance as the guests mingled. Alex gave him another of those cool looks.

"Everything okay?" he asked deliberately.

"Kala." She lifted her chin. "Everything's going perfectly. Don't you think it's perfect?"

"Perfect," he agreed. "I came over to say thank you."

"It's the least I can do." The words rolled off her tongue in swift, robotic fashion, stirring the antagonism roiling his insides. "Galina would like to watch the game," she said. "Can I watch it with her?"

"Women are distracting."

"Then why do you have the two beautiful waitresses? I saw them earlier."

"Because they're meant to distract, entertain the men. You are not."

Her mouth firmed. "I will stay in the background. Firmly in the background. Let me come."

His better judgment told him no, but this was Alex and her big blue eyes he was up against—an unfair battle.

"In the background," he underscored. "You blend in with the paint."

The high rollers' room glittered with opulence: Brazilian-wood floors shone underfoot, the marble showpiece of a bar was lined with hundreds of colorfully hued bottles and the arched, elegant glass doors that lined the wall to the terrace were magnificent, cut crystal shimmering in the muted lighting.

The air was tense, thick, the players bent in concentration over their cards. Aristos, Dimitri, the sultan she'd met earlier, a senator from New York and six other men sat around the table in the center of the room. Whiskey glasses littered the surface of the table, ties lay discarded on the backs of chairs and the aroma of cigars lingered alongside the overpowering scent of competition.

One of the beautiful blonde waitresses clad in a black dress far sexier than Alex's ushered her and Galina around the edge of the room to the bar.

"Is it always this quiet?" Alex whispered, sliding onto a stool.

"No. Tense game."

"Who's winning?"

"Kako, then the sultan, then Aristos."

Kako, the pro who had won last year… "How much is on the table?"

"Eight million."

Thee mou. She almost swallowed her tongue.

Ensuring Galina had a drink in her hand, she procured a glass of champagne from the bartender. Off duty now and able to relax, a victorious rush moved through her. Nina's performance had gone perfectly, Galina was ecstatic and Aristos had spent much of the party with the Smirnovs.

For the first time in weeks, she didn't feel helpless. Didn't feel carried along by forces far greater than herself. She had proven she could execute a charity event for VIPs and make it a success. It gave her the confidence that when she resumed her real life as a princess and her upcoming work with Nina, she could do good things in the world, that she could own the role.

It sank into her bones, that heady feeling, as she watched the game. Aristos, sleeves rolled up to his elbows, corded, muscular forearms exposed, took the round, pulling the pile of chips toward the stacks he had in front of him. Triumph glittered in his ebony eyes as he leaned back and drained his scotch.

The dealer set out the next hand. The senator stretched while he did, noticing her and Galina sitting at the bar and smiling a greeting. She returned the smile, keeping it brief. Blending with the paint, that's what she was doing.

But the sultan, who already had two wives although he'd been flirting outrageously with Alex at the party, noticed her, too. His overt stare caused a ripple effect around the table as the rest of the men turned to look.

Aristos narrowed his gaze on her. Turning on her stool, she devoted her attention to her glass of champagne and Galina.

The next round began. The sultan took it, Kako the one after that, then Aristos in a nail-biting hand that stretched the tension in the room to a breaking point.

The sultan looked most displeased. Kako gave a shake of his head, requested a break and headed out of the room. The tension broke then, the table dissolving into good-natured ribbing, one of the professional players flirting heavily with the blond-haired waitress as she served him a drink. The sultan remained silent, pouty, if a man could be described as that, sitting back in his chair, arms crossed over his chest.

"Maybe," he announced, setting his gaze on Alex, "we should up the ante for the next round."

Galina sucked in a breath. Alex sat up straight. Aristos followed the sultan's gaze to her, eyes narrowing. "What are you proposing?"

"Her," said the sultan, nodding at Alex. "Winner of the next round."

Her stomach fell to the floor. A silence filled the room. Aristos sat back in his chair, the expression on his face unchanged. "We don't play by those rules here. You know that."

They did somewhere else?

"Maybe we need to shake things up a bit."

"Not happening," Aristos drawled.

"Why?" The sultan gave him a belligerent look. "Is she yours?"

One of the pro players made a choked sound. The senator's eyes went round. The icy expression that passed across Aristos's face sent a chill down her spine. "Yes, as a matter of fact," he drawled, "she is."

The sultan held up his hands, a rueful twist to his lips. "Fair enough. You have to admit, Nicolades, you weren't making it very obvious."

Because she wasn't his. Because this was insane.

Aristos pushed his chair back, stood and walked over to where she sat at the bar. His spicy cologne infiltrated her senses as he barked a request to the bartender for a scotch, his eyes never leaving hers. He waited until the drink was poured, wrapped his fingers around the tumbler, clamped a hand around her upper arm and pulled her off the stool.

Her breath caught in her throat. Too intimidated to protest, she allowed him to guide her out onto the terrace while the whole table watched.

She waited until they were out of sight and earshot of the others before she pulled her arm out of his grip. "Enough of your caveman tactics, thank you."

He leaned against the railing and knocked back a gulp of scotch. Fixed his gaze on her. "I told you this was a bad idea. These men are a different breed, Alex."

As was he. It thrilled and intimidated her all at the same time.

"Did he mean it?"

"Undoubtedly."

"Did *you*?"

His eyes flashed. "Alex," he growled. "There are millions of dollars on that table. We are not doing this now."

"I know," she said, moving closer to him. "But I'd like to know the answer to the question."

"You can't be mine," he rasped, his gaze tracking her. "You want my list again? You are off-limits. I don't do relationships. My affairs are short-lived, transactional entities where everyone knows the score."

"What if I did, want that, I mean? To explore what's between us."

His gaze narrowed. "You are a princess. Third in line to the throne in case you'd forgotten…whom I'm supposed to be protecting."

"There's no threat here," she derided. "The only thing you're protecting me from is you."

"Exactly."

Her pulse gave a tremendous flutter, then took off at a full gallop. "And if I weren't…off-limits to you?"

"There's no point in discussing it, because you are."

She fixed her gaze on his. "I saw your face tonight. That night on the beach…"

"*Christos*, Alex." He raked a hand through his hair. "You've just walked right out of *Alice in Wonderland*. I am not the man for you. I don't do flowers and chocolate."

"I'm not asking for that…for a relationship. I want to explore what's between us. What that kind of passion feels like. That's all."

"That's all?" He stared at her. Set his glass down on the railing with a deliberate movement. "Are you trying to wreck my head?"

She shook hers. "I'm merely suggesting, as you yourself said, that we do what we both want."

"No."

She eyed him, frustration coursing through her. "You know what I think? I think you're all talk, Aristos. I think you throw these challenges at me, these scenarios of what it would be like between us, because you know I won't act on them. It's *safe*. And when I do, you run." She lifted her chin. "I think you're scared. I think you have no idea what will happen between us if we actually face up to this attraction."

"Oh, I know," he rasped, eyes flashing. "We would be incendiary together, angel. We would blow the doors off my bedroom, and this would turn into an even bigger mess than it already is."

"Or it would solve our problem… We could address it and put it behind us. No one would have to know."

A long moment passed. "Just so we're clear," he ventured in a silky voice, "you're suggesting we have an affair? Confined to this island?"

"Yes."

"No."

"Why?" She tugged her bottom lip between her teeth. "You said I was bored with Sebastien and you were right. You told me to define my life, to go after what I want. Here I am, going after what I want."

He uttered one of the filthiest curse words in the Greek language. She winced, absorbing his fury. Taking her by the hand, he marched her back into the room, issued an "all non-players out" command directed at Galina, then propelled her out of the room past a sea of amused faces, a palm at her back.

Across the beach they went, up the stairs to the Great House and down the hall to her room. Her heart was pounding like a freight train by the time he opened her door and pushed her inside.

"You," he said, "will stay here. You will not come anywhere near the game. I will deal with you when it's done." He pinned his gaze on her face. "Understood?"

"Yes." She tucked a stray chunk of hair behind her ear. "But you could tell me—"

Thud. The door slammed behind him.

* * *

Aristos stopped drinking after that. It had only been his second scotch; he'd been pacing himself, as had all the men, except the sultan, of course, who didn't drink. But any amount of alcohol in his brain after what Alex had just done to him was too much.

He set his second-to-last hand down, a good one. Sat back in his chair as Kako grimaced.

No one would have to know. It would just be between the two of them... Theos. A synapse in his brain snapped. *You told me to define my life, to go after what I want. Here I am, going after what I want.*

He wiped a hand across his brow. He had created this monster. This was his mess to deal with. The question was, what was he going to do about it?

He allocated half his attention to the sultan's hand, the rest of it sitting firmly back in that room at the Great House with the woman he now conceded he wanted more than he'd ever wanted one in his life. The same one who had just offered herself up to him for a no-holds-barred, private affair.

She was right, he acknowledged as the sultan set down a full house, a better hand than his. What he'd been offering were excuses, excuses that had been protecting him from her. From the lust he felt for her. From whatever else he felt for her that he refused to examine. Except for the king and his casino contract, of course. That was a very real deterrent to taking what she was offering.

But if he and the princess kept this between them, no one would have to know.

Kako set down a brilliant hand. Aristos scowled and took a sip of water. Examined the last point to be considered. He was afraid he would hurt Alex. Afraid he had no idea how to play this game when his feelings were involved. When it wasn't just sex. He knew he couldn't give her what she needed in the long run, but she'd said she wasn't looking for a relationship.

Could she handle an affair, however, that ended when his interest waned? Which it would once he'd solved her mysteries. It was always that way with him: the allure of a woman fading when she was no longer an enigma to him. The thrill of the chase in its most classic format.

If he agreed to what Alex was proposing, she had to be clear on the rules. The boundaries. Truthfully, he was starting to think a controlled experiment, like allowing a fire to burn under carefully monitored circumstances, was the only way forward for them. To burn this attraction out completely.

She was affecting his head. Impeding his ability to focus at the most critical time in his career. He couldn't have it.

An image of himself on his knees, his hands on Alex's delectable body, tightened his fingers around the tumbler. Those sexy moans she made when she couldn't help herself...

An impatient sigh broke through his fantasy. "I know she's hot," said Kako. "Hell, I'd be long gone by now, but could you please," he said, waving his hand at him, "take a card or pass so we can find a winner?"

Ignoring the pro's gibe, Aristos lifted his hand and requested two more cards. It wasn't enough.

The final result: Kako first, Aristos second, the sultan third.

He offered Kako his congratulations, his own mood rather surly now as he watched his millions piled in front of the pro. He intended to exact retribution for the result, in only the most pleasurable way, of course.

CHAPTER TEN

ALEX STOOD, FOREARMS resting on the terrace railing, contemplating the floodlit beach as the clock ticked past 2:00 a.m. The lap of the waves against the shore and the persistent song of the cicadas were the only sounds that filled the air, not enough to drown out the pounding in her ears.

She'd seen some of the players disperse along the beach toward their private villas, which meant Aristos would be done soon. Adrenaline coursed through her, tightening her skin, quickening her heart. Had Aristos meant tonight when the game was over they would settle this between them? Or perhaps when all the players had gone home? Since that wouldn't be until tomorrow afternoon, she thought it might actually kill her. She'd stayed dressed just in case.

A knock on her door ten minutes later had her jumping out of her skin. Waiting for it, anticipating it, she froze, all of a sudden utterly unsure of what she was doing.

It came again. Pulling herself out of her suspended state, she walked inside, crossed to the door and released the bolt. Aristos, tie slung over his shoulder, a bottle of champagne in his hand, stood leaning against the wall.

Apparently the intensity he'd been wearing hadn't ended with the game. The look he sliced over her was pure predator. It held her feet rooted to the ground, eyes fixed on his.

"You going to let me in, Princess?" His low drawl raked over her sensitized skin. "A discreet affair might not entail me standing in the hallway with a bottle of champagne in my hand."

Her heart skipped a beat. Is that what they were having?

She stepped back before it appeared she'd lost all her brain cells. Aristos straightened away from the doorway and moved inside, leaving behind a waft of that delicious spicy scent he wore.

She closed the door.

"Lock it." His evenly delivered command told her exactly how this was going to go. Made her stomach cave to the floor. She twisted the bolt shut with hands that weren't quite steady. Turned around to find him uncorking the bottle.

"Who won?"

"Kako."

"Oh." She pushed a chunk of hair out of her face. "I'm sorry about that."

"You should be." A *pop* as he worked the cork free made her jump. "I was in it up until those last couple of hands. You destroyed my concentration."

She searched his face for some sign he was joking, but there was none. Just that same intensity, clawing its way across her nerves.

"I really am sorry. I had no idea the sultan would be so…outrageous."

"I told you that game is no place for a woman."

"Do they actually bet *women* in these games? Isn't that against some sort of law?"

"There are no rules for some of these men. The sultan, Dimitri, they live in a whole other universe. It would never happen in one of my games, though, and they know it."

She shivered. "I didn't like him—Dimitri. Doesn't his background bother you? His unethical business practices? The rumors of far worse?"

"They are rumors, *paidi mou*. Exactly that. Show me a rich man who doesn't have shadows."

The casual endearment stirred the anticipation churning her insides. Her stomach lurched as he moved closer, the bottle of champagne in his hand. Close enough she could feel the heat of his big body. It moved through her, stung her with its all-enveloping warmth.

He raked his gaze over her face. "So here's the thing. I think you're right we need to tackle this problem of ours. Face up to this attraction we share. An affair would do that. But I need to know you can handle this, Alex. That you're not jumping in with this newfound confidence of yours only to realize it's been a big mistake."

She shook her head, heart battering her ribs so hard she thought it might break free. "I won't. I know what I want."

He lifted a hand and brushed the back of his knuckles over her heated cheek. "This starts and ends here. Nobody gets hurt..."

She nodded. He was protecting her with his caveats, but he was also protecting himself.

Aristos's eyes darkened, the only outward sign he had acknowledged the decision they'd just made. He took a long swig of the champagne straight from the bottle, then passed it to her. She closed her fingers around the ice-cold glass. "Not very princess-like."

"Nothing about tonight is going to be very princess-like," he murmured, snaking an arm around her waist and pulling her into all that solid heat. "Except me granting your every wish... I might be persuaded to do that as long as I have leeway to make some demands of my own."

She didn't dare even wonder what those demands would be. Had enough on her plate at the moment, quite frankly. She lifted the bottle to her mouth and took a sip of the dry, fruity vintage. It tasted intoxicating, heady. When Aristos cupped the back of her head and took her mouth in a kiss that wasted no time in getting to the point, her head spun.

His tongue dipped inside her mouth, sliding against hers in a leisurely exploration. His throaty murmur of approval skated across her cheek. "I love champagne on you. You taste so sweet, *moro mou*."

Bringing the bottle to her mouth, he fed her another swallow. Dipped his head to consume it with her. She had never experienced anything so erotic, so intimate. He fed her a few more sips in between those sweet, hot kisses until she had melted against him, completely under his spell.

He captured her bottom lip in his and bit lightly, the sharp reprimand catching her off guard. "This mouth," he growled, "does something to me... Every time I tell myself I have to stay away, I can't. You are wrecking my head, Princess."

Her stomach folded in on itself. She leaned back, drinking him in. "I love kissing you. It's almost...spiritual."

His gaze darkened. Setting the bottle down, he took the weight of her hips in his palms, dragging her closer. "Do it again," he instructed, covering her mouth with his. She did, kissing him back, exploring his beautiful mouth with teasing nibbles of her own. He tightened his hands around her hips and pulled her into him, settling her against the erection that strained his trousers. She gasped at the size of him.

"That's right, angel...your kisses do that to me."

That they did blew her mind. A light-headed feeling descended over her as Aristos buried his mouth in her throat, seeking out her pleasure points while his palms held her hips in place for the sensual, intoxicating slide of his thick length against her core.

When Sebastien had kissed her, it'd been pleasant. *These* kisses were turning her insides to molten heat. Making her forget she'd ever had nerves.

A low moan escaped her throat.

"You want more?"

"Yes."

He slid his hands down the back of her thighs and pushed her dress up. Easing his knee between her legs, his hard muscle found her throbbing core. The friction, his purposeful movements, the heat of his gaze as he watched her, sent bolts of pleasure rippling through her. The aching flesh between her thighs grew wet, supple, his to command.

"Aristos."

"You like that, angel?"

"Yes."

The helpless, raspy note to her voice sounded foreign to her. She didn't know what she wanted. Needed. She knew only that she wanted more.

He dropped to his knees. Her spinning head attempted to determine what he was doing. Closing his hands around her thighs, he nudged them apart, a look of such wicked intent on his face, her breath stopped in her throat.

"Aristos—"

He looked up at her. Read the hesitation in her face. "You've never had a man do this for you?"

"No." She hadn't had a man do anything to her beyond kissing her. But she thought the timing was all off to tell him that now.

"Consider it another of your firsts," he said huskily. "I'm pretty sure it was the thought of you, spread out for me like this, that lost me the game."

Theos. "It's too—"

"Angel," he said firmly, "trust me."

She did. Had trusted him from the beginning. She relaxed her thighs, giving way to the firm pressure of his palms. His hands pushed her dress up to her waist. The look on his face when he discovered the wispy black thong she wore made her stomach dissolve. "You kill me," he murmured. "You are so beautiful, Princess. I want to *know* you. Every part of you."

Any further qualms she might have had dissolved with those words. His thumbs slid under the sides of the thong to ease it off her hips. She stepped out of it for him, blood pounding in her ears. She closed her eyes after that as he parted her thighs wider. One hand on her hip, he slid a finger down the length of her most intimate flesh. She jerked against his touch, but he held her in place. "So aroused," he murmured, repeating the caress with a more insistent movement. "As hot for me as I am for you."

When he parted her with gentle fingers, she thought her heart might jump through her chest. His breath was a warm, heady caress against her skin, announcing his intention to touch her just before his tongue made a leisurely foray where his fingers had been. She bucked into his hold. He held her firmly, sliding his tongue over her again, finding the tight bundle of nerves at the heart of her this time. A white-hot pleasure exploded through her.

She buried her fingers in his hair as he nudged her nub with his tongue. Over her, against her, he moved, increasing his rhythm until the almost-impossible sensitivity dissolved on a hot rush of sensation.

"This is how I wanted you," he rasped, lifting his mouth from her flesh. "Completely at my mercy. Begging for the pleasure you know I can give you."

She was too far gone to respond. Her eyes flew open as Aristos slid one of his long, elegant fingers inside her.

"Easy, angel," he murmured. "I've got you. I promise."

Her hands clenched his hair as he moved his finger in and out of her in an exquisite torture that stoked the fire inside her higher. When he added another, filling her completely, she started sliding down a starry path of no return.

She moaned his name, the desperate edge to her voice shocking her. Keeping up that delicious rhythm with his fingers, he brought his tongue back to the tight nub at the heart of her. "That's it," he murmured against her flesh. "Let go, angel."

She arched her hips against his mouth. He took her apart with a deliberate flick of his tongue that pushed the white-hot pleasure to its peak. Her orgasm racked her, blinding her, her legs giving way beneath her.

He held her up as, spent, shaken, she recovered, waves of aftershocks shivering through her. When the earth had righted itself, he slid an arm under her knees and picked her up, carrying her to the bed.

Setting her down beside it, he reached for the buttons of his shirt. Rapidly, his gaze on her the whole time, he undid it and dragged it off, then reached for the button of his pants. Her heart jumped into her throat as he pushed them off his hips and stepped out of them. He was all solid, powerful muscle. Vastly intimidating. Not to mention the part of him that was fully aroused beneath his black boxers. It made her mouth go dry. Excessively dry.

She headed straight for the champagne bottle, picked it up and took a healthy swallow.

He sat down on the bed. "Nerves, angel?"

He had no idea. He really didn't.

She took another sip of the champagne.

"Bring it over," he suggested.

"No," she said, taking another drink, "I'm good."

Aristos had no problem waiting her out. He might be way past gone where Alex was concerned, but he intended to take his time with her. Play to her inexperience this time around. Later was another story…

When she eventually set the bottle down and walked back over to him, he took her in from head to toe, watching a flush work its way across her beautiful olive skin as he did. "Take the dress off, Princess."

She blinked. Chewed on her bottom lip. "I need help with the zipper."

He set his hands on her hips and turned her around. Reaching for the zipper, he slid it down to where it ended at the beginning of her delectable bottom. Snagging an arm around her waist, he pulled her against him, pressing his mouth to the delicate column of her spine. A shiver went through her. He moved his hands up to cup her breasts. She arched against him, seeking his touch.

Her responsiveness made the blood fire in his veins. "Take it off," he ordered throatily.

She lifted her hands and pushed the dress off her shoulders. It fell to her hips and caught on the curve of her bottom. Bending, she slid it past her hips to the floor, stepped out of it and kicked it to the side. When she turned around, he knew he'd never seen anything so perfect. She was petite with a Venus-like voluptuousness that was all woman.

He wondered if that was why he needed to possess her so badly. The dominant side of him. The need to protect, to claim what was his. And yet, he reminded himself, frowning past that errant thinking, she would never be his. This was a fling to put their explosive chemistry to rest.

He caught her hand in his and pulled her onto his lap. A tinge of apprehension still lingered in her blue eyes. He covered her mouth with his and kissed her until she was soft beneath his hands, played with the erect points of her nipples with his thumbs until she let out a low moan.

Depositing her on the bed, she landed in a cloud of cream-colored silk. Riffling through his pants, he found the condoms he'd stashed there. Fishing one out, he threw it on the bedside table, slid his fingers under the waistband of his boxers and pushed them off.

Alex's eyes were riveted to the proud thrust of his manhood. Ripping open the package, he slid the condom on, happy to give her a show. When he'd sheathed himself, he joined her on the bed. "This is where you get to tell me how you like it, Princess. Your choice."

Her eyes widened. "It—it doesn't matter. Just…slow, you know."

She was damn lucky he had some self-control left. *Barely.* "Maybe you don't know? Soukis was that tame?"

Her delicate throat convulsed. "I *don't* know. How I like it, I mean…"

Something twisted inside him. "No worries," he murmured, moving over her and caging her with his thighs. "I know how I want you. Underneath me. Wrapped around me, angel, so I can watch your face while I give you everything I have."

Her eyes were huge, sparkling sapphires. Bending his head, he took one of her perfect breasts in his mouth. Applied enough pressure to make her writhe beneath him. She thrust her fingers in his hair and hung on. Devoting the same attention to her other nipple, he slid his hand over her flat stomach, dipped into her warmth and found her wet and ready for him.

His control on shaky ground, he nudged her thighs apart. Guiding one of her legs around his waist, he lifted her bottom with his palm and slid his throbbing flesh against her slick opening. Alex closed her eyes, her fingers catching hold of the silk beneath her. Slowly, deliberately, he caressed her. Waited for the signal she was ready.

"Aristos." His name left her lips on a sigh. Sinking his fingers into the soft flesh of her bottom, he eased himself into her tight, hot body. She was small, petite here, too. He gritted his teeth and took it slowly, allowing her body to soften around his before he continued. The leg Alex had wrapped around his waist tightened, urged him closer. He sank deeper inside her, her snug body heaven and torture all at the same time.

"Okay, angel?"

She nodded, the hazy pleasure in her eyes inflaming his senses. Gripping her buttocks, he surged forward, filling her with all of him. Flinched at the resistance he encountered. His brain struggled to compute. Had it been physical? Mental? The shock spreading across her face, the different tightening of her body around his, the sudden easing now that she'd accommodated him, made it seem as if—

He froze. Surveyed the tension on her face.

"Alex," he said in a dangerously quiet voice, making those blue eyes flutter open. "Tell me you aren't what I think you are."

She bit her lip. He cursed.

Her fingers closed around his forearm. "I wanted it to be you. I made this choice, Aristos."

"And you didn't think to tell me?"

"I should have." She tightened her leg around him, holding him to her. "It's done now. *Parakalo*—I want this. I want *you*."

She was right. The damage was done. It was all his stunned brain could process.

"Please," she said again. "This is what I want."

It was the vulnerability, the hot desire in her gaze that did him in. The knowledge that if he was going to hell, which he surely was now, he was going to enjoy himself while he was doing it. He was going to make her first time the best experience it could be.

Palming her buttock, he began stroking inside her. Her natural eroticism, her passionate response as she lifted her hips to meet his thrusts, stoked the flame inside him back to life. Deepening his strokes, he brought his mouth down on hers and drank from her sweetness. Swallowed her low moans of pleasure.

"You like me inside you? How does it feel to have all of me?"

"Good. *So good.*" She dug her fingernails into his back. "Don't stop. Please don't stop."

There was no way he could now. There was no resistance left in him as he drove himself into her soft, willing body. *Spiritual*, she'd called it. He thought it particularly apt as he buried his mouth in her throat and tasted her racing pulse. Kissing Alex had been one thing. Possessing her another thing entirely. He had the feeling nothing else would satisfy him after this. That she would be imprinted on his brain, ruining him for anything less than what she was.

The tension in his body built to unsustainable levels. Lifting his mouth from hers, he filled his palms with her hips, angling her so he could find that pleasure point deep inside her that could give her an even more intense release than before. He saw it in her eyes, the way the blue turned deep indigo, that she felt it, too.

"Right there," he murmured huskily, stroking that spot again and again with deep, hard thrusts. "Feel me right there."

She started to tremble beneath him. He closed his mouth over hers as she came apart, her moan of pleasure raking through him, completing him in a way he'd never experienced before. It spurred his own violent release. Uttering a hoarse cry, he drove into her sweetness, slaking the lust that had been consuming him for weeks.

A thick silence filled the room as they lay spent, catching their breath. Shifting his weight off Alex, he went into the bathroom and cleaned himself up. When he returned, she was sitting up on the bed, her dark hair in wild disarray, blue eyes wary. "Are you angry?"

"Yes." He raked a hand through his hair. "You should have told me. *Diavole*, Alex, I just took your virginity."

"So?"

"So how does that happen in this day and age? You are twenty-five."

She lifted a shoulder. "I told you. There wasn't much of a chance to meet anyone in Stygos. Sebastien was my only serious boyfriend."

"And he never got you into bed?"

"That's why he asked me to marry him. Because I wouldn't."

She might have been worth it. He shook off that rather insane thought. "So you blithely decided to toss it all away tonight? Just for the hell of it?"

"You know it wasn't like that."

He didn't know anything anymore. Not one damn thing.

"Aristos," she said quietly. "This changes nothing. I'm an adult. I made a decision."

"A decision you didn't consult me about. A decision that has repercussions."

She frowned. "What repercussions?"

He didn't know that, either. Biting out a curse, he gathered his clothes from the floor and threw them on. Alex watched him from the bed, a frozen look on her face. But this time, *this* time, he wasn't going there. He needed to go find his common sense instead.

"Get some sleep. I have guests to see off tomorrow."

"Aristos—"

He left without looking at her. Before temptation led him astray yet again.

CHAPTER ELEVEN

ALEX WOKE WITH a pounding headache, sunshine from another glorious Larikos day streaming in through blinds she'd forgotten to draw. But it wasn't just her head that hurt. She was sore in places that made her cheeks heat.

Burrowing her aching head in the pillow, images from the evening before came at her fast and hard. Her night with Aristos had been hot, tender and passionate, had surpassed any expectations she'd had. Reading about that type of passion on a page and experiencing such heart-stopping intimacy were two entirely different things.

She felt different, changed, more of a woman in every way, as if the universe had opened up yet another facet of itself for her to explore. She didn't regret for one second giving her virginity to Aristos, but apparently he did.

Her head gave another vicious throb. Cradling it in her palm, she closed her eyes. The way he'd vacated her room with the speed of a hotel guest short of funds took the edge off her glow. Killed it dead. Spoiled what should have been perfect.

So she'd been a virgin. What was the big deal? It hadn't seemed to throw off what had surely been an extremely sensual encounter. Or maybe it had? Maybe it had turned Aristos off completely. Maybe she'd disappointed him with her inexperience. Maybe he'd just done a good job of hiding it.

Perhaps it hadn't been as spiritual as she'd felt it to be at all.

Ugh. Opening her eyes, she maneuvered herself into a sitting position. She wasn't going to be *that* girl. Not when she'd promised herself no regrets.

Untangling herself from the silk sheets, she padded to the bathroom, rooted through her toiletry bag and unearthed some aspirin. Downing them with a swig of water, she told herself Aristos's running had more to do with him being Aristos. Because he was a commitment-phobe and she had been a virgin. A deadly creature.

She dressed and went for breakfast on the main terrace, thinking perhaps it would help her head, but when the man in question strode into the dining room with Dimitri Smirnov, offered her a curt nod, then ignored her completely, her stomach shriveled up into a ball unsuitable for the consumption of food.

She gave up and left. Her head finally cleared in the cool breeze of the beach and a swim in the heavenly water. She would not backslide. She had vowed to approach her life with less fear. Taking risks sometimes meant making the wrong call. Getting hurt. And Aristos had always been a wild card.

Aristos's last guest left on a Cessna just after three. Only David remained beside him, waiting for his helicopter to take him to Athens, then Las Vegas.

"So how was Dimitri?"

"Hedging. He still wouldn't give me a straight answer at breakfast. Says he needs to look at his portfolio."

"The offer's still open. I can work my channels..."

Aristos shook his head. "He'll come around."

David raked a hand through his thick graying hair. "You'll pull this one out of the fire, Aristos. I've no doubt about it."

A faint smile touched his mouth. "It will be my biggest

magic act to date. Maintaining funding for an illusionary casino that may never be built."

"It will." David sank his hands into his pockets. "I like her, Aristos."

"Who?"

"You know who I'm talking about." His mentor shook his head. "I worry sometimes you think you don't deserve happiness. That you consider it unattainable to you."

"Maybe it is."

"And maybe you're just afraid to reach for it."

Maybe it wasn't worth it. He'd watched his family fall apart under the weight of the burdens it carried—financially, emotionally—his mother turning into a shadow of her former self when life had worn away at the very edges of her. Had watched the rosy glow slip from his life as a so-called revolutionary when it became clear the term was only used to perpetuate the violence, the control, those in charge had sought to exercise over them all as foot soldiers.

Happiness, those myths the storytellers liked to weave, they had always turned out to be lies for him. *How could you want what you didn't even believe existed?*

Returning to his office after David left, their conversation continued to dominate his head. *Content* was a state of being he could get on board with. Money went a long way toward providing that. Except he didn't seem to even have that state of mind in his possession anymore. Being around Alex reflected back at him the image of a man he wasn't sure he wanted to be any longer, a problem when you thought maybe that was all you had in you.

He'd thrown most, but not all, of his dark past at her and she hadn't blinked. Didn't seem to think any less of him for it. He wondered what she'd think if she knew the truth. How he'd walked away from the people who'd needed him most, not once, but twice. How being the man who always put himself first made him a selfish creature who wasn't about to change his spots.

He put his feet up on his desk and closed his eyes as he waited for Carin to put his call through. Allowed himself to consider the implications of last night after spending all day avoiding them. Alex had claimed her virginity changed nothing between them, that it had been her decision to make and she'd wanted her first time to be with him.

He could convince himself she had been right, it was that simple, that the damage was done and the only way was forward. The question was what *was* the way forward? Either he shut this down, likely the path he should take, or he made the conscious choice to do exactly what Alex had proposed—see where this thing between them went in a time-limited, short-term affair.

Expelling a breath, he hit the intercom and asked for an espresso to go with his call. His brain didn't seem to be in working order, because the only thing that did seem to be computing about this whole mess he'd predicted so accurately was that, in his lust, he'd recklessly claimed something that hadn't been his to own—the innocence of a royal. There would be consequences; he just didn't know what they were yet.

Alex was debating whether to go down to dinner alone or have it in her room when Aristos showed up at her door. Propped up against the jamb, all earthly male in khaki shorts and another of those T-shirts that showed off his muscles, it was all she could do to look completely unaffected.

"Everyone gone?"

He nodded. "Up for dinner?"

She eyed him. "Are you still angry with me?"

His mouth curved. "My feelings toward you are a whole lot of things, but anger isn't one of them."

"You walked out last night…"

"Because I needed to think."

Right. Where was that anger that had fueled her all day? The aloofness she so desperately needed? She looked down at the sundress she wore. "I'm not dressed for dinner."

His gaze slid over her. "You could wear a garbage bag and still look utterly edible, Princess. Grab your shoes. Sneakers, actually. We're going sailing."

"Sailing?"

"Thought you might like to see the sunset from the water. Chef made us dinner."

Her disobedient pulse fluttered. A sunset cruise would be intimate… But perhaps exactly what they needed at the moment to resolve last night. Slipping on sneakers and sunglasses, she walked with him to the beach. His gaze rested on her as they walked along the sand toward the dinghy waiting for them. "You look pale."

"Headache. It's going now."

"The champagne?"

"I didn't drink enough for that." Fire filled her cheeks. He'd consumed *her* before that had gone very far.

For once he made no smart comeback. Guided her instead to the motorized dinghy that took them out to the forty-five-foot sailboat waiting for them.

Once they were on the water, she found herself immersed in the rush of the wind. While anything but an accomplished sailor, she knew which sail was which and made a decent team member for Aristos, who *was* an extremely competent sailor, athletic and commanding as he guided them in a loop of the surrounding islands.

When they finally dropped anchor in a perfect little cove, the sun beginning to sink into the horizon in yet another of those spectacular blood-orange sunsets, another set of muscles she hadn't used in a while was making itself known. Wincing, she sank to the deck.

"Sore?" Aristos asked.

"Yes. And thirsty."

He unearthed a cooler from below deck, handed her a bottle and took a beer for himself. She eyed the vodka-based cranberry drink with amusement. "A girl drink for me?"

He moved his gaze over her in one of those totally inappropriate looks that made her breath catch in her throat. "Yes," he drawled, "definitely a girl."

Pinpricks of heat unfurled beneath her skin. She took a sip of the surprisingly tasty drink to cover her fluster. When Aristos stripped off his T-shirt to enjoy the dying rays of the sun, she followed suit. As far as bikinis went, hers was modest, far from attention-seeking. Aristos, on the other hand, sprawled out beside her, beer in hand, was the definition of the term in dark blue swim trunks, his long, bronzed limbs all tight, corded muscle. A couple of days' worth of stubble lining his cheeks and jaw added to his dangerous appeal.

"We should talk about last night."

She pulled in a breath. "Yes."

"First of all," he said, training that deadly dark gaze on her, "I wanted to say that you were amazing last night. Last night was amazing."

Her stomach clenched. "I thought what happened might have ruined it for you."

"It caught me off guard. I did not expect it."

"I was going to tell you but it didn't seem like the right time once we—"

"—consumed each other," he offered drily.

"Yes."

"Are you worried you disappointed me?"

She nodded.

"No chance of that, angel. It was off the charts."

A warmth engulfed her, radiating through her chest. "So why walk out?"

A long moment passed. "I'm insanely attracted to you," he said finally. "I care about you, Alex. I think that's clear. But anything beyond that, I can't offer. My longest relationship was three months—shorter than many of my contract negotiations."

Her jaw tightened. "To use your words, we've been through this. I've already told you I'm not looking for a relationship. I have a whole new life ahead of me I need to focus on. And second, as I said last night, me being a virgin doesn't change anything about our agreement. I was waiting for the right time. The right experience."

"Yes, but it creates…expectations."

"What expectations?"

"You gave me something special, Alex."

"Frightening, you mean."

"That's not what I said."

"It's what you meant. If you'd left my room any faster, you would have been running."

He sighed. "I'm not frightened. I'm concerned I'm going to hurt you. Relationships are messy, complicated entanglements I prefer to avoid."

"And now that we've reinforced the fact that I'm *not* looking for a relationship, where does that leave us?"

His dark gaze glittered. "I think that's up to you, Princess. As long as you're clear on who and what I am."

The antagonism that had been simmering just below the surface roared back to life. "I think that would be a difficult thing for me to swear allegiance to when you hide yourself behind your walls, Aristos. When you run at the first sign of intimacy. I wonder if *you* know who you are."

The glitter in his eyes intensified. "Oh, I know who I am, angel. An unashamedly, unapologetically solitary man.

Overtly ambitious and perhaps a bit spiritually corrupt. There is no redemption for me."

She blinked. Took a sip of her drink. "Actually," she said, "I think you forgot an inspirational success story for those who've walked your path, a person who gives back to others in need, a man who has a big heart he refuses to acknowledge."

A cynical twist curved his mouth. "I should make you my PR person. You'd have me on the most admired CEO list in no time, something even my own PR team can't seem to do."

She shook her head as he deflected again. "Nice try, Aristos. But I have your number now."

"Do you?" He downed a long swallow of beer, swiped his palm across his mouth, set the bottle aside and leaned back on his elbows. "Give it to me. I'm fascinated to hear what you think."

She took a deep breath. "I think David Tennyson might have picked you up off that street in Athens and helped build you a new life, an immensely successful life, but somewhere along the way, likely far before that, you closed yourself off from the broken relationships and promises that defined your life. You told yourself that love and relationships weren't to be trusted, were messy, complicated entanglements. To you they only meant hurt.

"You deflect people with sarcasm," she continued, "when they try to get close. You carry on your 'transactional' relationships because they are of no threat to you. You are a lone wolf, and you like to keep it that way."

She held his gaze. Found it full of an emotion she couldn't read. "How am I doing?"

Deadly accurate. Aristos waved a hand at her. "Keep going. I'll give my analysis at the end."

"Last night you ran because of the connection we share

as much as from taking my virginity. Because you've let me in and you don't like it. Because it breaks all your rules."

She sat back on her elbows and took a sip of her drink, apparently finished with her excellent summation of him. Her rosy cheeks, the nervous half glance she threw him, suggested she worried she might have gone too far. He thought that if it had been any other person on the planet, it might have been. But not her.

"Very perceptive," he drawled. "I like the lone-wolf analogy. But don't be fooled by our connection, Princess. It will only take you so far."

"I don't doubt it. But since we are only having an affair, if you've decided that's still going to happen between us, it's irrelevant, isn't it?"

He eyed her. Took another swig of his beer. "I feel like I've created a monster."

She gave him a self-satisfied smile. "Take the plunge, Aristos. Make the call."

Every muscle in his body coiled at the challenge. He was not unaware that indulging in what was in front of him meant taking his fledgling ability to be intimate with another person to the next level, but he couldn't have stopped himself if he'd tried.

"Get over here," he murmured.

Her lashes lowered. "I don't take orders from you."

"Yes, you do. Now get over here."

A flare of excitement lit those beautiful blue eyes. Setting her drink down, she pressed her palms to the deck and shimmied toward him. He snagged an arm around her waist and lifted her atop him so her legs were wrapped around him. His gaze rested on her quivering full lower lip, lust tightening his insides.

"I'm feeling a bit spiritually bankrupt," he drawled, lifting his gaze to hers. "You'd better send in the reinforcements."

Her mouth curved. "I thought you were a lone wolf."

"Don't you ever hear them howl at night?"

Her breathtakingly beautiful smile blinded him as he bent his head and took her mouth in a hot, searing kiss. Her hands clasped his jaw, anchored herself as he devoured her with a hunger he'd kept in check last night. She was with him all the way, arching into his hands when he stripped off her bikini top, moaning when he rolled her nipples between his fingers.

Then it wasn't enough, not nearly enough, because he needed to own her as much as she owned him in that moment as he pushed himself into uncharted territory.

Sliding his palm down her flat, quivering stomach, he moved his fingers beneath the waistband of her bikini bottoms and cupped the warmth at the heart of her.

Her breathing fractured, those long, silky dark lashes lifting to reveal a brilliant blue. "Aristos," she whispered, "we can't— We're—"

"—in the middle of the Aegean."

"Yes, but—"

He squeezed her soft flesh. Stroked her silky skin. A stifled gasp filled his ear.

"Like that, angel?"

"Y-yes."

His thumb found her core, rocking against her in a gentle rhythm that had her moving against his hand. Eyes closed, mouth parted, cheeks flushed, she was the hottest thing he'd ever seen, turning him hard as a stone.

She must have known he was watching her. Her lashes fluttered open, gaze meeting the heat in his. He increased the pressure of his thumb, moving in tight, deliberate circles now, his eyes seducing her as surely as his fingers.

A frown of concentration crossed her brow, her nails digging into his biceps as her orgasm built. Slipping his fingers inside her, he stroked her to the edge. *"Ei sai poly omora,"* he whispered, cupping her nape and bringing his mouth down on hers as he increased the rhythm of his fingers. *You're beautiful.*

A fractured moan left her lips, her hips pushing against his hand. Sinking his fingers deeper inside her, he whispered, "Come for me, angel."

Closing her eyes, she melted into him. Rocked harder until she came apart on a low cry he swallowed with a conqueror's satisfaction.

Fumbling in his pocket, he found a condom. He set her away from him long enough to roll it on, then lifted her with one arm and brought her down on him, his fingers pushing aside the thin strip of her bikini bottoms and guiding his shaft to her slick, hot flesh.

Her eyes widened, nails biting into his flesh as he penetrated her snug channel.

"Aristos. You're so big... I—"

"Slow," he muttered thickly. "We take it slow, *glykeia mou.*"

She closed her eyes. Trusted him with her body. Gradually, her body accepted his, melted around him until he was buried deep inside her. She opened her eyes then, an expression of wonder in those blue orbs that rocked him to his core.

Slowly, gently, he gripped her hips, moving her up and down on him, claiming her with every gasp-inducing thrust of his body. His eyes on hers, he reached between them and rubbed his thumb over the pleasure point at the center of her. Stroked her into another release.

When she came in a shudder, he claimed his own pleasure. A few quick thrusts was all it took, her pulsing, tight flesh shaking his body in a violent release that stole his breath.

She is mine. This time there was no going back.

CHAPTER TWELVE

ARISTOS TRACED THE perfect sloping line of Alex's voluptuous hip with a light touch designed to deify rather than wake. He'd had her in his bed for three days and still he couldn't get enough of her. It was like going to the well to drink and discovering you had a never-ending thirst that was impossible to slake. Like discovering something that might finally make you feel whole if you consumed enough of it.

In spite of that thought, or perhaps because of it, he eased himself away from her and slid his legs over the side of the bed. He was going to pin Dimitri Smirnov down to a meeting today. Spinning his wheels, wondering if the Russian was going to pull out on him, was killing his head, destroying his productivity. It needed to be settled. Cast in stone.

Showering and dressing, he left temptation alone, grabbed a croissant from the kitchen and made his way to his office. Carin greeted him, handed him a stack of messages and got up to get his espresso. Wandering into his office, he made for his PC.

Carin backtracked and came to the door. "Were you just whistling?"

"Whistling?" He frowned. "I don't whistle."

"That's what I thought." She gave him a look. "You *were* whistling."

"First time for everything. Anything urgent in this?" He waved the stack of messages at her.

"June. She said she sent you an urgent email."

Since his PR person bothered him only when something was truly important, he went right to his email, immediately thinking there'd been a crisis at one of his hotels. The last one had been a couple of rare birds who'd taken up residence in the facing of his London property. Threatened with eviction, the entire bird-loving population of London had revolted, placard-carrying activists and all. The birds had stayed.

He clicked open June's email, bracing himself for a political nightmare. It was a nightmare, all right, but not a political one. The photo June had sent made his head buzz. It was of him and Alex from that night on the boat, an intimate photo of them, Alex half naked, her legs wrapped around him.

His heart sank further as he read the caption from the European entertainment website it had been posted to.

Princess Aleksandra busy canoodling with billionaire Aristos Nicolades in the Aegean while Akathinia sits in wait.

Canoodling? Who used that word?

Thee mou. The enormity of the disaster sank through him as he sat back in his chair and wiped a palm across his brow. How had this happened? Paparazzi couldn't access the island. It was impossible. It had to have been a staff member.

His vision went red. "Carin."

She came in with his espresso. Took in his expression. "I take it the whistling is over?"

"Get Yolande in here *now*. And Rolf." His head of security.

His PA departed. He took a deep, fortifying sip of the coffee to kick-start his brain. The damage was done, but he could inflict pain on whoever had done this. And he *would* find them.

He was picking up the phone to call June in New York when his cell phone buzzed. Glancing at the screen, he replaced the receiver. *Nikandros.* He contemplated the buzzing phone, a tight feeling in his chest. He could ignore it, gather a game plan, then talk to the king. Or he could pick it up and get it over with.

He picked it up. "Nik."

"You have sixty seconds to explain why I shouldn't fly there right now and kill you."

"I care about her, Nik."

"*Try again, Nicolades.* You've never cared about a woman in your life."

"I care about her."

Silence.

He rubbed a hand to his temple. "You were the one who insisted she come here. *I* didn't want her here."

"And it was too much of a stretch to keep your hands off her? Off *one woman*, Aristos."

"Why?" Aristos wanted to hear Nik say it. That he wasn't good enough for Aleksandra. That he was below her.

"You know why. You are the most notorious womanizer on the face of the planet."

He digested that. Wondered for the first time if that was the core of Nik's issue with him, rather than his bloodline.

He closed his eyes. "It's done, Nik. But I intend to make it right."

"How?"

"We'll marry, of course."

Another long silence. *Had he just said that?* The *M*-word?

"I haven't given you my permission."

Ah, there it was. He raked a hand through his hair. "You know it's the right answer."

Another silence. "Get your PR team in contact with

mine. Put a lid on this. Meanwhile, Alex stays on Larikos. The press can't get to her there, and I need to focus on Idas. The rumor is he's had a stroke."

His heart lifted for the first time since he'd seen that damning photo. "Substantiated?"

"We're working on it."

He prayed it was true. Crown Prince Kostas of Carnelia was a known proponent of peace and democracy. It would be a godsend for the country and for his $2.5 billion investment. "Nik—"

"I need to think." The line went dead.

He pulled the phone away from his ear, a knot growing in his stomach at what he'd just done. Getting bigger by the minute. He should have ignored the call. Should have gotten his thoughts together, made a plan. Instead he'd just announced he was marrying Alex. He, who had once called marriage hell on earth, had just committed himself to that very institution.

Rising from his chair, he paced to the window, espresso in hand. Looked out at the glorious, picture-perfect vista he so often took for granted. Was too busy to even enjoy. He'd spent three of those sun-soaked, unparalleled Larikos days with Alex, working, yes, because he needed to keep things moving, but also using the opportunity to take a step back. To allow himself a breather from the obsession with business that had consumed his life.

He'd found himself more even-keeled, without his usual restless vibe, a perspective settling over him, a contentment. Perhaps those obsessions that had fueled him all these years had blinded him to other things…to the things he'd told himself he couldn't have.

He rubbed a palm over his jaw. Could he have them with Alex? Was this the solution to a problem he'd already known he'd had?

He watched the sun reflect off an impossibly blue sea.

Surprisingly, the idea of marrying Alex didn't fill him with horror. His interest in meaningless assignations had waned months before. Having a beautiful, intelligent wife by his side to fill the empty life he'd been leading held appeal, a woman for whom his desire was showing no signs of abating, who seemed to be chipping away at his cynicism with every moment he spent with her, making him feel almost human again.

And yet, he wondered, how far could he take it? Was he deluding himself he could ever be *that* man? The one who deposited his briefcase on the kitchen floor, received a kiss from his wife, went back to work the next day and did it over and over again? The man who stuck? Nik certainly seemed to be questioning it. He hadn't even given him his permission to marry Alex.

Memories, too close to the surface in recent days, bubbled their way to the surface. His last epic battle with his father before he'd left home for good...

This family is better off without you, Aristos. You have no substance, no honor. Go waste your life away with those infidels. You are one of them now.

And he had been. He would have been anything to get away from the toxic atmosphere at home. Even if it meant leaving everything he knew behind, including the brothers and sisters he'd loved. Even if it meant cutting those ties for their own safety, keeping them away from the lawless men he associated with.

But there had been more. He'd been angry, so angry at his mother for choosing his no-good father over him, for allowing him to turn him out. Bitter to the core. That was when the murkiness of the street had climbed inside and claimed his soul.

A text from June buzzed his mobile. Pulled him out of the past, the bitter taste of regret staining his mouth. He swung away from the window to answer it. Whether he deserved Alex, whether he was husband of the year material, was irrelevant. What mattered was repairing this situation before it spiraled out of control.

He'd been gone only hours and already she missed him.

Lifting her gaze from the text blurring in front of her, Alex acknowledged that disconcerting thought. She'd started a business plan for Nina as they'd begun to define their partnership, the need to plan her future a necessary distraction from her present, a grounding force she desperately needed given her current reality that involved long, hot, heady nights with Aristos and the very real fact that she was half in love with him. Possibly more.

Her risk-taking had taken her down a road she knew it wasn't wise to go, but it really wasn't the sort of road you just turned back from. Not when you thought the man in question might finally be letting his barriers down, slowly but surely. When you saw a potential there that was too bright and seductive to ignore.

With every day that passed, her decision to leave Stygos seemed more right. She still got homesick, still missed so much about its peaceful allure, but she realized now how much living she had to do. How her aversion to risk-taking had limited her experiences. And Aristos was a big part of that.

It was disconcerting how much she wanted to be the one to do the same for him. To be the one to open *his* world up—to show him what he was missing by cutting himself off from his emotions. To make him believe some people could be trusted, that *she* could be trusted.

Dangerous thinking indeed, but not enough to prevent her from putting on her shoes and making her way over to his office with the excuse that she needed a break. Peeking inside, she found him on the phone. He beckoned to her with a crooked finger. She walked in, perched herself on the windowsill and waited for him to finish barking out instructions on how to enter the airspace at Larikos.

"Who's coming?" she asked when he hung up.

"A jeweler."

"A jeweler?" She frowned. "Why?"

Aristos sat back in his chair and patted the corner of his desk. She eyed the open door. His mouth curled. "As appealing as that idea is," he drawled, "we have a situation we need to deal with."

It was then that she noticed the edge to him. The ruffled hair, the tight set of his mouth, the rapid-fire intensity to him.

She slid onto the edge of the desk, a feeling of unease whispering across her skin. "What is it?"

"The night we were on the yacht, someone took a photo of us."

She froze, graphic images of what they'd done that night filling her head. "You said no one could get anywhere near the island."

"They can't. A staff member must have taken it."

A staff member? Her stomach sank, a sick feeling engulfing her. "What kind of a photo?"

"The incriminating kind." He sat forward and clicked a button. Her brain went into lockdown. The photo on his computer screen had been taken with a long-range lens, her in Aristos's arms, legs wrapped around him, stark naked except for her bikini bottoms, head tossed back as she looked up at him. *Thee mou.* Her mouth went dry. The angle of the photo had been artfully done so nothing indecent was showing, but it was the look on her face that sent heat rushing to her cheeks. She looked…love struck.

"Where?" she whispered. "Where did you get this?"

"A European gossip site. But according to my PR person the rights have been sold to a handful of other daily newspapers."

"Can you stop it?"

"We're trying, but injunctions take time."

"What are we going to do?" Her voice had risen now. "I am *naked* in that photo, Aristos. I am a *princess*. You need to do something."

"I *am* doing something." His dangerously low tone warned her to pull it back a notch. "I've done about fifteen things in the last two hours."

She pressed her knuckles to her cheek. "I'm sorry. This is a shock."

"Nikandros," he said evenly, "called first thing this morning."

The blood drained from her face. "What did he say?"

"That I had sixty seconds to give him a reason not to kill me."

Theos. She stared at him. "And how did you...explain it?"

He calmly took a sip of his coffee. "The funny thing about a photo like that. It explains itself... So I didn't so much explain it as offer a solution."

She didn't like the hard glint in his eyes. "Which was?"

"We marry."

Her mouth dropped open. "You— I— *No.* That's not a solution."

"By all means," he said, his voice dripping with sarcasm, "come up with an alternative. I'm all ears."

She swallowed hard. "We simply explain to Nik things got a little...out of hand and I'm sure he will understand."

"And do we tell that to the rest of the world, too? A short little concise press release? *After lusting after each other for weeks, Aristos and Alex took matters into their own hands and—*"

"Aristos."

"You need a better plan than that, angel. Akathinia is still under the threat of war. It does not look good."

She shook her head. "Nik will calm down. It will be fine."

"Did I mention he threatened to kill me?"

She bit her lip. "He didn't mean that. He was angry."

"Yes, Princess, very angry, which is why we are going to defuse the situation. Now. This afternoon, in fact."

"I am not marrying you. This is insanity."

"Insane but unavoidable."

She stared at his determined expression. *Diavole*, but he was serious! The phone call she had walked in on flashed through her head. "Why is the jeweler coming?"

"So you can pick the largest, most outrageously beautiful engagement ring you want."

"Oh, no," she said, rising. "We are not getting engaged."

He snared an arm around her waist and pulled her down onto his lap. "Nothing is going to defuse this situation but an engagement. Nothing is going to defuse *Nik* but an engagement. So wrap your head around it."

She stared at him, attempting to process the unreality unfolding around her. And suddenly, she understood what he wasn't saying. He did business with Nik. Nik had granted him his casino license. Nik could also take it away.

"Let me talk to him," she said. "I'm sure he will see reason."

"Alex," he said softly. "It's not just Nik. It's your reputation you have to consider now. You are not a normal citizen anymore. You are a princess. The rules aren't the same. You know it and I know it. We're both to blame for this. We need to own the consequences."

There it was—those consequences he'd been talking about. *And, oh, how right he'd been.*

"You don't want to get married. You swore you'd never do it." She poked a finger against his chest. "You'll be miserable. Why would I want to commit myself to that?"

"I've had a couple more hours to wrap my head around

this than you have," he said grimly. "I'm about ten steps ahead. Besides," he said, shifting her so her bottom fit more securely within the span of his hips, "there could be worse things than having you in my bed...*every* night."

Her chest tightened. "This is not funny."

"Believe me, I'm feeling a lot of things right now, Princess, but humor isn't one of them."

She took a deep breath. "Aristos—this is crazy. We can't do this. You don't want this."

"It doesn't matter what I want." He tucked a stray curl behind her ear. "We are good together. We knew we had a problem—now we have a solution."

She shook her head. "You're mad. It's not enough for marriage."

"Why not? I find myself...bored with my current lifestyle. It can't go on forever. We could do good things together."

Her back stiffened. "So you want me to marry you to *amuse* you?"

"Yes," he said silkily, "that and many more things."

"No." She scrambled off his lap. "There has to be another way. I need to think."

Unfortunately, thinking didn't provide solutions. Particularly after Nik's phone call that afternoon in which he was short and to the point. The family didn't need any more scandals; an engagement would be ideal. They would take an engagement photo after she'd chosen her ring today and send it out along with a press release tomorrow morning announcing her and Aristos's engagement. The strategy was to replace the scandalous coverage with the happy news of a pending royal match.

Alex didn't even think about refusing. She was too busy staring at the wall wondering how she'd gotten herself into this situation. Cringing at the disappointment that had stained her brother's tone. Another Dimitriou royal scandal—a PR nightmare for the palace.

Her stomach twisted, tying itself into a tight knot. How could she possibly have been so careless? So unthinking of her position when her mother's lesson should have served as the biggest one of them all?

Three hours later, she found herself trying on rings from one of London's most exclusive jewelers. Numbly she chose a square-cut sapphire surrounded by diamonds, requested by her soon-to-be fiancé because it reminded him of her spectacular eyes.

Aristos put it on her finger, the cold slide of metal against her overheated skin sending a shiver down her spine. It fit perfectly because, of course, Aristos always got the details right. Which meant it stayed there. Which meant they were engaged.

If it wasn't the romantic proposal she'd always dreamed of, with her suitor down on one knee, she was too dazed to much acknowledge it.

When the photographer left, she and Aristos sat down to a late dinner and a bottle of champagne that tasted flat to her frozen senses. She told herself this wasn't set in stone, that once the furor died down, an engagement could always be broken. Couldn't it? But she knew in her heart that part of her decision had stemmed from her feelings for Aristos. Because she was in love with him, and maybe they *could* make this work.

"What?" Aristos arched a brow at her when she was unusually silent during the meal.

"Nothing. Did you get Dimitri tied down?"

"Yes. He and Galina are going to come stay this weekend with us."

"*This* weekend?"

"Yes."

It was the last thing she needed, to host the Russians

when she was grappling with all of this, but she forced a smile to her lips. "That's a good sign, then."

"Who knows with him."

She told herself not to interfere, but the research she'd done on the Smirnovs had been too revealing: rumors of drug-taking in his clubs abounded, that he perhaps participated in that drug trade highly debated.

She shot him a look. "He's a bad man, Aristos. Why do you do business with him?"

"Our dealings are purely financial."

"Yes, but him being an investor reflects on you. On your business."

His jaw hardened. "Do you know how many squeaky-clean sources of money there are in the world? Very few."

"So you choose to look the other way?"

His lip curled. "Are you picking a fight, Princess? And here I thought we were celebrating."

Being railroaded into an engagement was putting her in a funny mood. She pointed her glass at him. "Why is this casino so important to you? Why, with all the other properties you have, is Akathinia such an obsession?"

His gaze narrowed. "Because it is the jewel of the Mediterranean…because the world's elite vacation there…because no one's been able to crack it before now. When it's done it will put any other hotel and casino on the planet to shame."

"And," she pointed out, "it's your roots. It will prove to those who gave up on you how far you've come. That they were wrong about you."

He smiled, but it didn't reach his eyes. "Putting words in my mouth, Alex? Maybe it's not so insightful as that. Every developer in the world would kill to build on Akathinia."

She conceded the point with a dip of her head. Pushed the piece of fish she hadn't the appetite for around her plate, her engagement ring sparkling in the muted lighting.

"You done with that?" His low drawl brought her head

up. "Because if you are, I thought we could continue the celebration in private."

The look of intent in his sinful eyes vibrated through her. She lifted her chin. "I have a headache."

His gaze sharpened. "Is that so?"

She lifted a shoulder. "A tension one from today."

He threw his napkin on the table. "Good thing, then, that I am an expert at working the knots out."

She eyed him. He held out a hand and pulled her to her feet. They stood toe to toe, taking each other's measure. "It's been a long day," he murmured. "You get a massage. Anything more than that, you can let me know. You won't ever get anything you don't want from me, Alex."

Her heart went into free fall. Feelings she couldn't suppress bubbled to the surface, enveloping her in a warmth, a hot headiness, that threw her mixed feelings into a tempest. "That would be perfect," she said softly. "My shoulders are a mess."

Aristos's suite was bathed in a muted glow when they arrived, dozens of candles burning from tapered silver holders scattered around the room's sleek, luxurious surfaces. Roses of dark pink and red tumbled from vases, filling the air with an intoxicating aroma.

Her gaze moved to Aristos's. "You did this?"

"I asked Yolande to." He nodded to the bathroom, where a rose-scented bath had been drawn. "Go take a bath first. It'll help with the knots."

She stripped off her dress and underwear and stepped into the heavenly water. It did wonders for her stiff muscles and disposition. When she climbed out and wrapped herself in the silk robe hanging on the door, Aristos was typing out a message on his phone. He nodded toward the bed. "Be right there."

She perched on the edge. He tapped out the rest of the

message and tossed the phone onto the dresser, his gaze eating her up as he closed the distance between them.

"You know what I was thinking that first night we were here," he said huskily, his fingers toying with the lapels on her robe, "when you had that blue wrap dress on…"

She shook her head, eyes glued to his.

"That I wanted to unwrap you like a present. That you are so beautiful, any man lucky enough to get his hands on you should savor the opportunity. Recognize his good luck."

A shiver went through her. He captured her left hand, blazing with his sapphire on it, and brought her fingers to his mouth. "That makes me an exceedingly lucky man tonight, angel."

The maelstrom of emotions swirling through her intensified, until she felt as if she were in the eye of the storm. "Always?" she asked quietly. "Are you always going to feel that way? Or will it fade as 'evolutionary history dictates'?"

His mouth twisted. "I'd say we're both in uncharted territory here. The truth is, we fit. I know when to give you the push you need and you—" her heart sat suspended as he searched for words "—you show me what's possible. You show me the things I want to have."

Her insides dissolved. She saw it then in his dark-as-night eyes, the infinite possibilities for them. The spectacular and never-ending kind, if she was patient enough to wait for them. Brave enough.

He reached for the sash of her robe. Tugged it open. Her breath caught in her throat as he took her in, his gaze tracing a line down to her breasts, to the vee at the apex of her thighs, down over the curve of her legs to her coral-tipped toes. It turned her insides to liquid.

"I think," she said breathlessly, "the bath worked out those knots."

His mouth curved. "The head?"

"Better."

She waited, nipples hardening, body anticipating his caresses. Still he didn't touch her.

"What do you want?" he asked quietly, eyes on hers.

She stepped closer. "You."

It was like sealing her fate, the kiss that followed. Gentle, passionate, never ending—it was all of those things. His hands moved to her shoulders, slipped the robe from her. Her fingers dispensed with the button on his shorts. When she reached inside his boxers and closed her fingers over the hard, thick length of him, he was velvet over steel.

Tentative, then gaining confidence, she explored him. Stroked him. He closed his fingers over hers, tightened her grip, showed her how he liked it. It was so erotic, heated her blood to a slow simmer to do this with him. To share this with him.

His hand at the small of her back, he pushed her toward the dresser, setting her hands on its polished surface. Her gaze met his in the mirror. "Stay there," he murmured.

The ripping sound of a condom wrapper pierced her sensual haze. It stoked her blood even hotter. He came back to her, ran his palms down her spine to cup her buttocks. His foot nudged her feet apart. She allowed herself to be put where he wanted her, the blood roaring in her ears as she watched him behind her. He sank his teeth into her shoulder in a wicked caress.

His palm cupped her between her thighs. She was ready for him, more than ready. His low rasp of approval as he parted her silky flesh sent another shiver through her.

"*Thee mou*, but you do something to me." He sank his fingers inside her. She moved into his touch, reaching for him. He pushed her hands back onto the dresser. "Leave them there."

She did. If his intent was to make her vulnerable, to

leave her wide-open to him, to demonstrate how completely he owned her, he had succeeded. Her breath left her in a gasp as he placed one hand on her buttock and brought himself to rest against her moist, willing flesh.

"Arch your back," he commanded, eyes burning into hers. She did. He slid into her with a slow penetration that set every nerve ending in her body screaming for more.

"Aristos."

"Look at me, angel. I've got you."

She anchored herself in his gaze. His hands cupped her buttocks as he stroked his way inside her. Harder, deeper, until she could feel him everywhere, touching the very heart of her. He was so big and powerful, the places he hit inside her so intensely pleasurable, she started to shake under his hands.

He leaned forward, capturing her earlobe in his teeth. Scoring it lightly. "Relax, angel."

Relax? She was ready to beg for him to touch her, to push her over the edge, but it was his body that did it instead. The power of him that made her tighten with a desperate clench, the throb of her orgasm radiating out from her center as a scream left her throat.

He gripped her hips tighter and thrust inside her, pleasure exploding in his eyes. Just when she thought it couldn't get any better—it always did.

He carried her to the bed when they'd recovered their breath. The weight of her engagement ring felt foreign as she curled up against him, her hand tucked against her cheek. Made her feel fidgety, restless.

Aristos pulled her tighter against him. "You're mine now," he said roughly. "Forget about the rest."

How could she? The shock in her mother's voice when she'd called to give her the news replayed itself in her head. Her pointed question as to whether she knew what she was doing with Aristos.

She was taking the longest of long shots. Risking it all for a man who didn't commit. Who'd sworn he wouldn't. And yet with the slide of Aristos's hand against her back, sleep consumed her.

CHAPTER THIRTEEN

"The Sassicaia or the Excelsus?" Aristos's French chef lifted a brow. "Or both…?"

Alex surveyed the two bottles of wine. You really couldn't go wrong with either with the meal they were serving Dimitri and Galina Smirnov, but she was being a perfectionist because it was so important to Aristos, and he had put her in charge.

"I think both," she said, "but let me check with Aristos."

She made her way to the casino, the afternoon shower having given way to sunshine in anticipation of their guests' arrival. She had been happy to help with the dinner given the insanity of the past few days…the field day the press was having with both the nude and official engagement photos, although that sport seemed to play second fiddle to the fun they were having predicting how long the playboy billionaire's marriage would last.

They had been making bets. Taking polls. It was enough to make her think she *had* lost her wits in agreeing to marry him.

Carin's chair was empty, her fiancé on the phone when she walked into Aristos's office, his New York lawyer's voice coming through the speakerphone.

She sat on the corner of Carin's desk and waited, not wanting to hurry him as he and the lawyer went through a contract. Aristos, efficient as always, plowed through the terms in minutes. When they were done, his lawyer asked him if he needed anything else.

"Start working on a prenup for me."

Her shoulders stiffened.

"Sure. You got a ballpark figure in mind?"

Aristos named an outrageous number that made her mouth drop open.

"That's very…generous."

"I don't intend to give it away. I'm a lucky man. Not to mention Alex will bring considerable assets to the table herself. It's an advantageous union from all angles. A politically advantageous union for Nicolades Inc."

"No doubt," agreed the lawyer.

Her stomach tightened. *A politically advantageous union?* She told herself to focus on the "lucky man" part. But did that have more to do with what she brought to the table personally or her lineage as a Constantinides?

Aristos ended the call. She stayed where she was for a good couple of minutes so it wouldn't be clear she'd overheard the conversation, then slid off the desk and made her way into his office. She didn't mention what she'd heard. Wasn't sure why not. Maybe because she thought she was being oversensitive, that just because Aristos needed Nik's casino license for his current obsession it didn't mean that's all *they* were.

But it festered as she dressed for dinner that evening in a silver-beaded cocktail dress. Aristos came up behind her in the mirror as she stood choosing her jewelry.

"I haven't seen this one yet." He rested his hands on her hips. "I like it."

The smoky, intimate tone he'd undoubtedly used on every one of the women the papers had mentioned as notable exes inspired the usual flock of butterflies in her stomach, but she held herself stiff beneath his hands. "Stella chose it."

He gave her a long look in the mirror. "Anything wrong? More outrageous press coverage?"

Too much to count. She shook her head. "You should get ready. We need to go."

He surveyed the carefully schooled expression on her face. Pulled her back into him and set his lips to her jaw. "You playing hard to get, angel? I could like that game."

She pushed against him and stepped out of his arms. "No. I still need to do my hair."

The look he scorched her with could have stripped paint from a car, but he stepped back, made his way to the wardrobe and acquired a shirt. A fine pair they were going to make, she thought, grimacing, as she gathered her hair on top of her head. Aristos the powder keg in advance of the Russian's visit, her distinctly *off*.

The Smirnovs were waiting for them on the main terrace. Dimitri, a tall, thin, elegant figure with a sharp face and eyes that missed nothing, pressed a kiss to both her cheeks.

"Congratulations on your engagement. And here I had no idea you were a princess."

"We weren't broadcasting the fact given the political situation."

"Understandable."

Alex greeted Galina more warmly while her fiancé shook his nemesis's hand. They sat down to drinks, then dinner. Galina asked about her and Aristos's wedding plans. She tried to focus on the innocuous conversation, but her attention was captured by the cat-and-mouse game going on between the two men.

Aristos was direct and to the point. Dimitri was non-committal and evasive, a game player. One who flouted the law and who could someday become a liability to her fiancé, but he wouldn't acknowledge it. Not that she was anything but polite to the Russian, if coolly so, but as the dinner wore on, her patience wore thin.

"I'm opening a new club in Moscow in October." Dimitri

directed the comment at Alex as dessert was served. "You should come."

"I'm afraid I'm not much into clubbing," she returned evenly.

Dimitri lifted a dark brow. "Oh, but this one is like no other. Lions in cages. Waitstaff suspended from the ceiling. It's something to see."

"I'm quite sure you're right."

Dimitri gave her a long look. Aristos gave her knee a squeeze.

She could have stood up and given a cheer when the meal was over. But it wasn't to end there, unfortunately. Dimitri declared himself in favor of a nightcap. The staff relieved for the night, Aristos went off to procure a bottle of brandy. When Galina got up to use the ladies' room, Alex rose to follow her. Dimitri put a hand on her arm. "Stay and keep me company."

What could she do? She suggested they move to the comfortable lounge area that overlooked the sea. That used up some time. When she sat down on the sofa, Dimitri sat beside her.

"I get the feeling you don't like me, Princess."

She widened her eyes. "Why would you think that?"

"I've asked you to call me Dimitri twice. You refuse to."

She'd never been a liar, nor was she about to start now. Crossing her legs, she lifted a shoulder. "Your business is with my fiancé."

He sat back, a hard glitter in his eyes. "I've offended you."

"Not at all."

"My reputation offends you."

"Perhaps we should choose another subject of conversation."

"I'd rather finish this one."

Oh, but he was a piece of work. There was no escaping

this. She set her gaze on his. "I don't like your business practices, Mr. Smirnov. But what I have to say is irrelevant to my fiancé's business."

He took a sip of his wine. "You think my association with Aristos will tarnish your family's reputation."

"I didn't say that."

He pressed the rim of his glass to his chin, his eyes on her. "The press like to print a lot of garbage about me, Aleksandra. Don't believe everything you read."

His smug they'll-never-catch-me look was too much for her. "Where there is smoke," she said softly, "there is usually fire, Mr. Smirnov."

Aristos returned from the cellar to find that Alex and Dimitri had moved to the lounge. Alex's stiff body language immediately had his antennae up. She excused herself not long after that, Galina at her side, happy to leave the business to the men.

Intent on solving his impasse with the Russian tonight, Aristos poured a liberal amount of brandy into their glasses. He wasted no time in getting to the point. "I need a firm commitment you're in, Dimitri."

The Russian lifted a shoulder. "I'm finding I need a faster return on investment these days. Your casino could be delayed for months. Years."

Aristos's blood pressure rose. "It won't be. Reports say Idas is ill. His son will come to the throne any day and it will be over."

"And if it isn't?"

His gaze narrowed. "Either you're in or you're out."

Dimitri sat back in the sofa, taking his tumbler with him. "I don't think your fiancée likes me."

"I'm sure you're mistaken."

"She doesn't like my business practices. She thinks

I'll be a detriment to your reputation. The royal family's reputation."

His back stiffened. "Did she say that?"

"That she doesn't like my business practices? Yes."

Alex had not said that. She would know better than to say that. Aristos's fingers tightened around the glass. "What the royal family thinks or feels is of no bearing to my business."

Dimitri inclined his head. "Still," he drawled, "I think the gestation time on this investment is going to be too long, I'm afraid. I'm out."

With those two words, the Russian put his casino on borrowed time. "I think you shoulder reconsider," he said tightly. "The prestige of this project will be like no other."

"Funny thing about that, Nicolades. It always seems that way until the next best thing comes along."

Aristos sat on the terrace by himself, putting away another glass of the brandy as he worked to control his fury... contemplated his future. He thought he had his temper under control by the time he let himself into the room where Alex was up, reading, but just looking at her made his vision go red.

She put the book down. "What happened?"

He threw his phone on the table. "He backed out."

"Why?"

"He said the gestation time of his investment was too long given the political situation in Akathinia."

"But that might change soon."

"He doesn't care."

"He won't change his mind?"

"No." He pinned his gaze on her. "Did you say you didn't like his business practices?"

A flush stained her cheeks. "He backed me into a corner, Aristos. You saw the games he was playing tonight."

"Which is why you should have said nothing." His voice rose. "Did you also tell him his business dealings with me reflected badly on the royal family?"

"No. He intimated that. I told him your business dealings were your affair."

"After you told him you didn't approve of his business practices!" He was yelling now and he didn't care. "How could you be so stupid?"

Her face lost all its color. She sat there for a moment, silent, then pushed the sheets aside, got out of bed and walked over to him. "You need to calm down. They'll hear you. I didn't say that. He did."

"After you said it at dinner the other night. Don't tell me it wasn't in your head."

"Yes, because I care about you. Because I don't think he's the type of man you should be doing business with. Because I worry about him being your downfall, not because it has anything to do with my family."

"If you cared about me, you would have said nothing." He threw his hands up. "All I asked you to do was entertain him, Alex, but you spent the night being the ice queen."

Her eyes widened. "Is that what I'm supposed to do? Keep my mouth shut? Perhaps I was not enough of a *political asset* to you tonight, then?"

He blinked. "What?"

"A political asset. Like you said to your lawyer on the phone today."

"You were eavesdropping on my conversation?"

"I came to ask about the wine."

"It was a throwaway comment." He turned and paced to the other side of the room, his head too full, too hazy with the alcohol he'd consumed to think clearly.

Alex watched him quietly. "I understand you are upset. I understand how important this night was for you. But this has been coming with Dimitri. You knew he was iffy.

So perhaps it was meant to be. You are meant to find a better fit."

Blood swirled in his head, making him feel as if it would blow off. He swung to face her, giving her a scathing look. "Oh, that's right. I'll just go round up another hundred-million-dollar investor. Give me a sec."

She bit her lip. "Do you know he employs underage girls in his clubs? Lord knows what they do beyond serving customers."

"Now you're letting your imagination go wild."

"And you're not seeing what's right in front of you. Or do you just not *want* to see it?"

"Alex," he growled. "I've never pretended to be a Boy Scout. I told you my world is full of gray areas."

"But *you* aren't." She shook her head. "You forget I know you now. You are a good man, Aristos, an honorable one. But if you don't watch it, this obsession with proving yourself *is* going to make you spiritually bankrupt."

His mouth twisted. "That happened a long time ago."

"No," she said. "It didn't. You did what you had to do to survive in the world. But now you have choices. Power. You need to decide which road to take."

Silence reigned between them. Lifting a shoulder, he went to the sideboard and poured himself a glass of water. When he turned around Alex was gathering up her things.

"What are you doing?"

"Going to my room. I think we could both do with some space."

"Running away, Princess?"

"No," she said, lifting her chin. "Walking away is your specialty. I'm calling a time-out."

CHAPTER FOURTEEN

ALEX'S TIME-OUT WITH Aristos lasted for two days. She was too angry with him for insinuating she was responsible for Dimitri's desertion to offer an olive branch, Aristos too busy working day and night to replace the Russian's investment to do so, either, apparently. Which had left them in a standoff that couldn't go on.

He had shut her out completely, rebuffed any attempt to talk as he made phone call after phone call to his contacts around the world. If she didn't break the impasse, she was worried he would build his walls back up completely before they worked this out, and she was far too invested in him for that.

She ate dinner alone for a second day, then decided enough was enough. Picking up the sandwich she'd asked the chef to make, she headed for Aristos's office. She found him standing at the window, hands braced on the sill, gaze trained on the remnants of the spectacular sunset.

She stood there for a moment, struck by what a solitary figure he cut. It clung to him like a second skin, as though he'd been wearing it so long it was his permanent finish. *The lone wolf.*

Her heart throbbed in her chest. For a while she thought she'd stripped it away, but now it was back.

She cleared her throat. "Any luck today?"

He turned to face her, his dark, fathomless gaze taking her in. "No. A couple of potential leads, but nothing substantial."

She put the sandwich on the desk. "You need to eat if you're going to function."

He didn't even glance at it. She leaned against the desk. "Are there other solutions to the loss of Dimitri? Can you scale the project back?"

An emotion she couldn't read flickered in his gaze. "I would have to withdraw the plans, make major adjustments, something I don't want to do when I've been so public about my vision for it."

His reputation would suffer. He would lose face. His big gamble to prove he had conquered the casino world a failure... "You would still be first," she pointed out. "The first to build a casino on Akathinia. Isn't that enough?"

His lashes lowered, framing the dark circles that rimmed his eyes. It would never be enough. He would constantly be chasing after the next big thing until he destroyed himself. The realization sent a chill through her.

"The industry is about vision," he said finally. "About convincing the entertainment world you have the biggest and the brightest offering. You lose that cachet and you're done."

"Or you lose everything because you need to save face. You don't need to prove yourself anymore, Aristos. You have achieved a success beyond most men's wildest imaginations. Perhaps part of a dream is better than none."

"I will find another investor," he rasped.

"Or you will destroy yourself trying."

He lifted his chin, his gaze a smoky, dark cauldron of antagonism. "Is your lecture almost done?"

"Not quite." She folded her arms across her chest. "You're still angry with me about Dimitri."

He shook his head. "You were right. He was already lost."

And he hadn't bothered to convey that to her? To apologize? A wave of antipathy washed through her. "You can be a real *jerk*, you know that?"

He lifted a shoulder. "I come as advertised."

Wow. She shook her head. "You're shutting me out."

"I'm working, not shutting you out."

"Funny, it feels as if you are. If you weren't, you would have apologized. We'd be talking, working through this together like a normal couple. Maybe I can't solve it for you, but I can be here for you."

"I told you I don't do this well."

"Oh, that's right, your convenient no-promises excuse, yours to pull out of the bag whenever you don't feel like communicating. You'd rather tune me out than be in a real relationship."

His gaze narrowed. "My company is on the brink. Cut me some slack."

"You did it before the poker game, too. This is your routine, Aristos. Your MO." She shook her head. "I want to be that person you can trust. I want to be the other half of *us*. But if you can't let me in, this is never going to work."

A dark glitter entered his eyes. "Maybe it isn't. I've been clear about who I am, Alex, and you refuse to see it. You keep pushing your sanitized Hollywood version of me."

Her chin lifted. "It's not a Hollywood version. It's you."

"It's not." He clenched his hands by his sides. "You want to know who I am? Who I really am? I'm the man who can't stick. Ever. I'm the man who walked out on his family not once, but twice, because he couldn't stick. The one whose father told him his family was better off without him. And guess what? He was right."

"No." She shook her head, heart clenching. "No, he wasn't."

"Yes." His olive skin was ashen, drained of color. "When my mother kicked my father out, my older brother, Vasili, came to me and asked me to come home, *pleaded* with me to help because he couldn't handle all the responsibility he'd been given, and what did I do? I said no. I told him my mother had already made her decision. That I was done with them."

Her heart fractured, a million tiny shards scattering in every direction, piercing her with their jagged edges. "You were hurt. You expected your parents to put you first."

"I was a piece of dirt, that's what I was. A street kid who didn't care, and I haven't much changed." He wiped a hand across his mouth. "So do yourself a favor and walk in the opposite direction."

"Aristos—" She put out a hand to touch him, but he shrugged it off.

"I have a call coming."

In other words, leave.

"Kala." She held his gaze, its bleakness chilling her. "But you're wrong. You are wrong about who you are. You're trying to give yourself adult decision-making skills when you were a child. You were acting on emotion, hurt, and the people who loved you should have known better. Done better."

Turning on her heel, she left before he broke her heart.

Aristos did the conference call with California, with little hope that lead would go anywhere. Everything he could accomplish done, every avenue exhausted, he sat back in his chair and closed his eyes. He'd slept maybe six hours over the past forty-eight, his body felt as if it had lead weights attached to it, yet still he sat there, racking his brain for alternate possibilities.

There were none. If his Los Angeles–based investor didn't bite, he was done. He would need to scale the casino back or pull the project entirely. Either way, his reputation would be in tatters, everything he'd built subject to the whims of an industry that would call you old news before the year was out.

He wanted to believe everything Alex had said, to absolve himself of the responsibilities he'd had toward his family, but the guilt went too deep. At sixteen, he'd been old enough to know what he was doing when Vasili had come to him, and still he'd made the wrong choice, a choice he knew would haunt him forever.

He rubbed his burning eyes, attempted to think past the haze consuming his brain. He knew he should go apologize to Alex, but he was afraid of what he'd say in this state of mind…afraid of saying things he'd regret.

Being around her made it impossible not to look at himself, at what he'd become, because she was the good, the lightness in this world. She made him feel better than he'd ever felt in his life, so close to that magical happiness quotient he thought it might actually be attainable. But the more he allowed his need for her to rule, the more vulnerable he became; the more out of control he felt.

She had the power to hurt him. To twist his brain into so many directions he didn't know what he wanted anymore. Who he was. And that terrified him, took him back to a place and time where that was all he'd felt, to a chaos he never wanted to experience again. Had sworn he never would.

He stumbled to bed at midnight, his head no clearer. Sure he would pass out, he lay staring at the wall instead. When he could resist no longer, he got up, went to Alex's room, scooped her into his arms and carried her back to his suite.

She looked disoriented, confused, her big blue eyes searching for his as he tucked her into his bed. He couldn't have her there without touching her. Sliding his hands over her curves, he rediscovered her, memorized her. With a low moan, Alex sank into his touch.

Exhausted and sated, he fell asleep with her in his arms.

Alex woke by herself after a night wrapped in Aristos's arms, a night in which everything had felt right again and she'd thought she might have gotten through to him.

When dinner passed and he was still holed up in his office, she told herself she couldn't expect massive change overnight. She slept in his suite that night, hoping he would come to her when he was done. She was asleep before he came in, and he was gone before she woke the next morning. The pattern went on for two days before the ache in her stomach began to make her feel physically ill.

A phone call from Nik interrupted her ruminations. Kostas had taken over in Carnelia and declared peace with the region. It was over. They were free to come home.

She was deluged with a mix of feelings—happiness she could finally return home, anxiety about what this would mean for her and Aristos.

When he deigned to make an appearance at dinner that night, she told him of her conversation with Nik.

He nodded. "He called me earlier this afternoon. I've asked the pilot to be ready to take us at noon tomorrow."

Just like that. Her fingers tightened around her wineglass. "What are we going to do?"

He gave her a quizzical look. "We fly home. Resume our lives."

Her heart, breaking piece by piece this week, fell apart a little further. "No," she said deliberately, "I mean what are we going to do about us?"

He frowned. "I need to get the financing for the casino sorted out."

"I think you need to get *us* sorted out while you're at it." She pushed her glass away. "You have to decide whether you're going to give me a meaningful place in your life or let me go, Aristos. It's as simple as that."

"It's not as simple as that," he growled.

"It is. I don't want to be a convenient wife, nor do I want to be a politically advantageous one. I want to be your partner. I want to be the one you come to when you're happy or sad. The one who licks your wounds for you."

The silence that followed was deafening. Hot tears pooled at the backs of her eyes. "Do you know the tabloids are making bets about how long we last? How long you can stay married?"

His eyes flashed. "They are garbage."

"Yes, but the funny thing about them is there's always a vein of truth there. It's how they survive."

She threw her napkin on the table and rose. "Tonight it's me who doesn't seem to have an appetite. If you'll excuse me."

Alex stepped into the helicopter behind Aristos the next morning with nothing between them resolved. She steadfastly refused to look down as they took off, bound for Akathinia. At all the memories the island held for her... the terrace where Aristos had held her through that wicked storm...the beach where he'd finally opened up and broken her heart...the beautiful, magical suite where she'd given him all of her, sure they were different.

She had no idea if they'd ever be back here together. If they'd even make it.

The journey was painfully silent, Aristos with his face in his laptop, her staring out the window. When the white Maltese stone Akathinian palace came into view, she knew what she had to do. She didn't want to live with a husband who cared about her the way her father had her mother, only commanding a piece of his heart; she wanted, needed, all of him.

The helicopter touched down. Aristos planned to continue on to his home on the outskirts of the city, then to his office, so the pilot kept the helicopter idling as her fiancé helped her out and onto the cement landing pad.

Stella and Nik appeared on the steps. Desperate to keep her emotions in check, she turned to Aristos. His expression was hidden by dark sunglasses, but what did it matter? He'd been emotionally unavailable all week.

He lifted a hand to run a finger down her cheek. "I'll call you later."

"Don't."

His head snapped back. She bit her lip, summoning a composure she wasn't sure she had. "We need some space, Aristos. Time to figure out how we feel about this. *Us.*"

"Alex—"

She put a finger to his lips. "I know how I feel about you. You know I love you. Now you have to figure out how you feel."

She kissed him. A brief touch of her lips to his. When he would have pulled her closer, she stepped out of his arms, turned and walked away, fighting back the tears that blinded her path.

He had taught her to grab hold of her future. Now she had. She wondered where it would take them.

Aristos stepped onto the helicopter after Alex threw those three loaded words at him and flew home. He spent the next week working the same insane hours, rattling around his too-big estate on the cliffs of Akathinia when he finally came home, its soaring ceilings and twenty-five rooms empty and without soul. They always had been, but it struck him now how utterly barren the place was.

He knew the difference was Alex, the effervescent presence she was, the spirit in her that reached out and surrounded him, refused to allow him to retreat into himself. But she had just walked out of his life.

It had been on the tip of his tongue to call her back, to rectify the mistake he knew he was making. But he'd known he wasn't ready. He had ghosts to exorcise, a future to shape. Wanting something, even as badly as he wanted Alex, wasn't proving you could stick. And that he had to do.

When word came that his final hope for an investor to replace Dimitri had fallen through, it was like being handed a life sentence he'd known was coming. All you could do was slide your hands into the shackles and admit your mistakes. Your failings.

Alex had been right. He would destroy himself trying to prove something that didn't matter anymore. He needed to stop. He needed to find a peace he could live with.

A lightbulb went off a few nights later, pulling him out of bed and to a sketch pad, where he drew until morning. He sent the amateurish result to his genius of an architect, asking him what he could do to modify the current casino design with that direction to save costs but still retain his vision. Then he waited. And waited. When Barry Schindler flew in two days later, arriving on Aristos's doorstep to find him unshaven and ready to pounce, he gave his client a wry look.

"Losing some sleep?"

"Just a bit."

"I might be able to help."

Two strong espressos sitting on the table beside them, the architect took Aristos through the redesigned plans. His design was inspired, based on lighter, more versatile materials and brilliant, indiscernible modifications that would provide no less of an impact.

"How much?" Aristos asked, chest tight.

"I've saved you fifty million."

Which left him fifty million short. Perhaps he could get his other investors to kick in the remainder... It was worth a shot.

He made his first phone call to his biggest investor at a US bank. He said yes. He made more calls. A funny thing happened then. As word spread that Dimitri was out, his investors started calling *him* to offer to make up the gap. They'd never liked the Russian's involvement.

By the end of the week he had his fifty million and a go-ahead from the Akathinian government to break ground. A front-page story ran in the business section of the newspaper with the new schematic included. It was garnering universal acclaim.

The story also included a feature on the program he had committed his company to—what he called the Hector Rigatos Gambling Addiction Fund. He wouldn't call it that, of course, but he would forever think of it as that. For what Alex had taught him.

An intense feeling of satisfaction, of rightness, settling through him, he set the newspaper down, walked out onto the balcony and took in the hauntingly beautiful view of the mountains. In the shadow of that quiet, majestic presence he knew it was time for him to take *his* leap. He couldn't right the wrongs he'd made with his family—they would forever be with him—but he *could* change the future. If he wanted to be with Alex, to deserve her, he needed to face his demons. He needed to go home. He needed to learn how to stick.

CHAPTER FIFTEEN

SMILING AND WAVING at crowds during Akathinia's annual Independence Day celebration, even one as joyous as it was this year with the prospect of war lifted from the national conscience, was no fun for a princess who'd rather be on an Aegean island with the man she loved.

Alex was navigating her new role with care, loving her work with Nina, settling back into palace life with its intricacies and formalities. If only she didn't feel so miserable. If only she could put last week's newspaper feature out of her head.

Aristos had secured his investment, the casino was a go, the ground-breaking to happen in two weeks' time. But what had made her put the paper down and leave the breakfast room in tears was the gambling addiction fund he'd created to help those who fell through the cracks.

She was so happy for him. And still he hadn't come.

Her heart throbbed painfully in her chest as they navigated the final length of the parade route on the float upon which she and her family stood. Perhaps she'd been wrong. Perhaps it was just too difficult for Aristos to let down his walls after decades of shoring them up.

Somehow, she managed to hold her smile as they reached the end of the parade route, bade the crowds goodbye and were ushered into the waiting limo. Only her father was missing, his recovery at home an unexpected development as his archnemesis, Idas, lay on his deathbed.

Her father hadn't seemed to warm up much to her, but

her budding relationships with her siblings gave her such joy. Stella, who was becoming the best friend she'd always wanted in a sister. Nik, whose quiet, wise philosophy held so much she could learn from.

Stella pounced as the limo came to a halt in front of the palace and Alex slid out, heading for the stairs.

"You have to stop moping around."

Alex swept up the stairs and through the doors. "Aristos isn't coming tonight He's playing poker on Vardis Melonakos's yacht."

"You told him you needed space."

"That was a cue for him to give his head a shake."

"Maybe you should give yours one, too."

She pulled to a halt. *"Really?"*

"Yes, really. He's crazy about you, Alex. I saw it on his face when you walked away from him at the helicopter… when he pursued you at the press conference."

Her mouth pursed. "I'm not sure he's emotionally capable of acting on it."

Stella followed her up the stairs and into her bedroom. "Perhaps not, but moping around on the biggest day of the year isn't going to help. Are we going to have fun tonight or are you going to act like a limp dishrag?"

She straightened her shoulders. Gave her head the shake she knew it needed. "Yes," she said firmly, "we are going to have fun."

She channeled her favorite literary heroine for inspiration. *What would Scarlett do?*

She would *not* sit around pining for Aristos while he played poker on Vardis Melonakos's yacht with beautiful women serving him drinks. She would show him what he was missing.

"I think we should go shopping."

"Shopping?" Stella looked at her as if she were mad.

"My legs are about to fall off. The ball starts in four hours."

"Do you want to help me or not?"

The two princesses entered the Akathinian royal ballroom arm in arm after a firestorm of paparazzi flashes documented their arrival.

"A prior engagement," Alex had said tersely when asked where her fiancé was.

Stella shoved a glass of champagne into her hand. "Drink."

She did. Her sister scanned the room, her gaze settling on Crown Prince Kostas of Carnelia, standing beside Nik in a group near them.

"Look at him walking around the place as if he owns it. I *hate* him. I don't care what Nik says, what they said in their little *chat* together, there is nothing on this planet that could make me like him."

Alex smiled. Prince Kostas's unexpected appearance at the Independence Day ball had been a shock to everyone. Nik had invited the prince as a symbol of the healing that needed to happen between the two countries. Stella, still brokenhearted over her eldest brother's death at what she called "Kostas's hands," had not taken it well.

"Perhaps you should listen to what Nik has to say," Alex suggested. "He seems to be at peace with it all."

Stella scowled. "Kostas is a coward. He spent the last year relegating our two countries to turmoil, afraid to stand up to his father. I have no respect for him."

As if the extraordinarily handsome crown prince's ears were burning, he turned his head toward them. Elegant in a black tuxedo, he wore his dark hair short and cropped above a face that could be described as nothing short of spectacular: high, aristocratic cheekbones; piercing, narrow eyes beneath thick dark brows; and a straight, prominent nose.

"He's awfully stunning, Stella."

"If arrogant brutes are your idea of attractive, yes."

"I thought you used to like him. They say he is progressive, pro-democracy, nothing like his father. Apparently very witty and intelligent."

"*Used to* being the operative words."

Alex's eyes widened as Kostas broke away from the group and headed toward them.

"Don't look now, but here he comes."

Hot color stained her sister's cheeks. "Here? Why is he coming over here?"

"We're about to find out."

The crown prince stopped in front of them and inclined his head in a greeting. Alex smiled politely, but Kostas's gaze had moved to Stella and stayed there. "Perhaps you would do me the honor of a dance?"

A loaded silence followed. The flush in her sister's face deepened, her lips pursing as if to refuse. But then her manners seemed to kick in, as if she knew they were being watched, and with a stiff nod, she accepted.

Which left Alex alone. Alone in the very sexy dress she'd purchased, the plunging neckline of the champagne-colored sequined gown skirting the limits of what a princess might get away with. Worn perhaps to show the world she didn't care her fiancé wasn't here—or perhaps the man himself.

She stood, back against a pillar, watching Stella and the prince dance. It was better than TV. Two men asked her to dance, the duke Aristos had liked to make fun of and a friend of Stella's, but she turned them both down, pleading sore feet, a poor excuse, but she didn't care. She was tired of pretending.

"I was standing over there wondering why the most

beautiful woman in the room keeps turning down dances," a deep male voice purred in her ear. "Instead of allowing my imagination to run wild, I thought I'd come over and find out for myself."

Aristos.

Her heart jumped into her mouth as she turned to face him. He was not in a tuxedo like the other men, but in a dark suit that made him look so handsome her heart stayed lodged right where it was, deep in her throat, making speech nigh impossible.

The tears she'd been fighting swamped the backs of her eyes, threatening a full release.

"Oh, no." Aristos's gaze darkened. "No tears, Princess, not when we've come this far."

She swallowed hard, fighting them back. *What did that mean?*

"Aren't you supposed to be playing poker?"

"I was. I found my attention was elsewhere, so I left."

She scowled at him. "I am not available as a *diversion*."

"Funny," he drawled, his gaze sliding over her. "That dress screams it with a capital *D*. It's not fit for public consumption."

"Absentee fiancés don't get a say in the matter."

Fire lit his gaze. "Ah, but we know they do. Especially since I am not absentee any longer."

He curled his fingers around her forearm and directed her out of the ballroom to the terrace. Bypassing the crowd there, he led her down into the gardens. They walked until they came to the fountain, the little square at the center of the maze where he'd challenged her to take her big jump.

She sat down on the lip of the fountain, the sounds of the party muted now, the square deserted.

Aristos sat down beside her, splaying his long legs in front of him. The scent of his spicy aftershave made her want to crawl into his arms. She wrapped hers around herself.

"You asked me for space," he said, setting his dark, inscrutable gaze on her. "And you were right—I needed it. Needed to figure myself out, determine my priorities, whether I could be the man you needed."

Her heart squeezed. He always had been.

"What I discovered is that my life as I've been leading it is not the life I want to live. You made me see that, angel, made me see the possibilities…what I want, and I want more. I want to wake up every morning with you beside me. I want to share my life with you. I want you to be there to lick my wounds when I stumble, and yes," he added a devilish glitter in his eyes, "other parts of me, too."

Her heart turned over, leaping with a joy that sent it tumbling nearly out of her chest. "Aristos—"

He held up a hand. "I have a lot of baggage, Alex. Maybe more than I can ever fully overcome. There's never going to be a day where I'm not cognizant of the fragility of life—of how everything can be taken away from you in the blink of an eye. It will always make me a fighter. It will always push my survivor instincts to the forefront, making my first inclination to push people away. It's a reflexive thing I'm going to have to work on."

A tear slid down her cheek. "All of us have those things…those crutches we rely on. For me it was retreating. Not taking the chances I should. You showed me that."

"For me it was burying the past. Trying to pretend it never existed, that it couldn't hurt me, but it was always there in the background, chasing me. I knew after you walked away from me I would regret it if I let you go. But I had to face my ghosts first. Find out who I am now. Who I *was*. So I went home."

Her heart leaped. "You did? How was it?"

"Painful. Awkward. Amazing."

She could so identify. And yet hadn't it all been worth it?

"I'm so glad you went," she said softly. "Were they glad to see you?"

"Yes." The rasp in his voice made her cover his hand with hers. "I think there is…potential there. My mother—she was very emotional. Vasili—he—he will be the hardest. I broke his trust. I need to get it back."

She crawled onto his lap then, because she couldn't resist. Her hands framed his face. "You've made the overture. Give it time."

He nodded, his eyes so full of emotion her tears became a steady flow, sliding down her cheeks and soaking his shirt. She kissed him, a long, sweet kiss full of salty tears and the future she knew they had in front of them.

He pulled back, his hands grasping hers and dragging them to her sides. His gaze was so serious, so full of intent, it made her stomach grow tight. "You saved my soul, angel. I was very nearly spiritually bankrupt. I need you with me to make sure that never happens again, that my demons don't take over."

She gave him a tremulous smile. "I think I already made that commitment."

He lifted her ring-clad finger to his mouth and brushed his lips over her knuckles. "I think I missed something when I gave this to you."

"What?"

"I love you, *agapi mou*. I think it was love at first sight, if the truth be known. I did everything but say no to Nik when he asked me to take you to Larikos."

He loved her. Her brain latched on to those three words and held them tight. "I told him it wasn't a good idea," she breathed. "I knew you were trouble, Aristos Nicolades."

"I am," he murmured and proceeded to demonstrate with a kiss that had no sweetness to it, only hunger, an insatiable hunger that seemed to have no end. She moved closer as he slid a hand to her bottom and brought her to him, his sexy, fiery kisses leaving her short of breath.

"Your bedroom," he murmured as they came up for air, "where is it?"

Procuring a bottle of champagne along the way, they climbed the stairs to the royal suites. She was in his arms kissing him before they made it halfway up, then again outside her bedroom door before he pushed it open and shoved her inside.

She pouted as he lost his jacket. "I thought it was spiritual for us."

"Yes, angel, it is." He started working on the buttons of his shirt. "Now I'd like to take it to another realm."

She took a drink from the bottle. Eyed him. "I love you, Aristos."

His gaze darkened as he looked up at her. "I love you, too, Princess. Now put down the bottle and get over here."

She did. Because sometimes dreams *were* too expensive to keep. And sometimes they were all that mattered.

* * * * *

THE MISTRESS THAT
TAMED DE SANTIS

NATALIE ANDERSON

For my husband and family, and for the
laughter we share.

CHAPTER ONE

CROWN PRINCE ANTONIO DE SANTIS strolled along the dark street, savouring the stolen moment of freedom as he walked off the burn from the last eighty minutes in the palace gym.

Silence. Solitude. Darkness. Peace.

He checked the hood of his sweatshirt still hid most of his face. He'd soon have to turn back. In less than an hour this road would be crawling with workers frantically finishing preparations and testing the barricades they'd installed over the last day. The crowds would gather early too. San Felipe's car rally was prestigious, hotly contested and the starting gun for the annual carnival, which meant Antonio's next couple of weeks were even more packed than usual. State balls, trade meetings, society events, the carnival celebrations required a round-the-clock royal presence as the world's wealthy and glamorous came to indulge and experience his country's beauty. And with his younger brother away, Crown Prince Antonio was the only royalty on offer.

He'd do it all anyway; he always did.

He approached an intersection. The road to the left headed into the heart of the city and was the entertainment 'strip'—lined with restaurants and bars that would soon be packed for race action. He glanced up at the ornate exterior of the former firehouse on the corner—the latest building to have been reclaimed and refurbished into a hot night spot. But after only a week of business, the city's residents were debating the merits of this particular establishment more than any other.

BURN.

The four bronze letters bolted to the wall screamed both defiance and demand. He read it as a blatant statement of intent—she was here, she didn't care, and she didn't intend to hide.

Antonio frowned. Suddenly the window just ahead was flung wide open. The shutter banged on the wall right beside him. If he'd been one pace on, he'd have been knocked out cold on the pavement.

He halted. Even with the relaxed rules in carnival season, the club ought to be closed at this hour. He glanced into the open window, expecting to see a few intoxicated patrons still partying, but no noise streamed out. No endless thud, thud, thud of drum and bass. No high-pitched giggles, loud laughs or low murmurs. It seemed there was no one in the vast room—until something white silently flashed in the deep recesses. He looked closer, tracking the fast-moving creature as the white flashed again. The woman wore a loose white top and…nothing else? The most basic instinct had him locking on her legs—unbelievably long legs that right now were moving unbelievably fast.

Pyjamas. *Short* pyjamas.

His suddenly slushy brain slowly reached a conclusion. She opened another window down the side of the room and turned again. She wore ballet flats on her feet, not for fashion, but for function, dancing across the floor—spinning so quickly her auburn hair swirled in a curling ribbon behind her. She leapt and landed near the window on the opposite side of the room and opened that one with another dramatic, effervescent gesture before turning yet again. That was when he saw her face properly for the first time.

She was smiling. Not one of the usual sorts of smiles Antonio received—not awed or nervous or curious or come-hitherish… This smile was so full of raw joy it made him feel he should step back into the darkness, but he couldn't find the will to turn away.

Heat kicked hard in his gut.

Anger. Not lust. *Never* lust.

He'd have to have spent the last six months living under a rock not to know she'd moved to San Felipe. Given he ruled the island principality, he knew exactly who she was and why she was here. And he didn't give a damn that she was even more stunning in real life than in any of the pictures saturating the Internet. Bella Sanchez was here to cause trouble. And Antonio didn't want trouble in San Felipe.

Nor did he want Bella Sanchez.

He didn't want anyone.

Yet here he was with his feet glued to the pavement, watching her whirl her way round the room with glorious abandon, from one window to the next in flying leaps until she'd opened them all.

She executed another series of dizzying spins across the floor, and suddenly stopped—positioned smack bang in the centre of the window frame he was looking through.

'Enjoying the view?' Her smile had vanished and her voice dripped with sarcasm.

When he didn't move, she glided closer, her feline green eyes like lasers. She wasn't even breathless as she stared him down like a Fury about to wreak revenge on a miscreant.

Antonio's reflexes snapped. She thought she could shame him into scuttling away? Another hit of heat made him clench his muscles. He pushed back the hood of his sweatshirt and coolly gazed back up at her, grimly anticipating her recognition of him.

Her eyes widened instantly but she quickly schooled the shock from her face—her expression smoothing until she became inscrutable. Somehow she stood taller. She had the straightest back of anyone he'd ever seen.

'Your Highness,' she said crisply. 'May I help you with something?'

Unfortunately he couldn't reply; his tongue was cleaved to the roof of his mouth. How could she look this radiant so early in the morning? She had to have had an extremely late night and yet here she was without a scrap of make-up on, looking intolerably beautiful.

Antonio actively avoided being alone with women—especially models, actresses and socialites—but, given his single status and Crown Prince title, they littered his path and made their play nonetheless. Over the past few years he'd met hundreds, if not thousands, of stunning, willing women. He'd refused every single one.

But none had ever looked as gorgeous as Bella Sanchez did right now. And none had looked as haughty.

At his continued silence, she stepped closer. 'You were spying on me?'

His anger sharpened. He'd avoided meeting *her* most of all and now she made him sound like a peeping Tom. No matter that in part he felt like one.

'It is past closing hours,' he said stiffly.

'You're policing me?' As she stared down at him that haughty barrier locked fully into place, leaching the last of the vitality in her eyes. 'The club is closed.'

Her English accent was muddied. He figured it was from the years she'd spent abroad and the mix of people in her life.

'I'm merely ventilating the rooms,' she explained.

'Getting rid of suspicious smells?' He'd heard the rumours and he wasn't going to ignore them.

A small smile emerged, nothing like the earlier one. 'This is a non-smoking venue, not some den of iniquity.'

'There are other vices,' he replied with calm consideration. 'Salvatore Accardi warned me this operation was going to bring San Felipe nothing but trouble.'

'He would know all about trouble.'

She didn't so much as blink as she snapped back her answer.

He'd wanted to see her reaction to his reference to Accardi—but he'd got almost none.

Salvatore Accardi, former Italian politician, had taken up permanent residence in his San Felipe holiday home. And Salvatore Accardi was reputedly Bella Sanchez's father.

Twenty-odd years ago she'd been born of scandal, supposedly the love child of the married Salvatore and his sex-symbol mistress. Their affair had been splashed across all the newspapers of the day. But Salvatore had never acknowledged Bella as his baby. He'd refused to undergo paternity testing. He'd stayed with his long-suffering wife, pregnant at the time, and raised their daughter, who'd been born a mere three months before Bella.

Bella had been raised in the public eye, eventually dancing professionally before becoming chatelaine of this party house in the heart of Antonio's principality. And according to Salvatore Accardi now, her presence would attract nothing but sleaze to San Felipe.

'Is it so terrible to provide a place for people to have fun?' Bella asked, shrugging one of her delicate shoulders. She looked slender, but strong.

Antonio frowned at the direction—distraction—of his thoughts.

'This isn't about that,' he said coldly. 'This is revenge. This is setting up so you're right in Accardi's face.'

'Is that what he told you?' Her poise cracked briefly as anger flashed. 'Do you honestly think you can believe everything—or *any*thing—he says?'

At a gut level Antonio had never much liked Salvatore Accardi, but nothing had ever been proven. All those rumours of corporate and political corruption had remained only rumours. And if the man had the personal morals of an alley cat, that was his own business. He'd owned property in San Felipe for too long for Antonio to find reason to require him to leave.

Just as there'd been no reason to refuse a work permit and residency to Bella Sanchez.

And didn't everyone have the right to be believed innocent until proven guilty?

In her white short pyjamas Bella looked both innocent and unbearably sensual, because that white cotton was thin and she wore nothing beneath it. And when she moved? He could see the outline of her slim waist and generous curves.

'I'm not sure a venue like this suits San Felipe,' he said tightly.

'As if there aren't other clubs?' she questioned softly but her gaze was sharp. She almost leaned out of the window frame, making him acutely aware of her unfettered breasts. 'This isn't a sex club. There are no pole dancers or strippers.' She lingered over her quiet words, but then her eyes glinted. 'Definitely no drugs in dodgy back-room deals.'

Her voice shook with fierceness. He knew her mother, Madeline Sanchez, one of the world's greatest 'mistresses' in a time when such things had been scandalous, had overdosed more than a year ago in a Parisian apartment. Everybody knew all there was to know about Bella Sanchez.

'This is a legitimate bar and dance floor,' she added more calmly. 'And I'm a responsible club owner.'

'You're young and inexperienced.' He paused pointedly. 'In managing a commercial enterprise, that is.'

Her eyes widened, for a split second she looked furious. But he watched the change as she controlled her emotions once more—the stiffening of that already ramrod-straight spine, her smile so different from the one earlier, the hint of calculation as she glanced at his casual attire.

He braced. She was sizing him up and about to fire her own shot. And oddly, he was looking forward to it.

She swept her arm across her body in a dramatic gesture, drawing his attention to her attributes once more. 'Why don't you come in and find out for yourself?' she invited in a sultry tone. 'Come inside and see if you can find anything wrong with my club.'

It was a blatant dare—she'd switched into 'Bella Sanchez, Sex Symbol' without skipping a beat.

But it wasn't *that* challenge that did it for him. Not that coy smile of sophisticated amusement. It was the emotion lurking in the backs of her eyes. The anger she was trying hard to control—that slight tremor in her fingers before she curled them into a fist.

'Yes.'

He said it because she didn't expect him to.

She thought he'd politely and coldly refuse, smile distantly and retreat, like the conservative Crown Prince he was. She'd called his bluff.

So he'd called hers. Because at this moment, he damn well felt like doing the last thing anyone—least of all her—expected.

And she hadn't expected it. Her shock flashed for one satisfying second.

He waited while she unbolted the heavy door, opened it and stepped aside for him to enter. He paused just inside the room, watching as she closed the door and marched around him to lead the way.

'No suspicious smells, see,' she said pointedly. 'Nothing illegal.'

The ground-floor space was sleek and smelled clean, not yet permeated with the lingering, less than fragrant scent of five hundred sweaty clubbers dancing there night after night.

He glanced up—away from the back view of her never-ending legs—and saw the decadent wallpaper and the wrought-iron railings protecting patrons who wanted to party on the mezzanine floor. The chandeliers gleamed even this early in the morning. He hadn't been in a nightclub in a decade. He'd been crowned in his early twenties, but had been aware of the restraints on his behaviour for years before that. He'd always been dutiful. He'd had to be.

Only now he felt the stirrings of a desire he'd buried deep all those years ago. When *had* he last danced?

'You'll want to see the liquor licence.' She stalked over to the main bar. 'And there it is, exactly where it should be. The emergency exits are well marked,' she added, all officiousness. 'It was formerly a fire station, you know.'

He did know. But there'd be no putting out the fire in her eyes.

'The rest of the paperwork is upstairs,' she said defiantly, turning to face him.

'So lead the way,' he answered bluntly. He was committed now.

For a split second her shock was visible again.

Yes, Crown Prince Antonio would never ordinarily go up into the back room of a notorious nightclub in the sole company of a supposedly scandalous siren... but he felt like doing it just to see that reaction again.

He suppressed a smile as he followed her to one of the winding staircases that were like pillars at each side of the room. But as he climbed behind her his amusement faded.

He hadn't been so alone with a woman so barely attired in years. And it shouldn't have been a problem now. Except her legs went on for ever. He tried to tear his attention from them. Failed. Was relieved when they reached the mezzanine and she darted ahead to open another window. She then headed to a small alcove that hid a door marked 'Private'.

Another flight of stairs.

This time he gave in to the temptation to look. She would never know. But there was the faintest flush on her porcelain cheeks as she waited for him to walk into her office.

The top floor was clearly her private space and very different from the dark and sensual decor of the club downstairs. This room was lighter, with white walls and a cream rug covering the floorboards. A large desk dominated the room. A laptop sat open on it, paper files spread beside it. A filing cabinet was behind the desk, while a couple of chairs sat at angles in front of it. But Antonio remained standing because there was another door—open—through which he could see a small kitchenette. And given she was wearing pyjamas, he figured it was safe to assume there was a bed in there too. Tension hit. This had been a mistake. And Antonio couldn't afford any mistakes.

Bella stared. Crown Prince Antonio De Santis had accepted her challenge and was standing in her small office. She'd thought he'd decline, all unbending regal politeness. But it seemed he really had chosen this morning to inspect her business—obscenely early, name-dropping the man who refused to acknowledge her and dressed like *that*.

She'd recognised him the second he'd pulled back the hood of his sweatshirt but he looked nothing like the austere Crown Prince she'd seen on screens and in magazines. That man was tall and broad-shouldered, with not a hair out of place and almost always dressed in an immaculate midnight-blue suit. Perfect for the reserved, always polite but distant Prince.

The man in front of her now hadn't shaved. His hair was mussed. He must have been out running or something what with the old sweatshirt, track pants and trainers he was wearing. And the edge she'd glimpsed in his eyes? She never would have expected that. Nor would she have expected to feel breathless and hot in his company. Not so hyper-aware.

She never felt that around any guy.

'You'll find everything is in there.' She opened the file and turned it so he could read it, reading it upside down herself. She wanted him to see every single piece of paper and be satisfied and leave as soon as possible. She wasn't going down without a fight. She'd prove to all her doubters that she could manage this club. She'd prove it to *him*.

So never mind that she was in her shortie pyjamas, her top slightly too loose and with no bra beneath, because she couldn't be embarrassed. Never mind that she'd only managed two hours' sleep because she had so much to do. The club had been open only a week and, while it looked promising, she had a long, long way to go before it could be declared a success and she could sell up and start up the business of her heart.

But he didn't say anything about the paperwork. She glanced up and caught him staring at her. Again.

She was used to men looking. They all wanted the same thing, right? They all thought they knew everything there was to know about her. But the ice in this man's eyes was something else. It burned.

He stood silent. Guarded. *Judging.*

She'd not expected that from San Felipe's broken,

beloved Prince. Wasn't he supposed to hide a wounded heart? Wasn't he supposed to be kind and benevolent under the weight of all that duty?

Everyone knew his story. His 'One True Love' had tragically died of cancer barely two months after his coronation and the accident that had claimed the lives of both his parents. He'd not been linked to another woman since. The Prince had buried his heart with his girlfriend. And, according to the glossy mags, the nation believed only the love of a pure and perfect woman could heal him and bring him happiness...

That woman clearly wasn't her given he was looking at her like *that*.

Forbidding. Disapproving.

Thrown off balance, she felt goaded into provoking a reaction from him. Beneath the fifty feet of ice he hid behind, it had to be there—emotion of *some* kind.

She should have been intimidated. She should have remained polite. She should have respected the power he held. But she was too tired. And too hurt.

'Why are you staring at me like I've forgotten something?' She stepped out from her desk. 'Should I have curtseyed as you walked in?' She lifted her chin at his utter impassivity. 'Should I get on my knees before you?'

She regretted the sultry taunt the second she'd uttered it.

Because there was no reaction. He didn't move a muscle. Didn't speak a word. Just kept, ever so coolly, regarding her.

Her cheeks burned as shame grew. She'd been everything the world expected her to be—a scandalous, tarty temptress. But she was a big fat faker.

And he wasn't. He really was as frozen-hearted as they said. And every bit as breathtaking.

'You're going to have to do better than that,' he finally said. 'Do you think you're the first woman to try seducing me by stripping and dancing in front of me?'

His words hit like hailstones.

'I didn't strip.'

'Only because you didn't bother getting dressed properly.'

'And I didn't dance for you.' She ignored his interruption. 'I was just warming up alone. You're the one who stopped to watch. You could have kept walking, Tony.'

For a split second she got a reaction—his jaw dropped. Before he snapped it shut and then shot his words like bullets.

'What did you just call me?'

'Tony,' she repeated, refusing to back down. 'Crown Prince Antonio is too much of a mouthful.'

There was a pause, then his gaze skittered down her body—so deliberately. 'Too much of a mouthful,' he echoed slowly.

This time *Bella's* jaw dropped. Did he say that while scoping out her breasts? Which, yes, were on the fuller side. Especially for a dancer.

Crossing his arms, he continued to regard her, making her feel uncharacteristically vulnerable. His complete attention wasn't like any ordinary audience of thousands. His scrutiny was way more intense.

'I've seen it all, every artifice, every attempt to attract me,' he muttered. 'It won't work.'

'Because we're all out to entrap you?' she asked, shocked at his direct approach. 'You think I'm trying to use my feminine wiles to draw you in? Because you're the biggest prize?'

'Aren't you?' he answered, cocking his head. 'Or are you just trying to provoke me? You want to win a reaction from "the Ice Prince",' he mocked. 'Because you're all about getting the reaction.'

She drew breath at the accuracy of his hit.

'I've had every kind of play,' he continued with a quietness that belied the edge to his words. 'The sympathy, simpering agreement and the bitchy comebacks of the treat-me-mean kind…there's nothing I haven't seen or heard, so don't bother.'

Anger rushed along her veins, scalding her skin. 'You think I want you anywhere near me?'

His lips twisted in a coolly mocking look and he didn't bother to answer.

'You're unbelievably arrogant,' she said.

'You think?'

Yes, she did. But swirling beneath the frost-covered atmosphere was elemental attraction at its most basic. He was appallingly attractive—her body yearned to get closer to his. And when he didn't back away from her challenge?

Primitive instinct could be a powerful thing. But she had more of a brain than that. So her basic instinct could go bury itself back in the cave it had been dwelling in for the last three years.

'I have no desire to attract you,' she declared passionately. Totally meaning every word. 'This isn't some *ploy* with which I hope to gain your grace or favour or sexual interest. You do not interest me in the least.'

'You interest me,' he said softly, slicing the ground from under her.

Sensual awareness feathered over her skin.

'Why San Felipe?' He stepped closer. 'Why now?'

Her heart stopped beating as she looked up into his blue eyes. For a second he actually looked human—as if he actually cared. And for a second she longed to open up and just be honest.

But as if she could ever tell him. When he'd so arrogantly assumed she wanted to land herself a princely lover? When he chose to listen to the father who'd always refused to recognise her?

He'd be just another man who denied her.

She wanted him to leave but she couldn't tear her gaze from his. She'd thought she could handle anything. But she wasn't sure she could handle him.

He reached out as if to take her hand. 'Why now, Bella?'

Abruptly she turned to avoid his touch.

'Careful—'

His warning came too late. As she whirled to escape her weak ankle went and she stumbled, catching her thigh on the corner of her desk.

Antonio winced at the grimace of pain on Bella's face as she grabbed the desk to stop herself falling down. She'd gashed her leg, just above her knee. As he looked close he saw a long, jagged scar running in a wonky line up her shin.

She paled, her lips pressed together to mute any sound of pain.

It had been so long since he'd had any kind of physical comfort. Or offered any. He'd almost forgotten how. 'Bella?'

'It's fine.' She straightened and drew in a deep breath.

'I'm sure,' he replied, but he knew it wasn't.

'Wouldn't want you thinking this was another ploy.'

'It is my fault you fell,' he said stiffly, his hands at his side, wanting to help her yet feeling oddly impotent.

'You feel responsible? Rest easy, I won't sue you.' Her lips compressed. 'It's no more damaged than it already was.'

'It still needs dressing.' Blood was already oozing from the small wound. 'You have a first-aid kit?'

'Of course.' She didn't move.

He sighed at her reluctance. 'I need to see it. Or I'll revoke your operating licence.'

She gritted her teeth and limped behind her desk. His irritation smouldered. She really didn't want him to help. Was that because he'd really offended her or because he'd struck too close to the mark?

She *had* been trying to get a rise out of him, but she hadn't meant the vampish 'on her knees' offer—not when she'd jumped to get away from him.

She clutched the small container but he held out his hand. Sending him a death look, she passed it to him. Antonio bit back the smile of satisfaction and opened the lid.

'Lean on the desk,' he told her.

'This isn't necessary.'

He wasn't used to repeating instructions. He glanced up and her stormy expression clashed with his. 'Lean on the desk.'

Slowly, stiffly, she rested her body back.

'Thank you,' he said, ultra-politely.

He knelt at her feet, inwardly grimacing at the irony given her provocative remark only moments ago.

He knew an injury had ended her professional career. In the last decade Antonio had attended the ballet only out of duty but he could appreciate the strength and commitment it would have taken Bella to reach the level she had.

Her body was still incredibly athletic. This close he could smell her light, floral scent. It made him think of summer sun, not endless nights in a darkened dance club. In his mind's eye he saw her on the floor, bumping and grinding up close to her patrons. He gritted his teeth. Not jealous. And *not* aroused.

He was *not* aroused by her.

He wasn't like all the other red-blooded men in the world. He didn't have time to be. He didn't have the right. But just at this moment, he was every *inch* a mere man.

'Do you dance your way through all your tasks?' he asked, trying to distract himself from her sweet scent and delicate skin. He dabbed the blood and prepped a plaster as quickly as he could, not touching any part of her beyond necessary.

'Is that a serious question?' she mumbled.

'Yes.' Satisfied with how the plaster neatly covered the gash, he glanced up to read her expression. She was sitting unnaturally still—apparently holding her breath.

She met his gaze with those deep green eyes that were now almost liquid. 'You want to know if I dance while brushing my teeth?'

He inwardly smiled at the image. 'I bet you brush in time to the music playing in your head.'

Her eyes widened and *her* smile broke free—her

full mouth softened and her eyes sparkled. She looked fresh and beautiful and bright.

Heat flared from flicker to flame, urging him to touch those lush curving lips—

He jerked to his feet and stepped away before he did something colossally stupid.

'Have you been out drinking?'

He turned at the bitterness in her tone and saw her smile had vanished.

'I don't drink,' he said simply.

'No vices at all?' she mocked. 'No sex, right?'

That speculation was correct. It had been years since he'd had a lover. He was only about duty: to serve his country and to protect his people. *All* of them—dead and alive. That was his penance.

'And no drinking,' she added. 'I guess that just leaves drugs.'

'None of those either.'

'Fast cars?'

He shook his head. 'The Crown Prince cannot be injured or killed in a car accident. That can't happen in San Felipe again.' His parents' tragedy had cut the nation too deeply.

'So you're reduced to *watching*.' Storms gathered in her eyes.

'If you wanted privacy you would have kept your curtains closed,' he answered abruptly. 'But you didn't, because you like to be watched. You've made a career out of it.'

Anger flashed in her face. Before she could reply a short melody burst through the charged atmosphere. Then again. And again. His damn cell phone.

'Are you going to answer that or would you like me

to?' Those temptress tones returned—but so shaky this time.

She was trying to goad him again, using her voice, her eyes, her femininity to bring a man to his knees.

Not this man. He wasn't that weak.

Yet she knew that already. And that was the twist. She expected him to pull away—she wanted to drive him further back because she didn't want him too close. Because *his* nearness bothered *her*.

That realisation shocked him. His body had already betrayed him. She was so damn beautiful, for the first time in years his desire was stirred.

'It's my security team.' He cleared the frog from his throat and ignored the call.

'I'm amazed they let you wander the streets alone,' she said dryly.

'They know exactly where I am.'

Her eyebrows lifted. 'You told them you were coming here?'

'GPS.' His watch was tracked. It even had a silent emergency alarm button. Very spy film but he'd had to agree to it to get his morning walks alone.

'Your every movement is accounted for? So you're like a prisoner on electronic monitoring?'

'The concept is not dissimilar. They're concerned because I've not returned to the palace by my usual time.' He pulled the phone from his pocket as it began to ring again. If he didn't reply to this next call, a security team would be on its way in seconds.

'A change in the usual routine,' she drawled. 'Heaven forbid.'

'Yet here you are, doing the same warm-up dance routine you've been doing for years,' he answered blandly. 'We are creatures of habit, just doing what we usually do.'

Like falling back on old defences.

But as he read the message from his security chief he tensed. He double-checked the time on the screen—how had twenty minutes passed so quickly? He crossed the room to glance out of the window. In the space of a few minutes, the world had changed.

Outside people were lining the barricaded street, already standing two to three deep. He'd been so engrossed in dealing with Bella he hadn't heard the crowds gathering.

Swiftly he stepped back. To be seen inside Bella Sanchez's apartment at this hour of the morning would be unacceptable. But to be seen leaving it even worse. Especially given his unshaven, dishevelled appearance. The world would think he'd had another kind of workout altogether.

His gut burned.

Was this *want*? It had been so damn long since he'd wanted any woman. Clenching the phone in his fist, he faced her. She'd stilled, listening to the rising clamour outside. Given the way her features had tightened, the realisation the world had woken wasn't good news for her either.

'It seems it is your lucky day,' he muttered, feeling like provoking her the way she had him. 'I will have to remain here.'

Her eyes widened. 'For how long?'

Until his team could work out a subtle extraction plan. 'Until they've all gone home.'

'But that race won't finish for another six hours!'

Her obvious discomfort gave him a macabre pleasure. That she didn't want him near echoed his own unwanted feelings.

But he looked at her, outwardly unmoved. 'What do you suggest we do to pass the time?'

CHAPTER TWO

BELLA STARED. HE was joking, wasn't he? But Prince Antonio never joked; he looked as straight up serious and remote as ever. Worse, if anything.

'Why can't you leave now?' She still didn't understand why he was here at all.

He stepped further from the window, looking at his phone as it buzzed again. 'The crowds outside are already too big.'

'They love their Crown Prince. They'll be happy to see you.' He could do no wrong in his people's eyes.

'I'm not prepared for a meet and greet at this point in time.' He quickly sent a text.

'Because you're not in one of your navy suits? The track pants aren't all bad…' In the baggy hoodie he looked younger and more approachable than in any of the stills she'd seen. In fact dressed like this he looked alarmingly attractive. 'A prince at leisure—'

He glanced up and her words died in her throat. It finally dawned on her why he refused to leave.

'You don't want them to see you here,' she said. 'With me.'

He didn't answer. Didn't need to. She could see it all over his icy expression.

He was loath to be seen anywhere near her. Why? Did he think she could taint him in some way?

That hurt where she was most vulnerable. No one— not her old dance company, not her ex-boyfriend, not even her own *father*—wanted to claim a personal connection to her. Only those wanting instant Internet fame wanted to be caught near her. And as if that were what he wanted. Like her, Crown Prince Antonio De Santis had been born famous, but he was legitimately so—whereas she?

He steadily held her gaze. That unnerving reserve made her too aware of him, but she refused to let him silence her with little more than a stare. Not now or ever.

'You think it would damage your reputation to be seen exiting my club at this hour of the morning?' Her voice shook and she drew in a sharp breath. 'Maybe it would *enhance* it.'

He still didn't answer but his demeanour changed. He might be wearing worn workout gear, but now he looked every inch the powerful 'Head of State'. Clothes made no difference. Nothing could pierce that princely aura. Bella's anger flared. He was so protected, whereas she?

'No one would believe anything "untoward" of you. But me?' She laughed bitterly. 'I'm the vixen, right? But surely not even wicked little Bella Sanchez could trap Prince Antonio with her wiles…'

It was what he'd accused her of attempting only moments before. And he was right, it was laughable. Scathing, she stepped closer; her words tumbled unchecked, unthinking.

'I don't know why you're so worried,' she snarled.

'You're untemptable, right? You're the frigid Prince.'
She took no notice of his sudden frown or the muscle
jerking in his jaw; his wordless judgment had unleashed
the banked-up bitterness of so many betrayals. 'Your
absolute rejection of any physical intimacy is cowardly.'

Just as hiding here for hours would be cowardly.

And dangerous for her.

'In what way?' he asked icily, his words sharply
enunciated. 'Doesn't it denote self-control?'

Something burned in his eyes now, but she was too
hurt to take heed and too hurt to stop herself lashing
out. 'Maybe you're afraid that once you start, you won't
be able to stop.'

He said nothing. He didn't need to. His rigidity
screamed irritation and arrogance.

'Everyone loses control some time,' she taunted.
She'd seen it every night since she'd opened the club.
People got carried away. Just as she was now. But she
didn't care.

'Not me,' he finally countered.

'Because you're a robot?' she scoffed. 'You're just a
prince—that doesn't give you super powers.'

Silence strained for two beats before he broke it
with a soft-spoken, hard-hitting whisper. 'You want
me to prove it?'

He didn't move a muscle, but somehow he made
the room smaller. The subtlest change in his tone, the
darkening in his eyes put her senses on alert. He'd gone
from angered, to something else altogether. Something
more dangerous.

Goosebumps rose on her skin, but deep down satisfaction flickered. 'You don't have to prove anything
to me.'

'Don't I? When you've taken it upon yourself to judge me so completely?'

'You'd judged me before you even crossed my threshold,' she pointed out with relish. 'And you collude with other people's judgments when you react with concern about being seen in my company.'

'You're mistaken in many ways.' He frowned. 'I'm not a robot. And no, I don't have super powers. But I don't lose control, Bella.'

He walked closer, until he loomed in front of her. She held her ground and watched. *Dared.*

'I can start,' he promised with wintry imperiousness. 'And then stop.'

'Start what?' she taunted again.

'You're Bella Sanchez,' he murmured. 'You live for kisses and adoration.'

That stung. Her mother's reputation had stained her own from the start. Men assumed that as she'd inherited her mother's figure, she'd have her 'skills' too. But her mother had been discarded by every one of her many lovers. Which was partly why Bella was *not* the lover of anyone bold enough to make a move. And the truth was she was unmoved. Always.

She should shake him off with some glib retort and a smile and make her escape from a situation like this the way she'd done many times before. Or she should tell him exactly where to go and why.

'What if I don't want you to kiss me?' she asked, determinedly standing in place despite the adrenalin rush urging her to run.

'Don't you?' He laughed then. A low, sexy, mocking laugh.

That he'd laughed at all was a shock, but that he

laughed like that? She just gazed at him, stunned by this glimpse of someone else altogether—a gorgeous virile man.

His smile disappeared as he neared, but there was still that glimpse of human behind the pale blue. 'You are beautiful.'

Beneath that clinical assessment she heard huskiness. Heat washed over her, confusing her more.

'Beauty isn't everything,' she pointed out.

Glossy magazines and plastic surgeons would argue otherwise, but Bella knew the truth. Beauty faded. Beauty depended on who was looking. Beauty didn't count for anything at the end of the day.

'No,' he agreed softly.

The atmosphere thickened, building the tension both within her and between them. She wanted to duck and run. She already knew she wouldn't feel anything if he kissed her. She never felt anything. That was the point. She'd tried but she wasn't the hedonist the world wanted her to be. In ten seconds it would be obvious who the frigid one was. He'd know her secret. She gritted her teeth, angered by that old humiliation.

'Go on, then,' she finally snapped. 'Try it and see what happens.'

'Such an invitation,' he mocked.

'You're hardly bounding over with unbridled lust.'

'I don't do unbridled lust, remember?' He regarded her intently. 'You're not going to drive me crazy.'

It was almost as if he was challenging himself. Not her.

'I don't want to drive anyone crazy,' she retorted. 'People ought to take responsibility for their own actions.'

She just wanted to do her own thing. She hadn't asked to be raised in the glare of paparazzi flashes. Yes, she'd chosen the ballet stage, but it wasn't supposed to have intruded into her personal life as much. And now she did all that Internet sharing only to build something for the future—funding her escape route.

'Indeed they should.' He gripped her waist, his hands not too high or too low or too tight. He didn't step closer so there was a clear two inches between them. He held her in the position perfect for a formal dance. But they weren't in a ballroom. They were yards from her tiny bedroom.

Heart thudding, Bella fisted her hands and held them to her stomach, but she couldn't bring herself to say *stop*. Instinctively she knew that if she did, he would. But she was curious to see how far perfect Prince Antonio would take this. She kept her eyes open, focusing intently on him. It was a trick she'd learned when amorous dates had moved closer than she'd wanted. Guys didn't like to think they weren't wowing a woman with their sensual prowess.

But Antonio kept his eyes open too. As he inclined his head she found herself sinking into their surprising depths—they were such a pale blue, but there was an echo of that smile glinting in the backs of them. That smile was what she really wanted more of.

He pressed his lips to hers in the lightest caress, offering less than a heartbeat of touch. But it delivered a lightning flash of heat. Bella froze, teetering on the edge of something unknown, so tempted to tumble over—but he didn't take her there. He didn't touch her again.

He remained a breath away but she couldn't fathom his feelings in his unreadable eyes.

Finally it dawned on her that he had no feelings. He'd been teasing her. He'd intended to give her nothing but that chaste peck all along. Perfectly, bloodlessly executed. Any second now he'd step back and say, 'I told you so'. He was utterly in control at all times.

Disappointment spilled into that vast, empty space in her chest. She really shouldn't feel it, she really shouldn't care, she should concede his victory with laughing grace and push him away.

But she'd felt a glimmer of what might have been— a sliver of heat that had stunned her with its strength.

So she could only stay still, unable to move for thinking—for *feeling*. His eyes were so damn mesmerising but now she couldn't bear to look into them any more. Yet when she dropped her gaze, she saw his sensual mouth and his chiselled jaw roughened with morning stubble. He was picture-postcard perfect and it was so unfair because for one millisecond she'd actually *wanted*—

His fingers tightened, pinching her waist. She looked up in surprise but before she could speak his lips brushed hers again. Another soft, too brief—tantalising—caress. She got the smallest glimpse into his eyes before he bent to her again. His reserve crumbled as intensity flared. Her heart stopped at that flash of emotion.

When he kissed her that third time, he lingered. She lifted her chin, meeting him, her body instinctively yearning for him to stay. She wanted more—a *real* kiss. She wanted him to release the energy she sensed building within him and ease the need starting to ache within her. She wanted more of the magic she'd tasted in that first swift touch. She wanted more than disillusionment and emptiness and abandonment all over again. She just wanted *more*.

For the first time in her life, she *really* wanted it.

He didn't disappoint her this time. He stayed. He held. He kissed. His lips moved from gentle, to more insistent, to finally demanding. As she acquiesced, parting her mouth, his demands grew greater still. His hands shifted, shaping her curves and then possessively pulling her closer. Her heart struck up again, sprinting to a frantic tempo—in shock. In passion. She wriggled her hands from where they'd been squashed between them and reached up to his shoulders so she could literally hang on as he bent her backwards and kissed her more thoroughly still.

Oh, he kissed her. Her eyes drifted shut as she focused on the pressure of his lips—the teasing pleasure. His kiss lightened and she gripped his shoulders more tightly, afraid he was about to pull away. But he kissed her again and again in a series that mimicked that first—softly stirring desire, building her frustration until she couldn't control the small moan that escaped. Then he kissed her hard and long again. And he repeated the pattern—unpredictable, maddening. Delicious.

She'd never have expected Prince Antonio to be as playful. Or as skilled. But what did it matter when he made her feel like *this*?

She moaned in pleasure as he kissed her deeply again. It was as if all the empty places within her were being filled and heated and the sensation was so addictive. There was pure pleasure to be had in his arms. The kind she'd never experienced with anyone else.

Breathless, she wanted to say something, but couldn't. She didn't want to break the magic—uncaring of any consequences, of how crazy this had suddenly become. She just wanted to feel it—all of him—all of the gratification she could get. Instinctively she moved, circling her hips. His hand slid, pressing over the curve of her bottom and pulling her harder against the heat of his pelvis. Feeling how aroused he was made her melt all the more into his embrace.

His arms tightened around her but she didn't resist as he walked her backwards and then pushed her back against the desk. She couldn't remain standing anyway and she had no desire to stop. She only wanted more. Just here. Now. In this white-hot moment.

He shoved the files behind her to the floor with a sweep of his arm, pushed her back until she lay on the hard wood, and followed her down.

He kissed down the side of her neck, burying his mouth in that sensitive spot where her neck met her shoulders. His hand slid beneath her light pyjama top. The sensation of skin on skin made her arch involuntarily. His hand was heavy, then light, teasing as he traced small circles over her abdomen, up to her ribs, then higher still. She shivered as he neared the hard peak of her breast. He lifted his head from hers, breaking the kiss to look into her eyes. He didn't look down as he lifted her top to expose her breasts. She felt the cool air, felt her nipples tighten more—until they were almost painful. She licked her dried lips as she waited, splayed on the desk beneath him, until he looked down at her partially naked body.

A groan ripped from him when he finally looked. She looked down too, saw how her breasts thrust up towards him, her nipples tight and needy and erect—begging for more than his visual attention. They wanted touch. He muttered something unintelligible. Before she could ask him what he'd said he bent his head and took her nipple in the hot cavern of his mouth. Her breathing came quick and erratic as she watched him take pleasure in her body—in pleasuring *her*.

She closed her eyes, sprawled back on the desk, basking in the sensations as he explored her more fully. He pushed between her legs, grinding against her, and cupped her other breast in his hand, his fingers teasing that taut peak. When he pushed her full breasts together to lave both nipples with his tongue, she almost arched off the wood completely. All her restraints were now off, her need unleashed. She bucked, thrusting her hips against his, wanting him to strip her, touch her and kiss her where she was hot and wet and so, so ready.

Never had she been ready for a man the way she was for him. Never had a man made her feel this aroused. The ache between her legs burned, her blood ran faster in a quickening beat of need. She reached out, wanting to explore him too. His skin was hot to the touch. His jaw bristled but it was so good as it gently abraded her tender skin. She raked her hands across his back, the heat of him burning through his sweatshirt.

His muscularity surprised her. He was only ever pictured in suits so she'd never have guessed he'd be this defined. Granite muscles like these meant he worked out—regularly and hard. She wanted to see them. Wanted to touch. But he pressed down, smothering her attempts to pull his sweatshirt up, distracting her from that goal by simply kissing her again and again and again while running his hands over her bared breasts with wicked skill.

And she couldn't resist succumbing to the pleasure of it.

That it could be this man who pulled this feeling from her? This unadulterated *lust*. He left no room for regret or reason. There was only this, only now. His breathing roughened but he said nothing more. He kissed down her neck, then lower to tease with fiery touches across her quivering belly, then back up to her breasts. But his hand worked lower, slipping beneath the waistband of her flimsy short pyjama bottoms. She parted her legs further without thinking about it, aching for him to touch her there. He growled guttural approval as his fingers cupped her intimately. She shuddered at the intensity of desire that consumed her as he gently stroked. She was so close. The pleasure built so shockingly quickly. She'd never been so close with anyone.

'Antonio...' She breathed the quietest plea as she arched against him, right on the edge.

He froze, then glanced up to look into her eyes for a heartbeat. Dazed, she didn't register his tormented expression. But then he pulled away from her, his face now utterly impassive.

'You're stopping?' She gasped in disbelief. *'Now?'*

His lips twisted but he didn't reply. Running his hand through his hair, he huffed out a harsh breath and stepped back from her.

Astonished, she stared, realising what he'd done. He'd done this to prove a petty point. And he'd proved it already. But it was also a punishment. He was putting her in her place in a humiliating show of power—he could have her any way he wanted, however he chose.

But now he chose not to.

That he'd use his sensual dominance over her this way was most especially cruel because she'd never felt anything like this. No man had made her *want* in this way and this one time she'd almost felt pure, sensual pleasure, it had been snatched from her. She swept her hand over her belly, as if she could press away the ache deep inside.

'I don't need you,' she muttered angrily. So hurt. 'I don't need *any* man.' She didn't need any *one*.

He turned back, his gaze smouldering. Her legs were still splayed. She was so exposed, half-stripped and spread on her own damn desk for him to toy with but she refused to cover up and show how shamed she felt.

'What are you doing?' His words sounded raw and accusing.

She realised he was staring at her hand pressed low on her belly. Bitterness rose in her throat. Because yes, the only way she'd ever experienced an orgasm was by her own action. But as if she'd do that now?

Heat burned in his narrowed eyes. Outrage burned in her. She wasn't giving him the pleasure of *watching*. She curled her fingers into a fist, her vision swimming with acidic tears.

She heard his groan and a muttered word, but she didn't know what he said because suddenly he was there. Back where she needed him. Bending between her parted thighs, his spread hand raking up her body.

'It wouldn't be as good,' he muttered, leaning close, catching her gaze with his.

She tried to turn her head away but he moved too fast, holding her chin with a firm grip. He almost smiled as he moved closer.

This kiss was cautious and tender.

She didn't close her eyes and when he drew back a fraction to gauge her response, she kept glaring at him. But then he kissed one eyelid. Then the other. Making her close her eyes. Then he caught her mouth with his again. Not cautious at all. Not holding anything back. Just that passionate teasing, stirring her to react again. To want.

And heaven help her she did. So quickly she was there again, lost in the lust he roused within her. She couldn't wriggle away from him. Couldn't break the kiss. Rather she moaned in his mouth—a mixture of hurt and want and pleading.

In answer he slid his hand firmly over her stomach, wrapped his broad palm around her fist and lifted her arm, pressing it back on the desk beside her, clearing his path down her body. He cupped her breast, then teased his way lower again, to where she was still wet and hot and wanting. All the while his lips were sealed to hers, his tongue stroking and teasing and claiming her the way the rest of her wanted to be claimed.

She moaned again, nothing but want this time. She wanted him naked, wanted to touch him everywhere, wanted him to thrust deep inside her and ease this hellish ache. He didn't. He just teased—decadently, mercilessly until she was sweat-slicked and shivering and mindless.

She bucked against his hand—wanting faster,

deeper, more. He groaned in approval, kissing her harder, letting her feel more of his weight. She wanted to take it all. Her hips rocked, undulating in an increasing rhythm, matching the stroke of his fingers and tongue. She wanted to force him to break free of his control. She wanted him to stop holding back. She wanted him to just take her.

But he didn't relinquish his restraint for one second. He kept kissing her. Kept touching her where she needed him most. Stirring, rousing, until she was almost out of her mind with desire, until she was moaning a song of need into his mouth, her body trembling beneath his, her nails clawing into his skin as she hurtled towards the peak. Finally he broke the passionate kiss, letting her gasp as the rest of her arched, utterly rigid in that unbearable moment before release. Oh, it was here. He'd pulled her through the burn and made her feel it. Her eyes closed, she cried out as the wave of pleasure hit, sweeping her away in that powerful turbulent crest. She clutched him fiercely as the sensations tumbled within her, drowning her in almost unendurable bliss. He pressed hard against her as she convulsed, not letting her pull back from the intensity he'd stirred. His fingers rubbed relentlessly, ensuring she received every last spasm of pleasure from her orgasm.

Finally she fell back on the desk, limp as the warmth spread along her veins, sending her into a lax, dazed state. Raggedly she gasped, trying to recover her mind, but it was impossible to catch her breath. Impossible to wipe the smile from her face. Impossible to believe what had just happened.

Never had a man made her feel so good. It wasn't

just the orgasm, it was the heat and vitality he'd seemed to pour into her. He'd made her feel wholly alive, here and now. Twin tears escaped her closed eyes before she had the chance to brush them away but she was smiling at the same time, because it was so good and such a surprise and she was so happy.

Yet even now, despite that mind-blowing pleasure, the ache within burned anew. Suddenly she felt empty even with that elation still zinging around her. She wanted all of him. And she wanted him now.

Shocked at her surging hunger, she opened her eyes and looked into his.

'Antonio,' she whispered, shocked when she read what was so obvious in his unguarded expression. Torment—desolation and desperation. Feelings she understood all too well.

'Please.' She reached out to cup him—to make him feel as good as he'd made her feel. But he gripped her wrist and stopped her, his hand painfully tight.

'Don't touch me,' he ordered through clenched teeth.

His words hit like physical blows. It was utter, raw rejection.

She closed her eyes but his spurn had already slammed the lingering sense of pleasure from her. Emptiness ripped her open. Now their imbalance struck her forcefully. She was almost naked. He was fully clothed. She was vulnerable and exposed. He was sealed and silent.

But they were both angry.

He released her wrist, pulling away to put three feet of distance between them. He stopped and stood with his back to her, his hands on his hips, his head bowed. She could see the exertion in his breathing, as if he'd run a race to the death. He was trying to slow it, regulate it and recover his equilibrium. Well, so was she. But she was failing.

She sat up, yanking her top down to cover herself, confused and lonelier than ever. 'Maybe it's time—'

'I behaved like—' he interrupted her harshly, then broke off. He twisted to face her. Tall and proud and formal. Icy again. 'I behaved inexcusably,' he said in those remote, clipped tones. He bowed stiffly. 'I apologise.'

For a long moment she couldn't speak. Couldn't believe he'd become this remote statesman again. Did he feel guilty? Was he upset that he'd sullied the memory of his dead lover because he'd felt up the tart from the nightclub? Was that what this was?

Fury burned but oddly pity was entwined with it. She felt sorry for herself. Sorry for him. Sorry this whole moment had started.

But she only had to look at him to know any attempt at conversation would be futile. He'd scorched any sense of connection or compassion. There was simply nothing left. Yet he remained standing like a statue in the middle of her room, staring at her with that damned unreadable expression.

In the end she could only whisper, 'You behaved like a human.'

His nostrils flared but he didn't reply. He swiftly turned and strode to the door.

'You didn't want to be seen,' she called scornfully as this next rejection scalded her all over again.

He still didn't hesitate. He just walked out without a word, rapidly descending the stairs.

Bella closed her eyes until the sound of his footsteps receded completely. She understood anyway. He'd rather risk being seen leaving her club than staying another second in her company.

He didn't want to be near her ever again.

CHAPTER THREE

CARS ROARED: a relentless mass of humming metal and fuel. Distracted, Antonio almost forgot to applaud when the first passed the chequered flag. He'd not been looking at the finish line because she was down with the winning team's pit crew, and she was dressed not to be seen, but to stun.

Photographers called and clicked constantly, like seagulls incessantly circling a kid with an ice-cream cone. Bella paused long enough to send them a glittering smile, then turned to snap a selfie with the winner of the race. Doubtless she'd upload it once she'd filtered it to her satisfaction.

I don't need any man.

Her vehement denial replayed in his mind, but the vulnerability that the harsh-edged words revealed echoed loudest of all. Those tears after she'd come apart in his arms haunted him. He'd broken past that slick, sophisticated façade and found her to be tender and he'd been a jerk. Because he hadn't reciprocated. He hadn't been as honest with her as she'd been with him. And she'd been mortified.

But now, only hours later, her façade was back—beautiful and bulletproof. Grimly he fought the urge to take her somewhere isolated and break her walls down to get to that genuine, emotional response again. As if she'd allow him to now.

While he'd returned to the palace without detection that morning he was in no way pleased. He was a leader of not just an army, but a nation, and he never ran from a situation. Yet he'd run from the desire she'd aroused in him. Now regret and anger burned alongside it.

For the best part of a decade he'd staved off sexual want, using extreme exercise to gain self-control; his honed physique was a by-product of that intense discipline. Because he refused to hurt anyone the way he had Alessia and he refused to use women to satisfy purely physical desires. Discipline had become habit. It had almost become easy.

Until today.

Maybe his apparently uncontrollable desire for Bella had been a reaction to tiredness and stress. Or maybe it was because it had been so long since lust had burned him, it had been able to slip his leash like quicksilver...

He could come up with reasons, but they still didn't excuse his actions. And they didn't explain why he was unable to look away from her now.

She was ravishing, putting on a performance for more than the thousands in this crowd and her online audience of millions. This fortnight on San Felipe was packed with festivities and events, ones he had to attend while sandwiching in the vital trade talks and tax-exemption debates with the foreign politicians who'd come to work during the day and party at night.

Bella would use this fortnight to build her brand and define her club as the most 'it' venue on the island—

if not the world. This was the reason for the glamour, the smiles and selfie-central behaviour. All those society events that he had to attend, she would be present at too. There would be no avoiding her. Not in the immediate future.

His jaw ached with the effort of holding back his frustration.

As soon as the race formalities had concluded, he returned to his large office in the palace. He listened to the requests of his aides, read through the official papers in the scarlet box on his desk and braced himself for the celebration reception that evening.

As he'd figured, she was there, draped in an emerald-green silk dress that skimmed her curves before falling in a dramatic swathe to the floor. He was even less talkative than usual, preferring not to circulate at all. It would hammer home his icy reputation even more, but so be it. If only Eduardo weren't away—his brother had more social patience. Antonio just wanted to get back to the paperwork and the important decisions.

Except that wasn't quite all he wanted.

He endured her presence three more times over the next two days. At a charity brunch, at the unveiling of the plans to redevelop the marina, at the opening night of the new exhibition in the national art gallery...

Every time he saw her, the craving bit harder.

He avoided speaking directly to her, but more than once he met her gaze. Across the crowd in the gallery, during speeches, every glance seared, stopping that breach in his armour from sealing shut again.

Three days since that morning in her office, he seethed at his inability to wrest back his self-control.

His mind wandered every chance it got. When he should be focused, when he should be listening to someone else, when he should be thinking about things so much more important than himself, he thought about what he'd do to make her writhe in his arms until he heard her soft cry of release again.

That cry had made him harder and more wanting, yet more satisfied than he'd ever been in his life. He'd revelled in it for one incredible moment. Then he'd remembered. He couldn't have any kind of relationship.

Then he'd run.

But that cry had tormented his dreams day and night since. Now it was all he could think of.

He glanced at the valet pointlessly polishing Antonio's already buffed-to-brilliant shoes. He had a performance at the opera house to attend tonight and there was no way Bella Sanchez wouldn't be there.

'Leave me.' Abruptly he dismissed the man.

'Sir?' The servant looked nonplussed at the sudden command.

Varying from his schedule was impossible, given how crammed it was, but Antonio needed to pull himself together and cool this burn with a reality check. He needed to see *through* Bella Sanchez and remind himself she was merely a woman. And he'd refused hundreds, if not thousands of women. It was in their best interests that he had.

'I need ten minutes alone,' Antonio ordered.

His valet swiftly bowed and left. Antonio picked up the tablet he used to scan newspaper headlines. With a couple of swipes he opened up a video channel. The simplest of searches retrieved an endless list of clips. He clicked on the first. Lifted from a performance at one of the US's most prestigious ballet theatres, it had been viewed millions of times.

Bella Sanchez dancing the title role of Carmen. In this scene she was seducing a soldier to get him to do her bidding. Antonio watched, his gut tightening, as Bella sent the man a smouldering look over her shoulder—alluring, enthralling, *practised*. It was a move she performed on stage night after night after night, yet she made it utterly convincing. At the end of her solo the audience exploded, chanting her name over and over, stomping their feet, delaying the rest of the performance for a full five minutes while they called for encores. He stared at the screen, as spellbound as everyone in the audience had been, watching as she didn't break character for even a second. Haughtily she waited, accepting the adulation and keeping them in her sexual thrall as if it was only to be expected.

But when she'd lain before him, warm and exposed, she'd not been at all practised or polished. She'd been unrehearsed and real and what had happened had taken her by surprise as much as it had him. And the raw emotion in her eyes when he'd pulled away from her?

He'd hurt her. He regretted that. He regretted touching her.

Yet all he wanted was to do it again.

He tossed the tablet back onto the desk. Reduced to *watching* her like this, like some unbalanced stalker, was no way to find relief.

Why couldn't he end this aching awareness of her? The slow burn threatened to send him insane. He'd resisted already, hadn't he? He'd stopped before taking the pleasure he'd wanted so badly. He'd proven himself.

But he was tired of having to prove himself, tired of

devoting every minute of his life to his crown. Maybe resisting had been the wrong action.

Why shouldn't he have something for himself for once? He'd been restrained for so long. Every other damn prince took lovers. His younger brother had been a total playboy. In other countries princes, politicians, people with power and wealth indulged their desires. Ordinary people did too. It was *normal*.

But not for Antonio.

Not when he knew the heartache the inevitable intense media coverage would cause. Nausea churned in his gut from guilt as he remembered. He was sure Alessia's parents knew the truth of what he'd done to their daughter. They never discussed it, but they knew. So the least he could do was protect and honour both them and the memory of her. It was his duty. Having a public affair with a woman like Bella Sanchez would destroy everything he'd worked so hard to maintain. And an affair *would* become public.

Slaking this haunting lust was impossible.

But still his blood burned.

At the theatre he saw her immediately. She'd made that unavoidable. A scarlet petal in a sea of black suits, she wore the colour of seduction and vampishness, unapologetically sensual and attention stealing and a bold choice given the red highlights in her hair. Held up by thin straps, her dress was cut low over her generous breasts, their size and shape accentuated by her slender waist. Her strappy sandals made her almost tall enough to look him in the eye. Except tonight she refused to look at him at all.

Her shoulders were very square, her spine ramrod straight, her chin lifted. She knew every single man in the audience was salivating over her. That was the point, was it not?

She was here to be noticed, coveted, prized, but not claimed. This was a costume. Which was the real Bella Sanchez—the cotton-pyjama-clad woman stretching before six in the morning, or this carefully made-up temptress?

His heart drummed a fast, heavy beat. He kept his hands at his sides and didn't even try to smile. Unfortunately she was seated in the box to the left of the stage. Of course she was—it meant everyone in the audience could see her. As the royal box was in the centre of the dress circle, he could still see her even as he stared hard at the stage.

A violinist performed a haunting adagio, a choir sang, a soprano dazzled. But it was when a couple performed a *pas de deux* in the first half that he caught the first reaction in Bella. He studied her closer and saw the heartache in her expression as she watched them dance—was that the sheen of tears glistening in those blue-green eyes?

The downturn of her mouth arrested his heart. He gripped the armrests of his seat. He would not stand and go to her. He would not press his lips to hers. He couldn't let lust ignite again. But his imagination danced on, teasing him with the fantasy of her beneath him, smiling now as she looked up at him. How hot she'd feel, how she'd drink him in—

He gritted his teeth and glared back at the stage.

By the time the house lights came on for the interval she'd composed herself and was smiling again as she engaged with the city councillors she was seated with. The look she'd just sent one of them was straight from the stage. Antonio had seen it on that video clip only a couple of hours ago. It made sense. She'd spent most of her life studying how to entrance and entice and tell stories and emotions with her body. Her appearance tonight in the audience was just as much of a performance as any she'd done on stage. Just as he was performing as 'Prince Antonio' and masking the unruly battle swirling within.

He paced ahead of his aides, desperate to burn the energy building up inside, glancing at some of the other women present. They were as beautifully attired, but he felt nothing. It wasn't clothes, jewels, hair or make-up attracting him. It was that indefinable, unique essence. *Lust.* He grimaced. Why couldn't he just shake it off?

A throng waited for him to receive them during the interval. He listened and asked a few courteous questions. He'd got through five guests when Bella walked in alone. A murmur rippled across the room as people reacted. The crowd parted, giving her a halo effect as she moved into the middle of it. She didn't look to where he stood at the farthest end, but he was certain she knew exactly where he was. Her 'not looking' was too deliberate.

Now the crowd's attention was divided—half watched him, half watched her. The flamboyant Spanish entrepreneur who'd financed her club scurried over to speak with her. But it was the wolfish man trying to manoeuvre his way towards Bella who snagged Antonio's full attention—and animosity. Jean Luc Giraud was a predator out to amass as much money, and seduce as many women, as possible. But the man barely got five paces before his path was stopped by another, equally predatory-looking male.

Antonio stilled and watched closely. The ability to communicate was vital to his work and long ago he'd learned to lip-read. It was a useful skill, never more so than now.

'Don't even bother.' The taller man blocked Jean Luc's path.

Antonio couldn't see Jean Luc's response, but the blocker was facing him, and every word was clearly drawled with arrogant laziness as he answered.

'She won't give you what you want.'

Antonio's gut clenched. He waited while Jean Luc responded. The blocker shook his head in mock pity.

'Go ahead and try. She'll flirt, but won't follow through.'

Jean Luc turned, enabling Antonio to see the last of his response.

'...a tease.'

'Exactly. Looks hot, but is colder than an icicle. When you get her alone she drops the act and refuses. She's a fake. Like her injury was fake. She couldn't handle the demands of the company. The second she got hurt she was out of there so she could become the club queen.'

Red mist momentarily fogged Antonio's vision, blinding him to whatever the asshole said next. That this fool had been lucky to kiss Bella and made such a muff of it that she'd shut down? That he'd not treated her how she ought to have been?

Once more he remembered her look of surprise when that passion exploded between them. How often had she *not* got the pleasure she should have?

Compassion burned at the injustice. Just because he didn't indulge didn't mean he thought others shouldn't, but it should *always* be good. Wasn't that the point? And if it wasn't any good, then of course she was going to say no. And the jerk here should just—

'Your Highness?'

He turned to the man beside him, forcing on a polite smile. 'Forgive me, I was thinking of something else.' He drew in a breath when he realised who had stepped up to speak with him. 'Salvatore.' He inclined his head, making a conscious effort to unclench his fists.

'You're enjoying the show?' Salvatore Accardi asked with an obsequious bow.

'It is nice to see families out enjoying themselves together celebrating the island.' Antonio faintly underlined the word *families*. 'I enjoy San Felipe's festival season very much.'

'As do I.' Salvatore smiled. 'I'm sure you remember my daughter Francesca.'

His *other* daughter. The legitimate one who was a few months older than Bella.

Antonio turned slightly. Francesca Accardi was taller than Bella, her hair a glossy brunette, her slim figure beautifully dressed. 'Of course.'

'It is an honour to be here tonight, Your Highness.' She smiled brightly. 'The performances have been amazing and I'm sure the rest of the concert will be as incredible.'

'I'm glad you are enjoying it.' Antonio bowed, about to step away.

But Francesca suddenly spoke again. 'My father's new boat came into the marina after the unveiling of the new plans this morning.'

'Francesca is a designer specialising in marine interiors,' Salvatore chimed. 'Graduated top in her year.'

'Congratulations,' Antonio replied with a nod to Francesca.

'You might like to see our latest beauty,' Salvatore added. 'Her work is very unique.'

'I'm sure it is spectacular,' Antonio answered guardedly.

Everyone knew he liked his boats—thought they were his one indulgence. But the truth was he liked them because he could work in peace without interruption.

'I thought the plans for the marina expansion were very interesting,' Francesca said. 'Overcrowding is a problem of course, but I've had some thoughts as to how it could be made more efficient...' She trailed off and smiled up at him.

Was this politicising or flirting?

Antonio figured boldness was a family trait, but he felt none of the stirring he felt in the presence of her fiery half-sister. He couldn't resist glancing over at Bella to see if the wolf jerk had made his way to her. But she stood alone, looking right back at him, her green eyes stormy and accusing, watching him talk pleasantries with the man who denied that her existence was his responsibility. As his gaze clashed with hers, she lifted her chin and she looked away without so much as a blink.

Anger bubbled. She'd deliberately blanked him. He wanted her to look at him, needing to understand that emotion in her eyes. Instead he wrenched his attention back to the woman beside him. Bella's supposed half-sister Francesca Accardi was watching him too closely. He flicked his fingers and the aide hovering nearby stepped up.

'This is Matteo,' he introduced him briefly. 'Matteo, I believe Ms Accardi has some interesting ideas on the marina development. I would like you to meet with her to discuss them.'

There was no mistaking the disappointment in Salvatore's eyes as Antonio stepped back, leaving Matteo to arrange an appointment with Francesca. But Antonio was too used to people trying to make time with him, especially when accompanied by their single daughters. He turned back to spot Bella, but she'd vanished.

Bella sat in the plush seat in the exclusive box, one of the first to return for the second half of the variety performance. She'd intended to be one of the last—to maximise her exposure. As much as she loathed the tricks, she'd learned well from her mother. But her knees were now too wobbly to make that late entrance, her nerves too shredded from seeing Prince Antonio schmooze her father. The thing was, it was seeing Antonio that hurt more than Salvatore Accardi's customary rudeness.

Was she so stupidly weak she trembled at the mere sight of him?

Tonight she'd dressed with as much care as if she were still stepping onto a stage in front of thousands. She'd no shortage of glamorous dresses—people paid for her to wear their designs as long as she put her picture on social media. Getting the right look took longer than imaginable but it was a necessary part of the mystique and the 'lifestyle' her club was selling. Having lost her ballet career, she'd no other qualifications—*yet*—to call on. For all their fabulousness free dresses couldn't be eaten and she couldn't sell them for cash.

If she ever did clear her wardrobe it could only be to raise money for charity.

So if she wanted to eat, she needed to earn real money from a real job, study on the side and eventually save enough to move on to what she really wanted to do. And as much as she hated her inherited 'notoriety', she needed it, because without it she'd have absolutely nothing and she had to work it hard now because it wasn't going to last—some other model or actress or lifestyle blogger would be the new flavour soon enough.

She had to be seen. Flirt if necessary. Dance in her own club. But most importantly she had to avoid the heartless Prince who'd judged and punished her so personally.

But deep down she knew she'd dressed tonight with him in mind. She'd felt his gaze on her at those other events since that morning and his attention—his disapproval—stung. She'd tried not to care that he'd left her so abruptly but she did. Too much.

She'd wanted more but he'd reacted with such fury when she'd reached for him, he couldn't have made it clearer—she was so far beneath him.

And he was the ultimate jerk.

For a moment she'd actually thought they'd had a real kind of connection. He'd made her feel so good, then snatched it all away. She didn't know why but that one betrayal bit deeper than all the others she'd faced in her life.

She didn't enjoy the rest of the performance. She wanted to go and hide but she had to appear at the after-party backstage to show she wasn't down and out, had to smile at those she'd once danced alongside, know-

ing how they'd talked about her, and then had to go to
her club and tirelessly work it up.

When the curtain finally fell she escaped her local
council companions, telling them she'd meet them at
the party shortly, but it was to the now empty stage
she went rather than the powder room. Even with the
curtain down, that vast black expanse felt like home to
her, the one place she'd felt she truly belonged. Loneliness surged and she quickly ducked back into the wings
before anyone saw her.

Pull it together.

She had her new kind of show to put on tonight.

'Bella?'

She whirled at the low whisper, blinking to get rid
of the impending tears. How had he found her? Why
was he alone?

'You're distressed.' Antonio stood stiffly at a short
distance from her. In his black tuxedo he almost disappeared into the dark wings.

'I'm fine.' She tried to answer evenly, never wanting him to know how much she still hurt from his behaviour.

'Do not lie to me,' he said, very quiet and formal.
'Did somebody say something to upset you?'

'No one here could say anything to upset me,' she
muttered, wishing it were true.

'No?' He held her captive with a mere look. 'I just
told you not to lie to me.'

'Nobody has said anything to upset me. *Yet,*' she
elaborated pointedly.

The scepticism remained in his eyes. 'Then what
is it?'

She didn't answer—couldn't. He had no right to pry

and he couldn't expect her to open up to him now just because he was asking in that gentle tone.

'Bella?' He remained standing so restrained a few paces from her, yet there was that huskiness in his voice.

'I miss it,' she replied quickly, as hushed as he, because it was easier to talk about her ballet than what was really upsetting her. 'I miss the moment when I'm waiting in the wings and I take a last deep breath and step forward.'

'You miss the applause?'

She sighed inwardly at that edge. Of *course* she damn well did. She'd been seeking approval from someone—*anyone*—all her life. And she'd never got it from those supposed to love her, so yes, she'd sought it from the masses. She loved that applause and she'd worked so hard to earn it. But she heard criticism in his voice and knew he'd never understand.

'I miss the freedom.' The stage was where she'd felt most comfortable. 'The feeling of being in control.'

'Control of what?'

'Myself. Knowing I can move the way I need to… That I'm as strong and as fast… That I've done the work and the world is at my feet.' She stiffened at the look in his eyes.

'So you're the one who doesn't like to lose control,' he said softly. 'And yet you did.'

Anger burned—swift and uncontrollable. 'And isn't that just what you wanted?' she snapped. 'To make a fool of me.' His rejection had been her ultimate humiliation.

And she wasn't letting it happen again.

She pulled up and tried to speak calmly. 'You'd better go before someone comes looking and sees you talking to me.'

But he walked towards her, not away. 'I want to talk to you.'

'You want to gloat? To crow over your victory?'

He halted barely an inch away. 'I don't feel like a winner.'

'You started. You stopped. You wanted to prove your power—'

'I wanted to please you. I wanted to see you pleasured,' he interrupted in a rough whisper. 'That is *all* I wanted. I wasn't thinking of anything else.'

The words, the way he said them, silenced her. A trickle of warmth worked down her spine. He'd *wanted* to please her? It hadn't been about making her pay?

Confused, she gazed at him. Passion smouldered in the backs of his eyes, but the way he stood so still was so *controlled*. Was that because his emotions were awry? Was that because he didn't trust himself?

'Don't you think I might have wanted to do the same?' she whispered, unable to hold back even when she knew she ought.

'I *can't*.' The words were wrenched from him. His sharply drawn breath sliced into her.

'So you can give me pleasure but you can't receive it?' she asked, somehow feeling even more hurt than before. 'You punish yourself that much?'

A wild look flared in his expression. Her heart thundered but she refused to run; instead she stepped that last inch closer to stand toe to toe with him.

'That isn't it,' he muttered harshly.

'Then what is it?' she whispered, all caution lost. 'You don't like sex? Or just sex with me?'

She never talked back this way. She worked to keep men at arm's length, smiling and dancing but maintaining distance in a finely balanced art. But with Antonio she'd lost all that ability. For the first time in her life, she wanted a man to come closer.

He gripped her shoulders, leaning in to answer her. 'I haven't had sex in a long time. Thanks to you, it is all I can think of now.'

Satisfaction poured into her. Raw, feminine, sensual satisfaction. 'Then what stopped you?'

Why had he rejected her so brutally?

He didn't answer. He just looked at her. They both knew she would have let him do anything. She'd almost begged. And he'd jerked away. That memory burned. She wanted him to burn too.

'You're scared you won't be any good after so long?' she taunted.

His laugh was short and unamused. 'Don't try to provoke me into proving everything to you again. It isn't necessary.'

He gazed into her eyes, then his focus lowered to her mouth. Her limbs weakened with that languorous feeling. The low ache that had been with her for days now sharpened. She wanted a kiss. Then she wanted *complete* satisfaction. It was only a millimetre away. One tiny decision.

'This situation is intolerable,' he snapped, pulling her flush against his lean, hard frame. 'We have to—'

'Bella? Is that you?'

She jumped, stepping back as Antonio released her at the exact same time. A quick glance at him showed sharp cheekbones and a clamped jaw.

Erik, her former ballet partner, stood just to the side

of the wings. He was someone she counted as a friend, but he was the biggest gossip in the company. And with him—watching with eagle eyes?

Sebastian. Her blood iced. Of all the creeps she'd met in the world, Sebastian was one of the worst.

'I thought that was your dress…' Erik paused as he looked past her and saw who she was with. 'I'm awfully sorry. Are we interrupting?'

'Not at all. Ms Sanchez was kind enough to show me the stage on the way to the celebration,' Antonio answered with his customary quelling reserve, deflecting any suggestion of impropriety by demeanour alone.

For a split second Bella just gazed at him, amazed at his ability to revert to his formal 'prince' façade so quickly. And she now realised it *was* a façade. Why did he need such a remote, cold veneer? Did he never let anyone in?

He glanced at her, and she was shocked again to see that the heat had completely vanished from his eyes. A different expectation was within them now.

'Crown Prince Antonio, may I introduce you to Erik Lansing? He was the lead dancer tonight.' Bella obeyed Antonio's implicit order and acted as if nothing had happened. 'And this is Sebastian, the company's artistic director.'

Instinctively she straightened her spine as she faced her old boss. Sebastian had decided which ballerina got which part in each production. He was the man who'd assumed she'd be happy to become his lover, who'd been angered when she'd said no. She'd had to dance better than ever to prove her worth—to make it impossible for him to deny her the parts. But she could never shake that smoke of suspicion and innuendo amongst the other dancers. Sebastian had liked to let that smoke hang in the air, refusing to have it known she'd rejected him.

'I enjoyed your performance tonight.' Antonio grimly acknowledged the two men who'd almost caught him in a clinch with Bella.

He'd been a breath from kissing her. And if he had, he wouldn't have been stopping any time soon. Because she'd wanted it too. They'd have ignited the attraction sizzling between them and neither could have stopped until it had been fully assuaged.

He never should have followed her to the stage. But his curiosity—and desire—had been too strong. She fascinated him and he'd felt compelled to apologise and explain himself at least in part to her. Something he never did in a personal situation, because there *were* no personal situations. Until now.

But now he stood face to face with the 'blocker' who'd warned Jean Luc off Bella. This Sebastian slimeball was her old company's artistic director? That title meant power—over a ballerina in the company. Presumably he could offer promotion, or he could pass her over and give a prized part to another, more willing woman. Yet Bella hadn't given him what he'd wanted. And she stood straight, head held high, bracing herself in defiance in front of them all.

Antonio had known she had strength. Now he knew she had integrity too.

'Thank you.' Erik half bowed. 'I miss Bella though. I don't dance anywhere near as well with anyone else.'

He'd been Bella's ballet partner? Antonio watched as Erik slung his arm along her shoulders. Bella smiled at Erik but the look in her eyes wasn't the same as when she looked at Antonio. There was no desire, no anger, no passion. There was only a sorrow-tinged amusement. She didn't want the same thing from Erik as she wanted from him.

Even so, Antonio's stomach tightened. The jealousy was ridiculous. He was no better than any of the other predators in suits, sniffing around her.

'I must return to the other guests,' he clipped, his jaw aching. 'Excuse me.'

'Of course,' Bella murmured.

'We have to stay at this thing for at least twenty minutes, right? Then we're hitting your club.' Erik's voice carried as Antonio strode away. 'I hear it's full of beautiful young things.'

'Absolutely. Wait 'til you see my star barman.' Bella's laughter bubbled as she went back to her performance.

During the reception in the backstage lounge Antonio watched her execute those choreographed moves in real life again. But his bitterness receded when he saw that blankness in her eyes. It told him everything. This was an astute businesswoman doing what she deemed necessary to make her work a success. Beneath that determination, she had needs and desires that weren't being met.

So, thanks to her, did he.

An affair was impossible. But he wanted just one taste of the forbidden.

No one could know. And for that to happen, it could only happen the once.

Clandestine. Discreet. Finite.

There'd be no power games, threats or sleazy rewards. They would just be two people working out an intense attraction on their own terms and in private.

Five minutes later he watched her leave with her entourage of dancers. She was deliberately breaking royal protocol and leaving the reception before he, the Crown Prince, did. Showing him she didn't give a damn.

Which might be true.

But she still wanted him.

CHAPTER FOUR

BELLA RECOGNISED THE man immediately. Prince Antonio's aide might be immaculately and discreetly attired, but he still didn't fit in. His expression was as austere as his employer's and he clearly wasn't at her club to dance.

She wasn't dancing either. She was playing the 'exclusive VIP room' card, trying to let Erik distract her, but not even his endless talk could keep her thoughts from one tall, dark and handsome prince for long. And now here was Antonio's errand boy at almost three in the morning looking as if he was on a mission. Her pulse sprinted, swiftly overtaking the fast-thudding beat of the club anthem blaring from the state-of-the-art speakers.

From her seat on the mezzanine floor she saw him identify her bar manager. She immediately rose, discreetly radioing for that manager to escort the aide to the small private office at the back of the bar. She went down via the curling steps in the main dance space, taking her time to smile with some of her guests so no one could suspect how on edge she'd suddenly become. There were too many people and every single one of them had a smart phone with a camera app.

After another few minutes working her way past the bar, she entered the small private room. He stood waiting in the middle of it.

'Ms Sanchez, my name is Matteo. I am Prince Antonio's assistant.' He half bowed as soon as she'd closed the door behind her. 'The Prince requests your company.' He held a thick white envelope out to her.

Her name was on the front, inked in a scrawling hand and underlined with a couple of heavy pressed lines that suggested urgency. Demand.

Bella.

Her blood ran faster. She could hear his voice, whispering her name as he touched her, devastating her defences until she'd melted in his arms. But he wasn't here now. He'd sent a messenger in the middle of the night. Had he even written her name himself?

'He requests my company right now?' she asked Matteo carefully.

'Apparently an issue has arisen,' Matteo answered, still offering the envelope.

Bella stared, unable to be sure that she'd heard innuendo in his tone or not, but his face was a blank mask. He'd learned from his master well.

'And this issue can't wait until morning?' she asked.

'If you would take the envelope, Ms Sanchez.'

She took it from him and turned it over, breaking the seal on the back. She drew out the single thick card and, with a cool glance at Matteo, turned away to read the note. But the card bore only two lines of that harsh writing.

We need to talk.

The bald statement was followed by a number and an address—she recognised it as an apartment building near her club and her pulse was *not* accelerating, but her breathing quickened. Her nerves tightened.

'I will escort you there now,' Matteo said, as if he were offering her the greatest service ever.

'That won't be necessary.' She put the card back into the envelope with care. 'I can't go there now.'

The surprise that flashed on his face gave her an inordinate sense of satisfaction.

'Prince Antonio requests your company,' Matteo repeated.

'So you said,' she answered, determined to stay cool. 'And I will get there when I can.'

'You don't understand—'

'I understand perfectly.' She smiled at him though her mouth felt dry as dust. 'You're the one who doesn't understand and nor does he, obviously. I have a business to run. So you can tell him that I'll get there if and when I can.'

Matteo didn't reply but she wasn't bothered by his scrutiny. She wasn't afraid of him. But she was wary of how Antonio made her feel—and how much she wanted him.

'If you'll excuse me, I need to get back to my guests.' She clutched the envelope and left him to find his own way out.

But she didn't return to her guests. She climbed all the way to her own tiny apartment at the top. She put the card on her desk—the one he'd kissed her on—and stared at it.

Was this how a prince made a booty call? With just her name, an address and a lame 'we need to talk'? Did he do this all the time? Send his aide to set up shag-a-thons for him in a private apartment in town so no one would ever know?

So much for the myth of heartbroken, isolated Prince Antonio. Turned out the supposedly heroic, self-sacrificing Prince of the People had feet of clay. He just wanted it like any other guy. On the side when it convenienced him.

She was livid. And she was ignoring him.

She went back down to the dance floor. She wasn't going to drop everything at his beck and call. But she couldn't concentrate properly. Time crawled. It felt like hours until four a.m. finally struck—yet it was only forty-five minutes since Matteo had left.

It was another hour before her staff had gone and she'd locked up and could shower. The cascading hot water didn't ease her tension any. Sleep wasn't happening. So she dressed in skinny jeans, a light tee and ballet flats on her feet.

It was five-thirty in the morning when she finally made her move. She'd go and see him and tell him to his face.

No.

She wouldn't be his latest secret lover.

She walked out of the side door, ensuring the alarm was enabled, and saw Matteo leaning against the doorway of the building opposite. He crossed the street to where she stood.

'I will escort you there now,' he said.

'Have you been waiting here all this time?'

He nodded and turned in the direction of the apartment.

'You don't need to—' She started to argue but realised the poor man was only following orders. She was better to save her fight for facing Antonio. She started walking, pretending not to care that Matteo remained a half pace behind her the entire way. Clearly he *was* used to doing this kind of errand for his boss.

Fury pushed her faster.

At the apartment building the security guard wordlessly opened the door, not looking Bella in the eye. Matteo stepped in front and led her to the elevator.

Yeah, he'd definitely done this many times before.

He entered the lift only long enough to punch in a code at the keypad. It whooshed up swiftly, leaving her feeling as if her stomach were still on the ground. Ruefully she reckoned her brain was back at her club.

When the elevator stopped on the top floor she stepped out. The heavy door on the small landing was open. Antonio stood, resting a shoulder against the frame, staring at her. He still wore the jet-black tux, the jacket immaculate and tie neatly fastened; only the hint of shadow on his chiselled jaw gave away the passage of time—that and his glare. Serious, handsome, smouldering, he said so much in silence.

Too bad. She lifted her chin, because his rejection still *hurt*. 'You summoned. I came.'

She walked past him into the apartment, commanding the centre space.

'What do you want from me?' Years of training stood her in good stead; she knew how to fake confidence 'til she made it.

Antonio quietly closed the door, taking a moment to temper his response. She'd kept him waiting, he'd had zero sleep, and he didn't have the patience for endless debating. This was one situation in which action would speak louder than words.

But he needed the words because they meant he'd retain control. Of himself, of what was to happen, of how this would end.

And he wanted to hear her speak too. He liked her challenging edge, as if she wasn't going to agree to everything he had to say. At least, not immediately.

'Would you like to sit down?' He gestured to the plush armchair rather than the wide sofa. Enforcing social niceties at this moment would help keep him civilised.

'I'm not going to jump just because you said to.'

Her reply shredded the remnants of all polite pretence, exposing the sensual tension. Combustion was a breath away.

He gave up on civility and crossed the room to tower over her. 'And yet here you are.'

He'd known sending Matteo had been a mistake. His brother Eduardo had relied on Matteo for his discretion and reliability. Antonio had never had cause to before and should've known it would be better to do a job himself. He should've waited until later and gone to her club alone. Yet he liked this look in her eyes—baleful anger bubbling over sensual awareness.

'What do you want from me?' she repeated unevenly. 'You want me to dance for you?' She rolled her shoulders and took a half-step to the side.

It was barely a dance, more a suggestive movement, but Antonio was unable to answer. Another emotion entered her eye—determination, then *calculation*.

She moved ever so slightly while her gaze remained locked on his. There wasn't the freedom he'd seen when she'd not known he was watching her alone in the club. She looked every bit as beautiful, but he saw her self-awareness, her moves made for their intended effect on her audience.

On *him*.

'No,' he snapped.

Instantly she stopped. Her sultry mask fell, revealing her anger in full, making her all the more stunning.

'Not like that,' he added. 'I don't want to *watch*. I don't want a *performance* from you.'

'Then what do you want?' she flared. 'To humiliate me again?'

'Humiliate you?' His own anger ignited. He'd never intended to do that and he was furious he had. He grabbed her hips and hauled her against him. 'I want what we had. I want the real thing.'

He crushed her mouth under his, unable to contain himself a second longer. Energy radiated from her—resistance, anger, but most of all desire. In the next moment she melted, opening, pressing closer. Then she kissed him back—*hard*.

This was what he wanted. Her unrestrained reaction to him—negative and positive and the total eroticism that burst to life the second they touched. All the resistance within her transformed to passion. She burrowed closer, angrily clutching his jacket.

He lost his head in her heat. He ached to rip them free of their clothing. Have her exactly as he wanted—bared and welcoming with that fire-gilded hair tumbling free about her shoulders and her body hot and slick.

But he pulled away, brutally breaking the kiss because he had to put restraints around this. And he was damn well ensuring she had more than a quick, angry orgasm this time. He'd see her fully sated. Fully his.

Breathing hard, he held her at a distance, taking primitive pleasure in how long it took for her to regain her balance and stand on her own.

'This cannot go on.' He'd give in to lust, but only once.

'What?' she asked. Fury combusting, she shoved his hands from her shoulders.

'It only worsens with time,' he said quickly, before she continued to think he didn't want to resolve this in a way they'd both appreciate. He could hardly bear to look at the luminescent need in her gleaming green eyes; he couldn't resist her ferocity. 'We have to work this out.'

It had only been a few days, but Bella knew what he meant. The hunger, desire, and the *frustration*. The emotions he roused in her were the most intense of her life.

'So you sent your errand boy to make your booty call.' It was anger and arousal coursing through her veins now, a heady combination that made it almost impossible to think. She *felt* too much.

'I didn't want to attract attention,' he explained crisply. 'It wouldn't be good for either of us.'

'The publicity would be good for me,' she argued hotly, pushing forward what she knew would be his greatest objection to anything happening between them. Just because she could. 'Make my club even more popular. I could do with that success.'

'They would drag *you* through the mud and you know it. Don't act vapid. I know you care more than that.'

'Do you?' How could he really know anything about her?

He cupped her chin and tilted her face to his, capturing her gaze in his steely one again. 'I saw you. I felt you. You're more vulnerable than you wish to admit.'

Ever so lightly he touched the tips of his fingers to the pulse beating frantically just below her jaw. Not a threat, but a caress of concern.

Her heart stuttered. 'I don't need your protection. I can handle anything.' She jerked her head, forcing him to release her. 'It's your name you're worried about. Having an affair with me would ruin perfect Prince Antonio's holier-than-thou reputation.'

'I don't care what others think about me,' he said softly. 'But there are other people who would be hurt by my personal life becoming public. Discretion is necessary because it is kind.'

Silenced, she gazed up at him, her heart melting. He wanted to be kind? He wanted to protect people other than the two of them. She couldn't help but wonder who they were.

'And you do not want to be hunted any more than you already are.' His gaze narrowed, penetrating. 'You do not want to be treated the way your mother was. You do not want to have every detail of your life reported on. Invented. You do not want to have your ex-lovers paid fortunes to tell your sexual secrets. They would stop at nothing to get that information should you be known to be my lover.'

He hit precisely where she was most vulnerable. She never wanted to live the way her mother had. And yes, while she courted publicity now, it was one thing to manage her own media relations and give them enough to keep them interested but not have them hound her completely. But the way they would pry if they knew she was having an affair with Prince Antonio?

It would be unbearable.

'Yet you're still willing to take the risk?' she asked.

'I am talking only one night.'

Just once.

So this would never become an affair. It would be nothing more than a one-night stand. And there wasn't even much of this night left.

'I don't want to fight it any more,' he said ruefully. 'The last few days have been hell.'

That he felt as intensely as she did soothed her some.

'No one will ever know,' he added.

'Except you sent your man to fetch me at three in the morning in a club full of people,' she pointed out.

'I trust him with my life,' Antonio said.

'Because he's done this for you so many times before?' Maybe that shouldn't bother her, but it did.

'Never for me,' Antonio answered solemnly. 'But I cannot answer for my brother.'

Relief seeped into her stiffness. Prince Eduardo had been 'the Playboy Prince'. Of course.

'You do not need a man. A husband. A hero,' Antonio said quietly continuing his persuasion. 'You are determined to be independent. I respect that. But you want…' He paused. 'I have duty and obligations. I will never marry because I can never give a woman all she deserves. But I, too, want…'

'Do you?' She was somehow hurt, despite knowing everything that he said was true. 'But you don't have lovers. Or is that just the publicity line?'

'It's not just a line,' he said quietly.

She rested her palm on his chest, daring to intrude where she really had no right. Just to see if he could be honest with her. If he could share when only a few days ago he couldn't share anything. 'How long?'

'A long, long time. I've been busy. After a while it wasn't something that was important to me.' A glimmer of laughter suddenly lit his face. 'But don't worry, it won't be over too quickly.'

His ability to pleasure her was the last thing she was worried about. He'd already given her the best orgasm of her life, and proven his personal restraint at the same time. 'Why now, why me?'

That serious, brooding look returned. 'Because I can't think of anything *but* you. Because I'm tired of trying to fight it already. I know it's the same for you. I come near and your body reacts. You can't help the way you respond to me.' Unflinching, he demanded equal honesty from her. 'Do you have a lover currently?'

'Do you think I would be here if I did?'

'Of course not. I apologise.' His expression softened. 'There is more talk about you than actual action.'

'Does it matter?'

'No. But do you think I don't know how much of the Bella Sanchez "story" is made up?'

'You don't want to know the truth?' She straightened, determined to defend her scarlet honour even when really she'd never been that 'scarlet'.

'I know it already. You give yourself away every time I touch you. Every time I come near you. You react differently to me.' He put his hands on her waist and drew her closer. 'You cannot hide how you react to me.'

'That's not fair,' she said huskily. 'As if you're all that experienced.'

He laughed appreciatively. 'I might be rusty, but I'm not ignorant. And you're not the sophisticated vamp you try to portray.'

If this was him 'rusty' then heaven help her when he hit his stride.

He ran his hand up and down her spine, partly soothing, mostly arousing. Every touch seemed designed to torment her.

'The other morning…' He paused and looked at her with concern. 'I saw you. I felt you. What happened, how I made you feel…was more than you expected.'

She flushed, embarrassed that he'd known her orgasm had come as a surprise.

'I want to make you feel that good again.' Intent darkened his eyes.

'It's not wise.' But her body yearned for it.

'Because I made you emotional?'

'You were too.'

He froze for a moment; his hands stopped those teasing touches. 'I like being able to make you feel good. And you do want me to kiss you again.' Deliberately, lightly he rubbed his finger across her lip. 'And I want to. Everywhere.' He suddenly pulled her hips against his. Hard. Letting her know exactly where else he intended to use his mouth.

'You always get what you want?' she asked breathlessly, the feel of his body against hers was so good. The promise in his eyes exquisite torment.

'I'm the Crown Prince—most people are pleased to do things for me.'

'So I should feel honoured?'

He shook her gently then pulled her to rest against him again. 'Stop trying to stall and just admit you feel the same.'

'The same?' She stiffened, trying to hold back the desire threatening to overwhelm her. Did he really feel this as intensely as she? Did he want her the way she wanted him this second?

'I like how good you make me feel,' he muttered.

'I didn't do anything. You wouldn't let me.' She'd been so hurt by that.

A wry smile curved his lips. 'You need me to prove it? Again. Untrusting creature.'

'Do you blame me?' she asked. 'You ask me to admit things when you rejected me so harshly. You wouldn't let me near you. You made me—' She broke off. 'And then you left. You couldn't get away quickly enough.'

His smile faded. 'I apologise. You took me by surprise. You were right and I was wrong. I shouldn't have walked out and I have regretted it every second since.'

'You're the Penitent Prince?' She couldn't breathe.

'I want you more than I've ever wanted anyone. I wouldn't be here now if I didn't.'

At his words that last little knot of anger disintegrated within her.

'Nor would I.' But she shivered because somehow his admission made *her* feel vulnerable.

He slid his hand beneath the hem of her thin tee, tracing his fingers up her spine. His touch warm and firm.

'Chemistry like this…I didn't think it happened,' she confessed.

'Nor did I.'

It was just physical, right?

'You don't like it,' she muttered, her thoughts derailed by the swirling pattern he was drawing over her skin with his fingertips.

'It's a distraction,' he answered evasively. He slid his hand up to cup the nape of her neck and pushed her back over his arm so her shirt pulled taut. He gazed down at the way the fabric rubbed against her nipples, emphasising their hard outline.

'So you think if we have what we want, then we'll no longer want it?' She arched uncontrollably against him as he sucked one tight nipple into his mouth, bra and tee and all.

'Yes.' He bent to give her other breast the same sinfully good treatment. 'This cannot be anything more than here and now. You wouldn't want it to be anything more.'

She arched against him again, unable to resist rocking her hips against his hard pelvis. He was right. She didn't want any of what would come with this if it became public. 'Will you allow me to touch you this time?'

'I don't know how I got the strength to stop you. I don't know how I walked away,' he muttered. 'I want to see you naked.' His glittering gaze raked down her body, felt like a force—drawing heat from her, making her want to move in a way she'd never wanted before.

'We each take off one layer at a time,' she suggested. 'It's only fair.'

'Life isn't fair.' He smiled wolfishly and pushed her tee shirt up.

'*This* time, it is going to be fair.' She demanded it.

He didn't answer, but there was a glint in his eye

as he straightened her up, stood back and held out his arms, letting her peel the perfectly tailored jacket from his shoulders. Slowly, savouring the moment, she tugged his tie free, then unbuttoned the pearl buttons of his starched white shirt.

'That's more than one layer already,' he noted, his breath stirring her hair as she moved in close.

She didn't care. She was too busy exposing his chest. Heat balled low in her belly. He was gorgeous. Nothing but lean muscle and bronzed skin and a faint line of dark hair arrowing down the centre of his rigid abs to his belt. For the first time she took real pleasure in just looking. And then kissing. Then touching.

She traced over his ridged muscles. 'You're beautiful.'

'That's a word to describe you, not me.'

'You exercise.' She unfastened his belt and fumbled with his fly.

He moved to help her, toeing out of his shoes before shoving down both his dress pants, his briefs and socks until he straightened and stood utterly bared before her. 'Every morning.'

She stared, her mouth dry as she gazed on his honed, immaculate body. His regime had to be intense to be this fit—as if he ran or swam for long periods at a time. 'You're disciplined.'

'I have to be. I have a lot to do.'

And he was going to use that discipline and self-control with her now; she could see the intent in his eyes.

'You keep everything contained in its place,' she muttered. Work, exercise, sleep. She was in the sex box for him. And that was just fine.

So fine.

Except her heart was thudding and there was an ache within her that had never been there before.

'You're the same.' He lifted her tee, and she wriggled to help him. He unclasped her bra and briefly cupped her full breasts in his hands before moving to tug her trousers down. 'You're sleek, strong.'

'It makes me feel better if I've moved.' She nodded, lifting one leg, then the other, so he could take her panties off too.

In that they were a match—both physically driven, both worked hard. Both couldn't afford this messiness, but now they were both naked.

She licked her lips. She wanted everything all at once, but she didn't know where to start.

'Bella.' He muttered her name harshly and stepped forward, pulling her into his arms to French-kiss her senseless.

They kissed, touched, kissed again until she was all but delirious and weak-kneed. But then he dropped to his knees and pressed his mouth to her *there*.

She gasped his name.

'I can't wait to hear you,' he muttered approvingly. 'Again and again.'

Oh, no, this wasn't happening that way. Not again. She pulled back and fell to her knees too. 'I want to hear *you*,' she said.

But he was stronger. He lifted and laid her down on her back and moved between her splayed thighs. 'I can't keep my hands off you. Or my mouth.' He moved down her body, trapping her hands at her sides as he licked and kissed from her navel, to her most intimate curve where she was embarrassingly wet already. Then he rose onto his knees to study how he'd spread her beneath him. 'I want to taste you as you come again. Now.'

That devilishly sexy look in his eyes almost sent her over the edge then and there. But she didn't want to come before him. Not this time.

'I want *you* to enjoy it,' she moaned as he ran his hand over her breasts, gently cupping, then teasing.

'You think I didn't?' He shook his head and stroked her again with his skilful fingers. 'There's no greater feeling than knowing I've pleased you.'

'It's the same for me.' She arched uncontrollably as his hands worked further south. 'Can't you understand that?'

'I do.' He bent to her again and kissed her most sensitive nub. 'You can please me, right now. Come for me, Bella. Let me taste it.'

His tongue was so wicked there was no way she couldn't. Groaning, she ran her hands through his thick hair, holding him to her as he pleasured her with his mouth and hands. She rocked as she rode the crest of her orgasm, no longer embarrassed about how wet she must be, because the way his fingers were thrusting was so divine and the words of approval and pleasure tumbling from his wicked mouth were making her orgasm last longer than she'd have thought possible.

He cradled her as she recovered, small aftershocks making her quiver every so often. The pleased expression in his eyes called forth her own competitive spirit.

'My turn.' Suddenly energised, she rolled and moved onto all fours.

'Turn?'

'To taste.' She slapped her hand in the centre of his

chest and pushed, making him stay where he was, flat on the floor.

'Bella—'

'Don't argue with me,' she said fiercely. 'Don't deny me. Not this time.'

But he cupped the nape of her neck and drew her down to him, kissing her deeply. Almost she submitted completely to the desire to simply roll back and let him do whatever he wished with her. But she needed this. Wanted it.

She pulled away and looked into his eyes. 'I'm going to kiss you,' she said. 'Everywhere.'

He didn't answer, but nor did he stop her. She took her time discovering his body. He was strong, but sensitive too and she took pleasure in teasing out those secret spots. What he liked. Where he liked. His neck. His nipples. His thighs.

And slowly she honed in on his enormous erection. Licking her lips, she glanced up at him to gauge his reaction as she moved, curling her hand around the thick base of him.

'Bella…'

She utterly disobeyed the implicit order and opened her mouth to draw him in.

'Bella.'

There was no ignoring him that time.

She released him to glance up into his stormy eyes. 'Please.'

For a long moment he held her gaze, his expression strained. She realised he was holding his breath.

Then he sighed and an almost tender light entered his eyes. 'I'm the one who should be saying please.'

Almost shyly she smiled at him. Then she looked

back down at his straining erection. The single, glossy bead at the tip of his shaft told her he was close. Feminine pleasure flooded her. She wanted to taste all of it.

She heard his long hiss as she took him as deep as she could into her mouth. She sucked hard as she pulled back, and she rubbed and took him deep again. Oh, she loved to rub him. Loved to lick and suck and feel every powerful tremble she could pull from him.

She didn't stop. Rubbing, kissing, sucking, she lost herself in her rhythm, in the pleasure of touching him. His hips bucked, bumping her as she straddled his thighs. She shivered at the power beneath her. His legs were so strong, she couldn't wait to feel the full force of his lovemaking.

As his breathing grew harsher, she gazed up the length of his body. His skin gleamed from a sheen of sweat. His arms were outstretched to the sides; she could see the veins popping as he grasped at the plush carpet beneath him. Every muscle in his body was strained as he tried to hold back. She didn't want him to hold back.

'I'm going to drink every last drop.' She smiled with carnal promise. 'I'm going to watch and taste and feel you as I make you come.'

His muttered oath was mostly indecipherable but it made her smile deepen. Then she returned to him. He was so beautiful and all she wanted was to make him—

'Bella!'

His shout echoed in her ears, so filled with raw relief that she felt as if she were riding that crest with him. As the spasms eased she kept sucking him as deep as she could, holding true to her words and loving it as he shook beneath her.

'Bella.' He released a long breath and his body went lax. 'Bella, Bella, Bella.'

Still astride him, she sat up and looked down his length to his handsome face, tracing her fingers down her neck, between her breasts and to her belly, following the heated path of his seed within her. She felt so femininely sensual. And so aroused.

With shadowed eyes he stared back up at her.

Undaunted, knowing he too was finally sated, she smiled.

Swiftly he sat up and flipped her. She was flat on her back and he was pressing her hard into the plush carpet, kissing her breathless before she could blink. His fingers were between her legs and he made a guttural sound in the back of his throat as he felt how wet and ready she was. She writhed, riding his hand for a moment, so unbelievably pleased.

'Temptress,' he muttered and nipped her lips with his teeth.

He shifted onto his knees, reaching beyond for his trousers on the floor near them. In a second he was ripping open the foil package and rolling the condom on.

She lifted up onto her elbows, in awe of his already rigid erection. He glanced over and caught her staring. He smiled, but she read the determination in his eyes, felt the dynamism in his tense body as he covered her, and knew her moment of dominance was past. He was back in control. He was going to make her pay and it was going to be a heavenly price.

'I don't know how gentle I can keep this,' he muttered, stroking her intimately again. His eyes widened as he felt her body's reaction to his words. 'You don't want gentle?'

'I just want you in me,' she muttered low and harsh and hungry, unable to hold back her darkest desires. She wanted him too much. Only he had made her feel this way. And if she only had him this once, then she was holding nothing back. 'As deep and as hard as you can.'

He kissed her. His tongue lashed the cavern of her mouth with exactly the kind of fierce strokes she was aching for.

For the first time in her life she truly wanted passion.

'You have a hot, sweet mouth and a hot, sweet body.' He looked into her eyes as his fingers probed her wet arousal. 'But you don't want it all that sweet.'

She whimpered at his tormenting rubbing. But he was right.

'Answer me,' he commanded, pushing fractionally deeper and then pulling out.

She moaned in disappointment. 'Yes,' she admitted, aching for his return. For *all* of him.

'You want it hard.'

'Yes.'

'Fast.'

'Yes.'

'Now.'

'*Yes.*' Her head fell back as her blood burned. She writhed under him, desperate to assuage the ache so deep within her. 'I want you in me. Please.'

He nudged her thighs further apart with his knee and settled over her. He was so hard, so masculine and he smelt so good and she could feel him, almost there.

Never had she wanted a man like this.

She held her breath as she stared into his gorgeous

pale blue eyes. She saw the determined fire in them and wanted to be consumed in it. She saw his jaw lock. Then he pushed forward.

'Oh, yes.' She tensed, locking him in as an orgasm rolled over her in a sharp burst of ecstasy. 'Oh, yes-sssss.'

Her breath shuddered in the shock of it. He was finally there and he felt so good. She moaned again, convulsing in pleasure.

'What are you doing coming so quick?' He smiled tightly down at her as she gasped for breath. His expression was teasing. But strained too.

She didn't know. She'd never come during penetration before, let alone that quickly. But the amazing thing was, she wasn't far off coming again.

'What are you doing not moving?' she moaned breathlessly, stunned that she was on the edge again. If only he'd move. If only he'd give her everything. Oh, God, she never wanted this to end.

'Enjoying the view. You're so beautiful like this. I could watch you come all day.'

She shifted, wrapping her leg around his lower back, trying to pull him deeper.

'Don't tease.' She stroked his face and whispered what she wanted most of all. 'I want you to come with me. In me.'

'Oh, hell. Bella,' he muttered hoarsely. His wicked smile faded as he gazed at her. 'Then you might want to hold on, sweetheart.'

But he held onto her, sliding his hands under her back and gripping her shoulders to keep her with him as he pressed forward, deepening his possession of her.

Her breath hissed as he pushed to the hilt. She met

his gaze and knew she was in the eye of the storm. Hurricane Antonio was about to hit.

'Please,' she asked one more time. She wanted it all.

At last he moved, pulling back only to grind into her. Hard and deep he drilled into her, again and again and again. And it was so good. She met him thrust for thrust. Energy sizzled between them; their ride suddenly became frantic and wild. Their sweat-slicked bodies banged faster and faster.

'So good, so good,' she muttered over and over and over.

But then she could only moan in mindless pleasure each time he drove deeper. It was so carnal and so physical and so good. She kissed him everywhere she could with honest, unchecked abandonment. This wasn't sweet, this was decadently sensual and she had to curl her fingers into his muscled flesh to hang on as he forced his pace faster still.

'Come with me, Bella,' he commanded harshly, then kissed her.

His kiss held so much passion, it felt as if he were pouring his very soul into her. She felt him shaking against her even as he drove deeper still.

She arched, every muscle in her body straining. Her breaths were high-pitched moans as he pushed her nearer and nearer to that peak. She heard his breathing roughen, felt the rigidity in his whole body and revelled in it.

'Yes!' She managed to lock her arms around his back, fiercely holding him to her as she shattered beneath and about him, her screams unchecked and raw as that intense sensual tension exploded.

She heard him groan her name, then his hoarse

growl of intense pleasure as he thrust one last time, releasing long and hard into her.

When she could think again, she found he'd eased off her and was lying on his side facing her. Her heart thudded.

This time when he grabbed her wrist it was not to reject her. It was not to push her away. It was to demand the exact opposite.

'More,' he grated, his expression untamed. 'More now.' His passion was utterly off the leash now. 'You should have come as soon as you got my card.'

'I couldn't.' And she couldn't be more sorry about it.

'There is not enough time.' He moved over her, his body hard again. 'We didn't even make it to the damned bed.'

'This is all the time there is.' She parted her legs wider to accommodate his muscular strength. 'This is all there can be.'

She saw his reaction at the remembrance. Duty before desire.

'Then we'd better make the most of it,' he said, his jaw tight, his eyes savage.

His determination made her hot. His intensity made her tremble.

It was slower that time. And silent. There were not the hot, wickedly teasing words to start. He was careful not to bruise where she was most tender. But his gentleness was such exquisite torture. He made her feel so good tears welled in her eyes as she squeezed her muscles tight to lock him in place. She didn't want this to end. She didn't want him to stop holding her, looking at her. Didn't want him to stop ensuring she was out of her mind with pleasure. He could make her feel such unutterable, exquisite pleasure. She embraced him with all the fervour she could, yearning to return that favour. That was when it grew wild again. Loud and physical and fast.

But finally they lay slumped together, utterly spent. Silent again.

This time he was the first to move. This time he didn't meet her gaze. This time really was the end.

Quietly, carefully he left her, disappearing into another room. She sat up, curling her legs up and wrapping her arm around her knees. Dazed, she took in the discarded mess of clothing. He was right, they hadn't even made it from the lounge floor they'd been so eager and hurried. And it was all over already. Bittersweet melancholy filled her.

He walked back into the lounge. He'd swiftly dressed in jeans and a tee shirt. They might be casual wear for him, but he'd slipped back behind his reserve.

She wanted to kiss him. She wanted to fall back onto the floor and take him with her. She wanted that delicious feeling all over again. But she didn't dare.

'I am sorry, I must leave.' He glanced at his watch, his thoughts clearly elsewhere. 'I'm late already.'

'Of course.'

'Stay and sleep,' he instructed politely. 'The bed is through there…' He had the grace to look slightly sheepish.

'No, I have things I need to do as well.' She pulled her clothes nearer. 'I'll leave ten minutes after you. Will use a different exit from the building or something.'

He was silent. 'I would like Matteo to ensure you get home safely.'

That poor guy was still in the building ready for

service? 'That's not necessary.' Her skin burned anew with that all-over body-blush and she quickly pulled her tee shirt on, not bothering with her bra first. She just wanted to cover up. She just wanted him to leave already.

His jaw tightened but he didn't argue. He stood for another moment and she inwardly winced at the awkwardness.

'Goodbye,' he said stiffly, still frowning at her, looking as if he might say something more.

She didn't want him to.

'Goodbye, Prince Antonio.' She lifted her chin and threw him her most sophisticated 'Bella Sanchez' smile. 'It was a pleasure.'

CHAPTER FIVE

IT WAS ENOUGH. It *had* to be enough because he didn't deserve the pleasure she could give him and she didn't deserve the pain he would inevitably give her. He had to retain his control. She was out of bounds now. Once was a calculated risk. Once more could only be a disaster.

Antonio walked past the line-up of guests, greeting them as he went, determined to be as focused as ever. He was almost halfway through the continuous schedule of event after event in the festival fortnight. He'd been spared her presence at some occasions. But not this one. At his request she'd been sent an invitation and she had not refused. She was not stupid.

She wore a black dress that revealed nothing yet managed to imply everything. Her loose hair shone, the reddish strands glinting like threads of fire under the chandeliers. She stole his breath. And that was before she smiled. Or spoke.

If she spoke, he'd be lost.

But his desire for her wasn't the reason why he'd ensured she attend this particular function. It was in *her* interest to attend. It wasn't that he was desperate to see her again. He was simply helping her out, because he was in the position to be able to.

Salvatore Accardi was also a guest at this late afternoon's drinks, yet Antonio noticed the man didn't say hello to Bella. He was her father, Antonio was in no doubt of that, yet he didn't even acknowledge her presence with the politeness you'd afford a stranger. He acted as if she weren't there. Beyond rude.

But Bella was working the room with that bulletproof style of hers, refusing to let her father's ostracism daunt her. Antonio felt like cheering her. He understood social isolation and he didn't want her to feel the sharp edge of it. She'd done nothing to deserve it. He'd checked her out. Beyond that super-seductive façade, there was nothing. She'd not been caught lying or stealing or cheating...she was a woman—that was all. A woman who couldn't help who her parents were. A woman he still wanted.

He caught Matteo's eye.

'Ensure she's not left alone,' Antonio instructed as the aide came over. 'There are people here it would benefit her to meet and people who might give her a hard time.'

And then he decided to set the example for everyone. He deliberately walked over to talk to her; it would be too obvious if he didn't and he refused to be anything like her father.

'It is always a pleasure, Ms Sanchez.'

She didn't immediately reply but her eyes narrowed on him.

She wasn't appreciative of his efforts?

His focus changed, arrowing on the electricity arcing between them. He'd made a mistake. He'd thought he'd be lost if she spoke to him, but, really, it had taken only one look.

'It seems you have guests from every sector of San Felipe society here tonight,' Bella murmured, trying to regulate her racing pulse, but seeing him threw her balance completely. 'Business leaders, rally drivers, retired politicians…' Her voice trailed off. 'Even me.'

Antonio almost smiled. 'Why shouldn't you be here?'

'You know very well why.' She shifted, restless because of his nearness. 'You shouldn't have invited me. Our agreement was once only.'

She'd been a fool to think once would've been enough. The last few days since had been horrendous. And this invitation? It hadn't been in his hurried scrawl. It had been formal, printed and distant, yet she'd not hesitated for a second. The craving to see him had been too great. She'd applied her lipstick with a shaking hand, she'd been so full of anticipation. Now he was right with her and holding herself back was almost impossible.

But she hadn't slept properly in weeks because she'd been getting the club ready and now it was open she was frantically busy and the sleeplessness was affecting her more each day. So she didn't have the energy to build her defences; she couldn't control her own heated trembling.

'That wasn't why I invited you,' he answered impassively.

Bella's blood iced. It wasn't? Didn't he want her again? Had that one morning truly been enough for him?

'This is a reception for San Felipe's most successful local business leaders,' he continued with his customary distance. 'You are a businesswoman who's carving out a brand and a service that has seen unprecedented success already. That's why you're here.'

Rejection and bitterness bruised. 'To network with people who don't want my business in their town because I'm some kind of bad influence?' she asked acidly.

Salvatore Accardi had been sending hostile waves across the room since she'd walked in.

She curled her suddenly cold hands into fists. She wanted to leave. To escape Antonio more than anything.

'It's not like you're running a brothel,' Antonio drawled softly enough so only she heard. 'Entertainment is a large part of what San Felipe offers and you're drawing in large numbers of younger customers. We don't want the island to be famous for being the holiday destination of only the old and wealthy.'

'It's never been that. The old and wealthy men have always had their young and beautiful companions with them on San Felipe,' she mocked.

That was what her mother had been for Salvatore Accardi—the nubile young accessory. And in recent years with the two Princes in charge? Beautiful and ambitious and hopeful women had been visiting in droves. Bella was just giving them a place to display themselves.

Antonio's eyes gleamed but then he glanced over her shoulder and his expression became as remote as ever.

'You are not out of place here.' He bowed formally. 'I hope you enjoy your evening.'

That was *it*? No heat? No words with hidden meaning or secret smile? Nothing. Disappointment deepened as he walked away.

It *was* all over for him.

Well, she wasn't letting him see how that hurt. She'd stay, she'd 'schmooze' and show both Salvatore and Antonio she was made of stronger stuff than either of them realised.

To her surprise it wasn't dreadful. People talked to her. Complimented her on her past career and asked about the club. She became aware of Salvatore Accardi talking loudly on the other side of the room about the degeneration of inner-city San Felipe, but she wasn't going to engage. She knew people were watching.

Antonio was watching. But he needn't worry, she wasn't going to cause a scene. Despite what he thought, she'd not chosen to set up her business in San Felipe so she could exact some kind of patricidal revenge on Salvatore. Life wasn't that simple. She'd come here because it was the one place she could. And it was the one place she actually enjoyed being, other than the stage.

But Salvatore Accardi's voice was drowned out when a ruddy-cheeked older man arrived late and walked straight over to Prince Antonio and greeted him with an etiquette-breaching booming voice.

'Please pass on my congratulations to your brother Prince Eduardo on the birth of his daughter,' the man gushed loudly as he beamed at Antonio.

'Thank you.' Antonio nodded intently, seeming aware of the sudden interest from all those standing near. He lifted his head and spoke clearly. 'It is very exciting for us. I am informed she's very determined to maintain her own schedule and refuses to fall in with her parents' request that she sleep at *night*.' He paused as everyone chuckled, a small smile lightening his features. 'So I am confident she will make a wonderfully stubborn Crown Princess in the future.'

There was the tiniest silence before a woman ventured another question.

'Will we get to meet the little Princess soon?'

Antonio's expression tightened and he paused before replying. 'Princess Sapphire is very young and this time in her life is very precious and private for her parents. I'm sure you'll all agree.' He softened his words with another glimmer of that rare smile and absolutely everyone in the vicinity completely agreed.

But Bella watched as that small smile faded from his eyes and her heart smote. With masterful PR skills, he'd offered just a hint of something personal about the new baby Princess to satisfy public curiosity while protecting her privacy. But at the same time his words had underlined his own abdication from any family or personal life of his own. He had no intention or desire to marry and provide an heir of his own. His niece would one day take the throne.

Until then he would be alone. Because he was the Heartbroken Prince.

Her heart thumping unaccountably quickly, Bella turned towards a waiter to ask for a glass of sparkling water. But as she turned her gaze hit upon the man who didn't just deny his role in her existence, but who'd chosen to denigrate and torment her mother *and* her.

Salvatore Accardi was looking right at her with such undisguised loathing she stumbled. Her lungs malfunctioned. She straightened but couldn't turn away.

Salvatore Accardi could. With a final condescending appraisal, he muttered something indecipherable to the person next to him and deliberately turned his back on her.

It was the most public of rejections and yet probably—hopefully—no one would have noticed.

Except *she'd* noticed and she was so humiliated that not even years of experience controlling her emotions as she faced huge crowds could help her stop the blush from spreading like a sudden rash over her skin. She glanced at others in the group, unable to resist the curiosity—had anyone seen?

The person who stood next to Salvatore, a tall brunette, was staring. Her half-sister. Francesca. Beautiful and—with the way she too then turned her back—every inch her father's daughter.

Bella finally found the power to move. She walked almost blindly from the room. She didn't want to talk business and she definitely didn't want to banter or flirt or *be* Bella.

'Ms Sanchez.'

Bella blinked and paused. Matteo had materialised beside her looking bland, but he spoke with gentle courtesy.

'I thought I would introduce you to Tomas Mancini. He owns the island's most popular Michelin-starred restaurant here on San Felipe. He owns several others too, in mainland Europe.'

His lengthy explanation gave her a chance to breathe and as he slowly walked her to the other end of the vast reception room she had time to pull herself together properly.

Tomas was about seventy, accompanied by his elegant wife, also around seventy years old, and they were both charming, both talkative and standing with them was somehow soothing. She stood with her back to the rest of the room, relieved of feeling the pressure of vindictive, prying eyes.

'Tomas started out as a firefighter, you know. He was based at the station you have refurbished as your club,' Tomas' wife, Maria, informed her. 'That's when I met him. He rescued me, you know.'

'Did he?' Bella was diverted. 'From a fire?'

'A fire *alarm*. There was no danger but I was mortified.' Maria nodded in all seriousness. 'But I like to think of young people having fun there now.' She paused for a second then added quietly, 'I had fun there once.'

There was nothing in her tone, but Bella looked sharply into the older woman's eyes. There was the veriest hint of a wink. Bella finally smiled.

'Maria, Carlo has just arrived.' Tomas turned to Bella. 'He was our first chef who moved to an outer island to open a satellite restaurant for us last year. Would you like to join us?'

'Thank you, I will shortly,' she said, wanting to give them a chance to have some time alone with their friend. 'I'll freshen up first and then find you.'

'If you'll accompany me, I'll show you the way.' Matteo stepped alongside her again.

Bella glanced at him in surprise; she'd thought he'd been called away.

'Thank you,' she said, quietly appreciative of the way he walked between her and the group that Salvatore and Francesca stood in. Salvatore's voice still carried; she couldn't hear the words but just the tone oozed arrogance.

'It is in here.' Matteo paused by a discreet door out in the long corridor.

Bella stepped inside, drawing in a deep breath, but as she closed the door behind her someone loomed right in front of her. Just as she was about to scream she realised who it was.

'You gave me such a *fright*.' She clapped her hand on her chest, almost needing to thump it to get her heart started again.

Antonio stood a breath away, his customary reserved expression incinerated by the raw need in his eyes. But he said nothing.

Now her hurt heart raced—sending anticipation and hunger sparking around every one of her cells.

'What are you doing in here?' She licked her dried lips and watched that need in his eyes burn all the more intensely.

'I need to see you again. Alone. Tonight.'

Relief hit her like a tornado, blowing the roof off her tension. She released her breath in a shaky sigh. But just as relief hit, so did the impossibility of what he was saying. 'We *can't*—'

'Not now, no,' he agreed. But that didn't stop him taking the step nearer so he could pull her against him.

His hand smoothed down her back, as if he were trying to soothe her, but she felt the rigidity of his body and realised how tightly *he* was coiled. She rested her head against his shoulder, stifling her groan of sheer relief.

'I'm sorry I used Matteo again,' he muttered against her hair. 'But there are too many people—'

'It's okay,' she interrupted. 'I understand.'

She understood he was lonely and that for whatever

reason he wanted *her* to help him find physical release. That was okay; she wanted him for the same.

They were both hurt and lonely.

She placed her hand on his chest and looked up at him, willing to accept however it had to be, as long as it could happen again. Just the once more.

'Bella.'

She barely had a chance to hear his strained mutter before his lips were on hers.

Passion burst free at first chance. She wrapped her arms around his neck, wriggling closer for more heavenly contact. His arms tightened, lifting her clear off her feet, and she moaned. She never wanted this kiss to end. Always he made her feel so good, filling her with that incomparable bliss. Dangerously addictive and too good to deny. She rocked against him, using her body to blatantly offer him everything. Right here. Right now. She was beyond caring.

'Bella, we can't,' he muttered.

'We can,' she pleaded. 'Just quickly. So quick.'

He touched her, growling between his teeth as he felt her readiness. 'Without protection?'

She bit back her own moan and vehemently shook her head. 'You think I'd ever make the same mistake as my mother? Contraception is covered.'

He stared at her another second and then crushed her mouth with his. The kiss was nothing but raw frustration. But then he tore from her—lifting his head to look down at her, holding her in place so she couldn't rub against him any more. She felt his tension morphing back to that impenetrable self-control. He had no intention of having his way with her here and now.

The disappointment was appallingly deep. Again.

'I've missed you,' he said.

She melted. His completely. But she made herself pull back and stand on her own two feet. 'I'd better get back out there,' she replied, determined to be as strong as he.

'You'd better redo your lipstick first,' he replied, flashing a wicked smile.

'And you'd better remove it.' She eyed his pristine white collar meaningfully. 'Before you end up wearing more.'

His hands loosened from her waist and he stepped further into the beautiful powder room, allowing her space. 'I'm sorry Salvatore Accardi is here tonight. He is too loud.'

Bella shrugged as she opened up her small evening purse and stepped forward to check her make-up in the gold-framed mirror. Her fingers shook.

'Does he ever talk to you?' Antonio watched her carefully restore the glossy sheen to her lips.

'He only talks *about* me.' She grimaced at her reflection. 'He thinks all I want is money from him.'

'And do you?'

She turned and sent him a sharp glance. 'I'd rather starve.'

'I saw him look at you. Then blank you,' Antonio said.

Embarrassment burned through her again and she turned away, wishing Antonio couldn't still see her face in the mirror. 'The most cordial we've been in years.'

'Don't try to make light of it.'

'He doesn't hurt me.'

'Don't lie to me,' he said softly. 'Go ahead and give him a hard time. Just don't make a mess.'

She added a last swipe of gloss. 'I'm not here to give him a hard time. I want nothing to do with him. I don't care what he thinks or says or does.'

Antonio was silent a moment. 'I will make arrangements for tonight.'

She put her lipstick back in her small purse and then turned. 'I will deal only with you and Matteo. No one else.' But she would give him that.

'Thank you.' He cupped her face and gazed down at her for a long moment, as if reading her thoughts. But he resisted her silent request to kiss her again.

'I must go now,' he said apologetically and then swiftly left the room via another door.

Bella turned back to her reflection and tried to think calm thoughts to reduce the telltale colour in her cheeks. But flickers of excitement shot through her veins. She wanted him again. Couldn't and wouldn't say no to him or herself.

Maybe that made her his concubine. But she would take nothing else from him. Not a penny, a dress or a jewel, not a thing. And she was not his friend. Only his lover. And only for one more night.

CHAPTER SIX

THE HOURS THAT night stretched for ever. For the first time since she'd opened the club, she couldn't wait to close it. As soon as she'd seen off the last of her employees, she stood in the doorway. It was still dark, but in another hour or so the sky would lighten and the sun rise. A black car slowly cruised down the street towards her. Unmarked but opulent, it pulled in just by the main door, parking illegally. The driver's tinted window wound down a couple of inches. She'd expected Matteo, but it was Antonio.

Quickly she stepped forward and got into the passenger seat. He pulled away in seconds. She couldn't help but glance along the street, nervous that someone would have seen them. But the road was empty.

Silently he steered towards the very heart of San Felipe.

'You can actually drive?' She tried to make conversation with a tease, but her throat was dry and her voice tight.

'I am allowed, occasionally,' he replied in his formal way, but then he smiled. 'Ready?'

The giant gate before them opened without him hitting a button. She didn't see any guards or any officials as she stepped out in the internal garage that was bigger than the average-sized house and was filled with eye-wateringly expensive cars.

'This is the palace.' She whispered the obvious as he led her into the wide hallway. Even with the dim night lighting she could see the gilt-edged paintings lining the walls, the pedestals with priceless sculptures and the glass cabinets filled with antiquities and artefacts.

Her heart hammered. She'd never expected him to bring her to the palace. Wasn't it too risky?

The imposing building was incredibly silent and huge and she was paranoid there were security cameras everywhere snapping her with him.

'I know,' he whispered back. 'I want the comfort of my own bed.'

'But—'

'Be quiet.' He turned and quickly kissed her for emphasis. 'Someone might hear,' he whispered, then took her hand and led her through the maze.

Surprised, she glanced at him and saw the mischievous grin on his face.

He was Antonio, the ultra-serious Crown Prince, wasn't he? He owned this oversized, unbelievably opulent place and yet here he was sneaking around like a teenager.

He led her up some stairs, then more stairs and long corridors and finally came to a set of doors on the third or fourth floor—she'd lost count. He opened them and hung back to let her walk in first.

'This is your private apartment?' she asked, knowing the answer anyway, but feeling as if she needed to say *something*.

When he'd closed the doors she turned to face him.

But that gorgeous, elusive smile had faded and his expression was even more closed off than usual. Did he feel as awkward as she?

'When did you last have a…guest up here?' she asked.

That brought his smile back but he remained silent.

'You're just trying to make me feel special,' she joked lightly.

'You are special.'

She walked around the large room, mainly to hide the blush she could feel heating her cheeks. He didn't mean anything by it, but the gentle flirt was nice.

His apartment was a masterpiece of elegant understatement, the decor minimalist compared to the multitude of treasures in the cabinets lining the corridors. But it was so impersonal it made her heart ache for him again. Even she, with few truly personal possessions, had put her own stamp on her room. She had the flowers she loved to get from the early morning market, she had a small print from Paris to remind her of happier times with her mother, she had the ballerina jewellery box she'd won in her first ballet competition when she was barely five and had treasured ever since. But Antonio had a beautifully styled masculine lounge with nothing obviously personal that she could note. There were no paintings on the walls and no photos at all— not of him and his family and none of Alessia—which relieved her in one way, yet saddened her in another.

She turned to face him again and found he'd been slowly following her. Now he was only a pace away.

'You want to see all my rooms?' he asked, something veiled in his expression.

'I want to see everything,' she replied before thinking. She was so much more curious than she ought to be.

'There's not really that much to see.'

Well, there was beauty and incredible design and craftsmanship, but she wasn't here to admire an art gallery and she didn't want to treat him or his home as a museum exhibit. That was what his life must be like all the time and she wanted to understand more about him.

That was when she realised his place didn't matter; it was the *person* before her who held all the clues. If she wanted to understand him at all, she needed only to spend time with him. But they had only now. She gazed into his unfathomable eyes and wished she knew how to make him smile.

'I thought you wanted to see everything?' he finally prompted her.

'No.' She shook her head. 'Now I just want…' Her words faltered.

He took the last step towards her. 'Me.'

She nodded. 'Just you.'

She wanted to focus wholly on him, but they weren't here to talk. This was a clandestine convenience. A risky, stolen moment. Her heart tripped and thudded too fast. She waited, anticipating that burst of passion. They probably still wouldn't make it to his bed.

But he didn't kiss her. He took her by the hand. 'Let me show you one thing.' He walked down the hallway and opened the furthest door, waiting for her to walk in ahead of him.

'What's in here?' She summoned a tease. 'Your hidden den of iniquity?'

She walked in without waiting for an answer and stopped in surprise.

The room was large, its floor-to-ceiling windows protected by billowing drapes, protecting his privacy yet allowing the citrus-scented summer air to perfume the room. It was all but empty. Bella drank in the large expanse of polished wooden floor. And in the corner was a baby grand piano.

'You have your own dance studio?' That floor was begging to be danced on.

'Music room,' he corrected with a laugh.

'You're a musician?' She turned to look at him.

'You're surprised.' His rare smile flashed and stayed.

'You never seem to do anything other than serious "prince" things.'

'I appreciate many things. But especially music.' He walked over to the piano. 'It relaxes me. As dancing relaxes you.'

She was delighted to discover this and that he'd shared it with her. And she wanted him to share more. 'So will you play for me?'

He raised his brows at her.

'Please.'

'It would be my pleasure.' He sat down at the stool.

Bella crossed the floor and rested her hand on the smooth, glossy wood of the piano. It was beautiful to touch and she bet it would be an amazing sound. He glanced up at her for a moment then looked down to the keys. Intrigued, Bella leaned closer.

He began. After only a moment, Bella froze, unsure of how to react. He'd chosen an elementary piece and was literally banging it out. Two fingers smashed down on the wrong notes. He hit so *many* wrong notes, and it was so loud, Bella didn't know where to look.

But then a wicked smile spread over his face and his hand positioning changed. The melody changed. *Everything* changed.

'You tease.' She laughed, relieved, and moved closer to watch. He shifted on the piano stool, straightening.

'The look on your face.' He chuckled as he played, beautifully.

'Who knew solemn Prince Antonio would be a prankster?' She leaned over his shoulder, letting her hair brush against his cheek, aiming to distract him and make him hit a wrong note for real this time.

'You didn't know what to say.' He stopped playing and reached up to hold her in place near him, turning his head to press a kiss to her cheek. 'I was lowering your expectations. Now you think I'm better than I actually am...'

She pulled back to read his expression. 'My assessment of your performance matters to you that much?' She never would have thought he'd care.

'I've never played for anyone else.' He shrugged and glanced back to the black and white keys.

'I'm honoured.' And she was touched, that warmth in her soul that he'd let her into his secret life, just a little.

'Dance for me,' he softly requested as he began another piece. 'The way you were that morning I spied on you.'

'Okay.' Her heat soaring, she kissed *his* cheek in the lightest of caresses and stepped away from the piano. 'Barefoot, okay?' She kicked off her shoes.

'Don't feel the need to stop there.' He sent her a wicked look. 'Naked would be amazing.'

She laughed, pleased at his emerging playfulness. 'I never dance this way for just anyone, you know.'

He nodded, all seriousness again. 'I do know.'

She laughed again at the arrogance implicit in his reply but her heart fluttered, enjoying the lightness and liberty to just *be* with him.

He'd chosen a romantic melody and it was so easy to let go and lose herself in the streaming beauty of it. Smiling, she stretched her arms wide and simply moved, not showing any fancy steps, not needing to prove anything to him.

That was the thing, with him—physically, at least, she could simply enjoy the sensations, the moment. And now, the music.

But as the melody worked towards its crescendo she couldn't help looking at him to gauge his reaction. Her gaze meshed with his and was caught fast. His magnetism pulled her nearer. As the music grew softer, she danced closer. Softer and closer still until, as the last note died away, she slipped between the piano and him. He leaned back to let her straddle his muscular thighs. That wicked smile curved his lips and he began to play another piece, a teasing glint warming his ice-blue eyes.

She decided two could tease. She bent close and poured all the radiance she felt into her kiss. The notes of the piano continued to sound for only a moment. Then his magic fingers began to play her and she was so very glad she'd worn a dress.

He slipped the soft fabric up her thighs, exposing her to his touch. She wriggled and he slipped the silk right over her head.

'Antonio,' she breathed softly, so hot for him already.

'At your service,' he promised, leaning forward to kiss the crest of her breasts. 'I'm wondering if I can make you sound as good as my piano.'

'Play me and see.'

'I can already see,' he muttered in a pleased tone.

She felt his hardness beneath her and ached to free him from his clothing. She reached for him.

'Nu huh.' He shifted her above him with a laugh. 'I'm playing you, remember?'

'I was going for some harmony. Accompaniment.' She needed him with her. In her. Like now.

'Soon.' He soothed her with a kiss.

'No. Now.' She kissed him hard.

But he was ruthless. Relentless. He caressed, kissed, rubbed. Hard then soft, changing his stroke and rhythm, tormenting her until she banged the damn piano keys herself, trying to hurry him to get him to take her. When he finally relented and let her reach her release, she screamed long and loud until she slumped into his arms with a sigh.

'I can't take any more,' she begged. 'I need you. Please.'

He clasped her tightly and carried her through to another room. He set her on her feet and stood back from her.

'Take me, then,' he invited.

She noticed nothing at all about his bedroom. She was only focused on him. But he had to help her strip him out of his clothes. She was too frantic, too needy to get her fingers to work properly.

'Condoms. Pocket,' he muttered roughly.

She retrieved one and with a small smile set about ensuring he was sheathed. She took her time and used her mouth as much as her hands and when she'd finally finished he was swearing in a continuous stream beneath his breath.

She laughed and pushed him so he fell back on the bed. But the moment she knelt on the expansive mattress to join him he moved, as quick and powerful as a panther catching his prey. She rolled, letting him, welcoming him. She couldn't wait a second longer anyway.

'Hurry,' she called to him. 'Please.'

But he paused and smiled down at her and she knew what that wicked, gleaming smile meant.

Sheer, delightful torture.

'You're not going to do this fast, are you?' She shivered as her body geared up for more of his teasing onslaught.

He angled his head as if considering the plea in her words. 'It might end up that way. Eventually.'

She licked her lips and ran her hand down his rockhard abs. 'I'm willing to fight dirty.' She'd do whatever she could to make him claim her sooner rather than later.

That challenge sharpened the edge in his expression. 'Go ahead, darling, do your worst. I intend to fight dirtier.'

Oh, Lord, she was in trouble. She yelped in laughter as he tugged her further up the mattress so he could claim the part of her most begging for his attention again.

And then she just gave in to his desire to see her soar again. He might be reserved, but when he was fully focused on *her*—it was wicked heaven.

That magical hour later she smiled as he lay sprawled, sweat slicked and breathless, at the opposite end of the bed. The coverings were on the floor, the dawn light warmed the room and she'd never been as relaxed in her life. And she'd never felt as close to anyone else either. Not just physically, but it was as if she was in tune with him and they'd made the most beautiful music together.

He rested his head on his hand and ran a finger along the jagged red scar than ran down her shin and to her ankle. 'Does it hurt?'

'No. It just tickles,' she murmured.

'What happened?'

'Glass in my shoe.' She stretched her foot languorously, unutterably relaxed.

He frowned. 'Glass?'

'In my pointe shoe,' she explained briefly. 'Not much. I didn't feel it until I was partway through the performance. But, you know, the show must go on.'

He shifted down to her foot and inspected her toes.

'Don't.' She tried to curl them away because they were so ugly and now she was self-conscious and regretted telling him that much.

'You kept dancing?' He released her foot and she pulled her legs from his reach.

'Of course. When you're in the zone, you feel invincible. You don't notice until it's almost too late. At first I thought it was just a bad blister or something. In the end I fell and landed badly and broke my ankle and shin.'

And when she'd looked later, there'd been blood seeping through her pointe shoe. The cut had been so deep it had severed nerves and the chunk of glass they'd struggled to remove had been viciously jagged.

'The show went on.' She shrugged, playing it down with a casual smile. 'The understudy stepped up. I went to hospital.'

One of the pins they'd put in was still there and during those months in plaster she'd lost flexibility, muscle tone. Confidence.

Everything.

'There was no way you could build up your strength again?' he asked. 'Retrain and get back out there?'

'Not to the level I want.' And it had been ruined for her. That someone in her own company had hated her that much to do something so horrific?

She'd thought the company had been her safe haven but she'd been wrong.

So she was determined to be independent now. Any success she had, she would own in its entirety. She wouldn't be vulnerable by being reliant on anyone else. She had to control her own destiny and haul herself out of any problems alone. It was the lesson her mother had never learned.

'How did the glass get in your shoe?' Antonio asked ominously.

She didn't want to answer but she knew that look in his eye. The wickedness had vanished and he was in 'ruthless ruler' mode. She shouldn't have answered so thoughtlessly in the first place. 'I guess some people didn't believe I deserved my position in the company. That I was there because of my profile, not talent. Sex appeal, not technique.'

He looked grim. 'Did they catch whoever did it?'

'I didn't want to cause a scandal and nor did company management.' Sebastian had asked her not to go to the police, arguing bad press would destroy the company. And she'd had her reasons for agreeing with his request.

'*What?*'

She flinched at the fury in Antonio's tone.

'I didn't want people to know I was a victim,' she defended herself hotly. 'I didn't want the world to know I had enemies who'd do something that mean. I didn't want to show that.' She hadn't wanted *anyone* to know how vulnerable she was. How isolated. So she'd left and played up the party queen. 'I fell. My leg broke. End of story.'

And she'd trust no one now. Not even a prince.

She reached out and ran her hand over the small silver elephant that she noticed sitting on the nightstand, wanting to distract them both. 'This is pretty.'

He glanced at the trinket, still frowning. 'Alessia gave it to me for my birthday.'

Silently she wondered which birthday, how long ago and what significance the elephant held. All she knew about elephants was that supposedly they never forgot anything.

Maybe that was what it was—for him to remember her. They'd been school sweethearts for years before getting engaged, hadn't they? Bella returned the trinket to the table and looked back down the bed to Antonio.

His expression had shut down, of course. Remote, reserved Prince Antonio had returned. He might be lying at her feet, but he couldn't be further removed and it couldn't be more obvious that he didn't want to discuss it with her. Of course he didn't.

That sense of intimacy she'd felt only moments before—that closeness beyond the physical—dissolved. He'd never let her into his life the way he'd let his fiancée. He'd never love like that again. He wouldn't let himself. And that was fair enough. She too knew how much it was possible to hurt.

She smiled, determined not to let it show that *she* hurt right now. She was the distraction, the secret lover, the light relief for the royal workaholic. And she'd keep this private and fun because *he* was her distraction too. He was the one man who'd finally made her feel *good* and enjoy her sensuality and she wasn't going to let anything ruin this last stolen moment she had with him. Certainly not any stupidly weak emotion.

But how did she forbid her heart from falling for him?

CHAPTER SEVEN

THE HOURS AND days stretched ahead, empty and frustrating, loaded with meetings from European delegations and civic duties. Nothing he could get out of.

He'd certainly been unable to decline this afternoon's invitation to tour the new addition to the cancer unit at the hospital. While there, the staff had taken him on a tour of Alessia's Garden. Amongst the beautiful roses and serene seating in the heart of the hospital grounds, he'd given his speech and thanked the committee for all the fundraising they'd done over the years, and continued to do, in his fiancée's name. Because of them her name lived on.

They didn't know that because of him, she'd died.

Not even his brother knew the truth.

Desperation curled around him as he read through the next day's timetable. He needed a break from it. For the first time since he'd been crowned he wanted a holiday and an escape from the weight he carried on his shoulders. He'd never had more than a few days away and even then he'd taken work with him. It had been the one constant in his life, the one thing he knew he *could* do right. It was his calling.

But now he craved another moment of escape—

from duty, from his past, from the lie he lived day in and out.

He didn't deserve it, but he hungered for a moment of selfishness—the time to laze, linger and laugh on a bed with Bella instead of stealing a too-quick liaison in the last hour of the night.

He wanted just a little more. A whole night. A whole day. Enough of a feast to cure him and help him forget.

Three days since he'd done the unthinkable and brought her home, he sat alone in the palace, watching the hands of the clock slowly tick by.

There was no escape from his unrelenting schedule. And even if there was, he couldn't go to the island: his brother, Eduardo, was there.

Eduardo.

The brother to whom he'd never told the truth. The brother who'd repeatedly asked him how he could serve him better. The brother who'd changed so much in the last year since finding happiness with his soldier wife.

Antonio stared at his desk and finally picked up his phone. His brother answered immediately.

'I need you to come to San Felipe,' Antonio said quietly. 'I need you to attend a couple of events for me.'

'You're not well?' The shock in Eduardo's voice burned.

'I'm fine.' He couldn't lie about that. 'I only need a day or so out.'

'I will come right away,' Eduardo answered, still obviously stunned, but he didn't question more.

'Thank you.' Antonio rubbed the back of his neck. 'It's nothing serious. I just need a little time.'

'It's fine. I'm glad you asked.' Eduardo sounded as if he was moving already. 'If I need to make contact—'

'I'll be on the water.' Antonio gazed out of the window to the inky black space where the Mediterranean ebbed and flowed. 'You can radio me on the boat.'

Because he wasn't completely reckless. But nor could he wait 'til dawn.

An hour later he stood in the landing just outside her office, looking over the narrow balcony railing to where she was in the middle of the dance floor. It had been a risk, but at this hour the club was mostly in darkness, the lights flashing, confusing, disguising.

Everyone present was too busy noticing her to notice him anyway. In white trousers and a slim white top she danced in the centre of the main floor. There was a space around her, like a halo, as if somehow everyone knew they were forbidden to get too close.

But they watched. They *all* watched. And Antonio watched as Matteo told her. She stiffened and swiftly walked off the dance floor. Antonio stepped back into her office, anticipating.

'You shouldn't be here,' she said, striding in only moments later and slamming the door behind her.

'And yet here I am.' And he couldn't help but be aroused and amused as he drank in her energy. This was exactly what he wanted. Bella looking strong and fierce and crackling with fire.

'This is my club.'

'This is my country.' He crossed his arms, forcing himself to wait for her comeback.

'And you want to be seen here?'

'I thought this was the place to be seen. Am I going to inhibit your guests' pleasure?'

'They'll be thrilled to be in your presence. I'm sure they'll bust out their best moves for you. Especially our female guests. Will you be joining them on the dance floor or just *watching*?' Her eyes glinted.

He breathed in carefully, cooling his blood. But he was looking forward to the next twenty-four hours too damn much. It was all he could do not to reach for her now but if he did that, they'd never leave.

'Or is this another snap compliance inspection?' Bella smirked.

'Actually, this is an abduction.' He smiled back, hugely appreciating her not so subtle bite.

Her eyes widened. 'I'm sorry?'

'I'm taking you with me.'

'Pardon?'

'You don't need to pack. We're leaving now.'

'I can't leave *now*.'

Satisfaction thrummed. It was only timing she was concerned with? She wanted to come with him. 'Either you come quietly and right away, or I have the whole place shut down.'

Her gaze met his. Her face flamed at the double entendre he'd intended. He shifted on his feet, releasing the tension that was streaming through his body.

'Nothing like abuse of power, Antonio,' she finally responded.

'I have your best interests at heart.'

'Really.'

'Seriously.' He admired her independence but it irritated the hell out of him at the same time. 'We can leave quietly. Everyone is interested in the other celebrities on the dance floor.'

'Getting good at plotting, aren't you?'

'You look tired.' He frowned, because she did. And she looked paler than usual.

'Way to make me feel attractive.'

'When did you last get to bed before midnight?' he asked.

'What concern is it of yours?' She shook her head at him. 'You're not supposed to start caring, Antonio. That's not what you're about.'

It wasn't about *caring*. It was about having a very little more time for just the two of them. 'You work too hard and sleep too little.'

'So do you.' She shrugged. 'But that's not the point. It's no business of yours and I am not here waiting for your beck and call. I don't live for your summons. I have my own life to get on with.'

'Yes, you're right.' Every word she spoke was true. But there was something else equally true. He strolled up to her, framing her face in his hands and tilting her head so he could see right into her eyes. 'But you want this as much as I do.'

Her expression altered, the defiance drained and disappointment brought those shadows back.

'What I want doesn't really matter, though,' she admitted, a hint of sadness colouring her soft tone. 'I can't leave.' She gestured to her laptop open on her desk. 'Because I need to run the business. I need to understand it. I'm more than the face for it. I need to be the brains behind it. I need to make it work.'

Bella wasn't about to admit it, but Antonio was right: she was so tired and in need of a break. And that he was *here*, that he'd come to her once more?

That stunned her. Delighted her. *Distracted* her.

But if she could stay focused for just a little while she could pull her life back on track, *without* relying on anyone else. No one was taking her career from her again. No one was taking anything. 'I can't go with you.'

His eyes lasered into her, branding her even as she tried to resist him. She lifted her chin. It wasn't her problem if he didn't like hearing the word 'no' for the first time in his life. But after a moment her heart starting skipping.

'Don't look at me like that,' she whispered.

'Like what?'

'You know.' She shook her head. 'It's not fair.'

His smile appeared. 'You look at me like that.'

Her resistance wavered. 'Antonio, please,' she asked, determined not to let him dictate her world in this way. She needed to keep this on her own terms. She *wasn't* a plaything—for all that manufactured media representation. She had concrete goals and she had to meet them. He couldn't derail her long-term plans. 'Don't make me change my mind.'

But she was tempted. And he knew it.

'Bella,' he whispered. 'It's just for a little while. Little more than a day. Don't you think you deserve that? Don't I? Matteo will ensure the club is closed and secure. There's only another hour to go anyway. It will be taken care of.'

He was so high-handed and arrogant and confident. And kind.

'What do you want more?' he asked. 'To put me in my place or take just a moment for yourself?'

In truth her reluctance wasn't about making him pay, it was about giving herself the time to draw strength to cope with him. He was so overpowering, she couldn't let him tear down every last defence and get a foothold in her heart. She couldn't be that weak over him. But she couldn't say 'no' any more than she could stop breathing.

He smiled. He knew he'd won.

He took her hand. She curled her fingers around his and walked with him. He already had his phone in his other hand and was sending a message, presumably to Matteo.

'We need to go up to the roof.' He led her to the emergency exit door.

'Why?'

It became clear in only a moment.

'You landed a helicopter on the roof of my building?'

'And picked the lock on the door.' He chuckled. 'It was fun. But you need to install a better security alarm'

'It was *crazy*.' She walked up the stairs with him. 'Is it safe to fly at night?'

'I have the best pilot on duty, don't worry,' Antonio answered. 'And the sun is going to rise soon enough.'

He was right: the sky was lightening.

Suddenly shy, Bella didn't even look at the man in position behind the controls.

'Are we going to Secrete Reale?' It was the smallest island of the San Felipe archipelago, the Princes' private haven. It was the place his brother had taken countless women, if those rumours were to be believed.

'We can't. Eduardo's family is there,' Antonio answered briefly.

She watched as they flew low and fast over the water. It was only a twenty-minute trip and as the sun rose she saw the gleaming white jewel waiting on the water.

Her blood ran cold.

It wasn't a boat. It was a gargantuan palace. From

the air she could see the large pool and spa on deck, the surrounding plush furniture scattered with bright white cushions and, on one side, the helipad that they were now descending towards. It was the ultimate example of ostentatious wealth and luxury.

Cold horror slid down her spine as she realised that history was repeating itself in the most tasteless of ways.

She was his mistress and being 'treated' to a little more than a few stolen hours. Just as her mother had been so many times.

Her nerves jangled but she could say nothing under the noise of the engine. Antonio opened the door as soon as they'd landed and jumped out, turning to help her.

'I can't stay here. I can't be seen on here.' She wrung her hands, anxiously watching as the helicopter lifted off again within seconds of their disembarking.

'If you prefer, you do not have to leave the cabin at all.' He grinned wolfishly.

That humour tore the last of her control.

'You have no idea,' she turned to rage at him. 'How spoilt can you be?' She glared. Wounded and angry with herself for being so weak and willing. 'I don't want to be here with you.'

He visibly recoiled at the venom in her tone. 'I apologise.' His expression shuttered. 'We will return to town immediately.'

She met his gaze. The stiffness in his stance didn't hide the tiredness in his eyes. He was trying to do something nice. He'd just gone about it in princely fashion, arrogant as hell. And he didn't know or he would never have chosen this as their destination.

She sighed and sat down in the nearest seat, literally unable to stand any more. 'Antonio.'

His eyebrow flickered. 'Something you want to tell me?'

She rested her aching head in her hands. 'My mother went on a boat like this once.' More than once. Her mother had loved this kind of lavish holiday. 'With Salvatore Accardi.'

Antonio squatted in front of her so he could see up into her face. She couldn't hide from him.

'They took photos from a helicopter,' she said.

'There will be no helicopters other than the one we just arrived in,' he said.

'You don't understand,' she mumbled, her cheeks scarlet with shame. 'My mother and her lover were photographed on the deck of the boat. It was the moment of my conception.' Or so the papers had speculated at the time. That image—of her mother naked on her back with her married lover between her legs—had been one of the most scandalous images of the decade. The flaunting of an affair that had only hurt all the women involved.

Accardi had denied the dark-haired man in the picture was him.

Deny, deny, deny, was all he ever did.

'I should have talked with you first,' Antonio said quietly. 'I thought you would like it.'

'Anyone normal would,' she admitted. She closed her eyes. 'I'm sorry.'

Here she was on the same kind of symbol of opulence and wealth and corruption, with a man who could have anything—and any*one*—he wanted.

'I'm sorry too.' He caressed her cheek with his

thumb. 'But you're not her. And I'm not him.' Standing, he reached forward and scooped her into his arms. 'What we both are is very tired. You've been burning the candle at both ends. You need a rest.'

She half smiled at the stiff way he expressed the old saying. She rested her head on his chest, feeling his heart beating, suddenly unbearably tired. 'Yes.'

'Then let's get you to bed.'

She wanted to touch him and feel the mindless relief that he could bring, but the waves of exhaustion rolling over her were too strong and in his arms she relaxed completely. Her eyes closed as she felt him descend the steps into the body of the boat.

She felt him place her on the soft bed, felt his lips on hers. Too gently. Too briefly. But she couldn't win the fight to open her eyes again.

'Stay,' she murmured, at least she tried to say it but it might have only been a moan.

'I'm right here.'

And he was. Curled up beside her, drawing a soft blanket over them both.

CHAPTER EIGHT

BELLA HAD NO idea what the time was when she woke, but, given light was streaming through the beautiful window, she figured it had to be late in the afternoon.

'I didn't realise you were going to sleep for hours.'

She turned at the sound of Antonio's drawl.

'Hours.' He threw her a mock chagrined look.

With a sleepy smile she rolled onto her back and stretched her toes. 'Sorry.' She glanced back at him. *'Not* sorry.'

Silently he regarded her, his reserved expression more pronounced, when suddenly his solemnity broke and the sexiest smile spread across his face. He crooked his little finger at her. 'Maybe you'd better come here and show me how "not sorry" you are.'

Her body hummed in anticipation, but she couldn't resist attempting another tease. 'I can't make it all the way over there…' She stretched lazily again.

'Going to make me do all the work?'

'You seem to like to be in charge.' She shrugged, sending him a look from under her lashes.

'You like choosing not to do what I ask.'

'Maybe it's all in the *way* you ask…' She let her voice trail suggestively.

'How should I ask?' he asked. The ominous tone made her tingle all the more.

'With kisses, of course.'

He reached out and grabbed her foot, hauling her down the bed towards him. 'Good thing I know how and where you like to be kissed.'

Bella could only arch up on the bed and let him.

Slowly the sky turned from blue to a burnished gold as the sun seemed to sink into the water.

'Come up on deck,' Antonio invited gently. 'It's almost dark. No one is there to see us.'

He was right, there was no one there. He must employ incredibly diligent and discreet staff—because while she and he had slept, they'd worked hard to create a sheltered lounge area on the deck that had silk walls and sofas surrounding a sensual plunge pool. Silver platters were scattered on the low table, laden with freshly prepared treats. It was private and beautiful and *safe*. She wrapped herself in the robe he'd handed her and curled on the plush cushions. She bit into a strawberry, relishing the burst of flavour.

'Do you often come away on this boat?' she asked, watching in amusement—and unashamed appreciation—as he slipped into the warm splash pool.

'Not as often as I'd like,' he admitted, sweeping his wet hair from his brow and looking too sexy for comfort. 'I usually bring work with me.' He angled his head and eyed her wickedly. 'I guess I brought manual labour with me this time.'

'Manual?' She arched her brows.

He held up his hands, then wiggled his fingers. 'Hours and hours of hard, physical labour.' He sighed theatrically. 'Except you slept away so *many* hours…'

'I woke once or twice,' she informed him primly. 'And found you fast asleep beside me.' He'd been utterly gorgeous too—handsome and relaxed and not at all reserved. 'Admit it,' she dared him. 'It wasn't so bad.'

'I think we both feel better for it.' He rubbed his jaw with a grin.

She certainly felt better. She couldn't stop smiling. The more she was with him, the less she could believe this was real. That quiet, reserved, emotionally distant Prince Antonio was warm and funny and kind when relaxed. When alone with her and away from the rest of the world he was charming and witty. And so gloriously sensual.

It was better than any fantasy. She just had to remember it wasn't for ever.

He'd fallen silent. She realised he was studying her as much as she was studying him but that the laughter in his eyes had faded, replaced by a frown.

'What's wrong?' she asked before thinking better of it.

A shadow flickered in his eyes before he spoke. 'It's weird not to be working.'

She felt certain that wasn't what he'd been thinking, but she didn't challenge him on it. 'You're allowed a break. That's what you told me, remember?'

'You know what it is like to devote your life to your career. It would feel strange to miss a day of training for you, right? It's a calling more than a career.'

'I chose mine. You were born to yours.'

'It's in the blood, I guess.' He reached out to take her foot, rubbing her scarred skin. 'When did you choose ballet?'

'I got my first personal trainer just before I turned two. And a ballet coach.'

His hands stopped the delicious massage. 'A personal trainer when you were *two*?'

She chuckled at his outraged expression. 'I was my mother's cute accessory that she toted around until I grew too big for her to carry.' She'd been the pretty little girl. Until she started to attract comment that she was more attractive than her mother. 'I won a scholarship to study at a dance academy in England when I was ten and eventually she let me go. I loved it. There were no boyfriends, no cameras, no scandal. I could just get on with doing the thing I loved.'

'But you were away from your mother?'

'That wasn't a problem,' she said wryly. Keeping her mother's secrets had been a burden she'd been too young for. And she hadn't liked the vulnerability she'd felt as a teenager with those men around.

He hoisted himself out of the water to sit on the deck and reached for a towel. 'So you weren't close.'

'It was complicated.' Bella frowned. 'I loved her very much, but she had a lot going on in her life.'

'By a lot going on, you mean a lot of men.'

'Yes.' Bella refused to deny it. 'She spent a large part of her life looking for love and she never found it.'

She'd been used and had used lovers herself.

'Are you looking for love?' Antonio asked.

Bella laughed. 'I know what I'm not looking for.' She gazed out at the darkening water. 'Before I went home to Mother for a holiday one summer Matron at school taught me some self-defence moves. Ways to try to get away and a few lines to spin to get some distance if I needed them.'

'Did you need to use them?'

She shrugged. 'Fortunately I spent most of the holidays at other ballet summer schools or camps. I'd only see Mother for long weekends at the most. And when I did, there were lots of cameras. Cameras can actually make things safer.'

He inclined his head questioningly.

'People are more aware of their own behaviour when they know they're being recorded.' She stretched her foot. 'And I think my mother knew there was a safety net in having a boyfriend. It means you're taken.' She smiled. 'It keeps others at a distance. Mostly.'

'But you don't do that too—there's no safe boyfriend?'

'Only the one when I was young and thought I was in love.' She wrinkled her nose at her naïveté.

'But you weren't really in love with him?'

'I wanted to be.' She'd wanted to be loved. To feel secure. To be held and cared for. To be safe. To have someone want her—*all* of her—and just her.

'What happened?'

'I thought he was honest and strong. He wasn't. He let me down.'

'How?'

She didn't like the thundercloud that had appeared on Antonio's face. 'He didn't really want me. He wanted the…fame…of being with me. I was the prize.' She rubbed her arm. 'But he expected more from me. What with my family history…'

'More?'

'A sexpot between the sheets,' she said bitterly. 'Like my siren of a mother. The famous lover of all those powerful men…'

'And you're not a sexpot.' He leant forward and cupped her cheek. 'Not for just anyone.'

She felt her flush rising. 'Don't tease...' she whispered.

He gazed at her, his expression utterly solemn. 'I'm not a sexpot for just anyone either.' And then he smiled.

She laughed a little, as he'd intended her to. 'He was seeing someone else on the side.'

'Because he was a jerk,' Antonio stated simply. 'Not because of anything you did or didn't do.' He reached out and lit one of the candles in the table, casting a small glow in the darkness. 'And since then?'

She shrugged. 'There hasn't been anyone serious.'

'You don't like trading on your sex appeal.'

She paused. 'I don't want to be ungrateful. I know how incredibly lucky I am compared to so many other people—to live on San Felipe, to have secured the financial backing for my business, to have access to all those clothes...some women would love that. But I want to be able to do what I really *want* to do. So all this "show" is only 'til the club becomes a commercial success. I need to earn for a couple of years, then I intend to step back and do something else.'

'But you must love it in part—no one can fake it for that long. All those photos. All that dancing.'

'I adore dancing.' She leaned forward. 'And I guess I do quite like the clothes.' She chuckled. 'I like feeling like I look okay—it's the way I was raised and old habits die hard—it's a weird paradox. But I don't want that to be *all* I'm known for. When I was dancing, I had that as well.'

'So what is going to replace it?' He looked at her

curiously. 'You must have some ideas if it's not the club.'

'No, that's a means to an end. I couldn't get the backing I needed for what I really want to do.' It wasn't going to be a money spinner, but she needed only enough for herself to live on.

'And that is?'

She paused, then laughed at her own self-consciousness. What did it matter if he knew? 'I want to establish my own ballet school. I want to have my own academy and teach.' She felt her flush rising again. 'I know it won't exactly make me a fortune, but it's what I love and I want to share it.'

'You want to teach ballet?' Surprise glinted in his eyes.

'Yes.'

He nodded but then frowned again. 'Why San Felipe? If not to taunt Salvatore?'

'I came for some holidays here with my mother. She had another friend here, for a time.' She knew he'd understand she meant another lover. 'I always loved it here. The beaches are beautiful, the city old and majestic.' She shrugged with a soft smile. 'You know it has a magic about it.'

'And your mother's friend?'

'The relationship didn't last, of course. He passed away a few years ago.' She sighed. 'So there you have it, why I'm here. It's not that exciting at all, you see.'

Silent, he ran his fingers along her scarred shin as if he could somehow smooth it away. 'Why did you never ask for an investigation or press charges?'

'About the glass?' She faltered, but then pressed on. She'd worked hard to reconcile her decision. 'I didn't want them to see how much they'd hurt me. They'd win if they saw that. I'll never let them see how much they got to me,' she said in a low tone, keeping her head high.

'You're not bulletproof,' he said.

'It doesn't matter.' She tried to shrug it off.

'It matters immensely. You had the thing you love most stolen from you. You were stolen from us—the audience.'

She smiled softly at his support of her. 'It just is what it is. I've accepted it and I'm moving on. I'm a survivor.' She was determined, and proud to be.

The sun had vanished but now the stars had come out to shine. And the moonlight glittered over the water. He fetched one of the blankets that were folded on one of the sofas and brought it back to where she was nestled in the cushions.

He paused at the solitary candle flickering on the low table. 'You want to stay out here with me tonight?'

She nodded and watched him blow the candle out.

The dreadful thing was she'd stay with him wherever he asked, for as long as he wanted. Yes, she was falling for him, but she also agreed because he shouldn't be out here alone.

He'd been on the front page of today's paper, standing in the hospital garden that honoured Alessia. In his midnight-blue suit with his pale, emotionless eyes he'd looked so isolated. She wished he wouldn't shut himself away so completely. She wished he'd open up like this even more. There was a warm, funny, compassionate guy locked away in there and someone—never her—should help him be happy.

He should be happy.

But she wasn't the woman who could make that happen for him. She was the woman who had him only for now.

CHAPTER NINE

SHE WAS WOKEN with a kiss. She smiled—how could she not when he looked at her like that? He was tousled and stubbled and tired about the eyes and so very sexy.

She'd told herself she wasn't going to sleep at all during their night on deck under the stars, but he'd teased her so long and made her come so hard her body had waved the white flag not long before dawn.

'What time is it?' she asked him.

'Stupidly early,' he admitted apologetically. 'But there's something I wanted you to see.'

Holding the soft blanket to her, she sat up on the deck and realised he was in nothing but swimming trunks and a life jacket and was dangling a bikini from his hand.

'You think I'm going to wear that?'

'Or just the life jacket, I don't mind.'

She snatched the bikini from his hand and wriggled into it as he laughed.

The sky was pale blue from the first fingers of sunlight, the ocean still and beautiful and fresh and nothing could mar its beauty. She snuggled against his waist as he rode the jet ski, laughing at his show of speed and control. But he suddenly slowed right down and all but

cut the engine. Then she saw what was swimming towards them in a joyous streak of energy.

'Dolphins,' she breathed.

'A whole pod.' He nodded, turning to see her face.
'They're often out this way to feed.'

And *play*. The creatures leapt and somersaulted as
if it were the dolphin Olympics.

'There are hundreds of them.' She laughed in delighted awe. She'd never seen anything as beautiful or
exhilarating in her life.

'You want to swim with them?' He was smiling at
her, looking the most carefree and vital it made her
heart flip in her chest.

'Can we?'

'Sing to them,' he said, handing her a dive mask
he'd stowed in his vest. 'They'll come check you out.'

'Sing?'

'Anything.' He chuckled at her look.

But she slipped into the water and tried what he suggested. To her amazement three of the curious creatures swiftly circled around and around her. She floated
face-down, eyeing the beautiful animals until she had
to lift her head and gasp for breath. Antonio surfaced
next to her, smiling triumphantly.

'Antonio.' She breathed hard. 'They're amazing.'

'I know.' He hauled himself back onto the jet ski and
leaned down to give her a hand. 'You know they're one
of the few creatures to mate just for the fun of it?' He
chuckled. 'They feed and play and make love all day.
Not such a bad life, is it?'

'Not bad at all.'

She watched as he looked out over the beautiful waters again and that carefree expression slowly faded

from his eyes. He glanced at her ruefully. 'We'd better get back to the boat. Breakfast will be waiting.'

Their time was almost up.

Back on board, she showered, disappointed when he didn't join her in there. In the bedroom the clothes she'd arrived in were somehow cleaned and pressed and waiting for her. She blushed at the thought of those nameless, invisible servants knowing she was here and no doubt knowing why. She dressed then went to the lounge. Antonio sat at the laden table, already showered and dressed and waiting for her.

'I'll never forget that, thank you so much.' She smiled across at him.

He had been so kind to her, she'd never forget any of it.

For a split second he looked as happy as she felt, but then that reserve smoothed his features and that was when she couldn't hold back any more. She didn't want to see the vibrant man of the night return to that frozen state now they were about to leave.

'You shouldn't be alone,' she said softly.

Antonio carefully put his tumbler of juice back down on the table. 'Pardon?'

'I said, you shouldn't be alone. You should laugh more often. You deserve more happiness in your life.'

His blood iced.

'Do you feel sorry for me?' he asked quietly, but he was so close to the edge of anger.

Last night hadn't lasted long enough. While she'd slept, he'd watched, like some sick stalker. But he'd been unable to rest any more, too conscious of time ticking. And now?

It wasn't a clock but a bomb ticking. He did *not*

want her to go there with him. He didn't want to hear
that lie the world believed. Not from *her* lips. He didn't
want her to believe that damn pious story. He was un-
worthy of her empathy and her generosity. He was un-
worthy of *her*.

'Of course I do,' she replied simply. 'I'm very sorry
you lost her.'

Alessia.

His gut clenched.

'Is that why you're here now, because you pity me?'
He stood up from the table and walked away so he
couldn't see her face. 'You've been willing to let me
do whatever I want with you because you want to make
me feel better?'

He heard her small gasp of shock.

'Why are you so angry?' She stood too, following him to the centre of the room, standing defiantly
straight and in his face as always. 'I understand you
don't want to be hurt again—'

'You understand nothing.' It wasn't about *him* getting hurt. 'It isn't about me. It isn't fair to ask anyone
to share the kind of life I lead.'

'That's just an excuse.' She actually rolled her eyes
at him. 'Your kind of life can be managed. Media can
be managed.'

'Like how that worked out for you and your mother?'

She flinched but the cut didn't stop her. 'Look, I
know I'm not the right woman for you, but she's out
there. You're just too afraid to find her.'

Hearing her say that infuriated him. Did she really
think she was somehow not worthy of him? She had
no idea who the worthy one in this room was. It sure
as hell wasn't him.

He wanted to shut her up. He should kiss her. Have her. Fast and physical so he could feel the best he'd ever felt in his life for a few minutes again…but he couldn't because she was looking up at him all sincere and sweet and kind and *that* was what wasn't right.

Her eyes were so luminous, so genuine. 'You deserve to find love again.'

No, he didn't. And there was the killer—he'd never found love in the first place.

Bu she misread his silence. 'You do, Antonio. You're a good man. You deserve—'

'I deserve *nothing*,' he snarled in guilt-drenched fury. 'I *destroyed* her.'

Finally Bella was silenced.

And he was aghast at his slip and so, so angry. 'You think you know what happened? You think you know me?'

'Antonio—'

'Stop,' he said, wildly raising his hand. 'Stop and just let me say it. You want the damned, bloody ugly truth?'

For once in his life someone would see him as he really was and it might as well be her. It might as well be the one woman he couldn't stop wanting. And that was good, because she wouldn't want him once she knew. And this would be over.

'I broke up with her before she went away to university. The engagement thing had been more my parents' wish than my own and I was young and didn't want to be tied down. But Alessia was devastated. She begged me not to tell anyone. Wanted to keep it a secret until after she'd gone to England. And we'd let the press know we were no longer together after she'd been there a few months. I agreed. I could see she needed some time to compose herself…' But in his mind he'd been free and he'd been so damned relieved.

'A month or so later I went to see her when Eduardo first went over to study.' He dragged in a desperate breath and carried on fiercely, frantic to get the bitter truth out. 'She'd changed. She'd lost weight and was pale. She was nervy and wanted to get back together.' He paused again, clenching his fist as he remembered how he'd treated her that day. 'I told her that starving herself wasn't going to win me back. I told her to get a grip on herself and stop the drama-queen crap. I was *so* hard on her.' He'd told her he wasn't in love with her and that that wasn't changing no matter what she did.

He'd thought he was doing the right thing to make her pull herself together. Being cruel to be kind.

It had just been cruel.

He made himself look at Bella, made himself ignore the tears building in her beautiful eyes. 'Apparently she didn't see a doctor until another month or so later. She'd thought the weight loss and sore throat was just anxiety and heartache. Instead it was because of a fast-growing mass in her stomach. The kind of cancer that grows so fast, every day before detection matters. Every day missed meant she was closer to death.'

If found in time, treatment could work well. But if not found in time?

Too late already.

'Antonio—'

'My parents were killed the weekend she got the diagnosis. Her prognosis was dreadful. She decided I had enough to be getting on with, so she didn't tell me. Her parents didn't tell me. Eduardo didn't tell me.'

Because he'd been so arrogant to think he could handle the coronation and transfer of power all on his own. He'd refused to allow Eduardo to return to help. In his own grief for his parents he'd wanted just to *work* his way through it.

But he hadn't realised how much that decision would hurt those around him. And ultimately haunt him too.

'Not long after, I found out through the press, as the world knows. But the world still thought we were engaged...' He released a shuddering, painful breath. 'I saw her once more before she died.' He paused, hating that memory more than any other in his life. 'And the worst of it was, *she* apologised to *me*.'

When he'd been the one to break her. He had never regretted anything as much in all his life.

Bella walked over to him. But he was too on edge and he didn't want her compassion. He didn't want that caring. He didn't want anything from her. Not now. He held up his hand again. Desperate to control his damned emotions. *'Don't touch me.'*

Bella flinched at the raw agony in that command. But this time she was ignoring his rejection of her. She had to. She wrapped her arms around his waist.

'Don't.' This time it was a whisper. 'I don't...'

She held him in the gentlest, smallest of embraces.

'You didn't kill her,' Bella said softly. '*Cancer* killed her.'

'If she'd seen a doctor sooner...if she hadn't been stressed and heartbroken...if she'd fought harder...so many ifs. So many mistakes that were my fault.'

But as he spoke his voice went from emotional to expressionless.

He put his hands on her arms and lifted them so he

could step back, free from her. She gazed up into his shadowed face but she could see the determination glinting in his eyes. Goosebumps peppered her skin. He was so used to controlling himself. Even now, he could pull himself together. A cold fear rose within her.

'I will not hurt another person the way I hurt her,' he said softly, intently looking down into her eyes. 'Do you understand?'

'And you think keeping yourself isolated is the way to do that?' It was hard to talk past the giant lump that had formed in her throat. 'You think living only half a life is going to somehow make up for the loss of hers?'

'I lie,' he said harshly, his hold slipping for a second again. 'I live a lie. Every. Damned. Day.' He slammed his fist on the wall behind him. 'I'm not some heart-broken hero. I'm a cold-hearted bastard.'

'You're not that at all.' A tear spilt down her cheek. 'Because you *do* lie. You're protecting her memory. You're caring about her parents and her.'

'It doesn't make it okay,' he said roughly. 'It will *never* make it okay.'

CHAPTER TEN

HE NEVER, EVER should have told her. Because now it *was* pity in her eyes when she looked at him. And he didn't want that. He forced himself to walk away from her. It was over. There was no going back to their lovers-go-lightly affair now.

But she was more beautiful than he'd ever seen her. Her skin glowed, her hair hung in a long, glossy swathe, she smelt of sea and sun and when she'd first got back to the boat after the dolphins she'd looked supremely happy and relaxed. And he was arrogant and egotistical enough to take pleasure in that it was because of something he'd done. But now, the truth was out and she was in tears and their escape was up.

'The helicopter will be here in twenty minutes,' he said formally, determined to recover his equilibrium. 'We have to go back.'

'Of course. I'm ready now.' When he turned back to face her she'd dried her eyes and her back was straight.

He wanted to bring her glow back. That unadulterated happiness that for once had had nothing to do with sex. He wanted to know she was going to be happy *beyond* this moment. He hated the thought of her returning to that club and its exhausting demands.

He wanted to know she was going to be happy in her future.

'I want to give you the funds to establish your ballet school,' he said without thinking.

She stared at him fixedly.

'As an investment,' he clarified quickly. 'San Felipe is a cultural capital of Europe and we don't have a ballet school that could train dancers to professional level…' He trailed off as her expression hardened.

'It's a poor investment,' she said. 'You won't get the return that you would for almost anything else.'

He didn't want a damn return on his investment. 'Is that what that backer told you? He doesn't know what you're capable of.'

She would make it a success, he knew, because she would work herself to the bone to ensure she did. She was more determined than anyone he'd ever met.

'I appreciate what you want to do, but I can't accept it.' She was very, very polite.

'Why not?'

She paused, picking her words with care. 'I want to do it myself.'

'You don't have to do everything on your own,' he argued grimly. 'You want the academy, it's yours. No one will ever know where you got the backing from.'

Her eyes flashed fire. 'Are you trying to buy my silence? Are you worried I'm going to go back to shore and suddenly sell my story?' She paced across the room, turning back to berate him in a furious whisper. 'I will never tell a soul what you told me about Alessia. Not a word. Nothing about this trip. Nothing about us. Not *ever*.'

'I never for a second thought you would.' That

wasn't why he'd mentioned this at all. He knew he could trust her. She understood too well how it was to be judged.

'I don't want to be dependent on a lover for my life-style. I don't want to be my mother.'

'This isn't like that.'

'It's exactly like that,' she snapped back.

He paused as the *whomp-whomp-whomp* sound of the helicopter echoed. The boat's interior had amazing soundproofing, which meant that the helicopter had to have arrived for them to be able to hear it at all. Sure enough, within another second the whirring began to fade as the pilot powered the engine down. They wouldn't leave until Antonio gave the word.

He wasn't ready to do that yet. He walked towards where Bella stood glaring at him. 'I just want to help you.'

'Why? You won't let me help you.'

That was different. This was an easy kind of help. This was just money. 'Bella—'

'I'm not a prostitute, Antonio. I'm not your concubine or courtesan. Don't treat me like one.'

He drew up short, feeling out of his depth now. 'You're a *friend*. Friends help each other.'

'Not like this they don't,' she said. 'We're not friends. And I'm not using you for this, Antonio.'

'You won't be using me.'

Why did she look so wounded? His anger boiled over. He should have known she'd reject his offer. He'd never put himself out for anyone. Never offered another woman what he'd offered her. Couldn't she appreciate that? She was so damn stubborn and independent and now acting as if he'd somehow insulted her?

'Why can't you accept I'm just trying to help you?' he asked.

'Why can't you accept that that kind of help isn't something I can ever be comfortable with?'

'Then pay me back,' he exploded back at her. 'We can make it a loan. Just as you have a loan from the backer of BURN. He's not as nice a guy as I am and yet you're happy to accept his assistance.'

'Ours is a strictly professional relationship. Always has been, always will be.'

'And our relationship?'

'We don't have a relationship. We *can't* have a relationship.'

He knew she was right but her refusal angered him anyway. He loathed being told what he could or couldn't do. 'No?'

'Of course not.' She turned and walked towards the nearest door. 'We need to get on that helicopter. We need to stop this.'

'Stop?' He strode over to her. 'What do you mean "stop"?'

She paused and glared up into his eyes. 'You know exactly what I mean. It was fun while it lasted—'

'You're saying we're over?'

'I think that's for the best, yes.'

'Because I offered to help you?'

'It's really nice you wanted to help, but it's not appropriate.'

'What am I supposed to do?' he asked her in frustration.

'I've never asked you to do anything for me.'

No. She hadn't. And that angered him even more.

She didn't want anything from him. Other than hours in his bed.

Which was all he wanted too, right? Because as he'd told her just moments ago, he was never hurting *any-one* the way he had Alessia. Yet here he was, feeling as if he'd just hurt Bella. Badly.

'You're not ending this.' He turned her towards him, then backed her up two paces to the wall. 'This isn't finished. You know it. I know it.'

'Antonio—'

'Shut up and kiss me.'

He needed to vent the frustration rushing along his veins. Sex would help. Sex right now would help a lot. And he knew it would help her too.

'We're supposed to be leaving,' she argued, but her flush deepened.

'I don't care.' He didn't give a damn about his time-table. He needed her soft in his arms, looking upon him with sparkling, sleepy-eyed pleasure, not this hurt and annoyance.

He didn't want to feel guilt where Bella was concerned. Only pleasure. She'd only brought him a sense of well-being and that was the least he could do for her.

He couldn't make her accept his offer. He, who could make decisions that affected every one of the people in his country with the stroke of a pen, had no power over her. Not even to damn well help her. She would never forgive him for it even if he tried to force her. He couldn't make her do anything—except in this one area.

'In this you won't say no,' he said, aching for her sexual submission. Frustrated despite her warm will-ingness as he pressed against her. 'You will not deny me the permission to pleasure you. You'll come. Over and over.'

'Egotist.' Her eyelids were heavy but she kept those green jewels tightly focused on him.

'You want it too.' He sighed in gut-wrenching relief when she sighed and turned towards his touch. 'More than anything.' He leaned close. 'Isn't that right? Say yes.'

He needed to hear the words as well as see the willingness in her eyes and feel the hot softness of her body.

'Only to this,' she whispered back, her lips brushing his as she answered, her gaze still locked on his.

Oh, he knew that. He knew it and he hated it. Her slender body was hot and wet and tight as he pushed his finger into her sweetly slippery curve.

'We're not done,' he promised with another rough kiss as he pressed close.

'I know.'

But they were. And they both knew it. They were both lying now.

'Antonio,' Bella muttered as he pressed tiny little kisses over and over her mouth and his wicked hands tormented her and all the while he watched her. He watched and he *knew*.

Because she'd caught sight of the determination glinting in *his* eyes and knew he made all the rules as he pleased. And he was damn well going to please her now.

And she could no more deny him than she could deny her lungs air. She wanted to embrace him. Wanted him to feel as good as she. She was so hurt for him— more now she knew the truth of his past, than before. The guilt he felt? The burden he carried?

He'd denied it, but he punished himself so much—how could she deny him this last pleasure? How could she deny herself?

But it was too much.

'It wasn't supposed to be like this,' she groaned harshly as he made her come. So quickly. So intensely. And she was so hungry for more.

It was supposed to have only been a physical relief. A one-night stand to boost her sexual confidence, to make her smile, to be her secret. But it had become more. She *wanted* more. But *not* his money. Not his condescension.

And he wouldn't let her in where she really wanted to be. He'd made that clear. This had become too emotional for him. And for her.

Dazed, she leaned back against the wall, watching as he quickly shed his clothes all the while watching her, his ruthless expression so easy to read. He was ready to test her erotic limits again. And heaven help her she wanted him to already. Because that was the thing: she ached to be with him on so many levels—and she wanted to comfort and be comforted by him even if it could only be in this most basic of ways.

'You're sure you're covered?' he roughly asked, pausing just before taking her.

It took her a moment to realise he meant contraception. 'I am,' she assured him. 'But is it too much of a risk for you?'

'Everything about you is a risk.' He pushed her legs further apart and claimed her with a powerful thrust that made them both groan. 'But worth it,' he muttered hotly before kissing her. 'Worth it.'

This one last time.

Their hands locked together, their bodies locked, their gazes locked. He started, a searing, slow, devastating drill. He held her to him, teasing all her most sensitive parts with that skill and determination she'd come to accept was his strength. She couldn't stop herself muttering his name in a broken whisper over and over as he ruthlessly thrust her to that agonising, tense peak.

She didn't want to read all those conflicting emotions in his pale blue eyes. She wanted this to be the carnal affair it had begun as: they were here for orgasms only. Not for opening up emotionally and admitting old hurts that couldn't be healed.

But she couldn't look away, couldn't break the physical bonds shackling her to him. She should. She knew she should. But she couldn't. Because he held more than her body in his hands now. He held her heart.

And he was about to crush it.

CHAPTER ELEVEN

THE CONJECTURE ABOUT Antonio's twenty-four-hour absence was subdued, thanks to the valiant efforts of Eduardo, who'd surpassed his own legendary ability to charm an entire nation with his smile and good humour. He'd done that by simply bringing his wife and new baby to the event. As it was the first formal photo opportunity with the baby Princess, and was wholly unexpected, the press had a field day. Sure, there were questions about Antonio's whereabouts, but Eduardo had simply told them he was working on an important matter in the palace and had wanted Eduardo and Stella to have their moment.

'It went well. I appreciate your effort.' Antonio stood by the helicopter. Eduardo's wife and daughter were already safely strapped inside.

'There's nothing else you need me to do?' Eduardo asked, his gaze keen. 'I can stay longer…'

Antonio shook his head. 'Go back to the island with your girls. I'm in control here now.'

'You're never not in control,' Eduardo teased, but it was barely a joke.

Thing was, Antonio had never felt less in control. 'Thanks for coming,' he said gruffly.

'Thanks for asking me to.' Eduardo flashed the smile that had made millions swoon. 'See you in a few more weeks.'

The next couple of days passed in a blur of meetings and events, greetings and parties. As they rolled into one Antonio attended on auto. Too much of his mental energy was taken up with trying to forget. Trying not to want more time with her.

Trying not to miss her.

But at every event he couldn't help but cast his eye over the crowd feeling both the dread and hope of seeing her. Bitter disappointment flooded him every time.

But the San Felipe festival fortnight was almost over and his schedule would return to normal busy, not insanely busy. For the most part from now on, he ought to be able to avoid her. He ought to be able to stay in control.

Except the final event loomed tonight. There was no way Bella Sanchez would miss the annual San Felipe Masquerade Ball. Not when she was the nation's club queen. She'd be there in all her sensual beauty.

He buttoned up his starched shirt and fastened his tie. Each guest would hold a delicate mask, but he didn't bother. Everyone knew who he was; there was no escaping it.

He knew there was no escaping that public attention for Bella either. Not yet. But she didn't really want to be in this fishbowl world with a camera in her face every second and the press writing stories about every aspect of her life. She wanted to be free of it and once she'd funded her business she'd retreat into a normal life that had privacy.

That was what she wanted and it was best for her. So

she'd been right on the boat: it *had* to be over between them. No more stolen moments. No more kisses. No more laughter. And that was right for him too—he'd had his time.

He gritted his teeth as he fought back the wave of physical longing. God, he missed her.

The only way of getting through tonight was with no *looking*. Tonight he was going to have to avoid her completely.

Bella applied a final dab of mascara. She'd barely been able to eat a thing all day, and now the moment had finally arrived she was tempted to strip out of her glamorous dress and hide at home in her pyjamas.

She'd made a massive mistake in getting involved with Antonio. Why had she ever thought it would only be a simple, sinful moment of pleasure? It had become all-consuming and her heart *ached*. For him and for her. That he blamed himself so bitterly over Alessia's illness? That he isolated himself so completely?

And that he hadn't made any kind of contact with her since they'd left the boat?

Those last few moments together had been so intense, so profound but the memory of them was now so painful. Because despite his imperious argument at the time, it *was* over.

And she was devastated.

But she couldn't let her emotions get the better of her. She had to move forward. She'd long known how it felt not to be wanted or needed or loved, but she'd never let that stop her from doing what she needed to before. She'd go to the ball, hold her head high and continue building that swelling interest in her business. She might not have succeeded in many things in her life, but she was *not* failing at that. She had her gilt-edged invitation card, she had her dress and she had her years of standing on stage and being stared at. This would be easy.

As long as she kept her distance from the Crown Prince.

But when the liveried guards waved her in to the grand ballroom of San Felipe palace an hour later, she stood a second in the doorway and took in the sight before her. There was grand, and there was opulent, and there was majestic. This was more than all those things, but it wasn't the dazzling venue making her dizzy.

It was anticipation and fear and deep-buried desire.

She *ached* to see him.

Her heart thundered as she greeted a few people. Several society faces were now familiar to her and they welcomed her. She knew it was only because of her club's success and her social-media status, but she'd take it.

The first time she saw him, he was only a few yards from her but a crowd separated them. His immaculately tailored tuxedo emphasised his height and proud stance, and she saw he was intently listening to a tall brunette in a form-flattering black gown. Bella froze as she recognised the woman. At that exact moment Francesca Accardi glanced over at her. Time halted as she looked right at Bella, her eyes widening slightly, only then she turned to smile coyly again at Antonio, her face animated.

But she'd offered no nod or smile or any outward sign of recognition towards Bella.

That old rejection stung, but most especially because

Francesca was her own blood. Her half-sister was their father's favourite and now she was with Antonio?

Feeling cold, Bella stared at him. He'd turned to see what had caught Francesca's attention. Now his eyes remained on Bella even as Francesca tried to talk with him. But only for a moment. Then he too glanced away as he muttered something in response to the brunette.

There'd been no smile. No polite inclination of his head. No sign of recognition whatsoever. There was only a callous blanking. He'd seen her, but chosen to pretend he hadn't.

He hadn't acknowledged her at all.

Blinking, Bella turned, blindly moving towards the back of the ballroom. She would never, ever let him know just how much he'd hurt her in that moment.

And she would never, ever forgive him.

She spoke to more people. Made herself take a glass of champagne. She'd have a few sips and then she'd leave. But she wouldn't run immediately. She wouldn't give him that satisfaction. So she smiled. Talked. And the hurt morphed into an anger that grew bigger and hotter with every moment. She smiled more. Talked more. Laughed more.

She wouldn't show any of them any weakness.

Ten minutes later she glanced from the group of young businessmen she was talking to to find his fiery gaze on her.

Still no smile. No inclination of his head. But she read *his* anger this time. Adrenalin surged through her blood.

This time she was the one to turn her back.

She kept talking, but her awareness of him was more acute than ever. She sensed him near, looking icy, but she could feel the simmering fury coming towards her in waves.

She sent her own angry vibes right back at him.

As her smile brightened and her laughter rang her tension mounted. He stood nearer still, but still didn't speak. There was only the look, only the sharpness in the atmosphere and only the two of them felt it.

Finally he passed close enough to speak to her.

'You shouldn't be here,' he said in leashed, low tones.

'You're ordering me to leave?'

'As if you would if I did.' He kept walking past her but his quick glance back was rapier-sharp.

She answered with a death look. But her body felt charged. It didn't care whether it was anger or lust, her body just craved his attention. And she had it now— his gaze on her, his eyes watching as she talked with other guests.

For the next half-hour she talked and laughed and acted like the social butterfly she was supposed to be and it came easy. Every few minutes she glanced at him, their gazes clashed, held, *fought* until she turned away.

Still no smile. No nod.

She turned back, registering how crowded the massive ballroom had become. It was filled with people— women—craving time with Crown Prince Antonio. That tipped her tension from anticipation to unbearable.

She didn't want all these others to be here. She wanted to be alone with him. Fiercely, privately, intimately alone. And that wasn't going to happen. This was only a game, only for tonight. She wasn't going to get what she wanted. Not ever.

Her emotions crashed.

She turned, finally ready to leave. She shouldn't have come. She should have proudly kept her distance and encouraged her customers to come to her club earlier.

She'd miscalculated completely. She took the first door out of the ballroom that she could find. So many people, beautifully dressed, lined the corridor, laughing and talking. She brushed past them, following her instinct to get away. She'd got along its length and had just turned right towards the heavy doors when she heard him.

'Bella.'

She paused, but she didn't turn around.

'Second door on the left.'

It was a command. All her antagonism reared in a passion. But despite knowing better, she couldn't resist. She opened the door he'd meant and stalked into the room. It was a comparatively small meeting room—decorated with more gilt-framed paintings and opulent over-stuffed furniture.

He didn't slam the door behind him. But though he closed it quietly, he locked it, then stood with his back to it. Blocking her exit.

'You shouldn't have come here tonight.' He glared at her, all icy-eyed handsome magnificence in that onyx-black suit.

Despite the fact that she completely agreed with him, she wasn't about to admit it. 'You might be the Prince but this isn't some feudal village in the Middle Ages. There's such a thing as freedom of movement and freedom of speech and it's important to me to be here for my business and you *can't* stop me.' She glared at him, unable to hide her hurt or anger. 'You were so rude when I arrived. You didn't even say hello or nod or anything.' It had been the most pointed, painful dismissal of her life.

'You were the one who said it would be best if we kept this discreet,' he argued.

'You were the one who then kidnapped me for a night on your boat.'

'It was still discreet.'

'And hauling me in here is discreet?'

'I didn't haul you in here.'

No. He hadn't. She hadn't felt his hands on her at all.

'So because I didn't speak to you soon enough, you retaliate by parading round the ballroom in that dress.' He gestured wildly at her body.

'What is wrong with this dress?' She tossed her head and glared at him. 'It's a beautiful dress. And, not that it matters, it's a hell of a lot less revealing than the red one I wore at the ballet.' And she hadn't been parading. 'And what would be wrong with speaking to me?'

'I'm trying to protect you.' His teeth snapped. 'Do you really want those headlines—all the "The scandalous dancer and the Prince" stuff? All that rubbish they'll print on endless pages? Your life won't be your own if they find out.'

'I don't need your protection,' she argued. 'You think I don't know how to handle those headlines? You think I haven't been handling them all my life?'

'I didn't want you to have to handle more.'

'No. You just didn't want to acknowledge me at all.' Always she was denied. As if she were somehow shameful. Not good enough.

'I couldn't—' He broke off with a frustrated growl and then stepped closer, his whisper hoarse with absolute exasperation. 'I couldn't bear to even *look* at you because I cannot concentrate on anything else when you are in the room.'

'You're more of a man than that.' She shook her head, even more incensed by that lame excuse. 'You're the head of a country and have had to perform in way more difficult challenges than—'

'All I wanted to do is sneak you somewhere private and—'

'You're not an animal.' And he was hardly all over her now.

Only then he was, standing so close and squeezing her shoulders so she looked up into his face. And what she saw there made her gasp.

'All I wanted to do was sneak you in here so I could strip you bare,' he finished furiously.

The fire in his eyes made her so reckless. 'Then why don't you?'

She bared herself in that one sentence—bringing that desire right into fore.

He smiled. A small mocking smile. 'Always the provocation.' Swiftly he released her shoulders only to bend and pick her up. 'How much proof do you need?'

'All of it,' she demanded roughly as she felt his arms tighten still. 'I need all of it.'

He took three steps to the plump sofa near the wall. She hooked her legs around his waist just before he sat, so she then straddled him. He released her only to grasp her hair and tug so she lifted her chin and met his kiss. Hard and passionate and endless.

She writhed above him, aching to feel him there. Right there. Centring her, anchoring her. Completing her.

Their hands tangled as they sought to touch more intimately. His hands pressed against her curves, teasing, frustrating. She hated her beautiful dress, she wanted to feel his skin on hers. She wanted them both to be naked.

Neither were.

But their passion was utterly bared.

They moved quickly, angrily. He shoved her dress up to her waist with a jerky hand while unfastening his trousers with the other. She lifted herself off him only long enough for him to free his straining erection. And then she gave in again to the delight of rubbing against him. Of fighting to get closer, closer, closer still.

Their eyes met in a moment of frustration and desperation. She felt him move, his hand fisted around the crotch of her panties and he tugged hard. The silk and lace ripped. A moment later she sank onto him—fast and hard and utterly complete.

His hand squeezed her thigh almost painfully. His groan sent a shiver of raw delight down her spine. Now she was happy. Now she was with him. Now time could stop.

But it didn't. It couldn't. Nor could they stop.

He bucked beneath her, powerfully thrusting up, as if he could possibly get deeper within her. Desire for him burned—for more of how good he felt inside her. She pressed down to meet him, wanting more of him. Always more.

They fought to get closer, wild and desperate and so quick yet not quickly enough. And it wasn't slow enough either. She wanted him so much, *all* of him, but she didn't want it to end.

Except it was about to. She felt it coming—that unstoppable wave of pleasure that only he had ever brought forth from her. She arched back, whimpering as he bore it upon her. He thrust faster still until it was a frantic final coupling as frustrating as it was ecstatic.

'One last time,' he commanded. 'I need to see you come one last time.'

She stared at him in blissful agony, then closed her eyes against the despair in his. Bittersweet torture wracked her body as her orgasm hit. It was so good, but it tore her heart. Because this *was* the last time. Her mouth parted, but his hand pressed hard on her lips. In that final moment of release, he silenced her.

'I'm sorry,' he choked as he stiffened beneath her. 'I am so sorry,' he groaned in a harsh whisper as he too hit climax.

Bella dared not open her eyes. She didn't want to face this end. Through the door and walls, she could hear the ball in full swing but the silence between them in the private room was horrendous. She slipped from his knee, turning her back as she adjusted her dress.

'I didn't mean to be rude when you first arrived,' he said quietly, his voice still tinged with infinite regret. 'But I am not able to hide how I feel about you.'

'Is that so terrible?' She braced herself and faced him to ask, 'Would it really be so awful for people to know you'd finally moved on?'

He didn't answer. He didn't have to. Because for once his expression was so easy to read.

To her horror, her eyes filled with tears. He didn't want anyone to know how much he wanted her. Which basically meant he didn't *want* to want her. He didn't want to move on. He *hadn't* moved on.

She turned and ran, just getting to the door and

turning the key in the lock. But he must have run too because he reached above her head and pushed hard, so she couldn't open it.

'You're not leaving now,' he said.

'You're not stopping me.'

'I am. This time I am.' He turned her to face him. 'You can't go out there looking like that.'

'Looking like what? A slut?' With no underwear and kiss-swollen lips and the blush of orgasm still on her skin?

'I'm sorry.' He apologised again as he retreated into that damn formal reserve. 'This shouldn't have happened.'

She didn't want him to turn all princely polite. She didn't want him to regret what had happened. She just wanted him to want more the same way she did. But he didn't. She cared more for him than he did her. And she was heartbroken. She looked at the floor, unable to bear looking into that emotionless face of his.

'Forgive me.'

Angered, she lifted her head. '*I'm* not the one who needs to forgive you. *You* need to forgive *yourself*. You're a coward, Antonio De Santis.'

He actually lost colour.

'You think you're so damn noble, burying yourself in duty. You think you're protecting Alessia's name? You're only protecting yourself. You think you can keep yourself safe by not bothering to participate in life?' She shook her head, so angry with him for shutting her out. 'It doesn't work that way. Who's hurting now, Antonio? *Who* is hurting?'

'I'm sorry,' he said tonelessly. 'I cannot be the man you want me to be. I cannot be the man for you.'

It was the most humiliating moment of her life.

And he wouldn't admit that *he* was hurting either. 'I will control myself better in future. This won't happen again.'

'No.' She nodded painfully. 'It won't. I don't expect you to say hello or anything—you're absolved from any duty to be polite to me.' She half laughed bitterly at the heartbreaking mess she was in. He only wanted her for sex, whereas she? She'd gone fully in love. 'This can only be all or nothing. You can't give me *all*. So it has to be nothing.' For her own sanity it had to be nothing. But she was so, so hurt.

He didn't argue with her. 'I can have you escorted discreetly—'

'I'll go out the door I came in.' She straightened and pulled together the last shred of pride that she could. 'But I need five minutes alone first.'

He stared down at her, as if he could somehow break her and make her change her mind. But he couldn't. Her dignity was the one thing she'd leave this room with.

He had the intelligence not to apologise again, though she knew he wanted to. She could see that in his eyes. But she didn't want his pity. What she really wanted was the one thing he couldn't give her. He didn't want to give her.

And that wasn't his fault.

'Leave, Antonio.'

And then he did.

She locked the door again right away and took deep breaths to recover her equilibrium. She was not crying here. She was holding her head high and walking out of there.

No one would ever know how she'd been so crushed.

It took ten minutes before she was ready. Then she unlocked the door, squared her shoulders and walked back down the corridor and around the corner to where the people were thronging and still laughing, oblivious to the cataclysmic encounter in that room so close by. She got into the ballroom and began her trek along the edge to the exit at the end. She was walking so quickly, and with such concentration, she almost crashed into the broad-shouldered man who suddenly stepped in front of her.

'Do you really think you can ever belong here?'

She stared blankly for a second before realising who it was.

Salvatore Accardi. Her father. For the first time in her life he'd addressed her directly. And he wasn't being conciliatory.

Frantically she processed his words, wondering at what he'd meant.

'Look at you,' he snarled. 'You think it isn't obvious what you've been doing?' Salvatore sent her a scathing look. 'Like mother, like daughter. Giving it all to anyone who asks. No doubt you're aiming to get pregnant as quickly as possible and you'll blame it on the nearest wealthy man.' He stepped closer. 'You're the daughter of a whore and you're a whore.'

Oh, God, did he know? Had he seen? She glanced to the side, wondering if everyone here knew. How was that possible?

'You need to leave San Felipe,' Salvatore added.

She couldn't cope with this onslaught right now. Not after Antonio's rejection.

But as she stared at Salvatore, aghast and unable

to speak, she saw his eyes widen at something over her shoulder.

'Is there some kind of problem, Salvatore?' Crown Prince Antonio walked up behind her.

Salvatore's expression tightened.

Antonio took her hand, holding it tight. It was the smallest, but most pointed, of gestures and she was so shocked she still could say nothing.

'Bella and I are very close,' he said. 'So I'm glad to see you talking. I'm sure you want to make her welcome. But if you'll excuse us, we're going to dance now.'

Bella gazed at Antonio in utter astonishment. Why had he reappeared? Why had he taken her hand? And what on earth did he mean by dance?

She looked up at him to see, but he wasn't looking at her. He was coolly looking into her father's eyes.

For a single second there was complete stillness in the ballroom. The glittering guests were motionless, all looking at them, like a tableau at the start of an Ancient Greek play—though whether it was to be a tragedy or not was yet to be determined. Even the orchestra was silent. He'd chosen to move in that small gap between pieces.

Then everyone moved at once. Voices heightened, laughter rang. The excitement that had been palpable before was incandescent now.

San Felipe society was on fire.

Salvatore was now the speechless one. Everyone else surrounding her seemed to melt away. And then Antonio walked her away from him, holding her hand as if it were the most everyday thing in the world, when in fact it was the most intimate, most public display imaginable.

'What are you doing?' she asked as he led her through the crowd.

'As I said. I'm making my way to the dance floor.'

She stumbled and he paused, to put his arm around her waist and draw her nearer to him. Her heart thudded. *Why* was he doing this? Why when in private he had just ended *everything*?

He turned to face her and pulled her even closer to dance with him. His hold on her wasn't polite; it was the hold of a man who knew the woman in his arms intimately.

And the whole world was watching.

'Why did you say that to him?' Why tell him they were close? She stared up at Antonio. He was watching her mouth in all the noise—not the way he did when he wanted to kiss her, but with intent concentration. That was when she figured it out. 'You *lip-read* what he said to me.'

He'd heard that abusive 'whore' slur and he'd come running to the rescue.

But Antonio didn't answer her now.

'Antonio,' she prompted him.

She saw the muscle working in his jaw and knew she'd guessed right.

'Can you at least try to dance?' he said shortly. 'People are looking.'

Finally she understood. It was all about the *appearance*. Of course it was.

'You don't have to do this,' she choked.

'Do what?'

'Give me a Cinderella moment so you can control whatever scandal Salvatore might try to unleash. You're trying to protect my name, like what you did with Alessia.' And it was unbearable.

'This is different.' His words were clipped.

'I know.' She felt a blush burn her cheeks. 'This is far less serious. And far less tragic…far less…everything,' she whispered. 'But you're still trying to protect someone, and painting yourself into a corner. This time you don't have to.'

'What do you mean I don't have to?'

'I don't want you feeling obligated to. You've been through that once before and it affected years of your life. I won't be the reason for that happening again.'

'Bella—'

'You know, just because someone cares about you, it doesn't mean you're obligated to return those feelings. You don't owe that person anything.' He owed *her* nothing.

'You're wrong,' he said. 'You are always obligated to do no harm.'

Oh, God, he was trying to protect her. He was trying to be honourable. Even when she already knew he didn't want to be that man for her.

'Okay.' She struggled to keep breathing steadily and not scream at him. 'But you're to do no harm to *yourself* either.' She gave up on attempting to dance. 'This is harming you. This is not what you want.'

He'd just told her so in that private room when he'd promised that mad lust wouldn't happen again and broken her heart in the process. He'd wanted *nothing*, not *all*.

She knew he was protective of those he cared about, or those he felt he owed or who he felt responsible for.

She didn't want him doing that for her. She didn't want to trap him into something he didn't really want because he felt *sorry* for her. Not even for a short time.

The tears flooded her eyes and the lump blocked her throat. She could hardly see and she definitely couldn't speak.

'Bella—'

She forced back the burn in her chest. But the overwhelming heartache threatened to drown her. She wrenched her hand from his, turned and ran, forcing her way through the staring crowd, leaving him white-lipped and alone in the middle of the ballroom.

CHAPTER TWELVE

ANTONIO WORKED OUT in the early morning in the palace gym for the first time in days. A couple of times this hour had been Bella's and his whole body ached at the thought of her. Annoyed, he pushed himself harder, choosing to run on the treadmill to cool down instead of his customary walk through the pre-dawn darkened city streets. He both smiled and grimaced as he flicked the switch to increase the pace. No one had dared mention her—or the ball—to him but he'd not thought of anything since.

The look on Accardi's face when Antonio had taken Bella's hand? That naked fury? Antonio had revelled in it. He still did. But his smile faded when he remembered how she'd looked at him in that same moment. And when he'd hurt her so badly.

'Your Highness?' His valet ventured into the gym apologetically. 'You might need to get ready.'

Antonio glanced at the time and frowned. How had an hour gone by?

He stalked through to the shower. He had only two formal appearances this morning. Once they were done, he'd finally have the time to work out how to manage the intense media and public interest in Bella.

He was still livid that she'd walked out on him at the ball. Never had he met someone so determined to disagree with him and refuse his assistance. Independence was one thing. Pig-headedness another.

What had happened with Alessia was different. She had *died*. It was her parents and her memory he'd been protecting in the aftermath. And, he finally admitted, he'd been protecting himself.

He'd once told Eduardo that he would have married for love. Indeed it was the only thing he *would* marry for. But the way he'd treated Alessia? He couldn't risk doing that to someone else. He couldn't bear the thought of causing more pain and carrying more guilt. He didn't deserve happiness when he'd felt responsible for cutting her life short. He should have encouraged Alessia to seek help; time would have been the best chance she could have had.

But he'd failed her and he'd then chosen work. Bella had been right: it had been the easier option. He'd told himself that the constraints on him and the scrutiny he lived under meant there'd been no chance for love to develop with anyone else.

That had been an excuse too.

But then she'd danced into his life and challenged him on every level, hitting him hard and quick. With lust, certainly, but then there was everything else about her—honesty, strength, humour. She'd made him want to tease and laugh and live.

But in the moment when she'd needed him most, in that private room at the ball, he'd failed her. And when he'd put himself out for her in a way he'd never done for anyone else a few minutes later, she'd then questioned his motives. Of course she had. She'd rejected him. She was *angry* with him.

Well, he was *furious* with himself.

He slung a towel round his waist and stalked to his private music room only to find it now haunted by the memory of her dancing there for him. He sat at the piano and tried not to remember the way she'd straddled him on the stool. But all he could see in his mind's eye instead was the sweetness of her smile as she'd swum and sung with the dolphins.

He'd never felt as content as he had in that moment. Only he'd been too dumb to recognise why that was. And it wasn't about knowing he'd disarmed Accardi at the ball that had made him smile.

It was all about Bella—about making *her* happy.

This wasn't anger he was feeling now. It was *hurt*. He was hurt that she hadn't stayed, that she hadn't wanted him to help her. And it was fear, that maybe she'd hadn't really wanted *him* at all.

Yeah, he was terrified, because he was helplessly, utterly in love with her and he had no idea how to handle it. How could he get her to believe in him? She trusted no one. Now least of all him. And he didn't blame her. He was such an arrogant, ignorant idiot, who'd been so wrapped up in his own self-sacrificing, he'd not realised that he was sacrificing *Bella's* happiness too.

He picked up a phone and sent a message to his aide to cancel all his appointments for the day.

Because finally he'd figured out that his most important job of all was to love her.

CHAPTER THIRTEEN

NEEDLESS TO SAY the club was more popular than ever. Bella was reduced to barricading herself in her upstairs office. The number of people watching, wanting to get close to her, was terrifying. She was effectively a prisoner but she refused to call on Antonio to help her deal with them. He'd not made contact since she'd left the ball two days ago. It was over.

She'd employed extra security staff at short notice, enforced a strict entry policy and she'd hidden out at the top of the old fire station.

Coming to San Felipe had been a massive mistake. The paradise principality, all beauty and history, with its hint of pirate and sniff of Mediterranean magic, was supposed to have been the scene for her fresh start, but she hadn't even managed a couple of months before monumentally stuffing up by falling in love with the most impossible of men.

It wasn't because he was the Prince of the nation, but because he was so *principled*. He put duty before himself, put the needs of others before his own, and protected others regardless of the price to his own freedom, needs and desires.

She refused to let him do that for her. He didn't love her.

She also refused to give in to her weakest urge and run away. She couldn't. She was locked into the lease. She wasn't going to let the club's backer down. No quitting, no matter what. In a few weeks all the interest in her personal life would die down. The world would think they'd had a fling and that it was now over. Antonio had shaken free of her. And really, that was the truth.

She just had to grit her teeth and put up with the extra intrusion during that time.

But it wasn't that intense public interest that she wanted to run from. It was the heartbreak. She'd truly, totally, fallen for him but while she'd been the object of his lust, the only other emotion she inspired in him was pity. She had his courtesy, his misguided sense of responsibility. And that was almost worse than anything.

Energy—frustration, anger, futility—surged within her. She kicked the leg of her desk. But heat coursed through her rather than pain—he'd pushed her onto that wide expanse of wood and teased her to her first orgasm.

She didn't want to have it in her office any more. She might have to stay in his city for a couple of years but she didn't need this reminder of his sensual power over her in her home. She'd move the desk out this second. No matter that it was almost midnight and her club was full of patrons. She'd push the wretched thing out onto the landing and get the bar staff to take it away in the morning.

She shoved the paperwork to the floor behind her. Then she tried to shove the thing towards the door. It was so heavy, it took ten minutes to move it even two inches and even then it scraped a deep scratch in the wooden floor and she was furious enough to scream.

'Need some help?'

She jerked upright. Antonio was leaning in the now open doorway, watching with a soft smile curving the edge of his usually firm mouth. He was in jeans and tee, with stubble on his jaw, and his usually impeccable hair looked as if he'd been ruffling it with both hands for two hours. He had dark rings under his eyes as if he'd not slept in days and his pale eyes just burned right through to her vulnerable soul.

He looked *gorgeous*.

Her muscles liquefied. So not what she wanted when she was trying to shift a desk heavier than Stonehenge's largest rock.

'What are you trying to do?' he asked when she failed to respond to his first question.

'What does it look like I'm trying to do?' she answered heatedly. 'I'm moving this desk.'

His eyebrows shot up. 'It looks heavy.'

'Clearly.' She straightened and glared at him. 'And you're in the way.'

She didn't want him here at all—not looking like that. And looking at *her* like that.

It wasn't fair.

'How do you think you're going to get it through the door?' He didn't budge as she fruitlessly tried to move the behemoth another few inches. 'Ask me for help.'

For a split second she gaped. Then she snapped her jaw shut and stood upright to glare at him. 'No.'

He stepped into the room and kicked the door shut

behind him. Folding his arms across his chest, he mirrored her defiance.

'Ask me,' he dared, glaring back at her.

Something shifted deep within her when she saw that flickering expression in his eyes. Something she really didn't want to shift. He couldn't break down her resistance with just that *look*.

'I don't need to move it tonight,' she murmured weakly.

He leaned forward, planting both hands on the desk that stood between them. 'I need to know I can help you,' he said huskily, still pinning her in place with that unwavering, intense gaze. 'That you feel you can count on me. That I'll be there for you.'

Bella breathed gently, trying to stave off the emotion swirling too close to her surface. He still didn't get it, did he?

'I don't want to have to count on you,' she said. 'I don't want to use you in that way.'

She didn't want him to 'rescue' her. She didn't want to be any kind of 'duty' to him. She tore her gaze away, frowning down at the desk.

'It's not using me.' His spread hands snapped into fists, his knuckles whitening. 'I ache for you to need me. Because *I* need *you*.'

Stunned, she glanced back up to his face.

'It's okay to ask for help and it's okay to want to be loved,' he argued roughly. 'That desire doesn't weaken you in any way.'

'Have you been reading self-help memes on the Internet?' she croaked.

'Stop trying to push me away. I'm not going anywhere.' An expression crossed his face—one she hadn't seen in him before. 'I've spent the last two days racking my brains trying to come up with some elaborate way in which I can convince you. Considering what happened at the ball I figured a grand public gesture wasn't it. In the end I decided it comes down to just you and me. No audience. No performance. Just truth.'

At that vulnerable intensity in his eyes, her grip on her emotions slipped. Anguished, she broke. 'What do you want from me?'

'Everything,' he whispered. 'I want everything from you. Everything *with* you.'

'No, you don't.' She shook her head, haunted by all the constraints on them. 'Kings have flings with dancers. They date them. They don't—' She broke off, embarrassed at where she'd been heading. At her *presumption*.

'Don't what—' he smiled a little crookedly '—marry them?' He waggled his eyebrows. 'Isn't it a good thing I'm not a king?'

'You know what I mean,' she mumbled, mortified and unable to think further than her next breath. 'And you're a king in every other way.'

'You think I wouldn't marry you?'

'I think you *can't*.' She burned. He couldn't possibly be serious.

'Have you been reading the papers?' His gaze narrowed. 'You know what they say isn't true.'

'I haven't been reading them,' she answered his lecturing tone scornfully. 'I'm not stupid. I *never* read them. I don't need to read them to know what they say.'

And from his one comment she was glad she hadn't. It had taken sheer willpower and strategic unplugging of the Internet to resist the temptation. But she'd done it. She'd made herself focus on nothing but the club these last two days. She'd caught up on her accounts, her business studies and she'd paced for hours, alone and inconsolable. 'I'm not suitable for you.'

'You're the one declaring that you don't want to be defined by your past, or by the reputation others have foisted on you, yet you're the one saying that you can't be with me because of what others might think,' he said. 'I don't care what they think so why should you?'

'I care about what they say about *you*,' she said fiercely. 'I'm trying to protect *you*.'

'Why?' he shot back at her. 'Because you care about me?'

There was a moment of pulsing silence. In that one moment she was bereft of more than words, but everything.

'This isn't the Dark Ages.' He softened his approach and that wicked smile suddenly flashed across his face. 'There are no scarlet letters in my country. It's not like you have a sex tape.'

'My mother's one is still doing the rounds—' she interrupted, cringing inside.

'And you're not your mother,' he interrupted her back. 'Even if you did, I wouldn't care.' He leaned forward, pressing his fists harder on the desk. 'No more roadblocks. *I* choose *you*, Bella. If my people don't want you as their Crown Princess then I'll abdicate. You're more important to me than anything.'

'You can't do that.'

'I can. And I would. But the truth is I won't have to. Screw the scandal. They'll get over it.'

'No.' There was no way that would happen. 'I don't

think so. I think you should leave.' She needed him to go. Now.

His eyes narrowed on her. 'Do you know what I think?' he asked, bitterness sharpening his soft-spoken words. 'I think that no matter what I do, no matter what I say, I can't win this. You will still say no to me.' He blew out a harsh breath. 'You don't want me enough to fight for this. For us. For me.'

That tore her heart in two.

'Don't,' she begged him. 'Please don't.' Because it wasn't true. It wasn't fair.

She was trying to do what was *right*.

Large tears welled in her eyes, her breathing came uneven and quick and she wanted to run. But there was a huge desk and an immovable man in front of her.

And he wasn't going to let her run.

He watched her for a long moment, seeming to see right through her.

'This is fear,' he told her firmly. 'Pure and simple. You're afraid to believe in me. You're afraid to trust that I'm really here for you, because no one has ever been there for you before.'

Hot tears now scalded her cheeks. She couldn't stop them, couldn't stop him. She couldn't bear to look at him, yet nor could she tear her gaze from his.

'That changes, Bella. Tonight,' he promised her. 'I'm here for you now. And I have enough fight for the both of us.'

She blinked, spilling more tears, but she still couldn't get her voice to work. She still couldn't get her body to move. She still couldn't get her brain to believe.

'I have been such a coward,' he said quietly. 'I was a pompous jerk, believing that my "duty" was more important than anything when really it was an excuse not to let anyone get close. I have felt so guilty about Alessia and blamed myself for a long time. I felt like I didn't deserve this kind of happiness because of what happened. But you were right that I needed to forgive myself. To move on. And now I think maybe the way to make amends is to love a woman the way *she* deserves to be loved. To love *you* more than life itself.'

Bella closed her eyes, but he kept speaking and she couldn't block him out.

'It's very easy to love someone when she's the right person for you,' he added softly. 'I know you're scared to believe in this. In me. I know you don't trust me. Not yet.'

She wanted to hide because her skin was burning with pain and vulnerability.

'Give me time,' he added. 'We can work on that together, Bella.'

The sincerity in his voice compelled her to look him in the eye again. Hope did more than shift within her, it unfurled.

'You're not just saying this because you feel somehow responsible for me?' she asked. 'Because I'm okay. I'll be okay. I can survive—'

'Well, good for you, but I can't,' he snapped, his smile vanishing. 'I won't be happy without you. And I won't stop until you're at my side.' He growled at her. 'I never understood what love really was until I met you. Be brave. Trust me. Turn to me. Need me the way I need you. Love me the way I love you. Like nothing else matters. Because nothing else does.'

He was too compelling. Too honest. And nothing else did matter except that he was standing miles from her and while she'd heard everything he'd said, she needed to *feel* it too. She needed to experience that certainty in his strong embrace.

He'd fallen silent, watching her process everything, but his smile had returned. She realised he was waiting for her to come to him. Waiting for her to be as brave as he'd asked her to be. And she wanted to be, but her legs trembled as anticipation and ecstatic relief surged through her.

He met her halfway around the stupid desk. Reaching out, he framed her face with both hands and looked down at her for a long moment.

'Don't you want to kiss me?' She gripped his wrists hard, *dying* at his hesitation.

'More than anything this whole freaking time,' he muttered. 'But I was determined to *talk* to you. I knew you'd say yes if I made love to you first, but I didn't want to seduce you that way. I wanted to be sure you listened. And heard. You need to believe in me.'

He kissed her then—a soft, sweet kiss that breathed love and laughter into her once forlorn heart. Oh, Lord, was it possible to die from happiness?

She rose on tiptoe, refusing to let him pull back too far. She needed him near. She needed his touch. 'You thought you could seduce me into saying yes?'

'I can seduce you into saying anything.' He played up his wicked tease, his eyes dancing. 'Into saying yes, into saying how much you want me...but I wanted you to mean it.'

'Seduce me anyway,' she invited. 'I'll say it. And I'll still mean it.'

'What will you say?'

His question was barely audible, but she read the hunger in his eyes. Suddenly it was easy to be brave.

'That I love you.'

He too was so very easy to love.

'I do love you,' she repeated, no longer caring that she was crying again.

His kisses smothered her words but she kept on chanting them—in her heart, in her touch. And he met her, promise for promise, kiss for kiss, touch for touch.

He pulled her close. She'd missed him so much. They worked frantically, undoing buttons, pushing fabric aside, eager for skin, sensation, surety.

'No more secrecy,' he muttered. 'No more stolen moments.' He swiftly moved, spinning and lifting her onto the broad desk, his smile both tender and outrageous, his eyes filled with love. She parted her legs and pulled him to her, equally teasing and true.

'Love me,' she begged as he kissed his way down the length of her body and back up again.

'Already do. Always will,' he answered roughly, grabbing her leg and wrapping it higher around his hip so he could rub tantalisingly harder against her core, almost claiming her, but not quite. 'You're mine. I'm yours. Love me back.'

The pleasure was so exquisite she could barely comprehend his words. 'Yes.'

'Keep. Saying. Yes.' He thrust into her with each word, but not all the way, only teasing, arousing her beyond sanity.

'Yes. Yes. Yes.' She never wanted him to stop this torture—but at the same time she wanted it all. Now.

'Marry me,' he demanded as he thrust into her to the hilt.

She gasped and stared up at him, registering the brutally satisfied look on his face as he pinned her hot, willing body with his.

'You bully,' she breathed as she saw the laughing, loving determination within him.

'Not bullying,' he corrected with another devastating thrust. 'Seducing.'

'It's too soon.'

'Always you need convincing,' he teased. But he smiled tenderly at her and gently kissed away the tears falling fresh from her eyes. 'No matter. I'll seduce you every day until you say yes to this. To everything. To me.'

She gasped as he pushed closer still.

He looked into her eyes, his own revealing exquisite torment as he paused. 'We'll get there together, darling. You can count on it.'

He reached down between them to touch her. Merciless. Relentless. Utterly loving. Determination hardened his face as she trembled, shaking in his arms. There was more than an orgasm coming. There was bliss of the for-ever kind.

'Yes,' she sobbed. 'Yes, yes, yes.'

EPILOGUE

Two years later

'YOU'RE NOT A good accompanist for my beginner classes,' Bella admonished her laughing husband once the last of her students had left the studio.

'I thought I did pretty well.' Crown Prince Antonio spread his hands in an innocent gesture as he left the piano and sauntered over to where she stood in the middle of the wooden floor.

Bella tried not to be swayed by his gorgeous casual jeans and tee combo but she just loved seeing him this relaxed. 'Breaking into Happy Birthday in the middle of the warm-up was not helpful.'

'But it is your birthday and they loved singing it to you.'

It was his smile that was her undoing—that wickedly tempting glint that flashed from behind that formal reserve and hit her like sensual lightning.

'I've cancelled the rest of your classes for today.' He walked past to lock the studio door and turned back to face her with an arrogant wink.

'You haven't,' she breathed, outraged and delighted at the same time.

Two years in and he was still stealing moments for them alone.

'I have,' he confirmed with zero apology. 'Not only is it your birthday, it's our first wedding anniversary and I'm in charge of all celebrations. Especially the private ones.'

'You do love to be in charge, don't you?' she murmured as he came close enough to kiss.

'I've had a lifetime of experience.' He nodded as he brushed his lips over hers. 'Don't hold it against me.'

Laughing, she curled her arms around his neck and snuggled close. She'd never have thought she could feel so happy and so secure.

Salvatore Accardi had sold his property on San Felipe, loudly declaring he preferred Sardinia. Which was more than fine as far as Bella was concerned because Antonio had been muttering about banishing him from San Felipe for ever on some pretext and that would have only caused scandal and pain, neither of which she was interested in.

Antonio's brother Eduardo had welcomed her with rakish charm and she'd bonded with his wife Stella over her beautiful baby daughter Sapphire.

But the best thing of all was the man in front of her. That her Prince had become so playful still amused her. When the crowds weren't around he was filled with warmth and laughter, but it had spilled over into his public persona as well. The press headlines gushed over the transformation in the Prince—he smiled, he laughed, he was so obviously happy, they seemed to think she was Wonder Woman... So to her absolute amazement, the people of San Felipe had welcomed her completely. Speculation about Princess Bella's possible pregnancy was rife. But that was the one thing she wanted to share with him alone.

She looked up into his beautiful eyes, unable to keep her secret a second longer. 'I have an anniversary present for you.' Even though she was so excited, she was suddenly shy and couldn't get her voice above little more than a whisper.

But he could lip-read and, besides, he knew already, didn't he?

Her eyes filled as he dropped to his knees before her.

'Tell me it's true,' he muttered roughly, wrapping his arms around her legs so tightly she almost toppled.

'I thought we didn't read the papers.' She couldn't resist a final tease as she ruffled his hair gently.

'I haven't read the papers. I've read here.' He placed his hand on the very gentle swell of her stomach. 'And here.' He cupped her breast. 'And here.' He cupped the side of her face, wiping the tear from under her eye with the gentlest finger and then tracing the full curve of her lips. 'So tell me it's true.'

She smiled a watery smile. He groaned, a raw sound of heartfelt longing and wonder. She bent to kiss him quiet, pouring her heart and happiness into it, into him. She could never give him enough—not when he'd given her so much.

'Dance with me,' he whispered against her mouth, pulling her down to the floor with him.

'Any time,' she promised.

Because the music between them played for ever.

* * * * *

LET'S TALK
Romance

For exclusive extracts, competitions and special offers, find us online:

 facebook.com/millsandboon

@MillsandBoon

@MillsandBoonUK

Get in touch on 01413 063232

For all the latest titles coming soon, visit
millsandboon.co.uk/nextmonth